BLA... [BLACK WIDOW]

Bart Davis was bo... [obscured]
After graduating h... [obscured]
specializing in disru... [obscured]
eleven years. Along the way he acquired a Masters degree in Social Work, a brown belt in karate, became a licensed hypnotist and a therapist. He has lectured frequently on education, social work and writing. His first thriller, *Blind Prophet*, was published in 1983, and this success was followed by *Takeover*. *Black Widow* is his third novel. He and his wife live in New York State.

TAKEOVER

'A first-class thriller which encourages frantic reading'
Liverpool Daily Post

BLIND PROPHET

'One of the best international thrillers to appear in recent years'
Library Journal

Also available in Fontana by the same author

BLIND PROPHET
TAKEOVER

BLACK WIDOW

BART DAVIS

FONTANA/Collins

Acknowledgements

I am deeply indebted to the following people and organizations for their unselfish aid in the writing of this novel. First and foremost to General Ransom E 'Reb' Barber (ret) – above and beyond; and to the AF10/New England Chapter; The North American Aerospace Defense Command/Public Affairs; The United States Air Force; Sensei Daniel D'Agostino; Col Alan Shoemaker, USAF; Lt Col J Wagovich, USAF; Col A Forster, USAF; Col R Mickelson, OSUSD; Tricia Meeks; Mr Anthony S Makris, ICD; Sharon Davis and Robert Gottlieb.

First published in Great Britain by William Collins Sons & Co. Ltd 1988
This continental edition first issued in Fontana Paperbacks 1989

Copyright © Bart Davis 1988

Printed and bound in Great Britain by
William Collins Sons & Co. Ltd, Glasgow

CONDITIONS OF SALE
This book is sold subject to the condition
that it shall not, by way of trade or otherwise,
be lent, re-sold, hired out or otherwise circulated
without the publisher's prior consent in any form of
binding or cover other than that in which it is
published and without a similar condition
including this condition being imposed
on the subsequent purchaser.

With deep affection to my friends at the PWTA,
Hy, Annabell, Katie, Bob, Susan, Dick, Madeline,
and, especially, Michael

The more violent the age, the more violent the crimes committed in it.

HANS KIRST
The Night of the Generals

ONE

It was the kind of June evening where dusk stole in slowly, settling over the marshland next to David Hallam's house on the East End of Long Island quietly, but all Hallam was aware of was the steady throb of the motor he was working on and the fact that his heart was hammering in unison. Hallam shut off the outboard. Only thirty feet separated the channel bank and his house, but he feared not hearing the evening news opening theme. He glanced at his watch. Enough time. His eyes swept over the boat and the water. The marshy reeds swayed like metronomes in the evening breeze. He got up from the ageing, weathered planks that formed the small dock, wiped his strong hands on his ripped T-shirt and shoved his still dark hair off his forehead.

The water was the main reason he and Janet had bought the place. Fight fire with fire, the saying went. Nope – fight it with water. The narrow boat channel reassured him. Somewhere to run to? Maybe. In any event, its presence was a comfort.

Until two nights ago.

He turned round at a sound from the house and saw his wife, Janet, watching him from the kitchen window. She turned away, the venetian blinds snicking back into place disapprovingly. Ever since nursing him back to health in the veterans' hospital two decades before, she'd known this time would come. She understood its inevitability as one understands deep down that pets always die, that houses constantly need fixing, and that someday the children will leave home telling you how little you know.

Hallam turned back to the stream and watched a water beetle scuttle Christ-like across its slow-moving surface. Maybe he'd always known it too – but he hadn't been certain, really certain, until the eleven o'clock news two nights before. He was sitting on the living-room couch half reading a book, half listening to the nightly news that was such an ingrained habit. The newscaster's words hit him in the guts the way the cracking of a big tree hits you – deep down – or the unmistakable feeling of an earthquake.

The water beetle continued its movement, pincers dancing. Inside, he could hear the commercials that preceded the news. The skin on Hallam's back itched where . . . he pulled his thoughts back.

Two nights before.

This just in – the newscaster had said – *a brutal murder in Colorado Springs has police baffled and the local populace terrified. The mutilated corpse of a young female university student was found tonight . . .*

Hallam listened. It was like some terrible lottery, waiting for details to match instead of numbers. His stomach knotted tighter at each congruence. Janet came out of the bedroom. The TV was on in there and she'd heard it, too. She came and stood beside him, lifting the shirt off his suddenly damp back where he could still sweat. There had been a lot of newscasts over the years. He could feel her fierce hope that this was just another. But it wasn't. Detail after detail matched. The news was as sketchy as the news always is, but there was enough for Hallam to know that the madness was back.

For a day he waited, following the story. Suspicion became certainty. He wasn't surprised at the phone call that followed, only at the ease of reconnection. No private fiction had blocked what happened all those years ago, or the certainty that it would happen again. Action was swift when it did. He took the call in his office. 'Why are you closing the doors, Daddy?' his eldest girl asked, sensing peril, as children do, in the slightest difference. Hallam did his best to smile it away. Inside, he picked up the phone from his desk.

'Have you seen the news, David?' asked a voice he hadn't heard in twenty years.

Hallam was surprised. 'Paco?' It wasn't the one he'd expected.

'Yeah. It's Paco.' A long pause. Then a quick, ragged breath. 'You coming?'

Hallam heard the clock ticking from its perch on a pile of his law books. He turned on the desk lamp and watched the dust motes dance in a column of light. His partner would have to handle his cases. He looked to the safe where his important papers were stored – the deed to the house, his will.

'You coming . . . Orpheus?' asked the voice again.

A longer pause. 'Yeah,' Hallam said finally. 'Who's running us?'

'I am, for now. Maybe . . . well, we'll see when you get here.'

That surprised Hallam. The little Italian with a hard-on for the Dow Jones in charge? Things had changed in twenty years.

'Some details. Listen up.'

Hallam made notes on a yellow legal pad. When it was done he could hear the other man breathing, waiting. Twenty years . . .

'Paco—' Hallam began. He was cut off.

'When you get here.'

The line went dead.

Janet was already in bed when he came upstairs, the children in their rooms. His wife took refuge in sleep. It was safe under the covers. Some people broke or cried or went hysterical. Janet slept. Already, he could see her eyes glazing.

'I love you very much,' he said, sitting beside her.

'But you're going.'

He nodded, saw her hope fade.

'I love you,' he said again.

She touched her eye, her chest, pointed at him and made a 'V' sign. Married sign language. I love you, too.

He pulled the covers tighter round her and said, 'Everything's arranged. Two weeks or so.'

Her eyes were closing. They fluttered. 'Or not at all,' she said.

What could he say to that? He watched her eyes close, seeing in them the helpless terror she was fighting before they did. Moments later, she was asleep.

Hallam was too anxious to sleep. He stripped off his clothing and went to the bedroom window naked, looking out at the stream and the night sky. Twenty years changed a man. Life was narrower, it had less of an edge. He heard himself saying, 'Look, honey, I don't care how you decorate the place as long as you keep my big chair in front of the TV.' He grimaced. Another victim of the inverse proportion of middle age: bodies went from hard to soft as political sympathies did the opposite. He wondered how things had affected his friends. What was Hu like these days? How had Paco managed? More to the point, what would they all think of him?

The other side of the coin was this: last time he almost died. He grappled again with all the inevitable questions. Why should a married man with a comfortable life risk it all to pay debts over twenty years old?

He didn't have an answer.

'You coming?' Paco had asked.

Yeah. He was.

He didn't think it was bravery. Yet he was placing himself at risk. He didn't feel brave. Maybe courage had ceased to be an internal quality, not something you felt any longer, like anger or love, just something you did. Twenty years ago, he *felt* things. Now he *had* things. Two decades had turned bravery into just another decision.

Maybe that wasn't totally fair. Comfort was damn hard-earned. He was a long time recovering from Vietnam. After Law School it took them five years before they could buy a new couch, ten before they had a new car. Maybe in this day and age you had to be really goddamned courageous to risk those things.

In the end, Hallam decided, soldiers and sportsmen were required to be brave. The rest simply had to be willing.

At the least, he was that.

He pulled his suitcase out from the big bedroom closet and began to pack.

The house was empty when the taxi came to take him to the airport. Janet was at work, the kids in school. He tried to lock the sounds of the kids playing by the breakfast table that morning into his memory. Janet and he had eaten wordlessly. Everything, which is to say nothing, had been said the night before.

He boarded the TWA flight to Colorado Springs. Apart from his suitcase he was travelling light. Most of the things he needed couldn't be taken on a commercial flight. They would be waiting for him at his final destination, a place he had never been before. He hoped it wouldn't kill him a second time.

He was scrutinized by a stewardess in the first-class section. The pilot, who had lately taken to checking all the entering passengers for signs of knife- or gun-wielding desires, studied Hallam and was glad his sense told him the man's intensity had nothing to do with him or his aeroplane. The girl who sat next to Hallam decided the firm planes of his face were handsome, but saw his wedding ring and lost interest.

Everyone has a public fiction put in place against discovery. Hallam was conscious of his own being examined. He knew what the various totals were. He compared that to his history. *That* bit like a shark, never resting.

Hallam leaned back as the plane raced forward and up into the sky. He hadn't seen these men in almost twenty years. How would they look? The policeman, the paraplegic, the clown. What was left of them?

Public and private fictions. Fictions, because neither is true.

History confuses us and we are, at most, collections, trophy rooms where moving objects disturb only dust.

For a long time Hallam thought about what was drawing them together. Occasionally, he leaned down to shift the pointed carbide spike that was taped to his leg and didn't show up on metal detectors. The tape irritated his skin. It disturbed him to think he'd lost the knack of carrying weapons gracefully.

The jet broke through the cloud layer and sunlight flooded the cabin. Hallam accepted a drink from the stewardess and thought about the things that a man thinks about when the last connection to home has been severed by thirty thousand feet. The future approached at six hundred miles per hour and churned up his insides in a hot, liquid way.

Hallam thought about a lot of things. Mostly, though, he thought about how it all began . . .

THE FIRST PART

TWO

1968

The entrance to every flesh parlour in Saigon's red-light district was lit by rows of naked, glaring bulbs. To David Hallam's tired eyes, they looked like the teeth in a carnivore's mouth. Making the comparison complete were short hallways extending back like throats, where soldiers were swallowed up, drawn in by sloe-eyed, lithe women in tight, wrap-around *ao dai* dresses. All around him the district heaved and bucked in the summer night's thick air.

Hallam observed all this from the rear seat of the old yellow Datsun he'd been assigned from the 5th Battalion's motor pool. Out this late he had hastily appropriated one of the Nung Chinese guards to serve as driver, and now they were making their way slowly through the dense crowds that flooded the streets, pushing aside a wake of Midwestern farm boys, broad-backed Southern blacks and their wise-eyed Northern cousins, crafty blue-collar Italians and pencil-thin mustachioed Hispanics. They all travelled in small bands. Some wore jungle fatigues still caked with the red clay of the Central Highlands. Others wore loose-fitting, gaudy civilian shirts. Their arms and necks were two-toned from the sun. Hallam thought they looked slightly frightening with their harsh, angular crew cuts and slightly wild eyes – murderous juveniles all sharing some secret, guilty knowledge.

The car made a turn, heading into the district's harshest quarter. Buddhist neon failed to illuminate the corners where peddlers pulled GIs out of the light into the shadows, bartering for every conceivable whim and taste, filling in all the cracks in this morally garish universe. It was a disturbing sight; a mudslide of amoral wandering that lay beneath a cloying mist of Asian intrigue.

Things grew less chaotic as they left the centre, heading for a fringe area to the south. Hallam leaned back, pensive in the darkness. The war had unleashed something he had not yet been able to define exactly. It was new to his experience, a thing from beyond the normally charted borders of his inner country. He knew only that it was sick and depraved and . . . Hallam shook his head, searching for the right word. Had he been more religious, or the times less secular, the word Evil might have come to mind more easily.

'Captain-san?'

The driver's voice broke Hallam from his reverie.

'We are almost there. A few blocks.'

Hallam nodded. 'Thanks.'

He watched the city pass by. It occurred to him that it might not even be the war entirely, or at all for that matter. Maybe it was everywhere, the times themselves. All around him human interaction seemed to be losing its familiar shape. Old forms died, struggling for relevance. Hallam wondered about the changes, dwelled upon them in the dim hours of the night. Was the vaunted new direction inward leading to the light? Or just to some fetid inner swamp where motives were so closely allied to the slime as to be indistinguishable from it.

The driver pulled the car to a stop and turned. Hallam started; his skin was so bloody-hued. He suddenly saw it was the red glare of the police cordon's flashing lights. He scanned the streets. It was a block of low, ugly buildings – some clubs, brothels, a few rooming houses. It was bad to be here, worse to have been summoned.

Hallam shoved the door open and climbed out. The National Police had set up striped wooden barriers around the building that was Hallam's destination. Policemen in pale blue uniforms trimmed with white held their rifles at chest level, guarding the entrance to the four-storey wood frame whose paint was peeling badly. Their nickname of 'White Mice' seemed inconsistent with the rat's nest they were guarding. There was a smell in the air from beyond the barriers where a crowd had gathered, the odour of overly perfumed bodies packed too closely together. The gabble of voices captivated by disaster was like the buzz of fat, blue flies.

Another universal, thought Hallam sadly, eyeing the crowd. He flicked open his ID for the ranking policeman. The Vietnamese saluted smartly and led him through the cordon. Hallam felt the crowd's interest swing his way. He didn't like it.

'Who lives here?' Hallam asked as they entered the lobby. Narrow wooden stairs led up to a series of landings and hollow doors, none of which had numbers. The walls were stained white with mildew.

'Place for medium-long stay,' said the policeman. 'Girls from the district, from the bars, they live here. Men, too,' he added. 'Lieutenant Hu is on the third floor. You want me to show you?'

'I'll find it.'

Hallam walked upstairs. The door to one apartment was open and a small group of immaculate brown policemen was gathered on the landing. Hallam observed the camera, the tapes, the print stuff. Dragnet – transposed ten thousand miles; forms gone crazy again. They looked at Hallam with stares designed to remind him of the late hour. He knew they couldn't begin until either he or Hu gave the okay.

Hu was with the Vietnamese Military Security Service, MSS, and Hallam's joint case officer. Most intelligence activities in Vietnam were joint operations. In parlance, he and Hu formed a bilateral agent-handler team, with Hallam providing the greater technical expertise and Hu the necessary facility for translation. Hallam nodded to the police technicians. At the first whiff of anything related to an intelligence matter they would have had to summon Hu, who in turn was obliged to call in Hallam.

Hallam saw that Hu was inside. He was as wiry thin as most Vietnamese and his dark skin was the texture of river stones. Hallam knew that Hu's uniform would be crisp and fresh even at this hour of the night and he saw Hu's hard, black eyes tighten a bit at his rumpled civilian clothing.

He extended his hand to Hu who took it without reserve.

'Thank you for coming so quickly, David. The police apologize for the late hour. They would not have called this late, but they believe she is one of ours.'

'Is she?'

Hu gestured to a closed door on their right. Hallam assumed it was the bedroom. There was a small kitchen behind them, and a bath, with a toilet off that. 'Inside, please.' Hu ushered him towards the bedroom.

Hu usually wasn't so perfunctory and Hallam took notice of that fact. Their relationship was cordial, albeit professional, and both had seen enough corpses. Usually together. This was something else. He tried to read Hu's face but he was showing nothing. All right. Hallam shrugged. He would find out soon enough. He opened the door.

The air in the cramped bedroom burst out with a wet, bloody smell that caught at Hallam's stomach and threatened to convulse it. He grabbed at his handkerchief and balled it under his nose, wavering. For a moment, as he walked into the room, he didn't recognize the object on the bed. It failed to register as anything but a shapeless, bulging sack. Then he focused. What remained of the body of a dark-haired Vietnamese woman lay huddled on the bed, face turned away as if deeply ashamed.

As Hallam's senses began to discriminate further, the enormity of what lay before him hit him hard. He reacted viscerally, shock riding up his body from his stomach to his heart and clutching painfully at the muscle with sharp, scaly hands.

For a second Hallam had difficulty breathing. He felt like there was a bag over his head.

She was naked. Most of her blood had drained away. She had been stabbed so many times that Hallam could not see six inches of skin free from brutal penetration marks. Heels, calves, thighs, belly, chest; all had been pierced repeatedly. The fingers of her right hand were almost severed. Her arms – Hallam had to lean closer to make sure he was seeing what he thought – were covered with *teeth* marks. The flesh was torn open in a dozen places, rent by a human animal. Hallam had seen jungle shows on television, animal pictures like *Wild Kingdom* where they showed lions feeding on a just-killed zebra. It was like that here.

It got worse. There was sexual mutilation of the breasts and genitals. Her ribs had been stomped in and the bones poked through the skin. Hallam had never seen a human form treated with such disdain.

He thought about Hu's coldness. It was obvious that whoever had done this had a pathological hatred of women. But to Hu, coming from a land where troops on both sides often treated his countrymen as subhumans, this was also a crime against the Vietnamese by a killer who could deny his victim even the most basic recognition of common humanity. Race murder. Transcendent brutality. It made Hallam wince with a kind of hot, liquid fear. Something alien had done this.

He forced himself to search the room. The woman on the bed could be one of their people, but the face was too mangled to be certain. Her gaping mouth told him nothing. Her wide-open eyes reflected only terror. He began poking through her meagre belongings.

In a chest of drawers by the bedside table was a sack containing some money, a few personal items and her identification. Hallam read the name alongside the picture and for a moment she was alive again, her image swimming in his mind. He had debriefed her less than a week ago when she returned to Saigon. She was one of a number of lower-level agents he and Hu ran, whose trips to the countryside to visit relatives provided valuable information about Viet Cong movements in the area. More memories rose up with the recognition. She was an only child, the daughter of a farmer, and both parents had been killed by the VC. She worked as a prostitute in the Hung Dao hotel, a miserable three-storey shack on Tu Do street. And she worked for Hallam.

He looked back to the bed. The fetid sweetness of her blood suffused every breath he drew and he knew he couldn't stay there much longer. A thought struck him. If Hu was directing his anger at Hallam, was it possible he suspected the killer was an American, perhaps an American soldier? Hallam wondered if there was anything to support that belief. He checked the room more carefully but found nothing.

It was time to go. He took one last look at the poor bashed-in face. It regarded him blindly, asking for the compassion in death it had not received in dying. Hallam steeled himself, leaning closer, reaching out to shut the unseeing eyes . . .

The breath caught in his chest and the bile he had been fighting to hold down since walking into the room suddenly coursed hotly into his throat. He ran from what he saw – the head lolling freely, coming towards him, open, empty. The crusty, matted hair had swung away . . . The word Evil finally exploded screaming in his mind and he could control himself no longer. He burst out of the room past the waiting policemen and – in the brief instant before he lay huddled over the toilet retching in great gasping heaves – saw Hu's thawing look of . . . gratitude, maybe, that at least this soldier had not been able to look upon such slaughter with impunity.

As a parting gift to the tormented creature inside, the killer had severed her head from her neck and cut off both ears. For Hallam, the worst part of it was the sure and certain knowledge that he had taken them for trophies.

Hu watched him walk out of the bathroom with a wet cloth pressed to his face.

'You feel better?' he asked solicitously.

Hallam tossed his soiled handkerchief into a corner. The police were already in the bedroom. The hard, white glare of their flashbulbs strobed the doorway.

'Sure. Better. I don't want to stay here.'

Hu inclined his head. 'I've seen what there is to see. Before you arrived. The police can do the rest.'

'Let's go find a bar then. And you're buying.'

Hu reached for his cap and followed Hallam out. 'Why so?' he asked, cocking an eyebrow.

'For letting me walk into that without any prep,' Hallam said angrily, clumping down the stairs. 'I don't like to be treated that way. What was it, some kind of test?' He saw something flicker behind his partner's eyes. 'Yeah. And don't try and take cover behind that fucking ever-present smile. It was a lousy thing to do.'

'Will it damage our relationship permanently?'

Hallam thought it over. Hu looked genuinely concerned, but who the fuck really knew? 'Maybe,' he said. 'Depends.'

'On what?'

Hallam let it hang.

They reached the hall and Hu conferred with the senior man. They all walked outside and the police officer steered them past the crowd. On the pavement Hu said, 'Let's walk, David. There's a bar round the corner that isn't too bad. We'll be called if needed.'

'Okay, I could use the air.'

They walked in silence, Hallam's six-foot frame towering over Hu's smaller one. The American was built like a swimmer, lean-hipped and lanky, with short brown hair surmounting a face that was pleasant to look at. Women called his looks 'sweet', and men weren't made overly jealous by him. Best, there was warmth in the small lines by his eyes, with only a hint of the hardness he was capable of, seen fleetingly, like a tracer shell. But the dark brown eyes were bitter now.

'Fuck you, man. Fuck you,' he swore, shaking his head wearily, the words escaping in a long, drawn-out sigh.

'Don't be angry, David. I had to know.'

'Know what? That I couldn't look at that obscenity and keep my lunch down?'

'More than that. I admit to ulterior motives. But surely you know I wouldn't risk your goodwill lightly.' Hu didn't try to evade the American's steady gaze. Hallam had a way of peering out from behind those dark eyes that evoked a sense of the man's quiet intelligence and the full spectrum of his emotions. Hu saw the anger was undiminished. 'Why do *you* think I did it?'

The question turned Hallam's resentment back in on itself. He stopped for a moment, letting the night air flow into the still-hot space between his neck and collar. His nose twitched at the odours on the wind.

'You're taking this one personally,' he said slowly. 'I think you wanted to see how much it bothered me. To see if I would take it that way too.'

Hu's grunt was noncommittal, but Hallam again saw the fleeting look of gratitude that flashed across his features only to disappear just as quickly. 'We are here,' he said simply, turning down a short flight of stairs to the bar's doorway. Hallam took a few deep, cleansing breaths, less angry, more in control. He followed Hu in.

It was quiet inside, and cooler, and almost as dark. They sat in a booth. A girl in a cutaway body suit came for their order. Hallam smelled the sweet odour of marijuana. Hu put money on the table without protest. Hallam knew it was the closest thing to an apology he was going to get.

'David, do you know what a *double veteran* is?' Hu asked.

Hallam frowned. Even though they had worked together over a year, Hu still had a tendency to treat him like an innocent. The irony was, technically at least, Hallam was his superior in the chain of command.

'I'm familiar with the term,' he said with distaste. 'You think something like that figures into this?'

'Not precisely in the same way. A soldier who takes a woman by force and then kills her, a double veteran in the vernacular, is revelling in his power. The ultimate power trip. We understand it; you take a young boy who is not yet fully mature, who does not yet fully understand his drives, and give him a weapon and nothing to prevent his using it — no law, no punishment, no moral sanction from his peers. Sooner or later even the most previously good-natured will be tempted to force his will upon others. Some succumb to the temptation.'

'But many do not,' David objected.

'Many do not,' Hu agreed. 'But that's not my point. Up in that apartment, that was the work of no misguided boy. It was done by someone who brought his own hatred to this country, inside, like a furnace out of control.'

'And you thought I wouldn't react to that? Feel the same way you do?'

'I had to be sure.'

'Why?'

'Because the girl's position with us makes any police investigation, or even any investigation on my part, subject to your approval. You write her off and it ends here.'

Hallam mulled that over. 'How did the police get to us so quickly?'

'They got the woman's name from a neighbour and checked it through as a matter of routine. She figured on the hands-off list. They routed the call to MSS, who notified me.'

'The police ask you questions?'

Hu shook his head. 'That would exceed their authority.'

'All she really did was to keep her eyes and ears open when she went to visit her relatives. She took back the money she made in the Hung Dao and what we gave her. She was a fair source,' Hallam said speculatively, 'nothing spectacular.'

'But she was vulnerable two ways. As an agent and as a whore.'

Hallam was still reflective. 'If I had to choose, it would be the latter. Nothing about her activities for us would merit such a killing. Not this way. If the VC suspected her, they would simply have waited till she returned to her village, shot her in the head and dumped her in the road.'

'Could this be a cover for that?' But Hu offered the thought without real energy.

'No. Like I said, not important enough. Anything she had we would have got during her debriefing anyhow. You know, I liked that girl. She was strong. A survivor. I think what we see is what we got.'

Hu's nod was firm. 'A straightforward killing, the work of a sexual psychopath.'

'At first glance anyway. I want to see the police reports and get the experts' opinions, but this has a bad taste to it. It just doesn't *feel* intelligence-related.'

'Nevertheless, it's our jurisdiction.'

Something in the way Hu said that brought Hallam's glance up sharply. 'Not if this is a purely criminal matter.'

'Even if the crime concerned a member of the armed forces?' Hu pressed.

Hallam eyed him closely. 'In that case, yes, we'd be obliged to investigate. And to notify the internal security people if we came up with something.'

The answer seemed to satisfy Hu, but the exchange opened up questions Hallam could not ignore. 'Listen,' he said, 'I'm starting to resent your dancing around. You know something. Or at least you think you do. What are you probing for? Sooner or later you're going to have to tell me, you know.'

When Hu finally spoke, his voice was low and fraught with violence, like when the winds still before a storm. 'I want this man, David. I want him very badly. And I have to know if what he did to that nobody up there, that expendable nothing of a whore, bothers you enough so that you want him that badly too.'

'Christ, Hu. Of course, I—'

'Wait, don't say it yet. First understand what this means to me. Why it's personal. You don't know where it may lead. So wait and hear me out. Okay?'

'Sure.'

Hu started slowly. 'Foreign troops have been killing here for over a century, did you realize that? The French, then the Japanese, then the French again and now the Americans. A hundred years of slaughter, David, culminating in a war whose violence is so random, so without pattern or rhythm that even the most stable man is affected by it. Atrocities have become the order of the day. Each side seems bent on out-horrifying the other, like making raises in a card game. But it's ultimately the people, *my* people, who end up less than human in the minds of both sides. Walking targets, moving *things* to destroy as easily as a tank or a stump. Have you ever seen what is left after one of your squads that has been out in the field for a week or two has cut through a village in a free-fire zone?'

Hallam looked away. 'I've seen the reports. But this is war, and the VC—'

'Are worse,' Hu said sternly. 'Far worse. I agree, of course. I'm well aware of the geopolitical issues at stake also. Christ, David, I went to school in California. And I'm a military officer. My personal politics are extremely conservative. I have no desire at all to answer to a party or to be forced to spout meaningless rhetoric. But this killing is above all that. Or maybe beside it. The killer represents something to me. He's what is worst on both sides, on all sides. He's the kind who can turn people into objects or conflicts or battles or just *things*, but not people . . . living and breathing and crying over lost sons and ravished daughters and tormented children . . . Jesus, David, the children . . .' Hu's voice broke and he lowered his eyes.

Hallam said quietly, 'You're right. To the killer, the girl was nothing at all. The violence was savage, bent only on its own satisfaction and beyond any reason. Like drowning cats or tying cans to dogs' tails or pulling wings off butterflies.'

Hu's face was as tight as drumskin. 'Yes, I felt that, too. The self-absorption.'

'And it's somehow worse because the girl didn't even play

a part in it. Not her feelings or her pain. Not anything about her. She was only meat,' Hallam finished sadly.

'And he was her butcher,' Hu said. 'Unhappily, we agree. I am no poet, David, but nowhere else do I see so clear a metaphor for what is going on around us. We are a pile of bones the dogs fight over.'

Hallam felt nothing but sympathy for the man. Bright, professional, competent, and caught up in a situation so choked by the war he couldn't even follow his instincts without getting permission from the warriors. It was like having to ask the man who crippled you if, please sir, you might be permitted to feed yourself. There was injustice in that and Hallam was angered by it.

He also found that the crime tapped a deep feeling of revulsion in him. He was a soldier, here to do a job, committed to certain principles and ideas. Brutality was not one of them. This had the all-too-familiar feeling of something unleashed, something from beyond the normal or permissible. The Swamp beckoned again. Didn't someone have to stand in its way? Qualities acceptable in animals could not be tolerated in men.

He grew aware of Hu's scrutiny. 'You want to go after the killer.'

Hu nodded.

'It's not part of our brief.'

'But we account for our own time.'

Hallam heard the plea in Hu's voice. He didn't want to make it harder. To a man of Hu's precise dignity, the whole self-revealing conversation must have been difficult. Hallam sipped his drink slowly, aware that the alcohol and his lack of sleep were combining into a dangerous fog where judgement was questionable. But Hu was waiting.

'Okay,' Hallam said slowly, nodding. 'Okay.'

Hu's expression softened somewhat. 'I hoped you would say that. You're a decent man, David. And a fine soldier. I will do my best to see that this matter brings you no dishonour.'

Hallam suddenly felt a cold wind lick at the nape of his neck. Hu thought it might bring him dishonour? He began to look at his partner in a new light, saw a disturbing pattern for the first time and knew all at once there was still a piece of the puzzle missing.

'You bastard. You're holding out on me and I just this second realized it. All this crap about morals and psychology. Jesus! You're leading me down the garden path and I'm too stupid to ask what that hand is doing crawling up my leg. What else is there, friend? Right now.'

Hu's smile was often the normal Vietnamese refuge; it could mean anything. But he was not smiling now. He reached into his shirt pocket and brought out a clenched fist which he rested on the table.

Hallam could see that he was holding something, but he could not see what.

'Under the girl's bed,' Hu said. 'Between the floorboards. Only chance revealed its presence to me before the police. I thought it best we should have it. I suspect it is the murderer's.'

The fog around Hallam was growing denser. He stared at Hu's hand, transfixed. 'Show me,' he said.

Hu spread open his fingers and what lay dark against his palm made that simple act as dangerous as the unfolding of some deadly, carnivorous bloom.

'Jesus Christ, Hu,' swore Hallam feelingly, suddenly as wide awake as if he'd been slapped. 'Jesus fucking Christ.'

In the centre of Hu's slender brown hand was a single, black, 'subdued brass' star from the uniform of an American general.

THREE

The rest of the night was a blur for Hallam, punctuated by moments of outrage, temper, and deep, enervating depression. Through it all, the general's star hovered like a sort of sinister Holy Grail, fascinating, and at the same time repelling.

He had a hazy memory of getting back to his team house, a two-storey villa within a walled compound in downtown Saigon, and of being not-so-gently handled as Hu turned him over to the Nung guards for deposit in his rooms. He slept badly, and awoke without any sense of having rested. Enough of the alcohol's residual effects remained to leave him feeling dark-tempered and desiccated, and he found himself mumbling while he showered and shaved, an acerbic string of syllables, all meaning that he remembered too much of what had been done to the girl.

For the first time in his life, the blade against his skin prodded his imagination in disturbing ways and gave rise to disquieting thoughts.

What did it feel like to do such things to another person? What did it take inside? Millennia of prohibition against murder had left its mark on almost everyone. It was one of the pillars of Western society. Even those given sanction to violate that taboo for God-and-Country, with an automatic weapon at a distance, suffered some kind of reaction. In Hallam's experience, there was some part of every man that felt, well, bad about it. Regardless of popular fiction's mythology, it just wasn't that easy to kill.

Hu used the term psychopath to describe the killer. Strictly speaking, though, neither of them had a real understanding of what that term meant. In this overly Freudian error . . . Hallam smiled, the word he meant was *era* . . . people tossed around psychological jargon with little regard for its meaning. Therapy was party talk, pick-up lines; the strategy of 'let me impress you' replaced by 'let me tell why you do what you do'. Like always, I really just want to slip you the dick, but this way you're disarmed by my 'sensitivity'. Hallam sighed. In the land of the confused, even the remotely certain could be king.

He knew such pleasant observations about the nature of his fellow men were the product of feeling so mean-tempered, and he tried to force his thoughts into more professional lines. If indeed the killer was a psychopath, they were going to need competent counsel. He started running through the staff of the 5th Battalion in his head. Jimmy O'Rourke was a staff psychologist in the Analysis Section and a friend since intelligence school at the Bird – Fort Holabird in Maryland. A crime like this had complex motives and Jimmy would help him and Hu to understand them.

Complex motives. Hallam frowned. He was already sounding like a policeman rather than an intelligence officer. A nagging thought caught his attention and it occurred to him that he could still hide behind that. Leave the case to the National Police and walk away.

He sat down on the bed to draw on his socks. For Christ's sake, this wasn't his *life*. In a year or two he'd be back in the States to finish grad school. Did he honestly care if one more person died here, even as gruesomely as the girl had?

He picked up the phone and dialled Hu's private number. He had no doubt that the Vietnamese would be at MSS already. Probably a damn sight more clear-headed, too.

The phone was answered on the second ring.

'Hu?'

'Yes, this is he.'

'It's Hallam. Look, can you tell me why we should give enough of a shit about this to put our asses on the line?'

'Ahh.'

'Ahh, what?'

'Ahh, I think you've had a rough morning.'

'That's true enough,' Hallam said tightly. 'My night wasn't so good either.'

'"Weary is the path that fails to challenge", David,' quoted Hu philosophically.

'Who said that, Confucius?'

'As a matter of fact, yes.'

'Yeah, well, he also said that baseball was impossible because no one could walk with four balls. I say fuck him.'

'David, you know he never—'

'Yeah, I know. But I was stalling till I figured out what the hell what you said meant.'

'Do you know now?'

'Sure,' Hallam said. 'So fuck you, too.'

'David,' Hu sighed. 'We're not getting anywhere.'

There was a long pause. 'Yeah.'

'Do you want to listen?'

'I called, didn't I?'

'Yes,' said Hu, 'You did. Why?'

There was another silence. 'David?'

'I keep thinking about that general's star,' Hallam said slowly. 'I don't know. It makes me cold inside. Angry and afraid at the same time. It's crazy. A goddamned general. Why do either of us want to buy that kind of trouble?'

'In part, because if we don't stop him, he's going to do it again.'

'You can't know that,' Hallam said quickly.

'You think last night cured him?'

'Well, no . . .'

'Then it will happen again,' Hu said with certainty. 'And when he gets back to the States it will happen there.'

'All right, that's pretty compelling.'

'More so than if it happens again here?'

'C'mon, Hu. You know I didn't mean it that way.'

'I'm sorry. I know. I'm being overly sensitive.'

'Forget it. The last thing I said was, "That's pretty compelling".'

'Equally so is the notion that such a man may be in command of hundreds, maybe thousands of troops. We have a responsibility to them, don't we?'

'Yes. Probably.'

'Then for those reasons and another even more compelling, you should want to find the killer.'

Hallam could picture Hu's hard black eyes. 'And what might that be?'

'Put very simply, you would never forgive yourself if you didn't.'

Hallam let the phone slip from his hand and watched it dangle on the coiled black wire, first one way, then the other.

'David?' The voice was small and far away.

Hallam picked up the receiver and put it to his ear.

'David? Are you still there?'

'I'm here,' he answered. 'Not bad, Hu.'

'Thank you.'

Hallam ran a hand over the back of his neck. 'I'll set a few things up and call you there later. When will the police have something for us to look at?'

'Around noon, they say.'

'Okay. Sit tight . . . and thanks.'

'Not at all. But, ahh . . .'

'What is it?'

'The cursing, David. Really, your vocabulary is becoming almost completely vituperative. It's out of character.'

'Not to worry. It just reflects a general personality trend. Really, no big deal.'

'Very well. David?'

'Hmm?'

'Fuck you also.'

The line went dead. Hallam had to laugh. Fuck you also?

He glanced at the clock. Major Reiman would be at Battalion HQ by now. That would be his first stop. He finished dressing in his usual civilian working clothes – MI officers in the field did not wear uniform – loose-fitting tan trousers, a blue, button-down shirt open at the collar with its sleeves rolled up and its tails untucked, and a pair of old loafers. He went downstairs to the kitchen thinking about the phone conversation. It had helped.

Fuck you also. He loved that.

Hallam shared the villa with four other case officers, and as ranking officer was the team chief. There was also a cook, a housegirl, several Nung Chinese guards – hired mercenaries – and a caretaker. Three of the four other case officers were non-coms; many career officers considered that training for MI was too extensive a commitment to a specialization to be good for their upward mobility. 'Six-eights', as MI officers were called because of their Military Occupational Specialty number, 9668, were also subject to unusually close scrutiny and selection. A bounced cheque in a man's record might be enough to disqualify him.

This morning, Lieutenant Fred Burris and Sergeant Paul 'Paco' Gallo were perched over the breakfast table reading the paper while their French-Eurasian housegirl, Miette, was finishing the breakfast dishes at the sink. Both men were engrossed in the *International Tribune*, but in different sections; Burris in the Sports, and Gallo in the Business for his daily self-torture.

Burris put down the paper when Hallam entered, but Gallo, cursing softly under his breath, didn't even look up.

'Morning, gentlemen,' said Hallam.

'Morning, David,' responded Burris, looking him over with a critical eye. His brow creased. 'You look lousy. Something wrong?'

Hallam smiled dryly at the big Southerner, a former varsity lineman. 'No great surprise to me they put you in MI.' He thrust his chin towards the muttering Gallo. 'Dow up again?'

Burris nodded happily. 'Twelve points. He's really miserable.'

The two men were close friends, though an odder match could not be found than the rumbling, farm-bred Georgian and the cunning little New York Italian. Burris found Paco's daily agony tremendously amusing. But Paco was as helpless in its grip as any addict. He looked up desperately and waggled a finger across the table at Burris.

'It kills me. It really does. And it should kill you, too. But you sit there on your enormous ass with four print shirts you could stuff any five normal humans into and eleven bucks to your name while everybody else is getting rich. Twelve points. Twelve! You know what we could have made if we invested right? God, it kills me. Fucking Dow.'

'Don't take it personally, Paco,' Hallam counselled. But he knew it would be in vain. When the Dow was up, Paco was like a runaway train, unstoppable.

He was agonized. 'It's like making money out of air,' he said mournfully.

'You should invest too, Paco,' prodded Burris, stoking the fires of discontent. He'd earned his code name: The Clown.

'Isn't feasible,' Paco said bitterly. 'You gotta have thousands of shares to make anything, dickbrain. Maybe millions. You know how much an eighth of a point is on a million shares? That's money. On ten or twenty shares it's bullshit.'

'You got to stop putting yourself through this,' Hallam said, accepting a cup of coffee from Miette and smiling at her in thanks.

She motioned towards Paco and Burris. 'I think they like it, *bien*? Why else do this every day?' She took in Hallam's helpless shrug. '*Fou!*' she pronounced finally, and went back to her work.

Hallam turned back to Paco and Burris. 'I lost one last night,' he said sadly. 'Murdered in her room. I'm going over to Battalion to talk it over with Reiman. You got anything to go over?'

The mention of serious business caused Paco's thick Milanese features to harden into serious lines and his brown eyes regarded Hallam sympathetically. 'I was there yesterday. Took what I had over.'

Burris tossed over a manila envelope that had been resting on the table. 'You could take this.' He was running a pair of low-level agents deep in the countryside, roadrunners, they were called, and some usable product was beginning to come in.

'Tell the good major,' he added, 'I think we can address that new stuff Requirements sent over. Maybe three, four days.'

'I'll tell him.'

They all tried to make as few trips to Battalion as possible. It was true they were under very light cover – a group studying Vietnamese hospital administration – but there was no sense in pushing it. They usually went over only to liaise or for status reports, which they typed and hand-delivered knowing that each piece of paper was also a death warrant for an agent in the field if it fell into enemy hands.

Hallam tucked the envelope under his arm. 'If Hu calls, tell him I'll be back around noon and to come over if he has the police stuff. Fred?'

'Sure, David. Noon.' But Burris's attention was shifting back to Paco, who cut off further conversation with his anguished cry of protest.

'Another fucking joke! This guy Picasso? A quarter of a million for some bullshit he did with a pencil and paper before breakfast. Ten lines, it says here. Ten lines? That's twenty-five grand a line!'

Burris grinned and waved a hand at Hallam, then turned back to needle his friend again.

'Damn, Paco. Can you imagine? Just waking up and deciding to make a quarter mil in about a minute and a half. Wham. Bam. Like printing money.'

'Goddamn. God damn . . .'

Hallam couldn't repress a smile. He walked out as Paco began yelling for a pencil. The Dow and Picasso? You didn't have to be MI to know it was a goddamn conspiracy.

*

The 5th Battalion of the 525th Military Intelligence Group was headquartered in a nondescript building about a mile from the American Embassy in the heart of downtown Saigon. Operational control of the group was vested in J2, commanded by the Assistant Chief of Staff for Intelligence, and J2 was part of Military Assistance Command, Vietnam – MACV, pronounced MAC-Vee. The word 'Assistance' indicated that the command in Vietnam was a joint one, shared between the American and Vietnamese forces. MAC-Vee was made up of officers and men from the Army, Air Force, Navy and Marines and was the largest component of the United States Mission, or 'Country Team'.

Nowhere was the joint nature of the command more apparent than in military intelligence. Both US Army and ARVN, the South Vietnamese army, needed the same intelligence on the enemy, the weather and the terrain. Each had capabilities and limitations affecting their ability to collect and produce the needed intelligence. The Americans had experienced men, money, professionalism, management techniques and rapid communications. On the other hand, there were very few linguists who could either speak or read Vietnamese.

Further, the South Vietnamese were sovereign. They controlled sources of information, property and archives. They had greater insight into the workings of their own citizenry and perhaps a better understanding, at least initially, of enemy tactics and modes of operation.

MI was a complex business, roughly divided into Collection and Production facilities, that is the gathering of information, often called 'the take', and the rendering of that sometimes voluminous and contradictory mass of raw information into meaningful intelligence which was the *raison d'être* of all military intelligence – providing the commander with the knowledge he needs.

The Intelligence Division of J2, MAC-Vee, had four important branches. The Current Intelligence and Indications Branch provided the MAC-Vee commander with significant current intelligence from all sources through daily briefings and published the J2 Intelligence Summary and Weekly Watch Report. The Order of Battle Branch had primary responsibility for preparing guidance concerning composition, strength and identification of enemy forces. The Estimates Branch was a small, highly specialized group formed to answer such questions as: What is the enemy's capacity to adversely affect the accomplishment of our mission? What are his vulnerabilities? What is his will to persevere? And the Strategic Resources Branch focused on domestic events and activities in the Republic of Vietnam.

Below this level were four combined American/Vietnamese national collection centres. The Combined Intelligence Centre, Vietnam, CICV, produced long-range background studies. The Combined Military Interrogation Centre, CMIC, questioned high-ranking prisoners captured in the field. The Combined Military Document Centre, CMDC, examined all and translated some of the captured enemy official papers found in bunkers, tunnels and command posts; and the Combined Material Exploitation Centre, CMEC, examined captured weapons and material.

Hallam often felt that CMDC quietly produced product extremely useful to field commanders. It was not unusual for critical findings to be transported out by helicopter during the day, or by jeep at night. A source might be a personal diary or an unsent letter home taken from the corpse of an enemy soldier, but the information contained within might pinpoint an enemy division or a massive counter-attack, or alert a squad of American soldiers to a planned ambush.

Hallam's unit, the 5th Battalion, ran human sources of information – HUMINT – and was involved in every facet of the war from the location of enemy forces, logistical supplies, base areas and sanctuaries, to the VC political infrastructure and counter-intelligence. Specific collection requirements were generated by units all over the country and validated by J2, then boiled down to their essential elements of information, EEI, by the Requirements Branch. These EEI were passed to battalion commands like the 5th which in turn delegated them to case officers. It was the case officer's responsibility to do a mission analysis and assess individuals who might have access to the required information. Sometimes these individuals had first to be spotted or cultivated as sources. Often, they were already in place.

That was the structure which provided the case officer with the 'what' or 'why' of the operation. The 'who' and 'how' were his day-to-day responsibilities. After the mission analysis, and assuming that a potential agent had been spotted and, further, was vulnerable to recruitment, levers of persuasion had to be established. These might be offering extra food in a war-torn city, exploiting the desire for money, blackmail, or even, though it was rare, ideological conversion.

Hallam was passed through the security cordon and sent up in a restricted lift, only to be checked again when he emerged. Around him were large rooms where legions of clerks, typists, translators and analysts worked daily. Most people not involved in intelligence work had no idea how many people it took to perform the necessary activities. It took thousands. Every scrap of information, every written report, was to intelligence sections what nickels and dimes were to a bank – it took a lot of them to make the business profitable. And like money, each and every piece had to be precisely accounted for and confirmed or rejected as genuine or counterfeit. The only alternative was stopping peasants in the road and asking, 'Seen anybody interesting?'

Hallam was greeted by a few friends as he walked through one such area on his way to Reiman's office. The department noise around him had much the same chattering rhythm as its corporate analogue in any Xerox or General Motors main office back in the States. He walked up to the familiar sergeant whose desk was a fixture outside Reiman's door and whose handle separated him from the usual stereotype: Sergeant First Class George Washington Janokowski.

'Morning, Sarge.'

Janokowski looked up, his broad, black face splitting into a grin. 'Morning, sir. How's my favourite jive captain?'

In a time when racial conflict was unsettling the entire Army, Hallam, the sergeant, and others like them had set their own private tone based on mutual respect. Much of the tension resulted from the new waves of recruits brought over from the States, mirroring the difficulties that had emerged there. It was like importing a virus that, once spread, was increasingly hard to stamp out. It was not the first time this kind of thing had happened in the armed forces, but it was the first time it was occurring on such a scale.

Hallam laughed. 'Clean up your act, you black Polish ham,' he snapped with a knowing grin. 'Now get me into Major Reiman's office before I'm too old to enjoy the beating you got coming.'

'My, my, the good captain is a slow learner,' shot back Janokowski. 'You should know Major Reiman is one of your best sponsors. Though I can't see it myself, word is you're always welcome in there. Go right in, sir.'

'I thank you, my mother thanks you . . .' Hallam let it trail off, smiling. The encounters with Janokowski reminded him of the plaque given to one particularly well-liked colonel rotated home: 'To Colonel Red Shaver, Honorary Nigger of the Year, 1967.' It was said he valued the gift from the black NCOs more than any other going-away present.

Major Reiman's office was a chart-covered, pale green cubicle with windows overlooking the street. Now, as usual, the blinds were drawn. There was the standard issue grey steel desk and filing cabinets of the embassy variety, fireproof and equipped with combination locks. There was a picture of his family on his desk, a phone and an in/out basket. The rest of the surface was covered with maps, charts, reports, files, and glossy aerial photographs, as was the top of the green metal table against the far wall.

'Come in, David,' Reiman said. He was a small man with sharp eyes that missed little. 'How are you?'

'Fine, sir. Yourself?'

Reiman's sleeves were rolled up and his glasses perched on top of his balding, grey head. He was holding a magnifying glass which he passed to Hallam. 'Puzzled. Here. Look at this.'

He pushed over an 18 × 24 inch photocopy produced by an Itek variable viewer. Hallam spread it out in front of him. 'What are we interested in here?'

'You do any image interpretation at the Bird?' Reiman asked.

'Some.'

'Well, look here. Intelligence and Indications says these are farm buildings. We've got information says it's a camouflaged NVA surface-to-air missile site. That got it kicked back to us.'

'Lose a lot of fighters and pilots if II's wrong,' Hallam observed.

'Or wipe out a shitload of civilians if we say hit it and they're right. Opinion?'

Hallam ran the glass over the photocopy. The ideal altitude for high panoramic reconnaissance was 15,000 feet, but that resulted in a photo scale of 1:15,000, too small for tactical interpretation. The Itek increased the scale to 1:500 at 30× magnification without appreciable loss of resolution.

Hallam took a long time with the Itek copy. Reiman said nothing, calmly waiting for a verdict.

'I think I'd send in a strike, sir,' Hallam said finally.

'Why?'

'Look here,' Hallam pointed. 'And here. Those ruts are over a foot deep. See the shadows? Something a lot heavier than farm produce has been pulled over that road. And where are the water buffalo? Now this dark area here, see? II says it's a barn but I disagree. If it was, there'd be an entrance and fenced-in yard facing south, for the sun. Dries out the mud. That's best for the chickens.'

Reiman was intrigued. 'You store that kind of stuff in your head?'

'Not usually,' Hallam grinned. 'Just something we run into in the boonies. Locals taught it to us spotting other VC camouflaged posts.'

'I'll be damned.'

Hallam's grin faded. 'Maybe, sir. After you hear what I've got to say, maybe you and me both.'

Reiman's sharp eyes looked him over appraisingly. 'Sit down, David,' he said. 'Just give me a minute.' He picked up his phone and dialled a number. 'Bill? Get Danny Porter over at the 7th and tell him we say knockdown on site two-three-zebra Charlie. Knockdown. Tell him I'll send over the hard stuff later. Got it? . . . Okay.' Reiman replaced the phone. 'Shoot.'

It took Hallam only a few minutes to relate the details of his agent's murder. Reiman shook his head slowly. His revulsion was evident.

'What was she working on?' he asked when Hallam was done.

'Most specifically, VC infrastructure in her father's village.'

'How did you spot her in the first place?'

'She was a prostitute, brought most of the money home to relatives. Aunts and uncles. She was a survivor, basically. She had the right geography, parents killed by the VC. She was picked up by the National Police. They thought I might be interested. I was.'

'What'd you give her?'

'Food. Money. Nothing major. Like I said, it all went home.'

Reiman was thoughtful. 'When you first vetted her, any discrepancies?'

Vetting was something the British had taught American MI. Literally, to examine closely; it provided for running an untested resource past a known target and comparing the results with what you knew to be true.

'None,' Hallam said. 'Good as gold. She wasn't doubled, sir. I was sure of it and the polygraph never even wavered.

Hu and I have some thoughts on this, though. We don't think it's MI related.' He went on, explaining.

Reiman listened, mulling it over. 'I see. Makes sense,' he conceded.

Hallam took a deep breath and let it out slowly. 'There's one other thing, sir. Something that sort of pins it closer to home. Kind of supports the theory. It's why I'm here.'

Reiman frowned unhappily. 'I know you, David. I'm going to hate this.'

'Yes, sir. I think so.'

Hallam placed the general's black star on the desk in front of him. 'We found this under her bed.'

Reiman looked as if Hallam had placed a poisonous snake on his desk. He ranged a hand heavily over his face, resting his chin finally on cupped hands as the full magnitude of it hit him.

'God damn,' he said, shaking his head. 'God damn that to hell.'

Hallam said, 'Yes, sir. My feelings exactly.'

FOUR

Reiman nudged the dark star around his desk. 'What do you want from me?'

'Permission. To investigate,' replied Hallam.

'What else?'

'We're going to need access to personnel records, travel chits, open up MAC-Vee files. There are maybe seventy, eighty generals in Vietnam. It's going to be one hell of a job to narrow down the field.'

'In many ways,' Reiman observed, 'it's still an intelligence operation.'

Hallam nodded. 'We collect, you sort out. Closed file. You, me, Hu; minimal support staff. Nobody else.'

'CYA, David?'

'Cover *all* our asses, sir. This guy throws the rule book out the window. We flush him and he could just as easily come after us. Besides, he may have assets we're unaware of. This should be run tight as a drum. Eyes only. The whole nine yards.'

Reiman pushed his chair back and walked to the window. He pushed the slats apart and peered out. 'Gonna be waves, David.'

'Not if we're careful, sir.'

Reiman shook his head. 'Even then. First interview you do with a general officer the back channel messages will be flying all over 'Nam. The old boy net will activate and you could conceivably find yourself transferred so far out in the boonies you'll think you defected. And you will have, in a way. At least, some will see it that way.'

'Will you, sir?'

'No,' Reiman said, turning. 'I know you too well. And deep down I agree. War's like a breeder reactor. Feed in a little spark of sadism and it'll come roaring back out a hellfire. We can't afford to let ourselves go; it's too damn easy to start operating from your darker side. It's tough enough out here. We don't need more crazies.'

Hallam thought over Reiman's words. 'I'd like to bring Jimmy O'Rourke in on this, sir.'

Reiman nodded. 'A psychologist. Makes sense. Have him get a profile started. I'll see to shifting his work load. Quietly. No fuss. Where's Hu this morning?'

'MSS, looking at the police reports. After we link back up, I figure we'll start at the Hung Dao. That's where she worked.'

'Okay. But first a word of caution. Contrary to Christmas cards and Bing Crosby, the world is a fucking miserable place. You've been insulated. Most of us Americans have. But this thing could take you down into a pit so deep that mud's gonna look like caviar. We're talking bottom, David. No nice brick houses with chimneys and little league and Billy, Betsy and Bobby selling lemonade to buy Mom a pin for her birthday. Not in the pit. Only cunts and assholes and slime. And it can rub off.'

'I'm no virgin, sir.'

'David,' Reiman said sadly, 'you're a babe in the woods.'

Hallam stood up. 'I'd better be going.'

Reiman's voice was filled with world-weariness. 'I tell them. They just don't believe.'

'It's not that,' Hallam said plaintively. 'It's just what difference does it make? I go after him, maybe I end up in his pit. I don't, I maybe gotta start worrying about one of my own. Where's the choice?'

Reiman sighed. 'Very well. Your case number is zero six seven Echo India. Sign off everything as Orpheus. Hu is Eurydice. Use your real names and I'll know there's trouble.'

'Yes, sir.'

Reiman looked at him with the expression of a farmer watching the cow he raised go off to be slaughtered. 'One thing, David.'

'Sir?'

'The pits you spoke of? His and yours? Well, it's time for your first lesson.'

Hallam stopped by the door. 'I know what you're going to say, sir.'

There was a pause while Reiman studied him. 'Well?'

'They're the same pit.'

Reiman nodded. 'Take care, David, keep your head down.'

Hallam drove back to the team house to meet Hu. He found him in the comfortable living room, with Miette serving him a cold drink. Hallam accepted her offer to bring him one too, and plopped down into one of the big wicker chairs.

To one side of the large room was a dining room which opened onto a glassed-in veranda, both of which served as office space. Paco was in there now, reading reports. Burris was somewhere in the city.

'It went well with the major?' Hu asked.

'I think so.' Hallam reported the conversation. 'What do the police reports say?'

'Very little we couldn't surmise. The girl was torn up by a man; strong, right-handed. The wounds were very deep. He used a standard Army-issue bayonet. You could find thousands of them in and around the city. The teeth marks are no help because the flesh was literally ground up. Not enough contrast for an impression. He also did an excellent job of obscuring his presence: no clear fingerprints, nothing in the drains, he even took the cloths he used to clean himself.'

'Weird, isn't it?' Hallam said, 'that anybody could be so cool-headed after such animal frenzy.'

'It almost seems a contradiction,' Hu agreed. 'But one we would do well remembering. He is insane, not stupid. There is nothing illogical about any of his actions, except obviously the murder itself.'

Hallam got up and brought out a file folder from the office. 'He is now file number zero six seven Echo India. You and I are Eurydice and Orpheus. Real-name signatures flag Reiman.'

'Orpheus and Eurydice? That was Reiman's idea?'

'Yeah. His way of reminding us about the danger of falling into pits.'

'Not such bad advice.'

'Maybe.'

'And an interesting comparison,' mused Hu. 'Existentially speaking, it could mean . . .'

Hallam held up a hand. 'Enough. I want existentialism I'll call in a rock band.'

'David.' Hu sounded hurt. 'There can be great consolation in philosophy.'

'Sure. But can you dance to it?'

'Say again?'

'Never mind,' said Hallam. 'Besides, if I have to listen to any of it, I'd rather it be one of your usual murky Eastern parables or something.'

Hu smiled. 'No problem.'

'Well?'

'Tally-ho,' Hu said evenly.

Hallam pulled the Toyota into the kerb outside the Hung Dao. In the daylight the dilapidated hotel looked like its whores, flat-faced and cheap.

Hallam and Hu went in the front door. On either side were pictures of nude women, behind glass and backed with worn red velvet. Inside, it smelled of boiled rice and body fluids.

The 'management' had pulled a dozen beds onto the first floor and taken out all the interior walls, making one big room. The sheets were still soiled from the previous night and an old woman was moving slowly around the room changing them.

'Looks like an emergency ward,' Hallam said, nose wrinkling.

'For many, it is.'

Hallam snorted. 'Thank you, doctor. Do you now wish to ask this simple charwoman a few penetrating questions, or will you just prescribe intuitively?'

'You're doing it again, David.'

'Sorry.'

Hu went over to the old woman and began talking to her. Hallam poked around gingerly. 'Gotta have bacteria the size of dolphins in here,' he muttered to himself.

There was nothing of a personal nature anywhere in the room. Beds, washstands, a table with empty liquor bottles, shuttered windows, a staircase in the corner.

Hallam had mixed emotions about the place. Brothels for the troops were nothing new, but for some reason he had to confront a feeling that somehow he was responsible; in some way had an obligation to change things. Hu would have shook his head in disbelief at that and told him it was just his naive sixties social conscience rearing its silly liberal head. Hallam sighed. Maybe Hu was right. He decided not to go upstairs and teach the girls a few choruses of 'What the World Needs Now Is Love'.

'David?' Hu had finished talking to the old woman.

'Watcha got?'

'Names, numbers. The second floor has separate rooms. More private. More exotic, too. They're usually kept for officers or the really kinky. Girls live on the third floor.'

'We should get them down here.'

'I've already sent the old woman.'

'Think she'll try and escape? Could be the mastermind behind the entire bunch. And you let her go.'

'We can risk it, I think,' said Hu dryly.

Hallam smiled. It was a wonder Hu never chafed under his abrasive sarcasm, rightly regarding it as Hallam's way of calling for help. Hallam often wondered if Hu realized how much his presence steadied him, how much he needed the Vietnamese's objective view of things. He was the stepping stones Hallam used to cross this most treacherous river he'd been pushed into.

'Who are we today?' he asked.

Hu reached into his shirt pocket. 'I have National Police credentials.'

'Okay.'

The old woman was coming down the stairs with six girls, all in their teens, in tow. Some wore kimonos, some wore the sexy tunic-like *ao dai* dresses. They were all stretching from just having been woken, sleepy-eyed and sated like recently fed cats. But watchful.

Hu bade them sit, showed his ID and took down their names.

'Who's he?' asked one in English, bolder than the rest, pointing to Hallam.

'You the head girl?' Hallam asked.

She nodded. 'Yeah. But you no police.'

'*He's* police,' Hallam said. 'I'm a strange visitor from another planet.'

'Don't you make fun of me,' she said sharply. 'I'm not so stupid. You wanna see? The car outside, Toyota. Is yours, no?'

'The car . . .?' Hallam was caught off guard. The girl stared challengingly at him, pretty enough in a way, dark and silky-haired with a pout to her pronounced lips. He knew that to Hu she was just a prostitute; not his burden. After all, she didn't have to be a whore. And Hu would feel that with a mantle of moral superiority that never rested quite so easily on his own shoulders. Hallam couldn't help but see her as another of the war's victims . . . and that deprived him of Hu's insulation. It made her a fellow human. So instead of feeling superior, he felt slightly awkward in the extent of his power over her, embarrassed by his flippancy.

'It's my car,' he said and saw Hu frown.

'Then you military spook,' she said smugly. Her face creased into a knowing, confidential grin. 'CIA drive Pintos.'

Hallam needed a lifeline and Hu tossed him one. A terse fusillade in Vietnamese snapped the grin off the girl's face.

'What did you say?'

'I reminded her jail makes this place smell like roses.'

'Appreciate it,' Hallam muttered. He pulled the table away from the wall and pushed some chairs under it. 'One at a time, Hu. Tell the rest to wait over there. Let's start with Miss Car and Driver.'

Hu made the arrangements, then sat down next to Hallam with pad and pen ready.

'Name?' Hallam asked the girl.

'Daffodil.'

Hallam looked at her tiredly.

'Binh Lo Pac,' she said sullenly.

'Age?'

'Sixteen.'

'Come again?'

'Fourteen.'

Hallam produced a picture. 'We're interested in this girl. She work here?'

A crafty smile came over the girl's face. She looked at them. 'She sometimes talk about having big connections. You her connections, maybe?'

Hallam said nothing. Hu stopped writing.

The smile left the girl's face. 'She work here.'

'Last night?'

'Yes.'

'Was that the last time you saw her?'

The girl nodded. 'She left regular time. Not come back. Why you so interested anyway?'

Hallam was surprised the words left his mouth so easily. 'She was killed last night.'

The girl brought her hands to her mouth with a sudden wail. The others looked up, caught her rapid translation and the keening spread.

'Stop it,' said Hallam sharply.

'How?' the girl asked, quieting.

Hallam didn't really want to do it, but he needed her on his side. Outrage might put her there. He handed her the police photographs.

The girl was tough, he had to admit. He heard her gag but she looked at every one.

'Very bad,' she said finally. 'Poor girl.'

It was funny, Hallam thought, but that about said it better than anyone else had. Poor girl.

'Poor country,' said Hu softly, reading his thoughts.

'Who did she leave with?' Hallam asked.

The girl thought for a moment. 'Was very busy last night. Maybe two dozen in this room. More upstairs. She not live here. Left around one.'

'Why do you remember that?'

The girl looked at him oddly. 'She said goodbye.'

'Number one question,' cut in Hu. 'Who did she leave with?'

'No one,' the girl said firmly. 'She worked. She went home. Always.'

'Always alone?'

'Far as I see.'

'Did she always go straight home?'

The girl shrugged. 'Who knows what she does when she leaves?'

'Who keeps the books here?' Hallam asked.

'I do. For Mama-san.' Proudly, 'I read, too.'

'What did she earn last night?'

'I get records.'

It took her a few minutes to retrieve the 'books', a loosely bound collection of column-covered pages.

'Hundred-sixty dollars,' she said after riffling through.

'How many men?' Hallam asked, interested in spite of himself.

'Fifteen, twenty.' The girl shrugged.

Hu consulted the police file. 'She had two hundred in her bag.'

'She could have had forty from before,' Hallam said. 'You pay every night?'

She nodded. 'Girl keeps tally. It agrees with mine, we pay. If not, we argue.' She looked serious. 'I win most.'

'So she might have had money from the day before.'

'Yes, but she didn't. When I pay her, she count it and put it in her bag. Talked about paying rent that day. Had nothing from two or three nights. I tell her to move in here. She say, no. And left. Alone.'

Hu looked up. 'So somewhere between home and here she picked up forty dollars.'

'The killer's?'

'I should think so.'

'How did he spot her? She wasn't working the street.'

'Maybe from another time,' Hu responded. 'A different place. He sees her, makes an offer, it's accepted and she takes him home. Maybe the forty was just a down payment.'

'Even forty more than here,' the girl said. 'She come back here, we take piece.'

It made sense, at least initially. 'Pac, what's the highest rank you, ah, service here the past few nights?'

'Blew major yesterday,' she said reflectively. 'And did two captains the other day. That what you mean?'

'Yes. Uh, the major. He was the highest rank?' Hallam asked.

'You think we get big hotshots here? Look around. No goddamn country club. Major pretty good.'

'Prestige,' Hu said, stone-faced.

'You betcha.'

'Never a general?'

Hallam slipped it in effortlessly and for an instant would have sworn he saw something flicker across the girl's face. For a split second she was seeing elsewhere, then it was gone He would have given a lot to share that mental picture.

'Never,' she said.

'Never a general?' Hu asked. So he saw it too, Hallam realized.

'No. No general here.'

'Elsewhere?'

'Nowhere. No general.'

'You want the standard speech on how difficult we can make your life?' Hu said angrily.

'Don't matter, Ong. No general. I swear.'

'Hu?' Hallam smiled at the girl. 'I believe her. She's been very helpful. Let's move on. Thank you, Cô Binh. Please call the next girl.'

Binh Lo Pac smiled graciously at the unexpectedly formal courtesy. She made a polite bow and went to usher over the next in line.

'She's lying,' Hu said matter-of-factly.

'Yep. She's connected to a general some way. So let's get on with the others and see if anybody else here is.'

'Agreed.' Hu looked at the girl who had come over and sat opposite them. 'Your name?'

'Golden Dawn.'

Hallam let out a long sigh.

It was night when the two men left and Binh Lo Pac hurried to the doorway, scrupulously copying down the number of the old Toyota. Her face was harder now, less anxious to please. The lips had turned sharp and tight, a truer reflection of the drives which gave them shape.

There was a phone upstairs and she hurried to it. The two men could make it very hard for her if they came back and wanted to. She drew the curtains closed to warn the others to stay out of earshot. They would, too. Nobody angered her unnecessarily.

She dialled a number that even Hallam would have had trouble getting access to.

'MAC-Vee HQ,' said a voice.

'Extension five, please.'

'Please hold, ma'am.' A pause. Then a second voice, older, used to command. 'Hello?'

She was old beyond her years and jaded, but she could still feel fear. It was . . . arousing.

'Hello,' she said.

'Why are you calling me?' asked the voice coldly.

'A problem,' she said quickly. 'Two men came here. They said police, but I don't think so.'

'What did they want?'

'To know about the girl.' She went on, 'And about generals.'

'But you gave them . . .?'

'Nothing. You know better.'

'Tell me the rest,' he said simply.

She did.

FIVE

He crossed the alluvial rice fields bent low, travelling as silently as a snake through a marsh. What little skin peered out from his Ranger's suit was as blue-black as the river mud: camouflage paint. It was dusk and the setting sun flamed the horizon red-orange. The smell of human excrement in the low waters was powerful. There were peasants working nearby but they never saw him.

He reached the woods without the aid of his compass. He knew the way, having come often enough, slipping into North Vietnamese territory without fear of detection. He never knew when he was coming, never made a conscious decision to leave his posting at some specified time. Often, it was just a feeling that it was time again to sit in the master's presence. Or he had need to establish direction. This time it was the girl's phone call. He had to know how to proceed. Inevitably, the master always anticipated his arrival.

The knapsack was heavy on his back and he paused to shift it. It was filled with food and medical supplies. He sometimes wondered what the master had done before he made these visits and brought these things. He wondered what the old man would do if he stopped. The old man never went out, and over the past few months it had been seen to that no one else could get in.

He crept through the underbrush and came to the first string of traps he'd planted. In part, these were to keep the master safe from VC guerrillas and trigger-happy Americans; no one but a skilled Ranger or survival expert could pass through here without blowing off an arm or a leg. But they were also to keep the master *in*, like a greedy boy concealing stolen items, or maybe his collection of dirty pictures.

He picked his way gingerly through the finger-sized charges with pressure-sensitive feelers called 'gravel', usually dropped from planes. He passed the pits filled with sharpened stakes and the minefield, and finally the 'homemade' stuff that would tear your head off if you walked into it wrong.

In a small clearing in the centre of the booby-trapped circumference he came to the small, thatched cottage where the master lived. Alongside was a hut that housed his only servant. There was a fire pit out front, a pen with a few chickens, and a small garden. It was quiet in the clearing, surrounded by the trees. In the gathering darkness, one might miss it completely.

He knocked at the door and felt the first rush of excitement that always preceded an audience. As always, he left the food outside and removed his weapons and shoes. The smell of incense wafted out, slightly bitter yet somehow sweet. It was like a woman's smell and it tightened him.

The servant opened the door and ushered him into the tiny antechamber. He parted the curtains for the visitor to step into the main room. With a sudden intake of breath, the visitor saw that a tea service for two was already set up, and in his pattern – the oddly familiar pattern that the master said best reflected his particular soul.

'How did you know?' he asked.

The master just shook his head. He was seated cross-legged on a thatched mat, wrapped in silk robes. He was old, older than anyone the visitor had ever seen, with wispy, white whiskers straggling down a face so deeply creviced it looked like it could break apart at any moment.

His dark eyes spoke volumes. 'I knew,' he said simply.

'I have questions,' said the visitor.

The old man pointed to the tea. 'First,' he directed.

It was odd, the visitor thought, that the only sense of peace he had ever known came here, in an old Chinese's hut drinking tea in the middle of a war. He felt peace descend over him, cleansing, relaxing. He wondered, not for the first time, what it would be like to feel like this always. He might not have to . . .

He had first seen reference to the old man in an intelligence report on the area. Almost at once, he'd known he would come. Some mystic bond compelled him. He'd obliterated any further mention of the old man in that and subsequent reports. It became his secret, his connection to the mystical universe external to him which mirrored the universe within. He remembered his first pilgrimage . . .

'Focus,' commanded the master.

Very well. He emptied his mind, breathing in through his nose and out through his mouth until he achieved a steady rhythm. His needs, his drives, thoughts of the girl, all faded. When his mind was at last like the surface of a lake without ripples, the master spoke.

'The universe is always in a state of change, from one thing to another. Every moment becomes a different moment. All things change. Thus, every moment, every thing, contains within it the seeds of its own change. We strive to sense this, to understand what forces are at work and the changes that must occur because of these forces. This is the nature of the *I Ching*, the Book of Changes. Look down.'

The visitor opened his eyes and saw that the traditional white linen had been spread out before him and the tea service removed by the same unseen hands. In the centre of the white cloth were the many narrow sticks of yarrow root.

'Throw them,' commanded the old man.

In a movement reminiscent of the child's game, the visitor took up the yarrow sticks and let them fall back onto the cloth. They lay there, intertwined in a random pattern. The master scrutinized them. 'Again,' he ordered.

A total of six times the sticks were thrown. The pattern was different each time, unique. The visitor found himself drawn into the loose piles, pulled down as if each stick were a member in some strangely meaningful construction; till *he*, in some way, lay on that unsullied, white cloth.

'The Book,' said the master, nodding slowly.

The servant materialized and handed him the ancient volume of the *I Ching*, the Chinese Book of Changes. The master slowly turned its yellowed pages.

'It is the Shui hexagram,' he said finally. 'Look.' With a long stick, he traced six lines in the sand.

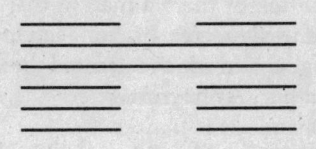

```
───────    ───────
───────    ───────
───────    ───────
─────────────────
─────────────────
─────────────────
```

'The Shui hexagram,' he said again.

'Do you not need my question?' asked the visitor.

'What would it matter?' shrugged the old man. 'Here is its answer.

'In Shui, the king repairs to his ancestral temple. It will be advantageous to meet the Great Man. Then there will be progress and success. The use of Great Victims will conduce to Great Fortune.'

This *was* interesting. So the one who hunted him was not just anyone, but a Great Man; one worthy of him. He savoured that. It was suitable.

The master continued. 'The first line, divided, shows its subject with a sincere desire for union, but unable to carry it out.'

Those who were after him. Yes, they would want 'union'. In a way, so did he.

'The second line, divided, shows advancement with sincerity. The third, divided, shows the subject in such a state that if he is greatly fortunate, he will receive no blame.'

So . . . Success would absolve him. He could win again.

'The fourth and fifth lines are undivided. Let his virtue be firmly correct and all occasion for repentance will disappear.'

'And the sixth line?' he asked.

The master nodded. 'Most important. Look here.'

'Yes. I see. It is good.'

'For one.'

'Which?' the visitor asked.

But the master said nothing.

'Which one?' he repeated.

The great, dark eyes turned to him. 'Whichever is more correct.'

He knew there was no use pressing. The fog of incense in the close quarters swirled around him. He stood slowly.

'Thank you, master. A direction emerges. I will come again soon.'

'As you wish.'

'You have need of something?'

'I am content. The food is appreciated. We will not starve.'

'No.' He hesitated. 'Sometimes I feel . . .'

But the master's eyes were focused elsewhere. The visitor knew he had been dismissed. He parted the curtains and walked out.

The night air was cold after the cloying atmosphere inside. He pulled on his boots and readjusted his camouflage suit. Without the pack he would make better time. He strapped on his .45 and made sure his knife was accessible in his boot top.

He left the clearing convinced of success. But to be pursued by a Great Man was no small thing. He would have to be careful. Firmly correct. Plans began to form in his mind. Intricate plans required much thought.

He moved deeper into the forest, his mind as clean and hard as glass. He revelled in the flow of his energies. He passed the traps without incident.

All the way home he kept remembering the sixth line of the hexagram. He began to see it more and more as a guarantee. The Great Man would fall before him.

The sixth line, the topmost, divided, showed its subject sighing and weeping; there will be no error.

SIX

Hallam looked over the English translation of the police report. 'What's this?' he asked, pointing to one of Hu's notations.

'Not all the wounds were made with the bayonet,' Hu said. 'Some were smaller punctures and the technicians found wood splinters in the wounds.'

'Wood splinters?'

'He may have hit her with other things in the room.'

Hallam didn't think so. 'We didn't see any damaged furniture. What'd he use, chopsticks?'

'Doesn't say. Only mentions the splinters.'

'Get on the horn and find out what else they have to say. Size. Type.'

'Why so interested?'

'I don't know, really. It just seems funny, out of place.'

'I can certainly check it,' Hu said.

'Okay.'

Hu picked up the phone.

'Maybe it's from a toothpick, or a match,' Hallam conjectured. 'Or a piece of his peg-leg. Maybe Long John Silver wasted her.'

Hu dialled the lab and spoke to the technicians for a few moments. Hallam sat back in his chair. They had returned to the villa well after dark. The prostitute knew something, of that they were both certain, but it remained to be seen how that could be put to use. Maybe the best bet was to pull her in and question the hell out of her. The Vietnamese had proved extremely vulnerable to the polygraph. The only problem was, this presupposed you had the right questions to ask.

'David?'

Hallam looked up. Hu was holding the phone away from his ear.

'The wood is yarrow root. Native to the northern hemisphere, found in large quantities in China. It is often used for medicinal purposes.'

'China's pretty far away,' said Hallam.

'Given our large ethnic Chinese population, there are plenty of Chinese products around here.'

'Okay. Hang up.'

Hu said brief thanks and replaced the receiver. 'What does this suggest to you?'

'Rudimentary, my dear Hu. The killer is a Chinese medicine man masquerading as an American general.'

'You're being facetious. But what about the possibility of his having visited a Chinese doctor? A herbalist?'

'Possible. All this Eastern mystic crap might be very appealing to a guy with bugs in the brain.' Hallam held up a hand. 'Don't say it. I apologize. A trip to the local herbalist might be a fine idea.'

'But not tonight,' suggested Hu tiredly.

'No. Not tonight. I'm beat, too. Tomorrow, after we meet with O'Rourke, okay?'

'Okay. Good night, David.'

''Night.'

Hallam sat for a while, enjoying the solitude and the company of the former owner's striking porcelain vases. On one hand art, on the other the killer. Did they express some kind of spectrum he had yet to comprehend fully? Miette came in to ask if he wanted a late supper. He declined. Warm breezes brought the scent of jasmine in from the courtyard. The house was quiet. Paco and Burris were out somewhere. Their fourth housemate, Maryk, still had a few days of R&R left.

What was the killer doing now? Hallam wondered. Did his

mind teem with lizards all the time? Or was he, too, just sitting somewhere now, doing some paperwork and feeling quite normal until it came time to erupt into insanity again?

Hallam felt his eyes beginning to shut and pushed out of his chair. He had hours of paperwork to do himself yet. There were other responsibilities that couldn't be allowed to fall by the wayside while they chased down the girl's killer. He had other agents in the field.

He went into the office and turned on the lights. Soon, he was engrossed in his work, grateful for the peace of mind the presence of the Nung guards generated. Report followed report . . .

It was after three when he stumbled upstairs and fell into a dreamless sleep until morning.

Hallam parked the Toyota and took the lift up to Reiman's office. Jim O'Rourke was already there and grasped his hand warmly.

'How are ya, David?' asked the big Columbia graduate. A former college linebacker in his native Minnesota, his big hand swallowed Hallam's.

'Fine, Jimmy. The major keeping you busy?'

'Pal, I got me a woman with tits like twin one-oh-fives. *She's* keeping me busy. The major here's just a part-time employer,' O'Rourke laughed.

'Always nice to know your priorities,' Reiman said dryly.

'Years of psychological training,' grinned Hallam. 'I'd send the insubordinate bag of shit home.'

'Don't I wish,' O'Rourke begged. 'This place assaults even my stable citadel.'

'Forget it,' said Reiman. 'You're fucking doomed.'

'Where's Hu?' O'Rourke asked. 'Or aren't you two doing Me-and-My-Shadow anymore?'

Hallam couldn't resist. 'Hu's on first,' he said with a straight face.

Reiman groaned. O'Rourke just shook his head sadly, 'They've broken the motherfucker.'

Hallam dropped into a chair. 'He'll be here any minute. Looks like there's a link between one of the girls at the Hung Dao and a general. But it's too early to tell more.'

'How's the paperwork end of things going?' O'Rourke asked Reiman.

'Ton of shit to sift through,' he said. 'But it's coming along.'

Further conversation was cut off by Hu's entrance. 'Sorry I'm late, gentlemen. Hello, Jim. Nice to see you again.'

'You too, Hu.'

'I dropped by the police lab,' Hu said, reaching into his pocket. 'David, our call about the wood apparently jostled somebody. They found a larger piece of the yarrow root in one of the wounds. Look at this.'

He passed over a plastic bag containing a three- or four-inch narrow segment of stick, splintered at one end and caked with dried blood on the other.

'What is this?' Hallam asked. 'Just a stick?'

'Could be,' Hu responded. 'Nobody knows yet. Research is being conducted. Ring bells in anybody's mind here?'

Reiman, Hallam and O'Rourke looked blank. Hu sighed. 'Me neither.'

'Okay,' said Reiman. 'In the absence of penetrating wisdom from anybody, let's let Jim do his thing. Captain?'

O'Rourke perched back on the table and his face lost its usual humour as his demeanour became professional. 'Let's understand something from the outset. I can't really explain the psychopath fully because we don't know enough about the condition. In a way, Papa Freud only mapped out the outlines of this very complex territory; much of the inner region is a mystery. But I can suggest a few things you'll probably find are true about him.

'First and foremost, a psychopath is conscienceless. He is motivated only by his own satisfaction. Nothing really exists for him but what he wants, fulfilling his desires. You, me, we feel others' pain. We would have felt the girl's pain. That's part of what prevents us from being able to inflict it. But the psychopath lacks our ability to empathize. To him, people are only objects and he sees the world only in shades of aggression. In some ways, it's as much a moral defect as a character disorder.'

'What causes it?' asked Hallam.

O'Rourke screwed up his face haplessly. 'I wish I could tell you we knew. Look, with all the Freudian bullshit that's tossed around these days, you know enough to know that the ego is the mediating function between our inner impulses and the outer reality. In the psychopath, the ego has been severely deformed. His mediating function has been locked into rigidly fixed terms at a very early age, so what should make reality clearer, actually distorts it. Imagine having had filters put over your eyes from infancy so you saw everything just in certain shades. The psychopath is like that. He doesn't know the filters are there, but they colour everything regardless.

'Studies suggest the psychopath usually suffers serious early-childhood deprivation, though that's not always so. For whatever reason, though, he's filled with rage – and has no way to diminish it. Continued abuse limits his flexibility. His entire judgement system is affected. The "filters" become welded into place and are soon characteristic of all his ways of thinking and feeling.

'The con-man who can marry a lonely old lady for her life savings and then kill her; the twelve-year-old street kid who tortures and kills his victims for pennies; the battlefield commander whose thinking is so distorted that he never plugs into the human costs. No weighing, no judgement. Most of all, no compassion.'

'And no God,' mused Hu softly, creating a deep, reflective silence.

O'Rourke picked it up first. 'In a way, I suppose. If morality is derived from the deity.'

'Compassion is,' Hu stated flatly. 'Can we argue any other source?'

'Like I said, Hu,' O'Rourke responded, 'Freud only gave us a very general map. If we find God inside the territory he outlined, I'll be first in line to trade in my couch for a collar.'

'Or an incense burner.'

O'Rourke smiled. 'That, too.'

'So what can we count on from this guy?' Hallam broke in.

'He'll be smart and clever. Above average intelligence. Probably quite charming, too. Externally, he can be a helluva fellow. But be clear. First, last and for ever it will all be an act. His intelligence has shown him how to function in the world, how to get what he wants. But he has no true feelings other than rage and no outlook other than gratification. Pierce the skin, look through the act, and underneath you'll see the furnace that long ago consumed everything human.'

'The hollow man,' said Hallam.

'Why, David,' said Hu. 'Eliot?'

'Don't be a snob, Hu.'

'The hollow man,' agreed O'Rourke. 'Yeah, with no "off" button.'

Reiman said, 'Enraged and compassionless and dangerous. Quite a package.'

'Any advice if we flush him, Jim?' asked Hallam.

'Sure, if you'll keep in mind that "dangerous" doesn't even begin to describe what your killer is capable of.' O'Rourke pointed a finger at Hallam to underscore his point. 'David, please believe me. If you threaten this man and can't run or get out of his way, waste the motherfucker without hesitation or he'll rip your heart out and eat it while you watch.'

It was too early for the whores to be out on Tu Do street, but late enough to send the peddlers packing for home. Carts got closed up and bicycled off. The streets grew emptier as the fat red sun slanted lower and lower. For a few minutes, the city was suspended between night and day and time grew as sluggish as the sedentary air.

He went in the side entrance of the Hung Dao, down a rubbish-strewn alley between the buildings. He used his key to open the door. There was a short flight of stairs to a second door, unlocked; he opened that one and passed inside to the large room on the first floor.

The old cleaning woman had finished her work and now fresh sheets adorned the over-used beds. She sat smoking a cigarette. At his entrance she looked up, eyes widening a bit, but she said nothing. She knew crazy eyes when she saw them. Hopefully, he would pass.

But he didn't. 'Binh Lo Pac,' he said. 'Where is she?'

The old woman had last seen the girl upstairs in her room about to take a shower. She said so; you didn't fuck with crazy eyes. When the man said nothing more she assumed he was satisfied. She returned her attention to her cigarette, enjoying the curl of acrid smoke around her nose, thinking about how tired her feet were.

An odd little *thrum* of air registered in her consciousness only as a passing insect. She never had time to reinterpret the sound correctly. She just died without ever seeing the source of the blow that killed her.

Travelling at over one hundred and forty miles an hour and delivering a ton and a half of force to a point the size of a button — in this case, her skull — the polished wooden butt-end of the *nunchukus* blasted into the exact centre of her forehead, crushing it, the shock wave turning most of the brain mass behind it into sodden, formless pulp.

The *nunchukus*, a pair of oak 'handles' about ten inches long joined at the end by a sturdy leather thong, completed its deadly arc. One shaft still in his hand, the other spun back into his grip in the completed motion so reminiscent of a 'flicked' towel or a cracked whip. Like most Chinese weapons, it was originally an agricultural tool; in this case a grain flail. Far deadlier now, it imparted almost all its force directly into the old woman's head. She didn't keel backwards, didn't even stagger, merely died where she was sitting and crumpled like a folding screen. The cigarette drooped from slack lips. He pocketed the twin shafts and went quietly up the stairs to the third floor.

Binh Lo Pac had her own room and he heard the sound of running water from her shower as he slipped inside. He settled down in a chair by her bed to wait.

She was naked when she emerged, towelling her hair dry. He had hoped she would be. He liked the tiny drops of water glistening in her dark pubic triangle. He rose up, aware of his own pulse beat. Time was slowing. She saw him . . .

She knew him well enough to know that if he was here he had come to kill her. He was pleased she made a final effort; the knife in her hand made it, well, not so much a challenge exactly, but at least a bit more strenuous than the usual squashing out.

The girl was no novice. She had learned to defend herself on the streets after being raped at the age of nine. She found the man later and killed him. She had been afraid but, like now, turned it into impetus. Never far away, the knife flashed into her hand and she dropped the towel as excess baggage. She came at him no-nonsense style, blade held low and flat, thrusting up for his vital organs.

The *nunchukus* flashed out, spinning in a circle and wrapping round the wrist of her outstretched hand. He caught one end and brought the handles together in a scissors-like motion that crushed her wrist. She cried out in pain, the knife dropping from her lifeless hand.

She tried to kick but he was prepared for that. The *nunchukus* flew up and round, disengaging from her wrist, only to blast back again in a staggering blow across her shin. The bone shattered like glass and sent her crashing to the floor in blind agony.

'But I gave the girl to you,' she gasped, pleading. 'Sent the other, too. Whatever you asked . . .'

'For money,' he explained as a teacher might. 'And you would sell out for even less.'

'Please . . . please, I send more.'

'No. You screwed up. The girl was connected to MI. Prepare.'

Her head bowed. 'Not like the others,' she whispered hoarsely, 'Please, just do it. Kill me.'

He frowned. Why was she still talking to him? She had sent others to him. What did she expect? Besides, there was a point to be made and he wanted to be creative. The Great Man deserved his best.

There was a glass on the night table, a heavy water tumbler. He put down the *nunchukus* and picked it up. The girl's eyes were glazed with pain and shock, but he saw fear flash in them. He reached down and grasped her by the hair . . .

Time was short. He was very inventive.

Hallam closed the girl's door gently behind him. Hu was talking to a policeman. No one in the hotel had heard a thing. No one saw a thing. The old woman downstairs, the girl up here; both dead, leaving a trail as cold as the killer.

Hallam took a deep ragged breath. Something was happening to him inside; hardening. He was able to look at the mess inside without throwing up, though God knew it was worse than the first time. But he was beginning to hate now, beginning to feel an inner shifting that told him he couldn't put this case down even if he was told to.

He was also severely shaken. You made assumptions about life in order to live it. The ground would stay put; buildings didn't fall on your head; people in cars didn't try and run you down. With his random, mindless terror, the killer denied all that. It got under Hallam's skin. No rules at all; psychic violation. It made you question all the assumptions you lived under, moved the earth under your feet, pulled your building blocks apart till there was nothing solid to stand on and no structure left on which to depend. Every movement became a fearful step into unknown regions. Nothing absolute could possibly remain – not even a loving God.

In that instant, Hallam knew what he would see in the killer's eyes when at last they met – and now he had no doubt that they would. The killer had used hanks of the girl's hair as a brush and painted on the wall with her blood the horrible bulbous Black Widow spider, bent-knife legs hooked in its web; the two figures trapped within the web could only be himself and Hu. The spider was feasting, and on the dresser, a glass filled to the brim with blood. Hallam wanted to gag it made him so sick with fear.

So he sought refuge in how much he hated this diseased maniac. In hate was strength. Invoke your own power, he told himself. Kill him yourself in a hundred ways in your mind. Work magic for magic. Fight back, he told himself; fight back. For the gory picture inside told him something else, too. One day soon he was going to come face to face with the spider and he would have to stare long and hard down into its empty eyes, stare without protection deep into a dark and churning place no man could ever witness and be unchanged.

Into chaos.

SEVEN

In a small, windowless room lit by rows of white-jacketed fluorescent lights down the hallway from Reiman's office, three two-stripers returned from their dinner hour and bent back to work. Over the past days the long list of names had narrowed. Seventy-eight generals became forty-six. Forty-six were condensed to twenty-two. Carefully, calls were made, reports checked, movements screened. Some generals were like the outer planets, visible only by their effect on other bodies. The aide, the request for transportation, the travel documents; all added up and another name could be crossed off the list. Nineteen. Eighteen. This one? Possible. Nothing to cross-check . . . The first.

The radio someone had smuggled in spewed background music; the Doors, the Rolling Stones, the Beatles. Rumour had it Paul was dead. It was hard to find anyone who gave a shit. Not so many miles away, nineteen-year-old soldiers scared shitless of the jungle were dropping acid and blowing up the countryside.

The movement of paperwork continued. The Moody Blues. Richie Havens. No Parisian wine cellars to get drunk in like our fathers did. All the rhythms were different. Whose dream was this, anyway? One day Vietnam's story would be told accurately. It was all just work, and some of it fucked you up. Seventeen. Cross that shitbag off. Sonofabitch was in DC. Here's the cable traffic. Verified. Sixteen.

It took a long time. One of them stepped out to the john and caught a quick buzz; spent some time trying to hunt up Suzy-Qs; returned and found others crossed off.

Ten.

One cursed mildly, pointed out that all of the music told them to question. Question what, for Chrissake? None of this shit was real. He missed *Saturday Night at the Movies*. A discussion ensued. Nobody could rightly remember. He missed Disney on Sunday nights. The Ponderosa. Ben Cartwright had to be real. Fucking white women was real. He was fairly sure his dick was real. Nine.

His girlfriend had written saying she was sure she saw him on the news last week. He wrote back no, he wasn't in combat and they didn't show what he did do on no fucking news. She wouldn't know the difference anyway – wasn't real to her either. What could be real to anybody raised on television? A whole generation wondering where the hell the soundtrack was every time they walked down the fucking street. Or took off their pants. No wonder you played the radio all the time.

A long three hours later; eight.

Somebody said breaktime. They ate by a window in another room with the lights out so they could watch the VC artillery flashes in the distance. It was moderate tonight. No major television news crews in the city doing documentaries. Otherwise, they'd put on a *really big show* for the folks back home.

Break over. Sure, sure. Back to the wonderful world of paper. Heard about a bunch out in the boonies under constant VC attack. Used to leave the bodies on the barbed wire till morning. Cut off the ears. Let 'em dry. Made necklaces. General shows up with CBS news; valiant stand and all that. Goes bullshit. Doesn't want the news to see. Says sew 'em back on. They do. Backwards.

Another guy tells me he knew an SAR guy gave up his rotation home to keep trying for a downed pilot. Can you believe it? Gave up *home*? Took two weeks to get him out. Saved his ass. Guy's Jolly Green got shot down twice. Had to walk out himself the second time. Brave motherfucker. Whaddya learn? I don't know. Takes all kinds, I guess. Seven.

Morning came and went.

*

Hallam and Hu drove into Cholon, the ethnic Chinese section of Saigon.

'You ever try any of this herbal stuff?' Hallam asked.

Hu nodded. 'As a child. I was very sick and the French doctors had no cure. Probably some kind of viral pneumonia. My father was a government worker. You can understand his reluctance. It wasn't, ah, upwardly mobile to seek folk cures. I suppose he was desperate. I ended up having to take some mouldy revolting mixture served up with so many needles stuck into me I looked like a porcupine.'

'Acupuncture?'

'Yes. But say what you will, I'm still here.'

Hallam held up a hand. 'You got me wrong. I don't claim a monopoly on this stuff for the West. Antibiotics or crushed lizard tail, a chemical's a chemical.'

'Remarkably egalitarian of you.'

Hallam grinned. 'I have my moments.'

The shop was on a side street lined with two- and three-storey buildings housing what could have been lawyers' or accountants' offices. Short flights of stairs led to wooden doors with glass inserts and even the street peddlers in front seemed neater and better organized.

The Chinese exercised a paramount role in the nation's business. Throughout Asia they were known as industrious, hard-working dealmakers, often called the 'Jews' of the Orient, not meant disparagingly. Hallam objected to the term as racist and anti-Semitic, but understood the comparison. In any event, the Chinese community added a healthy economic vitality to the city, although their favoured treatment by the government was sometimes resented by the local Vietnamese.

'That shop. There,' pointed Hu, reading the Chinese characters Hallam could not. He pulled the car over.

The shop was a mélange of dry, spicy odours and, visually, a conglomeration of oddly shaped, alien objects. Barrels of toothy, dried fish stood in groups and desiccated lizards hung from hooks, spinning slowly in the scented air. The bony legs of unknown animals protruded from wooden chests of drawers that looked like library file cabinets. Roots and mushrooms, mosses and dried noodles sprouted in profusion from coloured ceramic canisters.

Opening the door rang a small bell over the entrance and summoned a neat, plump man in a white lab jacket whom Hallam judged to be in his early fifties. He welcomed them in Chinese, conversed briefly with Hu, and then both switched to English as a courtesy to the American who, like most of his unilingual countrymen, was beginning to realize that his schooling had been the product of a remarkably restricted world view.

'How can I help you gentlemen?' asked the Chinese politely.

'We are here as part of an investigation,' Hu explained. 'But it is not one in which either you or your business figure except as a source of information. That is why we're here.'

The Chinese nodded. Hallam saw small tensions abate. 'I am Wu Lin. Please, how may I help?'

'We'd like to know what you can tell us about the yarrow plant,' said Hallam. 'You're familiar with it?'

'A medicinal plant,' Wu Lin nodded. 'In Western terminology, *Achillea millefolium*. It was named after the Greek, Achilles, to whom legend ascribes the discovery of its healing powers. We use it in the treatment of wounds. Its properties are what you would describe as antiseptic. Here.' He turned to a cabinet, opened a drawer and pulled out a small bag. 'This is the ground flower.'

Hallam spilled a bit of the white powder onto the counter. He bent closer and wrinkled his nose. 'Whew!'

The Chinese smiled. 'We list it as "pungent".'

'What about the root?' Hu inquired. 'Also medicinal?'

'No. There is a cousin to the yarrow called the sneezewort whose root was ground up for use as snuff in Great Britain. But that's all that comes to mind.'

'You've been very kind, sir,' said Hallam. 'Would you mind just taking a look at this and see if it means anything to you?'

'Certainly.'

Hallam brought out the plastic bag and passed it over the counter. The herbalist picked it up and examined it closely. Hallam could see the corners of his eyes and mouth curl with emotion.

'Yes?' Hu prompted.

'May I ask a question first?'

'Of course.'

'The blood here. It is blood, isn't it?'

'Yes.'

'Then this stick was used in a crime of some violent nature?'

'You may assume that,' Hu said.

'Very bad,' said Wu Lin, shaking his head. 'I understand your questions now, but you are on the wrong track. This kind of stalk, yarrow root indeed, has nothing to do with the practice of herbal medicine. It is more a kind of religious object. In some ways, I regard its use in a crime the way you, sir,' he gestured to Hallam, 'might feel about the use of a crucifix, though there are deep differences.'

'Please explain,' said Hallam.

'Stalks of yarrow root are cast in the most formal and ancient ceremony for using the *I Ching*, the Chinese Book of Changes. They yield images, hexagrams actually, which many believe can be used to foretell the future.'

'You know about this book?' Hallam asked Hu.

'About as well as you know the Bible. I'm aware of it. I have some sense of its functions. I've never studied it.'

'And you, sir?' Hallam asked, a request for continuance.

'I am no master, gentlemen. They are very few and regarded as sages, mystics. It is said they inhabit another plane. I believe they do. But I am somewhat versed in the *I Ching* and can explain further if you wish.'

'We do.'

The Chinese smiled. 'Then come inside and my wife will prepare some tea. I will get one of my children to mind the store while we talk. Please, the *I Ching* is no easy matter to sum up.'

They followed the herbalist into the rear of the shop, past hanging curtains, into a small but comfortable living area. There were several chairs, a television, and off to the right an efficiently arranged kitchen where a middle-aged woman was cooking. Wu Lin spoke to her and she nodded politely. A tea kettle materialized and she began to fill it. Wu Lin picked up a clay pipe and gestured for Hallam and Hu to sit.

'The *I Ching* is also called the Book of Changes,' the herbalist said, taking a seat and filling his pipe from a blue ceramic jar. 'Its underlying philosophy is the belief that in the final analysis, the world is a system of consistent relationships, a cosmos, not a chaos. This is the basis of all Chinese philosophy, ultimately maybe all philosophy everywhere.

'The foundation of the *I Ching*'s system of relationships is the distinction between Heaven and Earth. Incorporeal Heaven is the upper world of light, which regulates and determines everything that happens on the lower, dark Earth. This high and low, if you will, leads to the values of superior and inferior, yielding and unyielding, and are expressed symbolically in the *I Ching*'s hexagrams. You follow so far?'

'Heaven, Earth; superior inferior. That I follow,' said Hallam. 'But hexagrams?'

'Symbols composed of six lines,' said Wu Lin. 'At the outset, the *I Ching* was used as an oracle, a simple yes-no machine. Yes was indicated by an undivided line, no by a divided one. But greater differentiation was needed and the single lines were combined into pairs and finally a third line was added. In this way, the original trigrams came into being, conceived of as images of everything that happens in Heaven and Earth. All things, including the trigrams, are held to be in a state of transition, the same transition that is always taking place here on earth. Ice melts and becomes water, evaporates and returns as rain, freezes back into ice. You must look at the trigrams, these images, not as states of being but as movements in change.'

'Can you give me an example?' Hallam asked, sensing meaning, but needing something more concrete.

'The occidental mind,' smiled Hu smugly.

The Chinese laughed. 'Your friend suggests you are about to make a basic mistake, trying to understand the hexagrams as solid entities. They are not; only functions. The Western mind sometimes has difficulties with abstractions.'

Hallam smiled too, wolfishly. 'Tell my abstract friend this dull Westerner would be happy to compare their countries' infant mortality rate.'

Wu Lin looked back and forth for a moment, confused, as if at a tennis match and unsure who to route for.

'Please go on,' Hu urged. 'Like the legs of a horse, we often move in opposite directions to arrive in the same place.'

Not to be outdone, Hallam began, 'Confucius say man who keep finances in jock—'

'David!'

'Never mind. Please, go on.'

The herbalist got up to get a pencil and paper, amused. 'Perhaps an example would help. These are the eight trigrams which form the basis of the *I Ching*. Let me draw them for you . . . Here,' he held forth the paper for Hallam, who studied it:

```
━━━━━  Ch'ien, THE CREATIVE

━ ━ ━  K'un, THE RECEPTIVE

━ ━━━  Chên, THE AROUSING

━━━ ━  K'an, THE ABYSMAL

━ ━━━  Kên, KEEPING STILL

━━━━━  Sun, THE GENTLE
```

☰☰ Li, THE CLINGING

☱☱ Tui, THE JOYOUS

'Take the second trigram, K'un, for example,' said Wu Lin. 'K'un is The Receptive. Its lines are all divided so its attribute is devoted, yielding. Its image is the Earth. Now look.' Again he drew and held up the result.

☷☷

'This is the K'un hexagram, constructed of two K'un trigrams. Above and below, the Receptive Earth. Early on, the eight trigrams were combined with one another to achieve greater multiplicity. There are sixty-four in total. Each consists of six lines, each yielding or unyielding, positive or negative, divided or undivided, Yin or Yang. Each line is thought of as capable of change and whenever a line changes there is a change also of the situation represented by the hexagram.'

Hallam asked, 'What happens if you change all the lines?'

'In the case of K'un, you get its complement. Watch.' He drew again.

☰☰

'This is Ch'ien, The Creative. What could complement The Receptive more?'

'Now change one line,' Hallam requested.

'All right. Change the lowest line of K'un and we generate Fu, The Return.'

```
═══   ═══
═══   ═══
═══   ═══
═══   ═══
═══   ═══
━━━━━━━
```

Wu Lin continued, 'The Earth, strong in devotion, stands for Late Autumn when all the forces of life are at rest. When the lowest line changes, it represents Thunder, the movement that stirs anew within the Earth at the time of the solstice. It symbolizes the return of light.

'Each hexagram has an image, or idea, central to it. Also a judgement, which is the basic message the image conveys. We are concerned with unfolding events. With the help of the *I Ching*, we can discern the seeds of things to come and read in them a pattern of action.'

'Okay,' Hallam said slowly. 'I think I follow. But how do you use all this?'

'One begins by throwing the yarrow stalks. Fifty stalks are used but one is put aside and plays no further part. The remaining forty-nine are divided into two heaps. What follows is a complicated mathematical reduction generating certain numbers which in turn generate either divided or undivided lines. These construct the particular hexagram for the situation you desire to explore.'

'You have these stalks?' Hu inquired.

The Chinese smiled. 'I am a modernist. I use the alternative, three coins.'

The herbalist rummaged in a drawer behind him for a moment and produced a thick book that had seen much use and three old Chinese coins. Each had a hole in the middle and was inscribed on only one side. He handed them to Hallam.

'Before we begin, I must tell you again that I am no master. Few sages exist in the world, only one in this country that I know of. But even in my hands, what you would call an amateur's, the *I Ching* is a powerful tool. It should never be used lightly, not even now. That understood, you may throw the coins.'

Hallam picked up the heavy bronze coins and rolled them between his palms like dice. An odd sensation of power emanated from them, subtly rather than overtly felt. He hesitated, then threw. Two of the three landed inscribed side up.

'Each inscribed side has a value of two,' Wu Lin said. 'The reverse side has a value of three. From this the character of a line is derived. Six or nine yields a broken line. Seven or eight yields an unbroken one. Your first line is undivided. Continue.'

Five more times Hallam threw the coins. What at first had almost a sideshow air about it slowly began to pull at him in an oddly insistent way. He felt sweat bead up under his arms and slide in droplets down his sides; felt the shop's quiet dryness invade him, pressing at his senses. When he was done he felt weak and drained.

The Chinese nodded slowly. 'Here,' he said. 'As you choose to believe, see for yourself.'

Hallam looked at the hexagram.

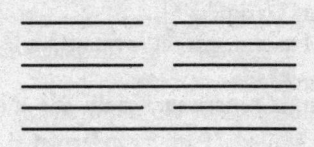

```
———  ———
———  ———
———  ———
———  ———
———  ———
—————————
```

'What does it mean?'

The herbalist's face was strained. Hallam saw worry there, concern; like a doctor who knew something he would rather not tell the patient.

'Tell me,' Hallam demanded.

'This is hexagram number thirty-six, Ming I,' intoned the herbalist. 'The Darkening of the Light.' His face grew tighter. Hallam could hear the creaking of the wooden building over his solemn tones. Wu Lin opened the *I Ching* and read formally:

'The six at the top stands for the greatest accumulation of earth, hence it is the line that damages and darkens the light of the others. It is the ruler determining the meaning of the hexagram.

'The judgement: Expansion will certainly encounter resistance and pain. Thus follows the hexagram of the Darkening of the Light. It means damage and injury.

'The first line is darkening of the light during flight. The judgement: He lowers his wings. The superior man does not eat for three days on his wanderings.

'The second line, darkening of the light injures him in the left thigh, he gives aid.

'The third and fourth line. Darkening of the light in the south. The Great Man is captured. He penetrates the left side of the belly.

'The fifth line. Small light. Perseverance furthers.

'The sixth line . . .' he looked at Hallam whose eyes were cloudy.

'Enough,' commanded Hu. 'David, snap out of it. David?'

'The sixth line,' intoned Wu Lin, 'not light, but darkness. He climbs up to Heaven, then plunges into the depths of the Earth. Not light. Darkness.'

Hu pulled at Hallam, got one arm under his shoulder. 'Get up, damn you. Get up.'

'I'm sorry,' the Chinese said sadly. He turned away.

'Hu? I . . .'

'Come on, David! Outside. Fresh air clear your head. Walk, damn it.'

'What? Oh, I . . . Okay. Outside . . .'

They stumbled through the shop. A barrel of mushrooms spun about and spilled. Hu swatted away a hanging lizard and sent it flying. The dryness caught at his throat.

'Come on, David. Back to solid earth. America. USA. Candy bars and concrete streets. Cadillacs. New York. LA. Two plus two is four, you stupid bastard. Four, do you hear me? David!' Hu forced him out of the door into the air.

Hallam shook his head, clearing slowly. The light made him blink. 'What happened in there?'

Hu lowered him to the wooden steps and sat beside him. 'You feel okay now?' he asked.

'Better,' Hallam acknowledged. 'It was like I was in a fog, breathing cotton.'

'Teach you a lesson,' Hu said angrily, with the relief of a parent whose child has narrowly escaped harm.

'Powerful stuff,' Hallam agreed soberly.

'Not that murky Eastern bullshit, David? That?'

Hallam let out a little laugh. 'I don't wear a hat, Hu.'

'Eating your words will suffice.'

'Fork, please.'

Hallam's irreverence did much to relieve Hu. He slapped his friend on the back. 'Your repentant attitude is sufficient. Seriously, you okay?'

'Yeah. Scary shit, though. How we gonna fight craziness *and* magic?'

'With great care, David. With especially great care. Nothing is fixed. Remember that.'

Hallam was silent for a while. Hu backed off. The American had ventured into dangerous waters, had seen a place not viewed by many. He had to return on his own.

'Hu?'

'Yes.'

'Got an idea. Wanna fight fire with fire?'

'I'm listening.'

Hallam told him.

'David,' Hu said, smiling broadly. 'It's even worthy of a murky Oriental.'

'Being around you, it rubs off, I guess.'

'You should be so lucky.'

For a second Hallam said nothing. Then he grinned. 'Candy bars and Cadillacs? That's what you really think of us?'

'I was under pressure.'

'In pressure *veritas*,' Hallam taunted.

'Eat dick, round eyes.'
'I disapprove of ethnic slurs, Hu.'
They got into the Toyota and drove off.

Down the corridor from Reiman's office, the last calls were made. Every other accounted for.
Three.
They called the major.

EIGHT

Major Reiman pointed to a closed and banded file on his desk. 'It boils down to this,' he said to Hallam and Hu seated before him. 'There are three general officers whose whereabouts we can't account for the night the girl was murdered. Any of them could have been in the city. All three are posted to MAC-Vee; two are Army, one is Air Force. All had access to transport which would have enabled them to get in and out of Saigon. None were in their billets till at least the next morning.'

He passed the file over and gestured for them to thumb through it as he spoke.

'The first possibility is Major General Carlton Mulrose, Deputy Commander of the 101st Airborne Division; age fifty-one, five foot ten, 170 pounds, fair complexion, light eyes. We've been able to get hold of some of the personnel records. You have them in the file there.

'Number two is Brigadier General Perry Hamilton, nickname "Rocky", Commander of the 14th Artillery, age forty-seven, six foot one, 180 pounds, brown eyes, brown hair. Combat scar under his right eye. He has several decorations for valour. Like Mulrose, he's a graduate of West Point. Good reputation. His men appear to like him.

Third is Brigadier General Arnold Wernicker, Deputy Commander of the 2nd Air Division. Five foot eight, 160 pounds, black, a former jet jockey in Korea. Much decorated. Graduate of the Air Force Academy.

'There you are, gentlemen. Like we say in the classroom, any questions and/or comments?'

'Nice job, Major,' Hallam said appreciatively. 'New York cops should have it so good.'

'They aren't required to account for every one of their citizenry. Makes it easier.'

'How do you suggest we go at these guys?'

Reiman looked unhappy. 'There's no easy way. What protocol covers asking a man if he's a murderer? Asking a general is going to be very sticky. These are career officers and not one is going to take kindly to some snot-nosed captain walking in and pointing a finger at him.'

Hu looked up from the file, smiled, and pointed a finger at Reiman.

'Excuse me,' Reiman said, 'one snot-nosed captain and a wise-ass gook lieutenant.'

'Mister gook to you, sir,' amended Hu cordially.

Reiman shook his head sadly. 'It's scary. You two are getting more alike every day.'

'Vietnamization, sir,' offered Hallam.

'He's won my heart and mind,' Hu agreed sombrely.

Reiman sat. 'It's worse than I thought.'

Hu turned a page in the file he was reading. 'This is interesting. Did you see that all three have sons in service here?'

'Not so odd,' Reiman observed. 'A quick call to the J-1 you play poker with and *voilà*, papers are born.'

'But why send them here?' Hallam took a look over Hu's shoulder. 'And those sure aren't out-of-harm's-way assignments. You'd think they'd protect their kids. Jesus, look at this. Mulrose's kid is a second looey with a light assault group, Hamilton's brat is a Ranger and Wernicker's is a Cobra pilot.'

'Got to deal with a lot of reverse prejudice if you're a general's kid,' said Reiman. 'They've usually got to prove something to somebody. Make it easier for them and you may ultimately make it harder.'

'This is very rough stuff, though,' said Hu.

'It's a rough war,' Reiman stated flatly. 'A good officer

risks in order to gain. Even his own son. Besides, how could you live with sending someone else's kid into combat if you didn't believe in what you were doing enough to send your own? Tradition, duty, they're not just bullshit. Say what you will about good wars and bad, David, the American armed services are still the finest trained, most awesomely equipped and best-led fighting force in the world. I'll tell you one thing for sure. In the end, if we have to pull out of here, it won't be because we blew it on the battlefield.'

'Yes, sir.'

Reiman lifted an eyebrow and gave a dry laugh. 'Okay, touched a nerve I suppose. Well, you got what you wanted. Go get this guy.'

'Yes, sir. Thanks, Major.'

'You'll hold the files?' Hu asked.

'Right here. Give me something solid to back them up with and I'll take them straight to the Judge Advocate.'

'You'll have it,' Hu promised, turning to leave. He was mumbling something softly that Reiman couldn't make out.

'What did he say?'

Hallam smiled. 'He was singing. You have to understand Hu, sir, to appreciate it.'

'Try me.'

'He was singing "We're Off to See the Wizard". Have a good day, sir.'

Hallam followed his partner out of the door.

They had to wait at the entrance gate to MAC-Vee headquarters to allow a general's car to pass. An omen, brooded Hallam. Stern-faced Marines finally checked their IDs and waved them in.

The MAC-Vee compound was a series of rectangular, pre-fab structures in parallel rows that looked like flat, metal ribbons from the air. Hallam pulled the Toyota into a designated spot. They walked across the hot asphalt and into the main building where their IDs were checked again and a desk officer tagged them. He directed them to the offices of General Carlton Mulrose.

Mulrose's offices were the same kind of green metal/grey-walled affair that comprised army and government institutions all over the world. Printed circulars announced blood drives, dances, rules of conduct. Rows of clerks pounded typewriters; administrative gunfire. The names of colonels and the initials of their respective commands were inscribed in green plastic strips on their doors.

'Captain Hallam and Lieutenant Hu to see General Mulrose,' Hallam said to the desk sergeant.

'Just a minute, sir.' He lifted his phone and spoke. After a second, he looked up. 'The general would like to know what this is in reference to?'

'Personal,' said Hallam. 'Tell the general we'd appreciate the courtesy of a brief visit.'

Again a brief exchange. 'Please have a seat, sirs. Be just a few minutes.'

Hallam dropped onto a brown wooden bench. Hu leaned on the arm. They had talked on the way over. Hallam would lead and both would try and play it low-key. So far, these three were guilty of nothing more than not being locatable. It was unwise to push without firmer footing.

Mulrose's office door swung open and several officers emerged amidst sounds of collegial familiarity.

'. . . don't like us anymore, General?'

'Not since you beat up on my three queens,' said a voice Hallam assumed to be Mulrose's. 'Consider this revenge.'

'Very petty,' joked another.

'But satisfying,' laughed Mulrose. Now he was standing almost opposite them.

'O-eight hundred!' he called after the departing backs. 'Remember that.'

'Yes, sir,' one called back. 'O-eight hundred.'

Mulrose turned. 'You the guys from MI?'

Hallam was already standing. He saluted. 'Captain Hallam, sir. And Lieutenant Hu. Yes, sir.'

They were both subject to Mulrose's appraising stare for a moment. 'Come on in,' he said finally.

Inside, he settled in behind his desk and Hallam had a chance to study the man more closely as his phone rang and Mulrose chose to take the call.

At first glance, Hallam could fix Mulrose in a certain category of general. He wasn't the golfer type, suntanned and looking like he spent his days on the golf course. They were well-barbered cardigan-sweater types with a dash of Andy-Williams-like civilian style. Mulrose belonged in another category. He was stocky and bulldoggish, with a flat-top crew cut so precise it looked mowed. He had the kind of slabby face that wouldn't ever give a damn about itself; it wore like an old hat. Except for the eyes. They were shrewd and amazingly clear; intelligent and animated. They would have an auditorium or a conversation searched for signs of danger or advantage in the time it took other men to shake hands. A smart man, nobody's fool. Put molten rivets in a clay mask and you had a general's face.

Hallam saw that Hu was also quietly observing. He waited patiently till Mulrose finished.

'Sorry, boys. Thanks for waiting. You said personal. What's this about?'

Hallam plunged in. 'Three nights ago, sir, one of our agents was brutally murdered in Saigon. I'll be candid, sir. Evidence indicates a general officer was involved. We'd like to know where you were that night.'

Colour rose in Mulrose's face like juice up a straw. 'You get your insolent ass right out of here this minute, Captain,' he threatened angrily, beginning to rise. 'Who's your CO?'

'Major Reiman, sir. But please, you know this isn't personal. MI can't account for your whereabouts on that night. We have to. We hoped you would understand.'

Mulrose's face was still deeply mottled. 'Understand? Now you listen to me. No smart-ass spook captain's gonna waltz into my office and accuse me of anything. You hear me?

Nothing personal, my ass. You bet I take it personal. Why the hell are you here?'

Hu stepped in. 'Because we don't think the sonofabitch who did this ought to get away with it,' he said, tossing the stack of police photos onto Mulrose's desk. 'Look at them. You decide.'

For a second, Hallam thought Hu had gone too far. Mulrose took a step round his desk and suddenly physical violence was in the air. But something in the photos must have caught his attention. He slowed, staring down at the top one. He stared for a long time, then pushed it aside to stare at the next. Hallam watched his rage get pushed aside by sheer revulsion.

'You know,' Mulrose said slowly, 'I've been around a long time and I never saw anything this bad. Christ. One of your agents, you say?'

Hallam nodded.

Mulrose thought about that for a while.

He said, 'Guy who did this is one sick mother.'

Hallam nodded again.

'And maybe you're just doing your job,' Mulrose said reflectively.

'We apologize for any lack of courtesy,' Hu said quickly.

Mulrose sighed. 'All right. What do you want to know?'

'Can you tell us where you were that night?' Hallam asked.

'Why me?'

'MI has run down every general in Vietnam that it can. Three are left whose time we can't account for. No one is saying we didn't slip up. Maybe someone has faked us out. But you signed out of here on the way to a dinner with Generals Winston and Hoyt at the Whey San restaurant in Cholon. Hoyt was there, he picked up the tab for the food. We have the chit. Same for Winston, he stood for the booze. The maitre d' served them and their, ah, two guests. Total, four. You signed back onto base at five a.m.' Hallam waited.

'What happens if I tell you?'

'Nothing. If it checks out you get crossed off the list.

Finished. Catching this guy is all we care about. You didn't do it, you don't exist for us.'

'I can make plenty of trouble for you guys if that's not true.'

Hallam nodded. 'We don't doubt it. Won't be necessary.'

Mulrose's gaze drifted back to the pictures. They were the key, Hallam understood. Smart old Hu. Somehow he'd seen that a guy like Mulrose couldn't stand to be associated with an illness like that, even peripherally. It pushed him to the point of going against his personal predilections.

'I don't like this,' he said, 'I think you know that. But you're right as far as it goes. I wasn't at that dinner. We're now off the record?'

'Yes, sir.'

'Okay. I keep a small place in Saigon. A friend lives there. I stay when I can. That's not a problem for her. This week my wife is over from the States visiting. So I was at dinner. You understand?'

Hu nodded. 'We'll need the address. A brief interview should verify things. No record will go into the files. We very much appreciate your help, sir.'

Mulrose drew himself up straighter. 'When you find this guy, what will you do?'

'We figure . . .' But the rest of Hu's response was cut off by the sounds of a commotion in the outer offices. Hallam checked his watch. It was time. Mulrose pressed the intercom.

'Sergeant? What goes on out there?'

The sergeant poked his head in. 'Outside, sir. Some pretty fancy skywriting. Just everybody going to the windows to see.'

Mulrose dismissed him and strode to his window himself. He yanked the blinds open. Hallam and Hu crowded closer. Hallam was watching Mulrose closely as the general stared up into the cloudless blue sky.

There, across the vault of heaven, the pilot of the old, prop-driven spotter plane was just finishing the last of the six lines Hallam and Hu had spent half a budgetary appropriation bribing him to skywrite; six bold ten-mile-long cottony white lines trailing defiantly across the sky forming the Ta Yu hexagram from the Book of Changes.

Mulrose stared at the enormous hexagram drawn across the sky. Confusion was so clearly written on his face that Hallam was certain in that moment that Mulrose was guilty of no greater crime than husbandly indiscretion. He saw that certainty mirrored on Hu's face.

'You two know anything about this?'

'No, sir,' Hallam lied.

'Pretty,' said Mulrose. 'Probably see it all over half the country.'

'I'd think so,' said Hallam, silently sending a prayer winging outward that somewhere the killer was at this very moment staring up into the same sky, seeing the hexagram and understanding its message as no one else would.

Ta Yu, the fourteenth hexagram: Possession in Great Measure. All lines undivided except for the weak fifth which occupied the place of honour and all the strong lines were in accord with it. Above, Li, The Flame; below, Chi'en, The Creative.

> ... *The fire in Heaven shines far; all things stand out in the light and become manifest. All things come to the man who is modest and kind in a high place.*

This was their message, this was their own magic thrown back in the face of chaos. Look, Hallam thought, read what we send you ...

> *Fire in Heaven above – possession in great measure. The superior man curbs evil furthers good and thereby obeys the benevolent will of Heaven. The Great Man will combat evil and promote good. In this way he fulfils the will of God who desires only good ... and not evil.*

You understand? Hallam sent urgently into the azure sky as if some mystic telegraph would bring the thought to the killer. See? This is what we invoke against you, your own black magic turned back towards the light.

Spin your web, spider. In the end you will lose.

Believe it, spider, Hallam thought grimly. We're coming.

In a place his pursuers could not have known, *he* looked up into the sky. Blazoned there across the heavens was The Message. He stood mutely for a long moment, knowing flooding him; understanding it was for him as if it had arrived in an envelope bearing his name. It overjoyed him, proof that the Great Man deserved the appellation. There was a warmth in his loins that was almost sexual, a need to join that almost doubled him over, it was so sharp.

Ta Yu. A wise choice. A very clever and brave statement. They were threatening him. He understood that. Somewhere inside a switch was thrown. The Great Man was worthy. What joy! They would be meeting soon.

He breathed heavily in the sun. Sweat trickled down his sides. He was conscious of every drop. Every breath was a sweet, self-realizing effort. Events were moving, he felt that. He would be moving too, quickly now. That was in the message also. They were coming. He felt their pursuit as a young girl might experience an amorous boy's – all passion and rage and fear; the cruel edge of sensuality. He welcomed it.

First, he decided, a visit to the master.

Then action.

NINE

'You caught his expression when he saw the hexagram?' Hallam asked Hu.

'Yes. It meant nothing to him, I thought.'

'Me, too.'

They had been waiting in Brigadier General Arnold Wernicker's outer office for over fifteen minutes. The winds outside were beginning to blur the lines. Already the hexagram was vague and diffuse. They had called on Major General Perry Hamilton before coming here, but discovered he was in the field. He wouldn't be back for at least forty-eight hours. Reiman was attempting to arrange transportation.

Wernicker had passed by several times, in and out of his office. When his door was open they could see models of Air Force fighter planes and bombers on plastic stands adorning file cabinets and table tops. Wernicker himself was a short, lean man with muscle laid on his narrow bones in layers like leaf-springs, hard against his wiry frame. He moved with quick, lithe movements and he had a voice that was deep and resonant and as clear as a disc jockey's.

He disappeared back into his office. A few minutes later, the intercom buzzed. The desk sergeant looked up.

'The general will see you now, sirs.'

Hallam followed Hu. Inside, Wernicker was facing the window, his back to them. 'Please sit, gentlemen,' he said without turning.

Hallam folded into a chair and Hu followed suit. Hallam said, 'Thank you, sir,' and was about to begin when Wernicker cut him off, turning on them with all the menace of an attacking jet and fixing them with a disgusted look.

'Don't thank me, Captain. You think I don't know why you're here? Two minutes after you walked out of Carl Mulrose's office everyone knew why you were here. Back channels, boys. You come at one of us, you come at all of us. What the hell is this about, anyway? Some two-dollar whore gets whacked and you're ready to drag a guy who's given his whole life to the service through the mud? You don't think we got enough bad PR for this war we need this murder crap, too?'

'Sir, If I may—' Hallam began.

'Stow it, Captain. I'm talking. And I'm gonna talk freely. Just between us. How long you been out here, a year, two?'

'A little over a year, sir.'

'Well, you're a mighty slow learner. You should know by now in this jungle there are only two sides: theirs and ours. When the fuck you gonna decide which one you're on?'

Hallam was dead silent, frowning. Anger was warring with discipline; outrage with respect.

Hu saw the warning signs. 'David? I, ah . . .'

Hallam ignored him. 'Are we really off the record, sir?'

'You bet, soldier.'

'Then taking you at your word, sir, who the fuck do you think you are, questioning my loyalty? What side am I on? I'm on the side that came here in the first place rather than grab the first defence job that came along. I'll stand on my record. And his,' he pointed to Hu. 'So why not stop acting like such an incredible jerk and sit down and shut up and listen to what we have to say instead of making such a goddamned ass out of yourself. Sir.'

Wernicker eyed him narrowly. 'Okay, so you got guts. At least that's something. Well, Captain, you just bought yourself sixty seconds.'

But Hallam was not so easily mollified. 'Sixty seconds? What is that, some kind of bone to toss us? You think we like this, going up against a group of guys tighter than a gay men's choir? We knew this crap would start the minute we began poking around. Camaraderie,' he said bitterly. 'Esprit de corps. Well, it's bullshit, General. And I'll tell you straight out why.' Hallam took a deep breath.

'This guy isn't one of you. Not if duty and honour aren't just crap you stick on your school rings. Jesus, I read how back home they think we're killers here. Well, I don't think we are. Not most of us. There's a difference between soldiering and murdering. But not for this guy. He's lousy. Sick inside. The war's just an excuse; he likes to kill. That makes him nobody's friend, not yours, not the others; unless you're as rotten as he is. Now I don't think so, but it doesn't really matter. Not in the long run. Hu and me, we're gonna take him out of the game, sir. Maybe so we can say they're wrong back home, maybe just so we can look back on this craziness someday and think at least we did some of the right things for the right reasons. I don't know. Maybe you just can't let some shit happen without somebody saying no. Bottom line is this, General. Anybody tries to run interference for this goddamn freak is just as rotten as he is and we take them out too. Believe it. No noise, okay. No fuss unless we're pushed. But nothing in this life or the next stops this guy from going down.' Hallam looked over at Hu. Why in hell was he smiling? He gave a short expletive snort. 'Sir,' he finished.

Hu turned to Wernicker. 'Ditto,' he said simply.

Wernicker stared at him. Hu smiled, 'We still had two seconds.'

Hallam started for the door.

'Hold it,' Wernicker said. 'Wait a minute.'

'Sir?'

Wernicker looked at them closely. 'You straight about no noise? You're not just looking for a spot on the network news or an article for the local rag back home?'

'No, sir,' Hallam said. 'No way.'

Wernicker nodded slowly. 'Okay. Maybe. Maybe you're right about this. And maybe I was wrong about what you're doing.' He paused. 'What I've got to deal with is, well, a different point of view. We got a situation here threatening to blow this army apart at the seams. Combat refusals are up, drug use is growing, racial tensions are on the rise and back home they want us to fight the dirtiest war in history like it's some social tea. What do you think the media would do with a killer general? It'd be a goddamn field day, Captain. We just can't afford to have morale go any lower. Any senior staff is going to feel pretty much the same way.'

'We do, too, sir. Help us and we can be in and out like surgeons.'

Wernicker's eyes bored into Hallam like drills. 'Maybe I want more.'

'I don't follow, sir.'

'Trials. Publicity. Maybe if you do find him, and you're sure, we might want to take care of our own all ways. You understand? You tell me. Or Carl. We'll do the rest. It would be considered a great favour. Neither of you would regret it.'

Hallam rubbed his chin. 'We'll have to think it over, sir. Hu?'

'We'll talk. Perhaps a gesture of good faith for now . . . ?'

'For instance?' Wernicker asked.

'Where were you on the night of the twenty-fifth?'

Hallam had to laugh. 'For God's sake, Hu. We're not after the Maltese Falcon.'

Wernicker still hadn't let down his guard totally, but the humour dispelled some of the tension in the room and seemed to finalize some judgement for him. He looked at Hallam. 'The reason you didn't find me listed anywhere you could verify that night was because I was on a mission that didn't exist officially. No requests, no records. But for the sake of argument let's take a look at a map over here. Hypothetically, you understand.'

Wernicker drew down a rolled map fixed to the wall. There were no names of places on it, just numbers and grid lines set up into small squares. Wernicker pointed, 'You know what you're looking at, where this piece of real estate is?'

Hallam looked. Christ! It was Cambodia, a small curve of land north-west of Saigon called the Fish Hook. 'Reliable' intelligence had it that it contained the much-sought-after North Vietnamese headquarters known as COSVN – Central Office for South Vietnam. But US Forces weren't supposed to be in Cambodia!

'Saturation bombing, B-52s,' Wernicker continued. 'An interesting thought, no? And if you did go that way, you'd probably want to start with overflights, target identification, photo recon. Of course, since we're not going to go into Cambodia there's no need. But if there were . . .' He let it just hang there.

'You can verify this?'

'It can be arranged. It would have to be top secret, though.'

'We can live with that. As long as it crosses you off the list.'

'I'll see to it. Might go through your major. Reiman?'

'Yes, sir.'

'What's your next move?'

Hallam said, 'See the next name on the list.'

'Kind of narrows it down, though,' said Wernicker. 'Assuming you cross Carl and me off the list.'

'Assuming we cross you off,' said Hu, his Vietnamese smile-for-all-purposes back in place.

'Okay,' Wernicker held up a hand, 'whatever you say. But take some advice. Assuming it is a general who's the murderer, make book that he already knows everything about you and your investigation. Keep your heads down. Tell everybody around you to keep their heads down. Attacking is our business. If you get into trouble, call me and I'll send in the cavalry.'

'Appreciate it, sir,' said Hallam.

Hu thought for a moment. 'Does some quick transport come under that heading?'

Wernicker smiled. 'This is the Air Force, Lieutenant. It don't come any quicker.'

'In that case . . . ' Hu began.

*

On their way to the airstrip, Hu leaned close enough to Hallam to be heard over the wind whistling through the jeep. 'What did you think of Wernicker?'

Hallam thought about it. 'Tough, old school, loyal. Struck me he believed what he was saying. Could a psychopath act that well?'

'O'Rourke seemed to think so.'

'You?'

Hu shook his head. 'I don't know. It didn't feel like acting. And I value loyalty highly, even some of the misguided kinds. I sort of liked the guy.'

'I thought he was gonna hit me if I cursed him out one more time.'

'He definitely wanted to. Sweet talker.'

It was a hot, sultry afternoon and shadows had begun to lengthen. Hallam checked his watch. 'You sure we want to head out this late?'

'It's only about twenty klicks. We can make it back around sundown.'

'You're the boss.' Hallam leaned back, letting the sun make his closed eyelids glow red-orange. It felt good, the sun on his face, the wind.

'David? I was, well, very proud of you in Wernicker's office. It was quite a speech.'

Hallam smiled without opening his eyes. 'Shucks, Pa.'

'Very well, make fun of me. I have only one more question, though it grieves me to ask it.'

'Shoot.'

'Back at the herbalist's, what *did* Confucius say about the man who keeps his money in a jock?'

Hallam's grin widened. 'Has finances all balled up.'

Hu didn't move a muscle. 'You should be ashamed, David. Deeply ashamed.'

'I am, Hu. Often.'

Hu leaned back, too. He was thinking about how many

times Hallam had stood up for them over the past few days, how many times the investigation would have stalled if not for his friend's tenacity and strength of purpose. 'Not so often, David,' he said, his voice barely carrying over the wind. 'Not so often at that.'

The big Sikorsky, one of a kind dubbed Jolly Green Giants, lifted into the air and vaulted out over the low hills. Capable of transporting the big 105-mm howitzers, the helicopter easily ate up the miles to the 14th Artillery's position carrying a load as light as Hallam and Hu. Good as his word, Wernicker had provided first-class transportation.

Soon the fields gave way to denser forest as Saigon fell behind. Out here, the war had taken an interesting turn with the creation of a system of hilltop artillery positions called firebases. To construct one, the 'Daisy-Cutter', a monster 15,000-pound bomb, was dropped on a hilltop blowing a three-hundred-foot crater – the size of the Rose Bowl - in it, creating an instant firebase. Then the big Sikorskys ferried in men and artillery to occupy it. Acting as a kind of bait protected by the artillery, forward infantry patrols sought to engage the enemy, calling in the helicopter search and destroy battalions to obliterate the guerrillas as soon as they were located.

In theory, that worked just fine. But 'Charlie', as the Viet Cong were called, came to know American tactics well enough never to stand and fight unless trapped. Having no territory to defend and no fixed bases, they simply fell back before the Americans, drawing them further and further out. Ambush was certain beyond the range of the artillery.

In the end, though, it was the helicopter's mobility that went a long way to reversing the guerrillas' advantage. Within minutes of an engagement, attack helicopters, artillery and additional troops could be ferried to the scene in support. The VC or regular North Vietnamese Army was rarely able to reinforce. Used well, it frustrated the guerrillas' advantage and brought victory. Used well . . .

The landscape sped by beneath them, a green and brown blur. Hallam looked up to see the co-pilot clambering back from the flight deck. Ahead, the first sight of artillery in star formation glinted from the top of a nearby hill.

'Couple of minutes, Captain. Got the all-clear to head on in.'

'Out here often?' Hu asked.

'Pretty regularly. Rocky Hamilton keeps everybody jumping. Crazy sonofabitch to be out here, if you ask me. I'd be home eating steak instead of at a firebase eating C-rations.'

'Why does he do it?' Hu pressed.

The co-pilot grinned. 'Like I said. Crazy sonofabitch.'

'Really. I'd like to know.'

'Straight?'

Both Hallam and Hu nodded.

'Out here you got two kinds of people,' the co-pilot said. 'Working stiffs and REMFs. You dig? Hamilton hauls his ass out here along with the rest of us. Makes a difference. He tells you what to do, well, you figure he's been there. Brass don't like it. But like I said, to us it makes a difference.'

'You like the man,' Hu observed.

'I suppose so.'

'REMF?' Hallam requested translation.

'Rear Echelon Mother Fucker. And nobody needs another one of those out here. Whoops. Gotta go. Have you gentlemen downtown in sixty seconds.'

The helicopter suddenly dipped and then plunged in what felt to Hallam like a kamikaze dive. But the pilots knew what they were doing. They settled onto the brown dirt of the firebase as lightly as spring rain.

A pair of hard-looking black single-stripers in jungle fatigues scooted up to the copter. 'You the guys come to see the general?'

'That's us,' Hallam said, stepping down. 'But this don't feel like Kansas and you guys sure don't look like any goddamned munchkins. We got the right place?'

'Got us a live one here, Zeke,' said the one who had greeted them. 'The captain's got a sense of humour. You just saved yourself from the "A" tour, sir.'

'Which one is that?'

The other soldier grinned. 'The one with the snakes.'

'Appreciate it,' said Hallam gratefully. 'Save it for the news teams.'

'We usually do.'

The crater created by the Daisy-Cutter was surrounded by circles of barbed wire and sandbag emplacements. Ordnance was underground to prevent enemy incoming from setting it off. A system of trenches cut across the firebase and Hallam and Hu followed their guides into them. Overhead were the big howitzers covered with camouflage netting.

They passed groups of dark-faced, shirtless GIs smoking, eating, playing cards, cleaning weapons. The war was at its hottest here. Frustration, fear and moment-to-moment concern for survival outweighed all else.

No wonder they liked Hamilton, Hallam reflected as they approached the man. He was bent over a chart table erected from some planks and sandbags, outside a dug-in sandbag structure that served as the command shack. On a pre-fab tubular pole a few yards away, a torn American flag fluttered defiantly in the last rays of the sun.

They walked up the last incline. Hamilton didn't look up from conferring with his senior officers. Hawk-eyed body-guards watched the newcomers carefully, then returned to scrutinizing the horizon.

'General? Guests, sir,' said their guide.

Hamilton looked up. A quick glance of appraisal, a small frown tugging at the corner of his mouth that he should have to be bothered; clearly, he had better things to do than waltz around with them. It said another thing, too. He knew why they had come.

'Hold on a minute,' Hamilton called out. 'Be right there.' Returning to his group, he continued to confer for several minutes more. When he had finished, he gestured to the perimeter. 'Over here,' he said and walked away.

Hallam was getting a little ticked off trudging all over the goddamned hill. He didn't love Hamilton's attitude either. The man had an air about him like everybody else's concerns were bullshit and only he had the real line on what mattered. Even his being here smacked of grandstanding. Okay, so you get your ass out of MAC-Vee and visit the troops every now and then. It was good, maybe better than most. But was it so fucking noble everybody had to love you for it?

Knowing it could affect his judgement, Hallam tried to restrain his cynicism. 'Sorry to barge in on you like this, General, but I think you probably already know why we're here, sir.'

'I do now.' Hamilton gave an amused snort. 'I'm on the same list as Arnie Wernicker and Carl Mulrose.'

'Yes, sir. For the same reason. Nobody knows where you were three nights ago.'

'Look, it's Captain Hallam, right. And Lieutenant Hu?'

'Yes, sir.'

'Well, you're here because I gave you the okay to be here. Before giving that okay, I made Arnie tell me why it was so all-fire important. I got a lotta things to do before nightfall. You got questions, ask 'em.'

'Just one. Where were you when the girl was killed three nights ago?' Hallam took the pictures from Hu, but just held them, waiting.

'I know where I should have been,' Hamilton began, 'in some decent restaurant in Saigon with the rest of my esteemed colleagues. But I wasn't.'

He scratched at the scar under his right eye, a pucker of dead, white skin. 'This is a little hard for me. I'm out here a lot. It's good for morale. Good for knowing what's going on. But the C-in-C doesn't like it. Get my ass shot up, I'm not so easy to replace. Bad precedent, too. Front-line inspection isn't a general's job. Everybody should stick to their job. So sometimes I have to sign out to one place and be in another. You follow?'

Hallam nodded.

'Johnson!' Hamilton called out. One of the bodyguards came running.

'Sir?'

'Where were we three nights ago?'

Johnson thought for a moment. 'Firebase Papa Romeo. Captain Palmer's bunch. You remember, sir. There was the firefight and we couldn't bring in the Jolly Greens. Had to spend the night.'

'Where were we officially?'

Johnson looked straight ahead. 'We were in a strategy session at MAC-Vee.'

Hamilton looked at Hallam. 'Anything else?'

'Just these, sir.' He handed the pictures to Hamilton.

In the gathering darkness it was hard to read Hamilton's expression, but Hallam felt him stiffen. His brow knit tightly and a kind of rigid, fixed stare claimed his features. He stared for longer than anybody else had.

'Sir?' The bodyguard looked concerned. 'Sir, everything all right?'

Hamilton just continued to stare. He shuffled the pictures slowly, gazing at each one closely.

'This is . . . terrible,' he said at last. He was sweating.

He dabbed at his forehead with his sleeve. Hallam studied his reactions closely. What was there that bothered him about this man? He did have an alibi, but would it stand up to close inspection?

'I'm sorry, Captain,' Hamilton was saying. 'But I have to be going.'

'There's been another murder,' said Hu. 'Just as bad.'

'Jesus,' Hamilton swore. He was halfway to his helicopter. 'I hope you catch this guy.'

'We will,' said Hallam.

They watched the general climb into his helicopter. The rotors began to spin and the craft pulled itself a few feet into the air. Hamilton gave a short wave.

Hallam turned to Hu, but whatever he was about to say was lost in the frantic scream from the far side of the firebase.

'Incoming! Incoming!'

It galvanized everyone. The first rockets exploded over the noise of Hamilton's helicopter. Soldiers ran to man the guns, carrying the big shells to feed them. Small-arms fire crackled. Hallam looked around stupidly, heard a funny whistling sound getting louder . . .

Hu hit him like a tackle and they went down together as the first shells hit and the universe turned over. Down was up and the earth erupted in geysers.

All around them, the big howitzers were now opening up. Great blasts of sound and flame shook the deepening night. M-16s crackled from the perimeter. Hallam felt Hu pulling at him and they stumbled back into the safety of the trenches.

'Here,' somebody yelled, thrusting an M-16 into Hallam's hands and one into Hu's. They looked up and saw the face of one of their former guides. No grin now, it was all business. They steadied into a grim rhythm, pumping round after round into the surrounding foliage.

For over an hour the hilltop felt like it was attached to a rocketing roller coaster, bucking and screaming and exploding with a fury Hallam had never witnessed before. Faces streaked with sweat and dirt gleamed wickedly in the moonlight. Fires cast phantasmagoric shadows over running men. The VC screamed from the jungle like banshees. Suddenly, someone ran across Hallam's field of vision, spun round clutching his side and went down as his legs gave out from under him. Hallam was up and out of the trench even as Hu was screaming for a medic.

A column of flame erupted only yards away and something plucked hotly at Hallam's shoulder. He plunged on, bent low like a broken field runner, diving the last few feet. The soldier was still alive, though blood was streaming from a wound high on his chest. Hallam yanked out his handkerchief and wadded it under his uniform and into the hole. He felt the ruptured flesh, slick with blood, roll under his fingers like mud.

He pulled the boy to a standing position, got his shoulder under him and hefted him up in a fireman's carry. The air buzzed with bullets like angry gnats. The soldier was in shock, too dazed to help. Hallam staggered under the load.

Another burst close by slapped at him like a giant hand. He turned, dazed and confused, tasting a flat, metallic wetness. Where was the trench? The night was exploding. Shadows confused him. Another geyser lit up the darkness spraying dirt and gravel in his face.

'David! Over here!'

It was Hu, suddenly coming towards him, and a second man with a Red Cross armband on his sleeve. Together they grabbed him and rushed him forward. The ground shook again. Off to the left something . . . something . . . Hallam was pushed forward and his feet slid out into empty air as the trench suddenly opened up under him. He went down hard, the soldier's weight still across his shoulders, pushing his head into the rocky ledge.

Someone was yelling, but far away. Faces swam into view. Hallam felt light, free. He was no longer earthly bound. He tried to respond. There was something that Hu should know. Something . . .

Then, nothing.

TEN

The night was his friend; it told all the lies he needed. It covered him. Some people saw only a peasant dressed in common, loose-fitting dark 'pyjamas'. Shadows concealed him; most weren't even aware of his passage. He slipped into the alley behind the 5th Battalion's headquarters for the second time that day.

The first time, he'd been dressed in full uniform. In many ways that was even less conspicuous than the way he was dressed now. No one questioned a general. Guards tended to look away, the opposite reaction to the handicapped. Vietnam had underscored that lesson: don't fuck with power.

He reached behind the rusty drainpipe and felt the end of the silken cord he had secured there earlier. Attached to the thicker rope coiled on the roof, he had lowered it carefully into position. Now it came away easily as he drew on it. After a few pulls he felt the slight snag as the knot which joined the two lines slipped over the edge. Soon he had the thicker line in his hands. It was strong enough to carry his weight, attached to a solid pipe on the roof.

He hefted the rope. There was no hesitation, not even a review of purpose. He just drew the black hood concealed under his collar over his head and climbed.

Scampering up the wall he felt like his namesake, the spider. The line was his own silken thread. He wondered if the Great Man had got the clue that he would come this way when they saw the picture he painted on the girl's wall. Probably not. He was so much smarter than even the Great Man.

They would be seeing each other soon. Under his hood, the spider smiled.

He reached the window whose latch he'd broken earlier. One tug and it slid open. He dropped through, senses extended for the slightest danger. He waited in the darkened corridor but there was no noise, no alarm. He closed the window and padded down the hall.

Major Reiman looked at the two files before him and came to the same conclusion. The evidence was incontrovertible. Somebody had altered the final reports. The raw information, the 'take', just didn't jive with the finished product. It would have to be somebody very high up, but whoever it was had excised just the information Hu had requested.

It had been Hu's idea to try and locate the *I Ching* master that the herbalist had mentioned. Hu reasoned there might be some connection between the sage and the man they had all come to think of as the spider. So, using Wu Lin's approximations as a first lead, Reiman had pulled all the aerial recon photos on the area and all the MI reports and slowly narrowed it down.

It might have been impossible to trace, except he had proofed the take against the final reports and thereby spotted the glaring error. It was simply a gaping hole where a critical assessment should have been. The aerial photos showed two huts in a clearing just inside NVA territory. But no mention of the find showed up anywhere. It had been forgotten. But since that was virtually impossible, it was a red flag on an effort to conceal. Without any further proof, Reiman was willing to bet he'd found the location.

He pulled a map in front of him. Hallam and Hu were here at the firebase. It was less than twenty klicks to the clearing. A helicopter could make the jump easily and the 1st Cavalry had the area pretty secure. He pulled out a series of reports. The 1st Cav would be holding the area for at least two more days. Hallam and Hu could get in and out during that time.

Reiman spent the next few minutes encoding a cable to Hallam and Hu. It was dark outside his office and the typewriters were silent. Everyone else but the night clerks down the hall had gone for the day. He picked up the phone and called Signals to send up a runner. Like his two junior officers connected with this case, he had come to want the spider badly. The second set of photos had not only turned his stomach, it had convinced him of the urgency of the chase. It was not going to stop unless . . . what was that?

Reiman stood warily, then relaxed. It was only the runner. He pushed open his door and the light spilled into the outer office making a corridor for the boy's entrance. It vaguely reminded him of the opening to Perry Mason.

'Sir?'

'I want this out as soon as possible. Double quick.'

'Yes, sir.'

A quick salute and the boy turned back. Reiman watched him go. Lot of good kids here. He went back to his desk and started to reorganize the file. With any luck, Hallam and Hu would be able to get a description of the spider from the sage and he could bring the case to the Judge Advocate and be done with it.

Another noise picked his head up. What could the boy want now? He looked out, but saw nothing. He shrugged. He picked up the file to shove it back into his safe.

Something itchy passed under his nose, a little cloud of irritating powder. He felt it inflame his nasal passages and a wicked sneeze form. He threw back his head from the quick involuntary drawn-in breath . . .

The black shape that suddenly reared up in front of him was the last thing Reiman would ever see. Caught in mid-convulsion, he could only stare in helpless terror as the black-shrouded shape brought the short, wickedly curved blade slashing across his exposed throat. Skin and cartilage parted as easily as the rind of a watermelon slit by a razor. Blood and breath burst out of Reiman and one tortured gurgle later he was dead.

The spider gathered the file together. He read it quickly to understand their suppositions, to see where they were headed. Reiman's last entry made things a bit more difficult. He would have to get to the master before the Great Man.

He looked down at Reiman's body. Gravity was spilling its blood over the desk. He dipped a finger in the puddling fluid and drew the Black Widow's red 'hourglass' spot on Reiman's back. He liked signing his work. It was distinctive.

He repacked the sickles – two separate twelve-inch wooden handles with curved blades at the top that always made him think of a spider's pincer-like chelicerae. In this way *he* had pierced Reiman's throat and drunk his blood. He cleaned them on Reiman's shirt and replaced them in the black silk pack strapped between his shoulder blades.

He wiped the last traces of the irritating powder off his glove. An old trick, baring the throat like that. Then he fed the entire file into the shredder and watched the spaghetti strips flush into the incinerator. He put out the lights.

Ten minutes later he was back in the street, heading for Hallam's house.

Hallam was sure he was dead. Why else would he be lying on his back in the dirt with acrid wisps of smoke trailing over him? The world was black and very silent. He was alone. He started to cry because he figured he'd gone to hell.

'David?'

It was Hu. Poor Hu, dead too. But surely Hu would have gone to heaven. He was good and kind. So sad.

'David, what are you mumbling? C'mon. Wake up.'

Hallam sighed. Pity. All gone to hell. He tried to say 'pity', but his tongue felt funny and it came out, 'pithy'.

Hu's face swam into focus over him. It was tired and strained but not overly worried. 'C'mon. Sit up.'

'How come you don't care we died and went to hell?' Hallam asked, interested.

Hu's face split into a grin. 'It was only a brief sojourn. Welcome back, maniac.'

'Don't insult the dead.' Hallam tried to roll back over but Hu propped him back up.

'No sleep, not with the concussion you probably have. Medic says stay awake. He dressed the nick in your shoulder. Nothing serious. The boy you carried back is okay too. Pretty damn heroic. Hamilton wants to give you a medal.'

'I didn't know what I was doing.'

'That was obvious,' Hu said dryly. 'By the way, next time you dive into a trench, do it feet first, not head first. Save you lots of wear and tear.'

'You pushed me!'

'Hardly.'

'Well.' Hallam stretched a bit. 'Thanks anyway. For coming out.'

'I couldn't let others see the real bumbling you. Forget it. Look around. Everybody's a hero tonight.'

'Attack's over?'

'Yes.'

'Then let's get the hell out of here.'

'Can't,' Hu said flatly. 'Our helicopter took a direct hit. Can't send another because of the VC fire. Only way out tonight is to walk.'

Something prodded Hallam's memory but he couldn't bring it into focus. 'Damn,' he said.

'What is it?'

'Something, but I can't remember. All those shells going off. It's hazy. Forget it. Maybe later.'

Hallam brushed some of the dirt off himself. 'God, would I love to be home now in a hot bath with a bottle of Scotch.'

'Dream on.'

'Home,' Hallam said wistfully, thinking of the villa. He lay back in the dirt and stared up into the purple sky.

He sat in the shadows across the street and watched the villa. Three guards. One in front, one up on the wall, one in the back, maybe the garden. When he was sure of the number he moved off.

He'd traded his pack for a silenced sniper's rifle which he stored in the trunk of the car he was using. Driving over, he allowed himself to feel the exhilaration of Reiman's death. Such a rush. It was hard not to run over someone from the sheer pleasure of it. He had to remind himself to go *round* the crowds in the streets.

He shinned up a tree that gave him a vantage point over the villa's wall, about a hundred feet away. It was going to be an exercise in concentration and timing but he had no doubt he could pull it off. He put the rifle to his shoulder and peered through the starscope.

The first guard was clearly outlined in the bright orange glow of gathered light. He swung over. Number two crossed his vision as he traversed the wall, then passed out of sight. All right. One. Two. One, two. Get the rhythm. One then two. He swung the rifle back and forth smoothly.

Guard number three was the tough shot. He was furthest back and lowest, in the depths of the garden. But he too had a rhythm. First one side, then the other. One side . . . then the other. One side . . . a match flared. What luck. He would pause to light up.

He swung back. There was the first guard. Over now, the second. Steady, get set. The first . . . the second . . . the third lifted the light to his mouth . . . He swung back. The first . . . Where was the second? Damn damn damn. No. There. The second appeared on the wall. The third inhaled and the cigarette's tip glowed . . .

He swung the crosshairs onto the first guard and pulled the trigger, swung back and pulled it again, swung down and pulled it a third time.

Three soft 'phuts' whispered in the night and three men died almost as one. Leaves rustled undisturbed.

Happily, he studied his work. With no need to rush now, he put a few more rounds into each body just to be on the safe side. He enjoyed the little jerks as they hit and he was careful not to knock the body on the wall off. He climbed down out of the tree and hung the rifle across his back by the strap. He pulled the black hood over his head.

The villa was dark and nothing disturbed its tranquillity. He dropped from the wall and padded silently onto the terrace. He withdrew a knife from the sheath on his belt and jemmied the brass catch on the French windows without problem. Seconds later, he stood inside.

There was a thrill about entering a sleeping house. He'd first felt it as a boy. It was the thrill of violation, the sense of slipping inside someone else's defences. He had once gone into a house and stood watching the man and woman in bed for hours. When the woman turned, the covers slipped off and he could see her naked breasts rise and fall. The red tips on those flabby sacks hardened in the cool air. The man's hairy genitals repulsed him. The tufts of hair on his back and belly looked like weeds. Soon after, he began shaving his own emerging pubic hair.

Before leaving, he took their hairbrushes. It was a message. It meant, I have been here and I can come back. Whenever I want to. He buried the brushes in the forest and urinated on the spot. He wondered what they would think in the morning.

He experienced that feeling of freedom, of unchaining, now. Off the kitchen was a small room. A Vietnamese was sleeping. He unlimbered the rifle and pressed it against the man's head and pulled the trigger. There was only a single death tremor.

He walked up the stairs. A big man was sleeping in the first bedroom, snoring. Moonlight slashed across his sleeping form.

'Who's been sleeping in my bed?' the killer whispered, stifling a giggle.

He put the muzzle into the man's open mouth and pulled the trigger.

He padded back into the hallway. The next bedroom was on his right. Did it belong to the Great Man?

'Hey, mista! You no supposed to—'

He turned and fired all in one motion and the housegirl almost vaulted over backwards as the bullets slammed into her and carried her crashing down the stairs. He turned back and reached for the doorknob . . .

The noise woke Paco. For a moment he thought he was dreaming, but some inner sense prompted him to fuller awareness. He was reaching for his gun as the door began to slide open. He flicked off the safety on his .45 and slid a round into the chamber. He raised the gun.

If it hadn't been for the eyes, Paco might have made it. He had never seen eyes like that, staring out from the slash in the black hood. It scared him in a way only night-time monsters could, with a deep, paralysing, bed-wetting fear. He fired, but the eyes cost him precious seconds. It cost him everything.

He missed and there was an answering burst of flame from the rifle's muzzle and the .45 dropped from Paco's hand as the bullet crashed into his shoulder, pulverizing it. Paco looked up into the killer's face and knew he had only seconds to live. He took the only way left to him. He rolled desperately off the bed and leaped for the open window.

The first shot missed him, crashing into the glass casement and sending a shower of shards spraying over him. He had one last second to judge the height of his fall, one last moment to believe he might make it before something slammed into his back and sent him flying helplessly out into the air. The fall tore a scream from his throat, two storeys to the stone patio.

He felt no pain. The earth just swallowed him up into its darkness.

The spider came to the window and looked down. The lines between the stones spread out from the broken form like a web. Shards of glass twinkled magically in the moonlight. Jasmine.

He left the villa, first making sure nothing remained alive in it. The Great Man was waiting.

ELEVEN

In the morning the firebase was a compassionate old whore; used and ugly but still able to comfort. Tired men emerged slowly from bunkers and sniffed tentatively at the moist wind blowing in from the jungle. They cleaned themselves off as best they could. Eating was a cold thing, devoid of pleasure.

Hallam was stiff from sleeping on the ground and his shoulder ached irritatingly. Hu didn't seem to mind as much. He had decoded Reiman's cable and was anxious to be off. Hamilton assured them transport would be arriving soon.

'You about ready?' Hu asked.

'Yeah. Couple of minutes.'

'Problem?'

Hallam squinted into the dawn sky, unsure how to explain. Come to that, he wasn't sure he understood what he felt himself. Body bags lay stacked nearby waiting for transport back to Saigon. They would be flown back to the States where about now some parent was getting a visit from a sad-faced officer. Excuse me, ma'am . . .

You're always in two places at once, Hallam thought, and one place was still here – at the other end, the beginning. The dying was a part of him now in a way that MI had never quite made it. I was there, ma'am. Yes, I saw him die . . . yes, we thought of you back in the world, even if he didn't have time to . . . No, I'm sorry. I am somebody else's son. What's that? Oh. Yes, it was bad, but not for the reasons you think. It was bad because there was no drama and no bugles. No truth or anything. Just ants scurrying frantically to stay alive. Just everybody scared shitless throwing anything they could into a jungle suddenly alive with scary monsters. I know somewhere else it meant something. Here, it was just your kid dying.

Christ, thought Hallam, I'm glad as hell it wasn't me.

He suddenly wanted very much to get off this stinking hill. 'I learned something here,' he said to Hu, scooping up the M-16. It was his now. 'All those military cemeteries are wrong, Hu. Wrong to put up all those crosses and stars. Every one ought to be changed. A tricycle, that's what you put on a grave. A bat and ball. A Hardy Boys book.'

'You're tired, David.'

'That, too.'

'And no one is unaffected by carnage.' Hu put a hand on his friend's shoulder.

'I just wish I had some answers. I don't.'

'I know. You just hurt.'

Hallam looked away, felt his eyes brim.

Hu asked, 'Does it mean anything to you that you saved a life last night?'

'Some. I don't know.'

'Nothing means anything without context. You mustn't lose perspective.'

'I'd rather you weren't another person telling me to see the "Big Picture". It makes me feel mean inside.'

'That's just your cynicism showing. The truth remains; there are reasons for everything.' He gestured towards the corpses. 'Even those.'

'You really believe that?'

'I do. And you would too if you weren't such a naive, spoiled American know-it-all convinced everything in the world is fixable with just a little money or some good old Yankee ingenuity. Well, it isn't. This is the rest of the world and it's a pit just like Reiman warned you. It's time you came to terms with it.'

Hallam looked testy. 'Save the grow-up speech, will you?'

'It's a friend's prerogative. But it's more than that. No one has answers for what goes on here, at least no one I know of. It's just goddamned conceited of you to think you can figure out what nobody else can, don't you see that? People been wiping each other out for thousands of years, you're supposed to know why? Shit. You come from one of the only places in the world where bloodshed is rare. But the rest of the world? Jesus Christ, every day they're killing each other over food, over land, over religion, over politics,' Hu took a breath and continued, 'over shit like names, over power, over someone else's wife, over their own wife, over money, over whether to bow east or west, over whether to worship cows or eat them, over—'

Hallam cut in. 'So what's your point? Just accept it?'

'Even that implies a certain conceit, as if you had a choice.'

'I think I do.'

'You don't,' Hu said flatly. 'You can live your life or you can make yourself crazy living everybody else's. David, it's dark outside. Very dark. You find a little light, grab it gratefully and let it warm you.' Hu's voice softened. 'More than most, David, you have great virtue, which Confucius taught us was the ability to love men. Now you must have wisdom, too.'

'And that is?'

'The ability to understand them.'

Hallam felt something release inside. Not answers or conclusions exactly, it was too early for that. But somehow Hu made it easier to live with the pain of not knowing; what one poet called negative capability, being able to exist within a moral flux and not taking refuge in easy answers.

'Food for thought, Hu,' he said. 'I appreciate it. I'll let you know.'

'Fair enough.'

The sound of approaching helicopters reached them. A pair of Jolly Greens were on their way in. Hallam took Hu's arm solidly. 'C'mon. Taxi's here.'

They started off, but a shout from the senior officer stopped them. 'Captain, Lieutenant. Just a minute!'

Hamilton strode over, looking just as tired and dirty as everyone else. He regarded both of them respectfully. 'What you guys did last night won't go overlooked. I wanted you to know. The decorations will be put in for as soon as I get back to MAC-Vee.' He hesitated, 'Sort of in line with that.' He handed them a pair of web belts with .45s and survival packs strapped to both. 'General consensus. They belonged to some of our guys who didn't make it. In light of everything, well . . . you want 'em?'

Hu accepted the arms silently, only a short bow which Hamilton formally returned.

Hallam said, 'Thank you, sir.' He pointed to the M-16. 'I'm taking this, too.'

The general nodded. 'You earned it. One more thing, though. Where you're going things could get pretty hot. They tell me the 1st Cav has that area under control but it's really NVA territory and they could decide to try and reclaim it any time. I'm gonna send some men with you just in case.'

'It's not necessary, sir,' said Hu.

'My decision. They go.'

The helicopters settled in. They waited, rotors turning.

Hamilton flipped his cap back on. Soldiers began loading body bags into the second copter along with the wounded. They gave Hallam and Hu respectful looks as they climbed into the helicopter's belly.

Hallam and Hu climbed into the second craft as the first took off. It hovered for a moment, dipped, then shot off southwards. Hu gave their own pilot the co-ordinates. Hallam strapped himself in. Preparing to lift off he thought about how air transport was another weird part of this war. They could be back in Saigon in minutes. Guys killing in steaming jungles could be back in New York the next afternoon. He looked out of the hatch at the faces of those who were staying behind. So long, fellas, just dropped in. Every face held the same question: where's *my* ride outa here?

Hallam settled back as the helicopter jumped into the air. Lots of questions.

He had no answers.

Tired of watching a repetition of the green-brown foliage Hallam was about to unstrap himself when the co-pilot came back to him.

'Captain? Pilot needs you up front, sir.'

'Coming.'

Hallam made his way forward. The pilot was circling the clearing. In the distance, Hallam could see a broad ribbon of highway cutting through the terrain. Smouldering wrecks of NVA tanks, mostly Russian-made T-54 heavies and PT-76 light amphibs were still sending up plumes of black smoke.

Hallam gestured. 'Been a war here.'

'Got that right,' said the pilot. 'Major Commie highway to the south. Last few days the Air Force been pounding the shit out of it. Got a FAC up top directing traffic. Place sounded like the 1812 Overture gone berserk with the Sandys and F-4s coming down in waves. Ground forces only moved in day before yesterday.'

Hallam saw bivouacs a few miles away. 'Safe here?'

'You gotta be kidding,' the pilot exclaimed. 'Safe is Burbank. Here you get your ass shot off if you're not careful. Tell me where you want to set down. We'll get you in and stay with the bird. Do what you gotta do and let's get out quick. We're sitting ducks on the ground for snipers or VC patrols trying to infiltrate back in.'

'Put us down in the clearing.'

The pilot frowned. 'Gonna be a little tight, but the nearest field is over a mile away. We'll squash some chickens, I fear.'

Hallam shrugged. 'War is hell.'

'So they tell me.'

They came in fast and pulled up over the clearing. Hallam scrabbled back, watching through the hatch as they dipped below the treetops and dropped to the ground.

Hallam strapped on the .45 and shouldered the M-16. Hu had his weapon on, too. The two huts were behind the helicopter. They left one soldier on guard with the pilots and took the other with them.

It was quiet in the clearing. Dense foliage obscured the horizon. A thin column of white smoke rose lazily from the larger of the two huts. The soldier went into the smaller hut low and fast, rifle ready. He poked his head back out after a few seconds 'Empty,' he said, stepping back out, 'but it's a goddamn PX in there, sir. Food, medical supplies, soap, gasoline. Explosives, too, sir. Not a lot but some pretty heavy stuff. Thermite, dynamite. Also one sleeping mat and some personal items. Servant's hut?'

Hu nodded. 'Probably. Wait out here. We'll go in alone.'

'Okay, sir.'

Hallam looked over. 'What's your name, Corporal?'

'McDivit, sir. John C.'

'Well, John C.,' Hallam said, 'anything but us moves, don't be too shy about blowing it up.'

McDivit smiled without humour. 'Gotcha, sir.'

For some reason, Hallam knocked on the door. An odd gesture here, as if they were coming to tea. He felt an anticipatory thrill as he pushed open the door after getting no response, as if something were coming to a close. 'I'm going in,' he said to Hu.

The dry, spicy atmosphere inside evoked such strong recollections of the herbalist's shop that Hallam felt his chest tighten and his throat go dry. Fighting the closeness of the air in the hut, he swept aside the curtain in front of him and stepped through. He felt Hu right behind him.

The sage was seated cross-legged on a low dais. Hallam stopped to regard him. He looked almost translucent, dry and brittle as old bones. For a split second Hallam almost felt some recognition pass between them, as if the sage knew him, knew why he was there. He found himself staring deep into the sage's eyes, fathomless pits of desperate sorrow. Yarrow stalks lay in disordered piles on the ground. The eyes flickered once, almost closed, then opened to stare past them as if they had ceased to matter at all.

Hallam began, 'Hu, ask him . . .'

But it was then that he noticed the dark splotches on the master's voluminous robe, the dark stains that were not part of its design. And he suddenly became aware that the pain in those aged eyes was not the result of farsightedness only. The old man's mouth opened but words would not form. Hallam could only recoil in horror as the stump of what was left of the sage's tongue flapped at his lips like some fat, obscene worm.

Someone had cut out his tongue.

In that moment, Hallam knew . . .

He had observed the helicopter land in the clearing from a vantage point in one of the trees high overhead. All that time removing the mines and booby-traps so the Great Man could arrive intact – silly; he should have realized he'd come this way. Well, no matter. They were here now. He watched them cross the clearing and enter the master's hut.

Below him, about fifty feet away, the pilots were conversing with one of the soldiers. He placed one arrow on the branch in front of him, a second in his mouth like a dancer held a rose, and nocked the third. Drawing back the bowstring in one smooth motion, he aimed, feeling his hand slide against the camouflage paint on his face; black and green like the foliage around him. He stilled for a brief moment, then released the string straight back and followed through fluidly.

The four-bladed hunting arrow buried itself deep into the soldier's back, slicing through enough arteries and vital organs to kill him instantly. The pilots only saw the arrow protruding from the soldier's back as he fell, realizing too late that they were under attack. A second arrow hurtled down and split open the pilot's chest, the third took out the co-pilot in mid-stride as he turned futilely to flee. The spider waited. No noise except the buzz of flies drawn by seeping blood disturbed the clearing. On the other side of the helicopter, in front of the hut, Corporal McDivit saw and heard nothing.

The splider slid down from the tree and crawled to the helicopter. He sliced through bundles of wiring with his knife and cut the cables leading back. It was going nowhere. He slid back out, passing near enough to the three corpses to touch them.

Eyes aglow, he whispered, 'Welcome to *my* parlour,' and crawled back to the tree where the detonator waited.

Corporal McDivit was unhappy. They were spread out and exposed, increasingly vulnerable. He decided to take a turn round the hut. He held his M-16 at the ready but heard nothing to provoke action. He was concentrating so much on the surrounding jungle that he actually tripped over the servant's body before he saw it.

Seeing the arrow, he dived instinctively, shouting, 'Captain!' and rolling away. He came up firing, having no real location but trying to draw fire to himself to give Hallam and Hu cover. He rounded the hut and charged into the clearing low and fast. The helicopter! The only way out. He ran zig-zagging across the open space.

McDivit felt the arrow that pierced his shoulder as a white-hot burst of pain that made his vision dark. It blasted him off his feet but he managed to throw himself the last few yards and drag himself under the helicopter. He was panting, dizzy from shock and bleeding profusely. He saw the bodies. Anger flared in him, but he crawled past and into the helicopter without stopping.

Inside, the savaged controls completed the story. He tried unsuccessfully to staunch the bleeding. He fought the pain. Training took over. Rage cooled. Watching his life's blood drain away, he settled down to wait.

Hallam turned, shoving recklessly at Hu. 'Quick! Get out. He's already here!'

Hu was staring at the sage, his face looking like something from a Bosch painting, but he turned and bolted, galvanized by Hallam's cry. The curtain whipped at their faces and the sage's tortured gasping would follow them as long as they lived, but they stumbled out. Outside, McDivit was shouting something and they heard his rifle fire.

Hu burst out first but stopped uncertainly. He saw McDivit racing for the helicopter. Where was . . . ?

Hallam tackled him and sent him careening towards the second hut. With certain conviction he knew there was no more time, that they had made the last in what seemed like a series of mistakes. He shoved Hu again harshly; he stumbled and went down. Hallam leaped on him, rolling, covering Hu's body with his own.

The master's cottage exploded in a paroxysm of shock and flame. Burning debris rained down on them and Hallam smothered Hu's back as his clothing caught fire. He felt heat on his own body and rolled desperately in the dirt to put it out.

A rage like none he had ever felt flooded him and he had the M-16 in his hands before conscious thought compelled him. Something moved by the tree line and he fired, holding the weapon on full automatic, spraying the spot in a long barrage as if he held a garden hose. He heard Hu's .45 open up alongside and when the M-16's clip was empty grabbed his own and kept on shooting.

Suddenly, a dark figure in jungle camouflage was up and racing for cover. He ducked as he ran, diving, rolling, desperate to avoid their combined fire. He slipped and fell but came up kneeling, his own pistol discharging. Hu let out a pained scream and his fire died. Hallam's clip emptied and the .45 slid open. He saw the figure rise like an apparition, swaying, and knew that this was the creature they had hunted, even though the camouflage paint disguised his contorted features like a fright-mask. The spider steadied his aim on him . . .

It was the moment McDivit had waited for. He fired at the standing figure and saw him spin round even as his own weapon fired. McDivit's bullet rent the spider's flesh and saved Hallam's life. It cost McDivit his own. Falling, the spider pivoted away and his pistol barked once, twice, and McDivit died, his weapon continuing to fire from his death throes.

The spider crawled into the jungle.

Hallam's left leg was on fire. McDivit had been quick but not quick enough. Hallam jammed a fresh clip into the M-16 and steadied the weapon across Hu's fallen body. With his right hand he felt the jagged tear across his thigh, shoved bandage into the wound, then felt for Hu's pulse.

Hu was breathing raggedly. There was blood all over the left side of his head. Hallam saw the spider disappear into the bush. He shot at him though it was futile. He couldn't go after him with his leg untreated, nor could he leave Hu unprotected. Slowly, he dragged the Vietnamese back to the shelter of the undamaged hut. He had no hope that the helicopter was usable and the pilots were surely dead. He spent some time pushing earth up into mounds around them and steadied the rifle on one. He got out the first aid kit. There was more medicine in the hut. He dabbed at the dark blood on Hu's face and his rage rose again as he held his unconscious friend.

'Fuck you, number ten!' Hallam shouted. 'Fuck you dead!'

There was no answer.

Careless! The spider chided himself bitterly. How could he be so careless? Forgetting the last soldier was unforgivable. And now look. His left arm hung uselessly at his side and his knee throbbed painfully from when it had twisted as he spun and fired. Careless careless careless. He would never do that again. Never never. If he ever did that again he would . . .

He stopped himself. There was always a way out. Everybody was dead except the Great Man and his companion, and he was sure both were hit. It wasn't so bad and there was a kind of symmetry in all this. Not so bad. Forget the pain. Wait a while, then finish it once and for all.

He lay in the soft earth breathing deeply, feeling the fecund growth all around him, earth's fullness at once growing and decaying. Flies walked on his face and he made no move to brush them off. He heard the Great Man shouting. Good, great rage, too. Worthy. Worthy of his best.

He smiled.

Hu moved weakly. 'David . . .?'

Hallam's relief was so great he felt tears start down his cheeks. 'It's about time,' he said harshly, but it didn't come out that way. He put down the things he'd been examining from the hut. 'Nice to have you back.'

Hu coughed. 'I'm not dead?'

'Nope. But you might as well be for all the work you're doing around here. Head wound. I can't tell how bad. Lie still and let me talk.'

Hallam explained what had happened, where they were, what he'd taken from the hut.

'. . . He's hurt, too. Maybe worse than us, maybe not. But he's gonna come back to finish it. McDivit tagged him, I think one of us did too. We got four to six hours of light left. I think he'll wait until dark, use the shadows. He knows there are two of us. So maybe we got a little time.' Hallam motioned behind him. 'McDivit was right. There's a shitload of stuff back there and I've got an idea how to use it.'

'What you got in mind?'

'Well, we can't take this guy head on. You wouldn't have believed the shot he made to take out McDivit. And he's been ahead of us every turn. No more straight ahead, it's time we finessed the bastard. Can you cover us while I work?'

Hu pushed himself up. 'It's a little hazy, but I think so. Ammunition?'

'Plenty inside. This guy is a packrat.'

'Okay.'

Hallam slipped into the hut. It was going to be tricky. He'd read about the thing he had in mind, but never actually saw one first-hand. It might not work at all. But he'd come to a decision. Bottom line, they'd taken enough crap from this sick motherfucker.

It was hard to position the fifty-five-gallon drum of petrol with his bad leg and it took a while to position it over the shallow hole he had dug in the ground. He had to prop himself up to open the top spout but he managed it in time Interestingly, the exercise seemed to strengthen his leg. He picked up the first of the bars of soap and began grating it into the petrol with his knife.

Hu poked his head in. 'What are you doing?'

Hallam grinned. 'Cooking.'

When the soap was all gone, he stirred the mixture with a long stick. It would have to be stirred a lot to get the same consistency throughout. That made a better dispersion rate.

He took a stick of the dynamite and put a No.4 cap on it, then levered the drum back and placed the stick in the hole underneath, trailing the wires out from under as he lowered it back. Finally, bathed in sweat and with a blinding headache, he put a No.2 cap on a Thermite grenade and taped it to the front of the drum. That was all. Three hours to sunset and no other way out. Hallam had bet the ranch on this.

In theory it was simple. In the field they called it Fu-gas. It was a bastard weapon in a bastard war. The petrol and soap made a crude kind of napalm after sitting for a few hours. When the dynamite went off it pushed the napalm 'up', then the Thermite – a mixture of powdered aluminium and metal oxide that produced intense heat – ignited it. Anything for a hundred yards left and right, front and back was burnt to a crisp.

Hallam crawled out. After the hut, the air was cooler. He explained to Hu what he had in mind.

'No way,' said Hu flatly. 'You can't cover that much distance in thirty seconds through this goddamned bush with a bad leg.'

Hallam insisted. 'Longer than that, you give him too much chance to react. I know it's a bet. So is your making it out of here unseen. I won't know if you're clear till the damn thing goes off.'

'Assuming it does,' Hu objected. 'You could be racing right into his trap if he outflanks us and gets to me first. Or worse, he sets this monstrosity off right next to you.'

'I suppose you're right,' Hallam agreed. 'Let's forget the whole thing. Too risky. Just invite him over and tell him we're gonna punch it out. Past five o'clock anyway. He'll understand. I know he will.'

'Stick the sarcasm.'

'I'm open to better ideas.'

'Okay. My legs are in better shape. I'll stay and be the bait.'

'Fine.' Hallam held up two fingers. 'How many?'

Hu peered out from under the bandage. 'Hold them closer.'

Hallam snorted. 'They're a foot away from your face now. How the fuck you gonna run when you can't see? Look, let's cut the Laurel and Hardy stuff and get this straightened out.'

'Imperialist dog. Round-eyed tyrant.'

Hallam ignored him. 'There's two hundred feet of wire here,' he began.

He saw by his watch it was time to open the tourniquet on his arm again. The blood flowing back was painful but it helped to clear his head. Only an hour or so till dusk. There were two of them. He needed night's advantage.

Twice, he had tried to get close and twice their fire had driven him back. Too much open ground. The second time they put on quite a show, throwing most of what he had left in the servant's hut back at him. The clearing looked like the moon, there were so many craters from the dynamite and grenades. No harm done though, he just moved back till they exhausted themselves.

Now their fire was sporadic. Firing at all was good; it saved him the trouble of checking to see if they were trying to escape. Occasionally, the Great Man screamed nasty things at him. Silly to be so personal about things. But it didn't matter. Not now. His pulse beat faster at the thought; this was their wedding night.

Consummation was very close.

Hallam pushed more earth up in front of him and fired a few more rounds into the jungle. He missed Hu's presence beside him. He didn't like to admit how scared he was being alone.

Very soon. He felt it. The spider was coming. Twice he had tried, twice they forced him back, the second time using a Fourth of July barrage of explosives to cover Hu's leaving. He slithered out like a snake. Couldn't see much further to the ground than that anyway. Good enough. Just crawl till the wire ran out, then attach the detonator. Hide your ass and wait. When you hear me yell, count thirty seconds and let the damn thing blow. *But David* . . . But nothing. I'll make it. Now go, gook . . . Oh, yeah. I love you. Shhh. Go.

It was harder to see now and whatever Hu's response was had been cut off by the explosions. When Hallam looked back, Hu was gone. Don't die, Hallam prayed. For God's sake, don't die.

You're always in two places, Hallam thought, getting set to run the hundred-yard dash of his life.

Hu was past the hundred-yard zone, he was sure of that. Only a few coils of wire remained looped in his hand. He inched forward, one part of his mind screaming about the bugs in the soft loam, the sticky things under leaves that brushed his neck. The other part clamped down on primordial fears with icy control.

He crawled on his belly. One hand pushed, the other reaching out . . . He froze. What his mind had registered as a narrow vine under his hand had just moved. Sweat burst out on him as if he'd been sprayed. His stomach roiled. He hated snakes, hated the way they could crawl up your legs or under your shirt . . . Shut up! Stay calm. He peered into the grey mist that shrouded his vision. The snake rose up before him, swaying menacingly. He couldn't see it well enough to identify it. It might be poisonous or not. It was vital to know. One of the vipers and he'd die before Hallam's signal ever came. Harmless and he could flick it away like any annoyance.

It swayed enticingly before him. Couldn't use a gun; it would alert the spider. Couldn't see well enough anyway. Slowly, so as not to provoke it, Hu reached down and slid the knife from its scabbard. More slowly still, he began pulling his hand back, his fingers gathering the wire in tiny increments, ready to toss, to distract.

His breath was shallow and reedy. No more time. He had to get the detonator attached. Spots danced in the haze before his eyes. He moved, tossing the wire, rolling aside with the knife flashing out.

The snake struck.

Hallam heard the spider coming. In the night sounds it was a close thing, but suddenly he knew a presence had been added that was as alien here as he was. He felt another rhythm, heard faint wispy breath riding under the breeze, heard an animal cease its harsh cry suddenly. There! He fired, stopped, listened.

It was going to be a matter of seconds. He tightened the bandage on his leg and worked the muscles to keep them from cramping. Even in the darkness he could find the way he'd chosen earlier. There was also a bright moon to help.

Something snapped. Hallam opened fire again in the general direction, spraying carelessly. He stopped to listen. Another sound, closer. He got ready.

There were two sticks of dynamite left and he lit the first

and threw it out in a high arc. It exploded, sending a shower of earth back.

Hallam took a deep breath, dropped the M-16 and threw the last stick of dynamite. He bolted out like hell was opening up under him. 'Now, Hu! Now!' he screamed.

The dynamite exploded behind him as he ran. Branches whipped at his face as he plunged into the brush. Pain shot up his leg almost at once and he had to stiff-leg it over fallen tree trunks. He crashed into a cluster of bamboo stalks and cut his face and hands frantically trying to get himself out. He ran. Ten seconds.

His boots splashed into a stream and he slipped and fell, drenched. He tore out and plunged on madly, soaking wet, fending off the bugs that swarmed into his eyes, the vines that slapped at him. He fell again and felt something stab him in the left side. He muffled an agonized scream, pushed himself upright and lurched on again.

His hands were empty, the .45 long gone. He was panting furiously from the exertion and unable to get enough air into his starved lungs. He ran into a tree, smashing his shoulder. Never mind. Go on. Get up. Run! Hell was behind in fire *and* the devil. Shots behind him. Twenty seconds.

Hallam ran for his life.

The final explosion subsided and he leaped through the smoke before the debris even settled to get to the Great Man. He fired happily into the spot where he'd seen him rise to toss the explosive. Now! You and I. The Shui hexagram foretold it. Sighing and weeping.

But wait, where was he? Sounds off to the right. He liked that, running. So be it. The jungle was his element. But no more mistakes. Could be they were planning a trap. He went into the hut low and fast, prepared to fire if they were clever enough to leave one behind . . . and stopped dead in his tracks.

He knew what he was seeing, the petrol, the Thermite

grenade, and for the first time in his memory he was afraid. There was no time to study it, no time to disarm. It could go off any second. His blood turned cold. He fell back.

He bolted outside, stumbling over the earth mounds. A trick! Rage blinded him. He yelled like a wounded animal turning and clambering up to run. He roared again, knowing full well the range of the thing the Great Man had devised, admiring it even as he fled. Only seconds remained to him.

He held his useless arm tight to his side, dropped his weapon and ran blindly. His chest pumped like a bellows and his legs worked like pistons. He burst into the dense foliage and bulled his way through, tearing and scraping it from his path. Never never never. Never never never. Never never never. Never never never.

He roared his fury into the blackness.

Thirty seconds. Hu lay deathly still. The snake was in two pieces nearby. This close he knew what it was. The bite would fester and make him very sick, but it would not kill him. He could hold on. He heard Hallam's signal, heard the gunfire and the crashing through the jungle. Thirty seconds. He rolled on his back to stare at the night sky, unable to go any further. For luck, God, another five seconds. He would give Hallam that. Let him get clear in another five seconds. Let him get clear.

Time came. He pushed the plunger . . . and the jungle exploded.

Things went white and something picked Hallam up high and slammed him down hard. The air was a scorching inferno and he buried his face in the damp earth, sucking air through the dirt, burrowing in like some desperate mole. The sodden clothing was a godsend, protecting him from the worst of it. As it was, the skin on the exposed parts of his body blistered almost instantaneously, pulling tortured screams from him.

The hair on the back of his head burnt off with a sickly smell and he rubbed mud onto himself with frenzied motions. He was whining like a trapped animal, thrashing wildly trying to still the pain.

The jungle was burning around him. The acrid smell of petrol was everywhere. He lay in hell's periphery, only the road before him was open. Behind was the inferno.

The flames lit up the night. Hallam managed to stand. This much pain and the body went numb. He looked at the charred flesh on his forearms as if they belonged to someone else. His mind shied away.

Hu! That thought came clearly. To hell with the spider. Hallam looked back. An atavistic grin contorted his features. I hope you fried. I hope you saw what was coming as the flames burnt you alive. Enough, his mind counselled, you got him or you didn't. There is nothing left to do this night but survive. He took a tentative step forward and fell. His face was pressed into the cool earth. Good to rest. No more spiders. Let it go.

He managed to get his legs under him and sat up. It was blazing hot and he pressed more earth to his face to cool it. Gotta find Hu. Burning branches were dropping nearer now. The fire was spreading. He felt hot winds tear at his lungs and hoped he wasn't burnt there as well. He'd seen burn victims shed the inside skin like snakes. He shuddered. Please God, don't let me be burnt there. Please God, save me. Please God, get me out of this place . . .

He tripped over the wire. It took him a while to figure out what it was, staring stupidly at the thin cord. The connection was not sudden. Finally, he realized he could follow it to Hu. He got up and stumbled forward, sliding the wire through his hands like a belayed rope.

'Hu?' he called out over the noise of the crackling fire. 'Hu?'

Hu was face down when Hallam came upon him. He saw the snake and puzzled a while over what could have happened. He dropped down beside his friend and turned him over, filled with relief and worry at the same time. He saw the puncture marks under the bandage Hu had hastily wrapped. The trees around them were smoking; no time to do anything further.

'C'mon, dopey. Can't sleep.' Hallam was slurring the words, perilously close to his own end. He swatted petulantly at Hu. 'C'mon.' Damn, why didn't he get up?

Hallam sighed. He undid Hu's belt and strapped his wrists together. Hu mumbled something. Hallam mumbled back and got his head through Hu's arms, slid them round his neck like a yoke and levered him up onto his back. He waited for a second, testing the weight.

'Dopey dopey dopey,' Hallam said in a singsong. 'Don't know better than to play with snakes?' The thought amused him and he giggled. He lurched forward a few steps, got better balance, lurched a few more.

It was cooler now, away from the fire's edge. A few steps at a time, Hallam moved forward. He hit trees like a pinball, bounced off, struggled on. A few steps at a time. Ten yards. Twenty. Sometimes, now, he could smell a sweet breeze from far away devoid of petrol or burning. It buoyed him.

A hundred yards. There was no time, or distance, really. He just got one step down. When he could, he took another. Simple. One more. He knew they were dying. That was simple too. You walked until you died.

His conscious mind had shut down and only drive was left. Tenacity. Visual images registered but had no meaning. The burning tree, the moon, the animal blurting suddenly across their path. Just walk. And finally, when you can walk no longer, sink down into the receptive earth . . .

The squad from the 1st Cavalry sent to investigate the fire found them. Hallam was kneeling, with Hu on his back still, as if in prayer. He was swaying in the rhythm of exhaustion. When the soldiers untied Hu's arms and separated them gently, Hallam just looked up and smiled and said something, but it was too garbled to understand.

The squad leader was on the radio in seconds and had a helicopter on its way to the nearest open space at once. He gave them the best first aid he could under these conditions and had them carried out. He saw them strapped in when the Jolly Green landed and shook his head that anything that used up could still be alive.

Within half an hour, Hallam and Hu were wheeled into the 10th Evac hospital. Clusters of white-coated doctors cut away their clothing, drugs were pumped in, IVs attached. They were rushed into surgery.

Sometime during the night they were stabilized and guarded optimism spread. MAC-Vee headquarters had called. Someone called them back with the news.

You're always in two places, Hallam would have said, but the tubes down his throat wouldn't permit it. Nor would the blackness behind his eyes. But after-images of a terrible dark shape and a burning jungle followed him all the way to the hospital, folding back into him like a racing cartoon character whose many images finally catch up to a body strained to breaking point.

A long way away, made short enough to survive, the jungle was still burning.

TWELVE

The general conferred with the chief surgeon. It was a hasty conference, conducted in a corner in low tones. A special shift had been called in. The head nurse herself was on duty at the floor's station, summoned when the corpses began to mount. She was an oldtimer who could be counted on to run things and keep her mouth shut.

In more than a few conversations over the past twenty-four hours the words 'damage control' had come up frequently.

Mercifully, the body count was holding at twelve. Jesus, a goddamned dozen! In the morgue, the corpses of Major Reiman and three Nung Chinese, along with those of the team house's maid and gardener, had been joined by those of the two dead pilots, a pair of GIs from the 14th Artillery and two other unidentified Chinese pulled out by the same squad that had brought in Hallam and Hu. Elsewhere in the hospital, Sergeant 'Paco' Gallo hung onto life with a severed spine and most of the bones in his body broken. The best anyone had to offer him was life as a quadriplegic. Not unkindly, there was talk of just letting him die, too.

The general excused himself and found a phone. He was connected to a number at MAC-Vee with only a short wait, but his foot tapped impatiently anyway. When the connection was completed he spoke quickly and precisely, a kind of battlefield reportage. Later in the conversation things like 'Major Hallam' and 'rotation home' and 'honourable discharge' and 'full benefits' got said a lot. A lot was said about medals as well.

The general hung up. He returned to the doctor and issued

strict orders. To the doctor he said things like, 'a lid so tight on this you'd smell a fart for a week'. The doctor, who held the rank of captain, was there because he had signed a paper postponing service in order to be allowed to go to medical school. He already knew he wanted a *cream*-coloured Mercedes when he got the hell out of *here*. He said things like 'Okay', 'Sure', and 'You bet'.

It was raining outside, a rare occurrence at this time of year. It made the air uncommonly sweet. The general slipped his trenchcoat over his shoulders and walked out from under the portico to his car. His driver held the door open. Inside, he listened to the pattern of the raindrops hitting the roof. Random. Ceaseless. Chaotic.

Hallam would be going home, Hu to a Military Security Service sanctuary to recuperate. It was hoped the cover placed on the entire matter would hold. They'd got enough of the story from Hu to piece the rest together. Officially, the killer died in the fire.

A dozen corpses was not so many to hide in a war. Wheels had been set in motion, procedures begun. In the long run, it wouldn't even be a bulge in the week's statistics. He wanted to begin to think of it as over, put to rest.

He slid his hands deeply into his coat pockets and watched the hospital's lights slide by as they drove off.

The car carried him into the rain brooding uneasily.

THIRTEEN

Hallam's hospital room was darkened and he was alone in it though the facility was vastly overcrowded. Careful attention had been paid to his burns by doctors who saw this type of thing every day, but there would still be scarring though mostly in places clothing covered. One nurse made a face as she changed the dressings on the unconscious form and said how she thought it unlikely this guy was going to the beach again soon. The doctor nodded. She was transferred the next day.

Tubes fed him intravenously. The bullet wound in his left leg had been treated and it posed little recuperative problem. Of greater concern was the gash in his left side. A steady stream of antibiotics was being used to combat the infection that had set in.

Unaware, Hallam lay comatose.

Nurses were assigned to him around the clock and a guard was posted outside his door. From the beginning, their every move was monitored by the man who sat unmoving in a chair in the shadows by the patient's bed.

Hu didn't mind the odd looks, but he spoke to no one. He carefully checked each bottle of fluid before it was hung on the IV rack and looked at each ampule before he allowed it to be drawn into a syringe. He ate from a tray brought by a special MSS agent. He slept sitting.

In the middle of the fourth night he was awakened by a scratching sound at the window. He didn't hesitate, didn't call out or check or raise the blinds. He simply lifted the machine-gun he had been sitting with for four days and emptied the entire clip into the window and surrounding wall.

Glass exploded outwards and chips of plaster flew around like hornets. The noise in so small a room was deafening. It brought the guard running and hospital security only moments later. They took the weapon away, chastising Hu severely. 'You crazy, shooting at birds?' they shouted at him.

No, he said. Spiders.

One pointed to his head wound and made a circling motion near his temple. Hu smiled. They moved Hallam to another room.

Hu took his seat again.

In the morning he made three phone calls, each to one of the generals. It was over, he said. Bury the dead. No noise. He had struggled against this for days but the night had convinced him. He was making a trade: Hallam's life for walking away. He was letting whoever needed to know that it *was* a trade. He would call it off for David Hallam's life. Nothing less.

He hoped over the years to come to live with what he was doing. He knew he could not live with the alternative. He hoped Hallam would not hate him.

For the remaining time in the hospital, Hu stayed close. But now there was a difference. He felt it. The message had got through. There were no more scratchings at the window.

When it was time for Hallam to leave, they gave Hu a wheelchair and let him go down to the airstrip where the big C-5 waited. He rolled past the body bags stacked on the tarmac. His vision was still not perfect but things were clearer these days. He watched as Hallam's stretcher was wheeled onto the plane accompanied by a nurse who held the IV bottles steady. For a time he had hoped Hallam would wake. Then, more kindly, he had hoped that he would not.

He watched as the plane's nose was lowered back into place and the loadmasters decreed it ready to fly. Sometime later he watched it take off and climb into the cloudless sky on plumes of smoke and fire.

Sometimes you're motivated by big things, Hu thought, sometimes by small. Where was the life of a friend on that scale? Poor Reiman. He had been right from the beginning. The pit had risen up and consumed them all. In the distance, the guns of summer's slaughter continued unabated.

Hu felt the first tears since childhood. Hallam was gone. Orpheus had once failed to carry Eurydice out of Hell. Hu regarded himself, still thin and weakened from the ordeal, sitting on a runway in a land of lost souls. Orpheus had failed a second time.

He was still here.

He turned back. Wheels turn, he told himself. Paths twined would intertwine again. He was believer enough in karma to believe that.

FOURTEEN

It was warm enough in Colorado for Hallam just to toss his raincoat over his shoulder. Crossing the tarmac from the plane to the terminal he noticed that yuppies from his home state were still arriving carrying ski equipment in spite of the spring weather. Hallam couldn't help feeling the activity was basically unnatural so late in the year. No Easterner really believed snow existed because of something as whimsical as altitude. It was only supposed to come with the cyclic progression of the seasons, from December to March, with a little thrown into April if it was a bad year.

It was a relief to walk after so many hours in the plane. The airport wasn't crowded and he retrieved his luggage without a long wait. There were several drivers standing beyond the gate. They held signs with names scrawled on them in pencil or magic marker. One of them said HALLAM. Old cautions reasserted themselves. No one could be interested in him at this stage but he still wished they hadn't made any advertisement of his arrival.

The driver was in uniform. At Hallam's eye contact, he stepped forward.

'Mr Hallam?'

'Who sent you?'

The driver looked surprised. 'Mr Gallo, sir. I was told you were expecting to be picked up.'

'Yes. I was. I'm ready.'

How do you explain the old cautions? Hallam wondered briefly as the chauffeur took his bags. He started off towards the terminal door. Jesus, thought Hallam. The Terminal Door. He loved walking through that.

The Colorado sunshine helped soothe his tensions. He slid into the plush back seat of the Rolls in a slightly better frame of mind. He'd never been inside a Rolls-Royce before and the car was indeed magnificent. They drifted out onto the highway like a ship moving out to sea. The burled mahogany of the side panelling was more elegant than the wood in Hallam's living room. The seats were deeper.

Obviously, Paco had finally figured out the Dow.

Hallam watched Colorado glide by, as different from South-East Asia as the moon. Unresolved events were rushing to a conclusion. It telescoped the past twenty years. There had never really been an ending for him. His last memories were running through the jungle when the napalm device went off. Then the world exploded in white flames. Over the years, he stubbornly held onto the belief that the killer was caught in the trap – but he had always had his doubts. It hadn't been such a surprise when the news reports confirmed them.

The big car turned off the highway ascending a narrower, two-lane road. People they passed looked like people do everywhere, vaguely familiar. Occasional school buses made him think of his children and that made him think of never seeing them again and that made him sick. There was a bar in the Rolls. He started to reach for a drink to steady his nerves, then thought better of it. The fight started well in advance of any confrontation. He closed the bar.

They climbed through an area that was more forest than town, turning onto a wide apron between a pair of stone posts to enter a driveway. The car stopped at the gatehouse. After a check, an armed guard lifted the gate and they passed through a high fence which ran perpendicular to the road in both directions. They continued on through the pines for at least a quarter of a mile before coming to a circular drive. It left them in front of a huge log-cabin-style house which Hallam decided could be safely called a mansion. Beyond that was a shimmering lake with a pier and a boathouse and the sun flaring across it all like a beacon.

The door opened as he went up the front steps.

'Good day, sir,' said the butler. 'Was your trip comfortable?'

Hallam walked in. 'Yes. Very.' As an afterthought, 'Thank you.'

'Not at all, sir. May I show you to your room?'

'Where's Mr Gallo?'

'He will be joining you at dinner, sir. I was told he wanted to give his guests some, ah . . . space. Yes, that was the way he put it.'

Hallam smiled. 'Space appreciated.'

'Dinner will be at eight, sir. This way, please.'

Hallam's room was wide and uncluttered, with rough-hewn beams running across the ceiling. His balcony looked out over the lake. There was a small boat in the distance and Hallam could make out someone in it, fishing. He couldn't see who it was.

He turned away and unpacked. When he was done he lay down on the bed for a while. It was the kind of pensive moment that called for a cigarette, staring at the smoke curling past the beams like ideas escaping, but he quit smoking the year after his father died of cancer. He swung his legs off the bed, deciding a walk was the better choice.

It was a little cooler outside and Hallam turned up the collar of his jacket. The air smelled clean and fresh and the scent of the woods was a rich aroma. There was a trail of sorts and he swung onto it. It took him to a wooded bluff overlooking the lake. The boat was still out there. This much closer he could make out who was in it. An odd feeling caught at his chest. For a moment he just stood there letting his emotions wash over him.

In the boat, Hu cast out his line again and sat back down.

It was Hu that Hallam most wanted to see and for a moment he wondered if Paco had engineered the whole thing knowing his guests might end up roaming. It didn't matter.

In that mad landscape of old, it was Hu who had meant most to him and, if he could judge from his own reactions, still did. How did you pick up after so much time? He began to follow the path winding down towards the pier. Hu was still fishing quietly. Hallam sat down to wait.

Twenty years before, while Hallam was recuperating in the hospital, the veterans' network was still functioning pretty well. Even though the officials clamped a lid on the whole episode – in retrospect, he decided, for some pretty fair reasons – word of slaughter on such a scale could not be completely suppressed. Those who survived the killer's attack were in their respective hospitals somewhere, and Hallam was in his, but there were a lot of people left cleaning up the mess afterwards. Most of the 525th knew what had happened. So did the relatives of the Vietnamese involved . . . and so on. Stories came back with returning vets and Hallam was no less skilled an intelligence officer for his lengthy convalescence. What there was to know, he found out.

He knew Major Reiman had been killed and the files destroyed. He knew the body count for that night. When he met Janet, then a nurse in his ward, and their relationship deepened, she was able to check on Fred Burris and Paco Gallo for him. He knew what shape the killer had left them in.

Information about Hu ended in a blank wall. He vaguely remembered finding Hu and carrying him that day, but it was like a dream he couldn't quite bring up to full memory. The rest was nothing but rumour and inconclusive scraps of information. Hu had returned to the mountains . . . Hu was no longer with the MSS . . . something about gold . . . something about a decision that left Hu, well, *depleted* was how the source put it. Then, nothing for over twenty years.

Hallam watched Hu draw his rod in and place it in the bottom of the boat. He dipped the oars gently and headed back towards shore. Hallam stood, waiting.

It was a pristine scene, one that should have filled Hallam with a peaceful feeling. The setting sun cast a ribbon of light across the lake, the boat glided in slowly. Instead, he waited like someone at his first dance, unsure of what the reactions were going to be. Hu's back was to the shore as he rowed. He was wearing a simple white windbreaker and jeans. A few feet from the dock he turned to check the remaining distance . . . and saw Hallam.

The eyes have it, thought Hallam, as their gazes locked and emotions coursed along the connection like a wire. Hu sat without moving for a long second, then nodded slowly, a deep, thoughtful expression crossing his still benign features. His boat touched the dock. The warmth in his voice was unmistakable.

'Hello, round eyes.'

Hallam realized he was grinning. 'Hello, foreign devil.'

'Give me a hand?'

Hallam reached out. 'Won't be the first time.'

Hu stopped. 'No,' he said, balancing in the rocking boat. 'It won't.'

Hu passed him the pole and his fishing basket and Hallam stepped back to let him onto the dock. Hu leaped the distance lightly and the two men were finally standing face to face. There was an awkward silence at first. Where did you start?

'Hu, I . . .'

'David . . .'

They hugged.

They sat on the bench. The sun was half a red coin perched on the treetops.

'You remember carrying me?' Hu asked.

Hallam peered into the growing dusk. 'Barely. When the bomb exploded it sort of wiped out everything. The pain must have doped me up. I couldn't get it together to find you. I think I thought you were dead. When I tripped over the wire I didn't realize right away I could trace it to you. You were just lying there. What happened exactly?'

'Snake. Too dark to see it clearly so I didn't know whether

it was poisonous or not. In any case, I couldn't use a gun. It bit me. Up close I saw it wouldn't be lethal, but it was enough to knock me out. I held on as long as I could . . . to press the plunger. Then, nothing till the hospital.'

Hallam nodded. 'I vaguely remember the snake. You bound up the bite?'

Hu bared his arm to expose two faded white spots. 'The guys who found us said you tied my wrists together and slung my arms round your neck.' Hu looked at him closely. 'Later, when I saw the shape you were in, I couldn't see how you managed it.'

'It wasn't a fully conscious effort. I think I yelled at you about playing with snakes. It was kind of funny in a way. Like I said, the pain made me dopey. The rest was on autopilot.'

'Not autopilot. Inner resources.'

'That's too noble. I was just stubborn.'

Hu grew silent.

Hallam sensed disquiet. 'What's wrong?'

'You saved my life.'

'You saved mine. Who was counting that day?'

Hu's disquiet deepened. 'I was. And because I did, David, I fear I'm to blame for what has happened here.'

'I don't follow.'

'Twice I had the opportunity to kill that madman and twice, for the same reason, I didn't. For twenty years I've carried the weight of that decision.' Hu's head bowed. 'I need to confess.'

'I'm no priest.'

'You can offer absolution. Will you hear what I have to say?'

It was the time of day when even the wind was still. The water before them barely lapped at the pier. Hallam nodded.

'We set a time, you and I, that day,' Hu began, 'thirty seconds to get away from the master's hut before I set off our homemade napalm. Thirty seconds to clear almost two hundred yards of jungle. I had just crawled it, David. I knew you couldn't make it in that time.' Hu looked away. 'I gave you more time because I couldn't bring myself to kill you, David . . . and because of that, the killer was able to escape your trap.'

'How long?'

'An extra ten or fifteen seconds.'

'The snake bite, you were too groggy to know . . .'

'I knew.'

Hallam took a deep breath. 'You said twice.'

'That day, I knew he survived. I couldn't be certain, but I *felt* he had. You understand?'

'In some ways,' Hallam said, 'that was the worst part. The connection between us and that maniac, the sense that we were all a part of some insane design. The hexagrams were a part of it. It got terribly . . .' Hallam searched for the right word and found it, '. . . personal.'

'I know, and just as I knew that he was still alive I knew that he was going to come for you again. You were somehow special to him, the Great Man of the hexagrams. He was determined to destroy you. MAC-Vee assigned guards to your room but I slept inside anyway, with a gun. I tasted your food. I checked every bit of medication they gave you.'

Hu's eyes were seeing elsewhere. 'During the fourth night someone tried to get in your window. I didn't hesitate, David, I knew who it was. I opened up and kept on firing until I'd awakened the entire floor and the guards came running in thinking I'd gone crazy.

'The next day I made three phone calls, one to each of the generals. I'd been struggling with it for days, but that episode convinced me. I couldn't protect you much longer and in the state you were in you certainly couldn't protect yourself. Sooner or later, the killer was going to get you. So I . . . proposed a deal. I didn't know which one it was so I made the same promise to all three. No more noise, no more investigation. In return, your life. They all three told me I was crazy but I knew it worked. I felt a difference. There were no more attacks. You were shipped Stateside a few days later.'

It was dark now, but Hallam didn't need to see his friend's face to know there was pain contorting it.

'What happened to you after they sent me home?' he asked.

'I went to one of the MSS retreats in the mountains and worked on mending myself inside and out. A year or so later I returned to active duty, but my heart wasn't in it. I let the killer go, the one victory I wanted more than anything else in that stinking war.'

'There were other victories.'

'None that mattered,' Hu sighed. 'But by then it was all winding down to its inevitable conclusion. The smart ones saw the signs. When the Paris talks started, they got out. One of my last missions involved some illegal gold shipments. I broke the ring and started to have it shipped back to Saigon. This was a few months before the end, but the signs were clear. I decided I could leave it for the Communists, or use it myself. I managed to get some of it to a California bank. When I got out I used it to set myself up in business. I've lived in southern California ever since.'

'Married?'

'No. You?'

Hallam smiled. 'With two kids.' For a moment, visions of home filled his mind. You're always in two places.

After a while, Hallam said, 'I worried about you. I tried to find out what had happened to you. Why didn't you ever call or write?'

Hu looked away. 'Guilt. It consumed me. I escaped, but my friends died. I stole, and ended up prospering. I saved the life of the friend I loved most in the world but I let an evil continue in the world that's been waiting to re-emerge ever since. How could I call you and tell you that? Every year there were no reports and I breathed just a little easier. It made my decision just a little more bearable. After a while I was afraid to call you, as if . . . I don't know . . . as if it might *cause* the thing to reopen.'

Hallam just stood there and breathed in the clear air for a while. They would be waiting at the house.

'You've taken it all on yourself, Hu,' he said. 'It's too much. You got out because only a fool stayed after we sold you down the river. You stole because you had no choice – because the other country you served, this country, didn't have the balls to reward your service with anything even approaching what you deserved. Survival is no disgrace, Hu, it's an imperative. You want to wear sackcloth and ashes for the rest of your life because you prospered?'

The rest was harder. It took Hallam a few seconds to find a way to say it. 'My eldest daughter was twelve the other day,' he began. 'I watched her blow out the birthday candles trying to make her smile real tight so her braces wouldn't show. When I looked at her mother, I saw tears in her eyes. Simple things. That's what I've learned, Hu. Big things confuse me. I haven't used the word "cosmic" in over a decade. The world is a much more complex place than I ever understood and idealists in the eighties give me much the same feeling of discomfort that Corporation Men did in the fifties, they're missing something essential . . . Jesus, I'm rambling on.'

'It's instructive.' Hu managed a small smile. 'And reminiscent.'

'What I'm saying is, the older I get, the less I really know for sure. I was one arrogant motherfucker at twenty. Now I'm twice that age and you know what? I realize I don't know shit. Except for one thing.'

'Which is?'

'I'd rather be here than dead.'

'What about the killer? He wouldn't be here either if not for me.'

'Christ, Hu, it was you who first told me to leave the cosmic balancing act alone. Look, you did what you did out of love, that's got to count for something. We fought as hard as we could and almost died, that's got to count for something, too. You can have my absolution, I give it freely. But we both know it won't help. The only way to settle this for both of us is to get the bastard once and for all.'

Hu shook his head. 'You still talk like a Westerner. Action absolves. I've been tormented by this for twenty years. You lived and that caused others to die. In what philosophy am I given the power to make that choice?'

'Screw philosophy,' said Hallam. He enjoyed saying it, feeling some of the old spirited anger for the first time in a long time. Hu felt it, too. Hallam saw him settle into it like donning an old suit you once loved. In that moment, some of the old partnership returned.

'Confucius says—' Hu began.

Hallam cut him off. 'I've done some reading since Vietnam. Confucius didn't say half the things you said he said.'

'He would have said this.'

'I'm listening.'

In the waning light, Hu's smooth skin looked the same as it had twenty years ago. He had an odd expression on his face. Hallam read it as . . . release.

'The killer, David.'

'Yeah?'

'Confucius says fuck him dead.'

Hallam smiled.

It was a beginning.

FIFTEEN

There were lights on in the house and the same butler that had met them at the door showed them to the dining room. Fred Burris was the only one seated at the linen-clad table.

'Hallam, goddamn it! And Hu!' Burris cried delightedly, springing up from his chair. He enfolded them both in huge bearhugs. 'How the fuck are y'all?'

Hallam slapped his back warmly and even Hu shed his normal formality and hugged the big man.

'The gook and the spook,' said Burris warmly. 'God, you're a sight for sore eyes.'

'You, too, Fred,' said Hallam. 'Talked to Paco yet?'

'No, but goddamn it, you seen this spread? That little shit did right well for himself. Look at all this. What the hell am I going to tease him about now?'

'Keeping it,' observed Hu dryly.

'Not so hard as you might think, friend Hu,' said a voice behind them. They turned as one, and stopped.

'You might as well look,' said Paco Gallo. 'The only really hard thing is not touching the people you care about.'

Paco was seated in a motorized wheelchair. He was dressed in a dark suit and tie and a blanket was draped across his lap. His arms were folded in his lap and his polished black shoes rested on the metal footpads. It was visually disquieting, as if someone had drawn a border at the top of Paco's shoulders over which motion could not cross. From the neck up, he was an animated man. The chair's controls sat on a goose-neck cable rising up from behind his right shoulder so his chin could stab at them. From the neck down, he was motionless, a corpse-like form.

'Paco,' said Hallam softly and he heard the pain in his own voice.

Paco heard it, too. Hallam saw him wince. He covered it by nudging the chair forward.

'Hello, David. You look well.'

It was Burris who made things right. 'Fucking Eye-talian,' cried the big Southerner. 'With all this, couldn't you afford a goddamned car?' He came sailing across the room to land happily in Paco's lap. Hallam thought the smaller man was going to be crushed, but the outlandish action seemed to please Paco rather than hurt him.

'Get offa me, dickbrain. Can't you see I'm a cripple?'

'It's a joke, right?' prompted Burris conspiratorially. 'C'mon, you can tell me.'

'The only joke around here is you, asshole. Get off me.'

Burris got up with exaggerated dignity. 'Still no sense of humour,' he confided loudly.

'Hello, Paco,' said Hu warmly. He clapped the man on his arm and Paco smiled in return.

'Hi, Hu. Good to see you. Sit down. C'mon, sit. All of you. Let me get you something to eat. You must be famished.'

They took their seats and Paco moved his chair up to the head of the table. 'Thank you all for coming,' he said quietly. 'We all know why, but I propose that we simply dine first. Talk over old times. Bring each other up to date. All right?'

Everyone nodded. For Hallam it was an interesting performance. Twenty years had done amazing things for Paco. When he last saw him, he had a good, quick mind, but little formal education or confidence. Such control would have been highly unlikely.

'Tell us about you, Paco.' Hallam gestured around. 'How did all this happen?'

'No way you made this in your uncle's cement business,' said Burris.

A servant entered with a bottle of wine and filled their glasses. Burris downed his in one long gulp. It was immediately filled again. Paco's was served with a straw, placed in a clamp and swung up to where he could sip it. He was quiet until the servant left, staring at the amber liquid thoughtfully.

'Funny you should remember that, Fred. Funnier still, that's just where all this started.

'Remember how mad I used to get at people making money in the stock market? Well, I didn't know much about it. I suppose I didn't know much about a lot of things. After . . . that night, I woke up in a hospital with the doctor's telling me that I broke most of my bones jumping out that window, including my spine. Maybe in another fifty years they'll figure out how to regenerate nerve tissue, but until then there isn't a damn thing they can do for people like me. It took a while, but I learned to live with it. The Veterans' Administration was pretty generous. They gave me the chair and all the therapy I needed. Some headwork, too. Then I was out.

'I had full disability, so I knew I wasn't going to starve, but that's about all I knew. I sat around for a while. I couldn't work. I was an only child and my parents were both dead, so there wasn't anyone to bother me. I felt okay. My decision to do myself in wasn't really made out of despair, I just felt that this was too lousy a way to live, you know?

'That decided, I felt pretty good. Born 1946, died 1971. Twenty-five good ones. Why be greedy? A lot of good men had less. What was the difference if I decided to do it to me, or some NVA bullet had? The only problem was that I was a Catholic. I wasn't in a church since my confirmation, but what the hell, in the end, those priests left their mark on me. Suicide is the biggy, the one they can't forgive. I just couldn't risk eternal damnation.'

Paco paused while the food was served. It was wonderful after the long flight and the time outdoors. There was soup, and Paco's champagne was replaced with a glass of it. Steaks were brought with baked potatoes and vegetables.

'Whadja do?' asked Burris, in between mouthfuls.

'I hired someone,' Paco said simply. 'An Italian from the Lower East Side at least knows where to shop for that. Jews know Zabar's, I knew the right guys. I hired one. Nice fellow, pleasant. It was business. So we arrange it for one night and I'm waiting like he asked and all of a sudden, who walks into my place but that same Uncle Fred just mentioned, the one in the cement business.

'It turns out I am an amazing schmuck because although everybody in the city of New York knows that the cement business is Family run, I don't. My uncle turns out to be a top honcho and he's pissed as hell his nephew is trying to have himself whacked.'

'How did he know?' asked Hu.

'He knew because the guy I hired worked for him. He told my uncle about this crazy vet who wanted to whack himself but didn't have the nerve and my uncle knew right away who it was. He called the guy off and came to see me. He made me a proposition. Lots of guys have healthy bodies around that section of town but there is a conspicuous shortage of brains. He figures I still got the smarts he remembered and he offers to send me to school. See, trust is a big thing. You want to hide five or ten million dollars a year, you need guys you can trust to help you. Accountants and lawyers to set up dummy corporations, bag men and runners to get the stuff across borders and so on. He offers me a deal. Go to school, get a degree in Finance and work for him. In return, I want for nothing.

'I tried to explain I was in a position where there was really nothing I wanted. He just smiled and said to call him when I was ready. When he opened the door to leave, the most beautiful brunette in the world walked in. Well, that scared the hell out of me. I didn't even know if I could do it anymore.' He smiled in recollection. 'That girl was a pro. She took me places I hadn't gone when I had a body that worked. She left three days later and I called my uncle.

'The rest, as they say, is history. He had made a lot of

money. After I was done with school I showed him how to make a lot more. The market was next. Now I laugh at the Dow. Remember, Fred?'

'Sure do. I'm proud of you, grunt.'

Paco seemed pleased. 'I'm officially retired now. My uncle is doing ten to twenty in upstate New York, but I got out before he took the fall. I still watch some of his properties for him. Like I said, trust is an important commodity. I'm worth between thirty and fifty million, depending on prices on any given day. You guys know me well enough to know I'm not telling you all this because I'm bragging. I just want you to know what kind of resources you got behind you. That bastard stole my life. Sometimes I still see those eyes in my dreams. I've waited a long time to pay him back. It's worth . . . everything.'

Hu said, 'Let's hope it doesn't cost that much this time.'

'I'll drink to that,' echoed Burris. As far as I'm concerned . . . as far as . . . as far . . .' Like a motor suddenly without power, Burris was slowing down. His face froze into a dazed expression. The arm with the glass in it locked into immobility. Hallam was up on his feet at once, but Paco stopped him.

'Let him be, David. He's okay.'

'What the hell's wrong with him?'

'It's a kind of epileptic seizure,' Paco said sadly. 'The parting gift of our mutual friend. He put his gun into Fred's mouth and pulled the trigger. Fred was lucky, I suppose. His head was sort of twisted the way you sometimes do when you're sleeping. The shot blew out most of the back of his skull but didn't sever the spine. He's deaf in one ear and most of that side of his head is steel plate. Screws up the pressure in the brain. He can be fine one minute, the next . . .' He gestured with his chin, '. . . this.'

'How can he do anything . . . like this?' Hu asked.

'You mean like hold a steady job or maintain a relationship or things like that?'

Hu nodded.

'He can't,' Paco said flatly. 'You know those guys you see on television, the vets who are still so mindfucked they can't get it together except to walk around in old fatigues and talk about how the war fucked them over? Well, Fred's one of them. When I knew we were all going to be together again, I had him checked out.' He looked at Hallam and Hu and read the unspoken question in their faces. 'Yeah, I had both of you checked, too. It was interesting. Of all of us, you have the most normal life, David. I wasn't sure you'd come.'

'You should have been.'

A smile from the once quick Italian kid crossed Paco's face. 'Yeah. Sorry. Anyway, Fred's been in and out of most of the VA head clinics around the country. What the hell can he do if he keeps spacing out that way? The shrinks know he's not crazy, just too scrambled to hold it together.' Paco's face softened. 'Now that I know, I'll take care of him. Whatever goes down. He won't have to worry.'

'How long does this last?' Hallam looked closely at Burris. There was no recognition on his face at all. Just blank.

'Can't tell. Few minutes, fifteen at the most. Sometimes he doesn't even realize he's been out.'

'How does he feel about it?' Hu asked.

'He feels like shit.'

'And you?' Hu pressed. 'How do you feel about it?'

It took a while for Paco to answer. There wasn't any body language to read and, with less to control, his face was unreadable. 'Still come at people, eh, Hu?'

Hu said nothing.

'Yeah, sure,' said Paco after a while. 'Well, maybe it's okay. We got to get to know each other again. Form a team again. Nothing sacred, nothing that can't be asked.'

'That was the rule,' Hu agreed.

'Then listen. If you took all the atomic stuff that ever exploded and put it all into a little bag so it was compressed like to the ultimate degree and it was waiting, ready to go off at the slightest additional pressure, you'd have some idea of the force behind the rage that's inside me. Every day. No let-up. Not even a second where I don't want to scream from what's pent up in me even thicker than in that paper bag. I want to kick, but I don't have legs. I want to strangle, but I don't have hands. I could murder everyone that can walk and run and fuck and swim and eat like a human being and not a dog. You know what I found, Hu? I found out I could hate just like that psychopath does . . . and it almost scared me to death.'

Paco's breathing was ragged and sweat beaded on his face. Hallam watched him fight for control and find it.

'Almost . . . but not quite,' Paco continued. 'So I controlled it and used it, just like I've learned to control everything else in the last twenty years. In the end, I'm gonna see him dead.' He looked at them with eyes that had seen Hell and brought back a piece. 'I'm gonna dance on his grave,' he said in a voice as dry as bone dust. 'On his grave . . .'

'Paco, I—' Hu began, but a sound from Fred cut him off.

'Hey, what's going on here?' The big man looked confused. He looked around the table. There was no trace of his seizure. 'We friends, or what?'

Hallam picked up his glass and looked at him affectionately. 'Friends to the end,' he declared. The silence that followed was too short for Burris to notice.

Burris laughed, downing his drink.

Hu drank, pulling back inside himself.

Hallam looked at Paco and received a short nod in return. Protecting Fred Burris was suddenly everybody's responsibility.

Hallam watched the rage in Paco's eyes die slowly.

It never quite left.

SIXTEEN

They moved into the library when dinner was over. Somehow it seemed natural that Burris should slip behind Paco's wheelchair and push it. Hallam observed a satisfaction in the unanticipated symbiosis between Burris and Paco which seemed to please them both.

Hallam settled into one of the deep leather chairs and looked around the library. Floor-to-ceiling shelves were split by a walk-rail halfway up the room. The carpet was plush and the cut-glass lamps and rich wooden panelling harkened back to older, simpler times.

'Fred?' said Paco. 'The folders. Over there. Hand them out, will you?'

'Should I take one too?'

'Please.'

Hallam opened the folder. The first pictures were a shock. He hadn't seen the three generals in over twenty years. For a moment, looking at pictures of them from the Vietnam era, time stood still. He stared, and Hamilton, Mulrose and Wernicker stared back at him. Memories of that day at the firebase flooded back . . . and with them an odd memory pulled faintly from beneath the surface of his mind. He tried to reach it and it slipped away. He shrugged it off and thumbed through the file.

'What you've got there,' Paco began, 'is all the information I could put together regarding case number zero six seven Echo India, Hallam and Hu's last assignment. As you probably know, the original file was destroyed the night Major Reiman was murdered. Most of the stuff I got was from the investigation afterwards. Read it and see if there's anything you can fill in. For now, let's turn to the press clippings.'

The folder contained a series of photocopied articles mounted between plastic covers. They described the slaying of a twenty-year-old female student from Colorado State; a slaying so brutal that every correspondent felt moved to comment on the inhumanity of the mind capable of such an act. That alone, however, wasn't what had alerted the men in the room. The definitive fact that linked this murder to those of twenty years past was that most of the clippings made reference to an hourglass-type figure drawn in blood on the victim's slashed belly – the same mark the killer had left during his rampage in Vietnam.

'He's still alive,' said Hallam. 'Same gender of victim, same type of crime, same mark left behind. Can we get more, Paco?'

'Police report's in there, too.'

Hallam found it. The details were grim. Multiple stab wounds, tears, bites, mutilation. The old sense of an evil child tearing the wings off insects came back to him. There were photos of the mark serving as confirmation. It was the same one they had seen in Vietnam.

The victim's name was Veronica Lassiter, aged twenty, a student studying computer science. Nice-looking girl. Once. Her father was a Dr Morgan Lassiter, a scientist with the North American Air Defense Command, NORAD, in Colorado Springs. Hallam turned back to the pictures of the generals.

'Where are these guys now?' he asked Paco.

'I think I can tell you best,' Hu said, 'if you'll allow me a little background first. When I got here from Vietnam I was still an intelligence officer. I was cleared for government service, but too much had happened. I didn't have the same feel for the work. So I moved into the computer area. It was a developing, wide-open field. Simulations, military games. I was a contract employee for a while, then I left the government and started my own firm. We provide security and installation for the advanced experimental computers the Pentagon uses. My clients are some of the country's biggest defence contractors and my contacts in the government are excellent.

'Of our three suspects in Vietnam, only General Hamilton is still on active duty. He's attached to the Joint Chiefs' staff, a respected and much-decorated man. Word is, if the general presently holding the position of Chief of Staff, Army, is retired, Hamilton will get the post.

'Mulrose left the Air Force for a government position. He's head of the National Command Authority Administration, a little-known federal agency which monitors and evaluates the ability of the government to operate during a national emergency. If there's a war and the President is in Iceland and the Vice President is in Pakistan and the Secretary of State is in Idaho, just who the hell runs the show? And how? Worse, if they're all in Washington when the bombs hit and no one survives at all, who runs things then?

'Wernicker is the only one who's returned to civilian life, if you can call it that. He's a senior projects manager for Howards Aircraft, a company developing military hardware and computer systems.'

'Could you get a fix on their whereabouts during the time of the murder?' asked Hallam.

'I did, but unfortunately it was no help. All three were in the area and had been for over a month. They're attending a top-secret simulation run by Mulrose's agency called the Ivy League Command Post Exercise. It's designed to test the country's ability to function after an all-out Soviet attack – in parlance, a decapitation strike. They're holding Ivy League at NORAD and it culminates in five days of advanced computer simulations – game playing, to the uninitiated. The Secretaries of State and Defense will be there and there's even word that the President will attend. So far, it's mostly setting up communications tie-ins and testing remote units like the emergency airborne command post, a specially equipped Boeing 747, or the secret federal facilities in

Massachusetts and Texas. They're even establishing a miniature White House in Europe to see what would happen if a successor to the President was consulting with our allies when a war broke out. During the simulation itself, there'll be a lot of top personnel shuttling around, but NORAD will be locked up tighter than a drum.'

'And us?'

'We'll be inside, David,' Hu continued. 'My firm is one of several providing programmers and security for the computers being shipped in. The game starts in three days and lasts for five. Your name and Fred's have already been added to the list of my staff.'

Hallam felt his stomach tighten. 'We're going in after him?'

Paco leaned forward. 'While the game lasts, no one can get in, no one can get out. He can't run and there's no place to hide. Push all three. One will make a mistake. Then you get him.'

'Or he gets us,' Hallam frowned. 'If he can't get out, neither can we. Jesus, locked up with a madman who'll know soon enough we're coming after him? I don't relish that.'

'Want to back out?'

Hallam looked at him sharply. The comment annoyed him. It served no one's interest to be thinking like cowboys at a shoot-out . . . ageing cowboys at that. 'Don't push me, Paco. I won't be bullied. The fact that you can't get out of that chair doesn't make me your surrogate warrior. I won't be used.'

'You can be a shit, David.'

'Maybe, but not a stupid shit. I'm damned scared of this guy, you want me to say I'm not? I'm supposed to go charging off like some fucking knight?'

'I want this guy for what he did to me.'

'He did it to all of us, Paco. I want him, too.'

'You walked away without a scratch.'

'Bullshit.'

'Like you said, I'm the one who can't get out of his chair.'

'I'm sorry for that, but heroics aren't going to help.'

The angry light in Paco's eyes reflected his own inner demons. 'You know how many times I wake up in the night and I'm right back in that villa? I see those eyes, those crazy eyes burning like a cat's, staring at me, coming closer, and I remember going through that window and I realize . . . I realize if he came again, this time I couldn't even get off the goddamn bed. Want him? Jesus God, none of you know how much.'

'We know,' said Hu quietly. 'We know. We live with it too. How long did you have to remain in the hospital recovering from the burns, David?'

'Almost two years.'

'Show him.'

'Hu, I—'

'Show him!'

Reluctantly, Hallam untucked his shirt. 'How did you know about it?' he said to Hu.

'I sat by your bedside for four days, remember?' Hu stepped forward and yanked his shirt the rest of the way up.

'Jesus,' breathed Burris harshly. 'Looks like lizard skin. Legs, too?'

Hu pulled the shirt down. 'Legs, too. How long did it take for the lung tissue burnt up in the firestorm to regenerate?'

'A few months. When they took me off the painkillers it was like breathing fire. Every breath. After a while you stopped crying and just waited for it to stop. One day it did.' Hallam rearranged his clothing. 'It isn't as bad, Paco. I know that. But it isn't scot-free either. The smell of gasoline makes me nauseous. I still get sick if I walk into a Chinese restaurant. I haven't been to a beach in twenty years. He got me inside, too. Like Fred. Like Hu. Like you.'

'Don't deny me this, David,' said Paco, pleading.

Hallam moved to his side. 'I'm not. We'll get him this time. I want that, too. But slowly, carefully. With every move thought out. Like the pros we once were.'

'Or thought we were,' said Burris dryly.

Hallam saw the rage drain from Paco's face.

'The tie-in to Dr Lassiter's daughter,' said Hu, 'and his

working for NORAD and the fact that all three of our generals—'

'Former generals,' Paco reminded him.

'No such thing. Once a general, always a take-charge-son-ofabitch,' countered Hallam.

Hu continued. 'The fact that all three are there already is too much of a coincidence to be a coincidence.'

Hallam looked at him. 'When does the simulation start . . . what did you call it?'

'The code name is Ivy League CPX. The game begins in three days. Then NORAD slams the door shut.'

A cold shiver passed over Hallam's back. Paco noticed it. 'David?'

'NORAD. The thought of descending into that complex and being shut in . . . Shit, it reminds me of Reiman and the code names he gave us.'

'That's not in my file,' Paco said.

'It wouldn't be. It was personal, Reiman's way of warning us about what we could uncover and what it could do to us. He called us Orpheus and Eurydice.' Hallam had a far-away look on his face. 'Said we were going down into Hades to save a soul.'

'Or to lose one. Maybe we did.' Hu shrugged. 'Orpheus was never the same again either.'

'Neither were we,' Burris said, pulling the chair away from the table. 'You guys tired? Paco?'

'Yeah, good idea. We'll talk at breakfast. David?'

'Yes?'

'About before. I'm sorry.'

'Me, too.'

'What Reiman said, what you went through . . . I understand. I'm not the only one.'

'Same for me.'

Burris turned Paco's chair and began to wheel him out. 'Ivy League,' he snorted. 'Too nice a name for a war game. Makes it sound all pretty and old-fashioned.'

Hu stood up. 'Funny, the creators thought that, too. Ivy

League's not what *they* call it. For a couple of reasons. When they input all the relevant circumstances, the game always seemed to turn out the same way – total, final, nuclear war.'

'Seems more appropriate then,' said Burris, 'to call it the Total Nuclear War Game, no?'

'Close enough,' said Hu soberly. 'But not quite.'

Hallam grimaced. 'I can live without knowing this, Hu.'

'There is a proverb covering ignorance, David.'

'Spare me.'

'Very well. For five days they are going to destroy the world to see if what remains can function.'

'What does anyone call that?' Hallam asked.

Hu said, 'They call it the Doomsday Exercise.'

SEVENTEEN

The guard at the gate saw the familiar face behind the wheel and saluted sharply. 'Morning, sir.'

'Morning, Corporal.'

The gate swung open and the government car headed down the roadway. The snows were long gone and the mountain air smelled fresh and clean. His badge was activated at the security desk and he walked to his office jingling the change in his pocket as was his habit.

NORAD was a beehive of activity preparing for Ivy League. The scope of the simulation staggered the imagination. They were about to fight an entire war from the first notes of the engagement through to 'decapitation'. The amount of computer time it involved could run a medium-sized university for five or ten years, the paperwork could keep a corporation busy enough to do nothing but answer memos for about twelve months. At civilian rates, the phone bill would bankrupt a small city.

'Morning, sir,' said his secretary. 'Coffee's already on your desk.'

'Thanks. Anybody else in?'

'Not yet, sir.' She smiled. 'As usual, you're the first.'

'Calls?'

'General Powers and DepSec O'Grady. Call back?'

'In a few minutes.'

He went into his office and locked the door.

He sat for a moment behind his desk. He would have liked a window but of course this far underground that was impossible. He realized he was digging one of his fingernails into his palm, felt the callus there that the nervous habit had produced, stopped. The only key to his locked bottom drawer was on his own key ring and he took that out and unlocked it. The vial of cocaine was hidden at the back within a small Chinese puzzle box, one of the few souvenirs he brought back from Vietnam. He moved the intricate pieces of the clever little box to expose the vial. The cap contained a tiny spoon. He dipped it into the white powder and inhaled the small mound, first one nostril, then the other. He waited for the first signs of reaction, the clear sinuses, the feeling of expansion, the power. These days, it was less than ever. He wondered if that was why he'd had to go out again for the first time in so long.

It was careless. He saw that now. Too close to home. Damn careless. Then the press picked up on the story. But what else could he have done once she spotted him? What the hell was she doing in that neighbourhood at that hour anyway? Bad luck, and discrimination, that's what it was. Pure and simple. Nobody cared about a whore cut up and tossed away, but butcher a co-ed and the whole goddamned world came apart in indignation. Christ . . .

He was feeling the drug now. It was enough to get him through the morning at least. It relaxed him, brought certain . . . feelings . . . under control. He hadn't had the cover of a war for a long time. Without the drug all these years, more episodes like the last one would have occurred. Then where would he be?

He felt in his pocket for the coins.

Six quarters. Nice weight in the palm of his hand. He shook them in his fist for a while, like a gambler shakes his dice. When they were warm enough from skin contact, he tossed them on his blotter. Six times.

Six shiny circles against the green. He calculated the lines and formed the hexagram. From the same desk drawer he took out the *I Ching*. It was for comfort only, he'd memorized the hexagrams long ago.

It was the Hsu hexagram: Waiting, Nourishment. Above

K'an, The Abysmal. Below, Ch'ien, The Creative. He frowned. An odd combination, one he couldn't remember seeing before. What was the significance? The image was clouds rising up to Heaven, the idea of waiting. He read further. Waiting meant many things, among them, holding back. Danger could lie ahead. He turned to the commentaries and read further. *Waiting on the sand: there is some gossip; waiting in the mud: the arrival of the enemy; waiting in blood: the pit yawns.* He thought about that for a while. The lines at the top were the key: *One falls into the pit. Three uninvited guests arrive. Honour them and in the end there will be good fortune.*

'Sir?' The intercom broke his reverie.

'Yes?'

'Your nine o'clock appointment is here. Should I have him wait?'

'One moment, please.'

He swept everything back into his desk and locked it. The hexagram found a disturbing place in his thoughts. *Three uninvited guests.* Was he in some kind of danger? He pondered that for a while, letting the drug restore his equanimity.

Honour them.

If they came, he would indeed.

EIGHTEEN

Hallam woke the next morning with the odd feeling that he was in a strange bedroom. Disconcerted, he opened his eyes to find he was. Then he remembered why. He fought the impulse to cover his head and go back to sleep. Tossing off the covers he went through the series of stretching exercises that kept his skin somewhat more supple, then showered and shaved. His reflection had that kind of unfamiliar look like in a motel mirror, causing him to notice new lines and blemishes.

The others were already eating breakfast when he arrived.

'Morning, David. Sleep well?'

'Fine thanks, Paco.'

'Bacon and eggs?'

Hallam smiled. 'Bacon and eggs, country air, a good night's sleep . . . Christ, I could get healthy out here.'

'Unlikely,' said Hu as the butler put a plate of steaming food in front of Hallam.

Hallam looked over. On Hu's plate were six different-coloured pills and a glass of what looked like greyish mud.

'What is that?' Hallam asked. 'No, wait, don't tell me. Knowing you, you've become a vegetarian.'

'No civilized man eats his fellow creatures,' sniffed Hu primly.

'Most of your fellow creatures have no compunction about eating civilized men.'

'Good one, David,' chuckled Burris. He thrust a slice of bacon at Hu for emphasis. 'Never saw a hungry lion turn down a good meal.'

'Vegetarianism is a logical outgrowth of the basic moral concern for one's world,' Hu insisted.

Hallam pointed at Hu's glass. 'Vegetarians eat mud.'

'It's not mud. It's a blend of vegetables and vitamins.'

'Rabbit food.'

'You guys should take this act on the road,' said Paco dryly.

It was just an offhand quip, but it served to underscore that Hallam and Hu were a team again, or at least were becoming one. All at once, Hallam saw Hu's intent in needling him. He was re-establishing what had once been integral to their relationship, the verbal duelling, the sarcasm, the attacks on each other's traditions and, most of all, the ability to communicate emotions in a way that did not embarrass either.

'Wily Oriental,' said Hallam grinning.

Hu said, 'Great to beat your feet in the Mississippi mud.'

They had coffee outside. The morning was warm and the lake glimmered through the forest. Pots of wild flowers adorned the low wall surrounding the flagstone patio. Paco nudged his chair to the metal table using the control pad at his chin.

'I've given a lot of thought to this,' he said. 'It's obvious I'm not going anywhere, so you guys are going to have to do all the legwork. I will run our base from here. But remember, Ivy League is a button-up exercise. During the five days, you won't be able to get out.'

'Communications?' asked Hu.

'Radio telephones. Arrived yesterday. Direct satellite access or they can patch into any available line. As long as the batteries are good, just take them anywhere and dial.'

'Not like twenty years ago,' said Burris. 'What about transportation?'

'There are several vehicles in the garage, including a jeep. Use what you need. As for funding. Fred, over there please. Those packages.'

Burris brought them over. There were three wallets bearing their names. He took his and passed the others to Hallam and Hu.

Hallam looked inside his. There was over a thousand dollars in cash and several credit cards, including a platinum American Express card. Along with Hallam's name and the name of the bank which issued it, it simply bore the designation: Unlimited.

Hallam said dryly, 'So much for funding problems.'

'Not like the Army,' said Paco. 'Just buy what you need. Hu, you want to explain the data base?'

'One of Paco's companies entered into a relationship with my company and we were able to formulate a short-term lease arrangement and obtain some clearances that might have otherwise proved difficult.'

'Does that mean what I think it means?' asked Burris.

Hu's face never changed expression. 'It means Paco laid out so much money that certain computers destined for the Pentagon will be slightly longer in transit. I'm going to have to speak to my transport people about it.'

'Do that,' counselled Hallam.

'The long and short of it,' Hu continued, 'is that we have roughly the same computer power as a medium-sized nation. The units downstairs are some of the most modern and powerful in the world. Paco will keep them functioning. They can be activated by terminals in the house or reached remotely by the radio phones. We are also subscribing to an interesting array of data bases, setting back our host no small sum. The result is a capacity to problem-solve on a criminal or a technological level using the newest forms of AI.'

'AI?' queried Burris.

'Artificial intelligence. Human-type interactive capacity. I'll demonstrate later.'

There was only one category left and Hallam hated to invoke it. It was over twenty years since he had held a gun. The last shots he fired, in fact, were at the killer. Again the last twenty years dropped out of his life like a parenthetical clause.

'Weapons?'

'You can't bring any into NORAD, but there's a range and an instructor here to get back your skill. Hopefully, you won't need it.'

'Nice to be operating in friendly territory,' said Burris.

'Saigon was supposed to be friendly, too,' Hu reminded him.

The look on Paco's face said how much he thought anywhere was safe. He said to Hallam, 'Far as I'm concerned, you and Hu are still in charge of the intelligence aspects. You thought about your first move?'

'If possible, I'd much rather get him before Ivy League starts. If he's been there for a month already, he knows NORAD better than we do. He's got alliances, people who'll doubt our credibility, stories for cover and reasons that'll obscure. It's his parlour.' Hallam looked at Hu and got a nod of approval. 'We've got the police file. I think we'll go see the victim's father. Fred, I'll need you to pick up some things in town.'

'Can do.'

Hallam looked pensive. 'Maybe at Lassiter's we can pick up something the police didn't. After all, they didn't have Buddha here.'

Hu flared. 'Now that is insulting. Taking a religious figure and denigrating it beyond . . .'

Hallam was only half listening. Old rhythms. Patterns. He was still frightened as hell, but pieces were slowly falling into place and he felt better about it.

NINETEEN

Dr Morgan Lassiter lived in an elevated area with a splendid view of the mountains. The four-wheel-drive jeep took the inclines with power to spare. Hu was driving.

'How do you want to play this?' he asked.

'Straight. I think if we can help, he's going to level with us. Did you read the file on him?'

'Yes. A man of great accomplishments. I didn't even know the Vatican had a Pontifical Academy of Science.'

Hallam took his eyes off the tall pines. 'They're called the Pope's scientists. Over half are Nobel prize winners. More than that I don't really know myself.'

'You can now.'

'Can what?'

'Know. Or weren't you listening to me when I explained the data base?'

'Figure I'm stupid and walk me through it.'

Hu turned up a road. 'Take out the phone and dial Paco's number.'

Hallam did that. 'Now what?'

'Input your access code.'

'These numbers here?'

'Yes. Recognize them?'

Hallam stared at the numbers taped to the side of the phone. It took him a minute. 'My eldest's birthday! How'd you get it?'

'Social Security records.' Hu smiled. 'Even you shouldn't forget it.'

'Okay, now what?'

'Just wait.'

Hallam heard a series of buzzes and clicks, like a connection being established. Then, 'Good morning, Mr Hallam,' said a computer voice. 'How can I help you?'

'I need information on—'

'Won't work,' Hu interrupted. 'It's smart, but it will have to learn to pick through all that language. The simplest way is to use the word HEADING to precede all inquiries. SUBHEADING will narrow it down.'

'What's its name?'

Hu frowned. 'It doesn't have one. That button there, by the way, will put it on the built-in two-way speaker. Then it can pick up any voice around it. There's an optional earphone, too, for privacy.'

'Okay.' Hallam pressed it. 'Good morning, Griswald,' he said benignly. 'Heading, The Vatican. Subheading, The Pontifical Academy of Science. Whatcha got?'

The voice from the speaker was strong and audible. 'Searching.'

'Not bad,' said Hallam approvingly.

'The Pontifical Academy of Science,' intoned the voice suddenly, 'traces its beginnings back to the Academia dei Linci, the Academy of Lynxes, animals fabled for their keen eyesight, a small group of scientists including Galileo, who first met in 1603. Continue?'

'Continue,' said Hallam, impressed.

'After Galileo was condemned, the group was disbanded only to be re-formed several times over the centuries. Such notables as Corneille Heymans, Niels Bohr, Max Planck and the more modern David Baltimore and Severo Ochoa have been members. Pursuing the Academy's main function, that of advising the Pope on scientific matters, the Academy has lately considered such topics as parasitical disease, biomass fuel, mental retardation, genetic engineering and evolution. Continue?'

'Thank you, that's—'

'Just say no, David.'

171

'Continue?' the computer repeated.

'No . . . Thank you.'

Hallam turned the phone off and put it back in the glove compartment. 'Quite something.'

'The equivalent of the helicopter to warfare. Changes everything.'

Hallam's gesture took in the radio phone. 'All I can think of when I use one of those things is the Dick Tracy strip the *News* used to carry when I was a kid. Now it's real.'

'The amazing thing is how stupid these machines really are when compared to the things I've seen on the drawing board.' Hu slowed and squinted up at a road sign. 'Darby Lane. Isn't that what we want?'

'Number fifty-eight.'

The sprawling ranch sat on a wide piece of ground with a good view of the mountains. It was well landscaped, with a double-car garage and a basketball hoop set on a post in the driveway. A family house, Hallam thought. He noted that some of the shrubs weren't cut like the others, as if the chore had been interrupted, or, more likely, forgotten in the aftermath of despair. It was a good house. Hallam hoped someone would have the strength to preserve it.

There were several cars in the street and Hu parked the jeep behind a station wagon. They got out. This was the kind of visit Hallam might make to a client to get some papers signed and for a short moment he looked for his briefcase. Hu noticed the motion and raised an inquiring brow.

Hallam said, 'I feel like an actor.'

'A long time ago it was real enough.'

Hallam sighed. 'So was Captain Video.'

He knocked on the door.

It was answered by a thin, sad-looking woman.

'Please, come in,' she said, trying to smile but losing it almost at once in light of the reason for their presence.

There were a few people gathered in the living room, talking quietly. Hallam knew from the police report that there was no Mrs Lassiter. She had died of cancer several years before. There was only one other child, a son, Tom, who lived in Boston and had hurriedly flown back.

The woman who let them in gestured towards a closed door. 'Morgan is in the bedroom. Would you like me to tell him you're here, Mr ah . . .?'

'Hallam. And Hu. Yes, please. If it's not too inconvenient.'

Again she attempted to smile. 'Not at all.' Hallam decided he liked her.

He watched her open the bedroom door and go in. Inside was a man he assumed to be Dr Lassiter sitting in a chair. His posture was resigned, weary. A boy who had the same thin build was sitting on the bed nearby. Hallam saw them exchange words with the woman and saw Lassiter's brow crease. Obviously, the names meant nothing to him.

He rose stiffly and came out of the bedroom. He was a tall, gangly man with large hands. His thinning hair was combed straight back and there were marks on his nose from glasses, which he wasn't wearing. He squinted a bit as he came forward.

'Thank you for coming.' His voice was tired, but firm.

'Not at all.'

'I'm sorry, you have me at a disadvantage. Were you friends of Ronnie's?'

'No, sir.'

'Then . . .?' He opened his hands helplessly. His son walked out of the bedroom, sensed the confusion and moved to his father's side.

Hallam's gesture took in the people in the living room. 'Can we speak in private?'

Lassiter's eyes narrowed. 'Is this about my daughter?'

'Very much so.'

Grief hadn't dulled Lassiter. He gave them both a quick perusal, followed by some mental calculations. The judgement was in their favour.

'Tom, take care of things out here. This way, gentlemen. Follow me.'

'Morg?' It was the woman who answered the door. 'Everything all right?'

'Sure, Kate. Be back in a minute.'

Lassiter led them to a wood-panelled den with a couch, two chairs and a television. A family room. Hallam offered his hand. 'I'm David Hallam. This is my partner, Mr Hu.'

Lassiter sat in one of the chairs. Hallam sat opposite. Hu took the couch.

'I'm terribly sorry for your loss,' Hallam said. 'Please believe that. In some ways, we share more than you know.'

'That raises more questions than it answers,' said Lassiter.

'I can answer them,' said Hallam, 'but it will take a while.'

There was a terrible sadness in Lassiter's voice. He said, 'I have the time.'

Hallam began. 'Twenty years ago, during the Vietnam War, Hu and I were joint case officers in the 525th Military Intelligence Group. A young girl, one of our agents, was brutally murdered in much the same fashion as your daughter. We believe there is a connection.'

There was no disbelief on Lassiter's face, no scepticism, only the refocusing of his massive intelligence, like the turning of a great telescope suddenly given the right co-ordinates. It was as if an electrical discharge had suddenly tinged the air between them.

'Twenty years is a long time,' he said carefully.

'Certain signs are unmistakable,' countered Hallam. He held his hand out and Hu passed him one of Paco's files. 'Read this. I'll tell you the rest when you're done.'

Lassiter hefted the file. Hallam watched his face. Opening it would be an act of commitment, the first move towards belief. Hallam waited.

Lassiter opened the file and began reading.

Lassiter looked up when Hallam finished speaking. 'It's incredible. This has gone on for over twenty years?'

'I suppose we could have, maybe even *should have* pursued it after the war,' said Hallam. 'Maybe you'd need a psychiatrist to give you the real reasons we didn't, but what did we have, really? The officer in charge of the investigation was dead, I was hospitalized. Hu was alone in the middle of the war. The rest . . .' Hallam shrugged. 'Probably the truest thing I could say is that having been so badly burned, literally and figuratively, none of us had the balls to go back after him alone. When the war ended we all kept watch, so to speak. After a while, I guess we just accepted that he *had* died in the fire.'

'It was easier that way,' said Lassiter.

'I won't deny it.'

'It would be even easier to stay away now.' Lassiter was looking at him closely.

'I won't deny that either.'

'But you haven't.'

Hallam shrugged. 'No.'

Lassiter looked at the file. 'Why not go to the police?'

Hu answered him. 'You're free to do so. We'll give them all the material we have and testify as to the events contained in the file. We cannot speak as to the consequences, however.'

'What consequences?'

Hu nodded. 'Look what happened last time.'

Lassiter pondered that for a moment. 'You think he'll turn it round and come after his attackers again?'

'There isn't a doubt in my mind,' said Hu flatly. 'Moreover, this is the United States, during peacetime. Different rules apply. We have no police power here. Without proof and no military authority to back us up, normal legal procedures will apply. Even if we're sure, we won't be able just to point the cops in his direction and have him picked up. They'll launch their own investigation. That'll take time. He'll be warned. As God is my judge I swear he may even be able to *sense* it coming. Then he'll have space to move. You want to see for yourself what he can do with a little space? You want to push Paco's wheelchair or look at Burris's steel plate? You have a house and a son, loved ones . . .' Hu's eyes were hard. '. . . still. You want to risk what's left with him out on bail?'

'No.' There was a long pause. 'But if this has to be done . . . extralegally, I want to be certain it's the right man.'

'You're a scientist,' said Hallam. 'Compare the data. The police report and the MI reports from twenty years ago are almost identical.'

'Crimes committed by psychopaths would be.'

'What about the hourglass mark?'

'Inconclusive.'

'Maybe,' Hu agreed. 'But there's more.'

Lassiter was hungry for proof. He knew the odds of ever finding this kind of killer, a maniac with no more motive than his own twisted reasoning. He leaned forward. 'I'm listening.'

Hu opened the file. 'Here, in the police report. There were wood splinters found in the cuts. We're willing to bet they're yarrow root.'

Lassiter nodded curtly. 'There's no mention of that in the report.'

'Call the police,' suggested Hallam.

Lassiter crossed over to the phone and took a card out of his pocket. He dialled the number written there. It must have been a direct line because he spoke to no operator.

'Lieutenant Cosgrove? Morgan Lassiter . . . Yes, thank you. As well as can be expected. Lieutenant, I'd like to ask you a question. Has a complete autopsy been conducted yet? . . . It has? All right. The wooden splinters found in Ronnie's . . . in the cuts. Has the type of wood been identified? . . . Yes, I'll wait.' There was a long pause. Lassiter just stared at the wall.

'Yes, Lieutenant? . . . I see. No, I don't think it's significant . . . No reason . . . Okay, I'll call you if I do. Thank you. Goodbye.' He replaced the receiver.

When he turned, Hallam knew.

'Yarrow root,' said Lassiter tonelessly.

Hallam looked at Hu. It was confirmation for them as well. 'We have some questions. What was your daughter doing in that neighbourhood at that time of night?'

'Ronnie was headed into the sciences, but she had a minor in Sociology. Said it was to keep her head balanced.' He smiled, remembering. 'Yes, that was her phrase. She was doing field work in a project. A case study of people on the streets, prostitutes, the homeless. She was trying to prove a correlation between their life and early child abuse.'

'So she was in that neighbourhood quite often?' Hu asked.

'Often enough to get to know the people who lived there. Why?'

'Your daughter wasn't the killer's type of victim,' Hallam said. 'Mistaking her for a prostitute or for one of the regular residents might explain it. He's not stupid. Nobody makes the kind of fuss over a street whore as over, forgive me, your daughter.'

'I understand. Yes, it makes sense.'

'Did she have anyone special in the neighbourhood?' Hu asked. 'Anyone she trusted or had a deeper relationship with?'

'There was one she mentioned more often than the others. I think he was sort of her unofficial guide and protector. Juice, was the name. Hispanic fellow. A vet too, I believe.'

'That will help,' said Hallam. 'Hu and I are going into the neighbourhood.'

'You'll let me know if you find anything?'

'Of course.'

'And if you don't, what then?'

Hallam and Hu exchanged glances. 'In three days,' Hallam said, 'Ivy League CPX begins.' He ignored Lassiter's look of surprise. 'Yes, we know you work there. Here's what we're considering . . .'

Lassiter listened. When they were done and gone, he sat for a while thinking.

Then he began to gather the pictures.

TWENTY

Where do you go when the revolution dies? Colorado. California. Magic names. Lands of promise. Can't make it in New York, head out to Mecca. Unfortunately, Hallam thought as they passed through a section of Denver poor enough to rival anything in the East, job skills were job skills even here. A lack of them meant unemployment just as devastating, even with pretty mountains as a backdrop. Add to that one of the largest populations of transients in the nation and you had a mixture that smouldered like an underground oil fire, sputtering into ignition here or there, symptoms of the deeper explosive mass beneath.

One such place was Redwood. Hallam made some quick observations. Cheap hotels, cheap bars. Fat women in Spandex pants. Skinny guys with runny noses in fatigue jackets.

'Want to try the bars first?' he asked Hu.

'Yeah. Guy named Juice shouldn't be all that hard to locate.'

'Who are we today?'

'I'm Sherlock Holmes. Want to be Mycroft? You know,' said Hu, parking, 'it's interesting.'

'What is?'

Hu opened his car door. 'Once an asshole, always an asshole.'

It didn't take more than an hour to find Juice hung out at a bar called the Watering Hole. It was dark inside and smelled bad, with fans ineffectively stirring the smoky air. A couple of men were playing pool in an adjoining room.

Hallam and Hu sat at the bar.

'What'll it be, fellas?'

'Two beers,' said Hallam.

The bartender produced two bottles without asking the brand.

'We're looking for a man called Juice,' Hu said. 'Folks say he hangs out here.'

Hallam suppressed a smile. Hu sounded like a Western marshal.

The bartender shrugged. 'Now and then.'

'Is he here now?'

'Who's asking?'

'We were friends of Ronnie Lassiter,' Hallam said. 'We understand he was, too.'

The bartender took a dishrag from behind the counter, saying nothing, and wiped a few glasses. His thick forearms twisted. Hallam caught sight of a tattoo on his forearm. It stirred vague memories.

'We're not police,' Hu was saying. 'No hassles.'

The bartender's face might have been made of stone.

Hallam slid off the bar stool. 'Be back in a minute.' He nudged Hu in the side. 'Keep it up, he's warming to you.'

Hu looked sceptical.

Back in the car, Hallam took out the radio telephone, dialled the access numbers and hit the speaker button.

'Good morning, Mr Hallam.'

'Good morning, Griswald. Heading, Vietnam. Subheading, tattoos, uh . . . informal insignia, battlefield designs, outfit logos . . . something like that.'

'Searching,' said Griswald from the speaker. 'Specifics?'

'A tattoo of a big snake like a boa constrictor encircling a skull and crossbones, like on a poison bottle. Might have been words underneath, I couldn't tell.'

'Searching.'

Hallam waited through a series of clicks, whirs and pops. Then, 'Snake, skull and crossbones tattoo is the unofficial insignia of the so-called Death Head Rangers, a subgroup of the 14th Cavalry. Motto: To The End. Task was behind-the-lines search and destroy missions. On terrain self-sufficiency was stressed. Units often operated independently for long periods, returning to base only when unit numbers were sufficiently depleted to require replacements. Continue?'

'Who was the . . . Subheading, commander.'

'Captain James Garett, serial number 094—'

'No. That's enough. You're okay, Griswald.'

The voice sounded surprised. 'Why, thanks.'

'Don't mention it.'

The speaker went dead.

Hallam sat back down beside Hu. 'Any luck?'

'None.'

Hallam downed the rest of his beer and gestured to the bartender for another. When it arrived, he picked it up and tilted it toasting fashion.

'To the end.'

The bartender's eyes swivelled sharply. 'Say again?'

Hallam shrugged. 'Forget it.'

'No, wait. If you said what I think you said . . .'

'What's it to you?'

The bartender rolled up his sleeve. 'You know what this is?'

Hallam held out his hand. 'One of Jimmy Garett's boys! Well, now.'

'Jeez, you too?'

Hallam took the offered hand, smiling. 'Need some information . . .'

Hu shook his head as they walked towards the pool table. 'Sometimes you are positively pathological.'

'But effective.'

'That's what scares me.'

A small thin man in a T-shirt and jeans was crouched over the pool table shooting at balls with rapid movements. Hallam waited until he missed.

'Juice?'

He looked up. He had small, distrustful eyes. 'Who's askin'?'

Hallam pointed over his shoulder. 'Friend of Freddy's.'

'Yeah?' Juice looked to the bar and evidently got some sign that reassured him. 'Siddown.'

'Thanks. This is Hu.'

Juice's lips twisted. 'A gook?'

'Ex-gook. You knew Ronnie Lassiter?'

Juice nodded. 'She was okay. Wanted to help. I took her around. Showed her what's what, you know? Too bad about her.'

'Sure. You know who whacked her?'

'No way. I left her about ten, ten thirty. She wanted to walk around, talk to some of the girls. Next thing I heard, somebody did her.'

'That bother you?'

Juice sniffled. 'Sure. But it ain't like she used to have me over for dinner, you know?'

Hu asked, 'See anything out of the ordinary that night? Strangers?'

Juice looked at him like he was a child. 'People come here to get laid. There are always strangers.'

'C'mon, Juice,' Hallam shot back. 'Maybe she didn't invite you to dinner, but you liked the girl. You took care of her. Don't tell me she died and you just shrugged and walked away.'

'Well . . .'

'You checked. What did you find?'

'One of the girls said she saw her with some guy. A soldier.'

Hallam tried not to look at Hu. 'What else?'

'Nothing. That was it.'

'Old? Young? Tall? Thin?'

'Sure,' said Juice. 'All of those. It was dark, man. A soldier, that's all I know.'

'Okay. Thanks.'

*

Outside in the car, Hu said, 'You just dropped it. Why?'

Hallam rubbed a hand across his chin. 'All of a sudden, I was back in 'Nam. There we were, investigating, looking, going by the rules . . . and he turned it all round and got to every one of us. What if he's got someone planted here to alert him like he must have had in that brothel? Why is it every time we poke into this thing, he seems to know we're coming? Maybe he's psychic or that *I Ching* really does give him something we don't have. In there, all of a sudden, I decided we stopped playing by the rules. We have to think like he does.'

'And?'

'And that means no more thinking, no more being so damn careful. Hu, we're going to come at him just like he came at us. That's why we failed in 'Nam. We didn't understand what we were dealing with. You ever see an oil fire put out?'

'No.'

'They do it with dynamite. Some shit you just can't fuck around with. Same principle here. We gotta be bigger and scarier and more straight ahead than he is or we're going to end up dead this time. I know it.'

'Fight fire with fire?'

'With a nuclear bomb if we have to. I was wrong to think we needed to investigate. We're just repeating old mistakes. If we had a lead, fine. But there's nothing here but confirmation of what we already know and if we press it we'll lose the one advantage we have – he doesn't know we're coming. We have to keep *him* off base this time, keep *him* guessing.'

Hu started the car and pulled away. Hallam kept talking, suddenly feeling better than he had since arriving.

'I know I'm right, Hu. Look at it from another angle. Last time round, anybody got in his way, he killed them. No talk, no questions. There we were, making like good MI agents with our cute little notepads and our bright new procedures and every witness we questioned died. All these years I kept thinking he was smarter than us, so much smarter. And I couldn't figure out why.'

'Now you have?'

'I think so. I think I understand the psychopath for the first time.' Hallam paused for a moment trying to phrase it just right. His hands fluttered in the air for a moment, like birds searching for a landing spot. Finally, 'Hu, he just does.'

'Just does what?'

'Anything,' Hallam responded. 'And everything. He just does. That's his secret, that's what makes him so scary. You and me, there's something inside that makes us wait or watch or think, things like conscience or morality or some parent's voice reminding us about consequences. We hesitate before we act, sometimes so slightly it's hard to notice, but it's always there. A split second, half a beat, an intruding thought. Not him. He just does. You're in his way, you die. He starts to worry about you, you die. You pop up one day and scare him, you die. He's the simplest of all machines; no complexities, no moving parts and he'll always be a half-step ahead of us because of it. Christ, why didn't I ever understand this before?'

Hu looked sceptical. 'And now that you do?'

'We use it against him.'

'I'm not going to ask.'

'C'mon.'

'Nope.' Hu turned a corner. 'I won't.'

'You will.'

There was silence for a long while. Hu accelerated onto the highway back towards Paco's house. Hallam wore a smug expression.

Hu sighed. 'Okay. How?'

For the first time, Hallam felt on solid ground. 'We're gonna fuck with his mind for a change.'

Halfway back to Paco's house, Hu began to see it.

TWENTY-ONE

Dr Morgan Lassiter sat in church thinking about things.

Things were composed of progressively smaller elements, down to the basic building blocks of the universe itself. Laws governed those building blocks; it was an ordered relationship. Objects heavier than the fluid they displace must sink. Not just once or a few times; always and everywhere. They *had* to sink. If they didn't sink, it meant that the interlocking web of principles defining the relationship of all things to each other had in one terrible instant ceased to exist and things would, quite literally, fall apart.

Morgan Lassiter believed that the reason things did not fall apart was because God had written an indelible web of laws to govern all the elements of existence which He had created. Lassiter had always been a staunch Catholic and was gladdened by his work as one of the Pope's scientists. Though some of his colleagues found his ties to the Vatican odd, even anti-intellectual, Lassiter had no trouble reconciling religion and scientific inquiry. His job as a scientist was to confirm universal principles, regardless of their cause. His job as a Catholic was to believe, regardless of scientific confirmation. The former was an act of intellect, the latter an act of faith. There was no conflict between them. In the dazzling blaze of the laser lights he created, he could see the face of God.

Yet Lassiter was damaged by his daughter's brutal murder as nothing else could ever have damaged him. No pat repetitions soothed him, nor was there much comfort in the beneficent Heaven in which he believed so completely. He welcomed the cadence of the prayers, but found no solace.

The priests had been gentle and kind, but they hadn't been able to help either.

Lassiter sat up straighter in the pew and looked around him. This late in the service, heads had begun to loll. Sleeping noses twitched at the smell of the incense. The priests continued the Mass but Lassiter couldn't keep his thoughts from wandering.

One of his most basic beliefs was that evil was not just one of the two poles of the moral universe, but that it was an active principle. It was out there *doing* things, hurting people. Nothing in either his Church or his life taught him that he had to accept that. The Church stood against it. Good men of all faiths everywhere stood against it. Lassiter had no illusions about his humanity. He was no saint. Within him was a seething rage towards his daughter's killer that no amount of cheek-turning or forgiveness would dispel. He had prayed to God that the killer be punished, the evil expunged.

Quite literally, therefore, the appearance of Hallam and Hu was a godsend.

Lassiter had spent the two days since they came to his house preparing to return to NORAD. His colleagues were surprised when he called them to say he was coming back for Ivy League. 'To take my mind off things,' was sufficient explanation. They were glad he was coming. The most terrible thing, though, would be the acting. If Hallam and Hu's theory was correct, one of the men he was going to be facing daily was his daughter's killer.

He knew Carlton Mulrose reasonably well. Mulrose was head of the National Command Authority Administration and was in charge of the Ivy League simulation. Lassiter attended frequent meetings held by Mulrose's staff, some with Mulrose himself in charge. A tough boss, his subordinates said, a stickler for detail who ran his agency like one of his old commands. A gruff exterior – nobody said there was a heart of gold underneath.

He knew General Hamilton slightly, and only on a working basis. Actually, he knew Hamilton's son, Frank, better.

Frank's position with the Joint Chiefs' war games section made him a frequent visitor to NORAD and on one project Lassiter was working on he had even had the young man home to dinner. Could his father be the killer? Would Lassiter's face reveal his suspicions every time he was in Hamilton's company? Lassiter felt the first tinge of unreality. If the appearance of normality could hide such deviance, could anything be taken at face value?

Arnie Wernicker was a business friend, if that was the proper term. As Senior Projects Manager for a company with which NORAD did so much business, it was inevitable that they worked together over the years. The former jet jockey was an impressive individual with an intriguing knack for storytelling. There was certainly no sign of insanity. Ronnie had taken a liking to the older man. At social events, Lassiter had seen them dance together, apparently enjoying each other's company. Ronnie said she loved his stories.

Lassiter shook his head, picturing all three faces. Competent, maybe even gifted men. Now twist those faces into the kind of horror mask the killer's face must have been while he . . . No, he just couldn't manage it. Whether it was that he couldn't picture any man doing those things, or that he just couldn't picture these men, he didn't know. But one thing was clear. In his work, just as in his life, nothing would be the same.

Around him, people were standing and moving forward to receive Communion. It was an odd feeling, much of the comfort lost. The wafer was so cool on his tongue, the rage so hot in his blood. Lassiter remained kneeling, watching the priest move down the line. He was aware of the spiritual irony. Communion with the Prince of Peace while contemplating murder.

He'd have to worry about absolution some other time.

TWENTY-TWO

The morning was spent making last-minute preparations. Hu had issued Hallam and Burris their identification and 'smart' badges, a variation on the old ID badge that used to carry just some typed information and a picture. These new ones stored as much data as a bank computer card and contained service records, access levels, security clearance, current status and a host of other things to make a top-secret security-minded installation happy, not to mention a computerized, dot-matrix picture of the holder's fingerprints and retinal pattern that could be brought up on any terminal and compared on the spot.

Hallam worked late into the night refining the approach he wanted to take. Burris would already be inside by the time they got there. Hallam went over things again and again. So much had to be left to chance it filled him with the fear they were rushing ahead blindly, repeating past mistakes. The interview with Lassiter's daughter's friend, Juice, convinced him of the need for a new direction. You're always in two places at once, he used to say to Hu. In the bar, he was suddenly back in the Saigon whorehouse that day they interviewed the girls. He couldn't forget that immediately afterwards two at the Hung-Dao had died. Hallam decided he wasn't going to let that happen again.

They'd been driving about half an hour when Hu made a right turn off Highway 115 onto a smaller paved road with a sharp angle of ascent. The landscape was rocky, broken mostly by lonely scrub pines. Hallam looked around, reading the signs.

'This is Cheyenne Mountain?'

Hu nodded. 'The entrance is about four miles up this road.'

'Higher?' Hallam questioned, feeling his ears pop. 'I thought NORAD was underground.'

'It is. Inside a mountain,' said Hu. 'The entrance to the north tunnel is over seven thousand feet high.'

'Well, nothing's changed since we were in the service.'

'What do you mean?'

'Who else would put an underground complex seven thousand feet in the air?'

Hu ignored him. 'Wait till you see this place. Want some briefing?'

'Shoot.'

'It's fantastic, really. They carved a series of chambers out of a mountain of solid granite large enough to put an entire four-and-a-half-acre city into. There are fifteen buildings, David, and not one of them, not one walkway or ceiling or road touches any part of the chambers or the mountain itself.'

'What's everything made of, paper?'

'Three-eighths of an inch, continuous-weld steel.'

'Then it's all done with mirrors.'

'Better,' said Hu. 'With springs. Rows of them. The entire complex rests on over thirteen hundred individual coils made from three-inch-diameter steel rods weighing over a thousand pounds apiece. Shock absorbers were installed also, to hold down any bounce or sway resulting from a nuclear blast. Lot of delicate equipment in there. Can't let it be knocked about.'

'The whole complex floats?'

'Pretty much like a car on shock absorbers does. The buildings are free-standing and joined by flexible walkways. They won't sway enough to ripple your coffee if just about anything but a direct hit goes off outside.'

Hallam grimaced. 'If it does, this still might not be the place to be. What happens when the granite starts to fall?'

'Not a thing. The engineers drove one hundred thousand rock-bolts twenty feet into the cavern walls. The layer of compressed rock prevents the granite from creeping back in or dropping off. There's a wire mesh over that. If Chicken Little yells the sky is falling, don't believe him. It can't.'

Hu gestured ahead. 'Get out your ID. We're coming to the first checkpoint.'

Ahead was a blue breeze-block building with a large green band sweeping up its side containing white letters that said, WELCOME TO NORAD and SPACE COMMAND, Cheyenne Mountain Complex. On the hillside beneath it was a low granite semicircle with the Space Command insignia. A chain-link fence topped with coils of barbed wire rolled back from across the roadway and guards came out of the blockhouse to check their credentials.

'Ivy League,' said Hu to the guard, handing him their IDs.

He checked a list on his clipboard. 'Yes, sir. Button-up in three hours.' He passed the badges back and waved them on to park the car.

The main entrance into the complex was a tall, rounded concrete tube leading into a hole in the mountain. Hallam judged it to be about twenty feet high by thirty wide. The walls on either side of the tunnel were rough rock. Immediately, Hallam had the sensation of being closed in. Why not? He was beginning a descent that Hu had said would put from twelve to seventeen hundred feet of solid rock over their heads. He took out the phone.

'What are you doing?' asked Hu.

'May as well see now if this is going to work in here.' Hallam hit Paco's number and then input his own code.

'Good afternoon, Mr Hallam.'

'Good morning, Griswald. Read me all right?'

'Some signal distortion,' said the tiny voice from the phone's speaker. 'But all right. How can I help you?'

They were well into the tunnel now, at least a third of a mile. Before them were a pair of massive rectangular doors that looked like a bank vault's.

'Blast doors,' said Hu, seeing the direction of his gaze.

'As good a subject as any. Griswald? Heading, NORAD. Subheading, Blast Doors.'

'Searching . . . NORAD's blast doors are its final protection from the outside. Set fifty feet apart and framed by rock, they are over three feet thick and have a swing weight of more than twenty-five tons. Hydraulically operated, they can be opened or closed in forty-five seconds. Continue?'

'No.' Hallam hit the off button as they went past the blast doors into the main cavern. The area was a hubbub of activity. Compact three-wheeled vehicles driven by workmen in coveralls transported equipment, and Marine guards directed the traffic down various tunnels.

Hu led him over the steel grid walkways with an assurance that came from long association. An occasional officer stopped to say hello. One Army captain looked vastly relieved to see him.

'Mr Hu, sir,' he said, coming on them. 'General wants a preliminary run-through in about an hour. Your team set up the new units yet?'

'I just got here,' said Hu, 'but if it hasn't been done already, I'll see to it.'

'That'd be great, sir. Thanks.'

'By the way, this is David Hallam, one of my senior people. His first time in NORAD. David, Captain Pete Rizzo.'

They shook hands. 'Quite a place you got here,' Hallam said admiringly.

'You're seeing it at its wildest,' said Rizzo, gesturing around. 'The only thing worse than a button-up exercise is an actual alert. It's the logistics. We're sleeping over seven hundred people and the Granite Inn, that's what we locals call the dining facility, had to truck in enough food for ten thousand regular meals and God knows how many snacks. Our coffee budget for one of these exercises would support a good-sized Caribbean nation.'

Hallam laughed. 'Been a long time since I was on an Army cot.'

Rizzo grinned knowingly. 'Me, too, but if the truth be known, we're the lucky ones. Officers, VIPs, and senior techs – folks like you all – get to sleep in the dorm area. Isn't the Hilton, but look at the alternatives. Well, I gotta run. Gentlemen.' He trotted off.

'How come you get sirred like that?' Hallam asked as they went down a flight of metal stairs. It was quieter here.

'Government service rating gives me a rank equivalent to colonel. You were restored at your old rank and enough service credited to you to give you rough standing as a major.'

'You outrank me?'

Hu grinned.

'And you're happy about it,' Hallam said with mock surprise. 'Where's your traditional Eastern disdain for that kind of bullshit hierarchical orientation?'

'Be nice to me and I'll put in a good word for you,' Hu advised him.

Hallam made a rude sound.

They entered an area of white, pre-fab sectioned walls with brightly painted numbers and letters on them. Hu said, 'We want B3. Anywhere in the dorm complex, just follow the wall signs alphabetically. Here we are.'

Their room was a tiny six by six cubicle with beds mounted against the wall like shelves, one over the other. There was a built-in closet/dresser on the far wall and opposite the beds was a mirror with a narrow shelf under it. Like outside in the corridors, the walls were white, but the woodwork was a pleasant light grey, and there were dark grey blankets folded neatly on the beds.

Hu began storing their gear in the closet. 'Bathroom's communal, down the end of the corridor. You might want to take a look at the wall map a few doors down. It'll help you visualize the layout of this place faster than I can explain it.'

Hallam finished tossing his things in the closet and went to find the map. It was a bright orange and blue plastic cut-out, attached so that it stood out from the wall. There was a bright green arrow with the designation, You Are Here, on it.

'Just like the Zoo,' Hallam muttered to himself.

Hu was right. This helped to visualize the overall layout. Apparently, the engineers who designed the complex decided against excavating just one huge cavern and chose instead to mine three separate chambers, cross-cutting them with three other chambers in a kind of noughts and crosses board design. You didn't have to be an engineer to see that this enabled the chambers to have rock pillars between them, giving far greater support. With over a quarter of a mile of rock overhead, this was a comforting thought.

Hallam measured the map's feet-to-inches scale against his index finger and did some quick measuring. The three main chambers were about fifty feet wide by sixty feet high by three hundred and forty feet long. The cross-chambers were about fifteen feet narrower, five feet lower and maybe two hundred and fifty feet shorter. A tunnel almost a mile long linked the north and south portals. They had come in the north section. The map indicated the south section was used mostly for air intake.

He studied the map for a while. Something began to nibble at his consciousness. Three chambers crossed by three chambers. He turned his head sideways, peering at the map. You know, if you looked at it another way. Three lines crossed by three lines . . .

'The Lord will provide,' he said, wonderingly.

He went back to find Hu.

Hu looked sceptical. 'It's a simple thing for the computer to work out, David. Do you want to do it instead?'

'No, after. The second time around. Do you have the roster of offices on file?'

'Yes, but can you get in and out without being seen?'

'I'll certainly try,' Hallam said sincerely. 'I don't want to tip our hand this early either. But it's a neat move after this place is closed up tight. It brings it to *him* again. Maybe it'll keep him off balance.'

'It also lets him know we're here.'

'Not us, just somebody. That's the beauty of it. All that rage to go out and smash and kill, bottled up with no one to vent it on. He can't leave to find a victim. I want to frustrate him. Last time he had it too easy. This time *he* has to make the mistakes.'

Hu looked at the drawing Hallam had placed in his hand. 'Okay. Let's do it. Just be careful, eh?'

Hallam smiled. 'My watchword.'

'Since when?'

'I am older and wiser.'

Hu tactfully refrained from comment.

TWENTY-THREE

NORAD gave Hallam a feeling he was in some vast body where life-support organs pumped continuously to serve the needs of the facility's brain – the three-level Aerospace Defense Command Post and the men who ran it.

Hallam knew he had some breathing room right now. The killer was unaware of their pursuit. He wanted to use that time to explore the facility. Once he delivered the message he carried, the killer would know the hunt had begun. That might prove a far more dangerous conflict than the one NORAD was hosting. Ivy League was only going to blow up the world electronically. If the killer got his hands on Hallam or Hu . . .

He reached the bottom of the complex, plugged the speaker/receiver earphone jack into the phone, put the receiver in his ear and dialled Griswald.

'Good afternoon, Mr Hallam,' said the speaker in his ear.

'Hi, Griswald. Heading: NORAD. Take me through this place if you can.'

'Searching . . .'

Hallam was impressed once again with Paco's preparation. Using the earphone, the computer delivered its responses directly into his ear and the tiny receiver in it was so sensitive he could speak normally and it relayed his voice.

'Searching . . . Yes, I can. The general plans for NORAD are on record. I can access them and give you most of the gross features and statistics. Pinpointing your location by use of the satellite NAVSTAR ground location system, I have your position within twenty feet. Please clarify further.'

Hallam looked around. 'I'm next to some big things that look and sound like engines.'

'Gotcha,' said Griswald. 'You are looking at the power station. Six diesel engines each turn a seventeen-hundred-and-fifty-watt generator. Over to your right is a fuel storage reservoir carved from the rock. It has enough fuel to keep the motors going for a month. Look around. See an array of pipes and valves?'

'I see them.'

'Water from underground springs is pumped into reservoirs beyond those rock walls. Over six million gallons are stored there, most of that for cooling the power plant. What you're looking at is the water monitoring facility which checks for contamination and regulates the flow.'

'What about air?'

'The air, Mr Hallam . . .'

'Forget the Mister Hallam, just call me . . .'

'Boss?'

Hallam grimaced. 'If you like.'

'Yes, boss. NORAD is designed to survive a nuclear attack, so incoming air is processed through a system of chemical, biological and radiological filters to remove impurities.'

Hallam thought it over. 'Air, water, power . . . What's left?'

'There's a medical facility two levels above you. It's got an updated surgical suite, a dental office, a pharmacy and a two-bed hospital ward. There's also a snack bar, a barber shop and a physical conditioning centre. Please follow my directions and I'll lead you past them.'

Hallam spent the better part of an hour familiarizing himself with the layout. It was remarkable, really. In the midst of NORAD's enormous and far-reaching responsibilities, an off-duty officer or workman could get a haircut, have a snack and work out for a few hours before retiring – all in a complex a quarter of a mile inside a hollowed-out mountain.

Hallam made his way to the centre of the complex. He found a perch out of everybody's way where he could observe the command post.

'Griswald?'

'Still here, boss.'

'Can you tell me what I'm looking at exactly?'

'Extrapolating from your position, a closet.'

'Readjust your sights, genius, that's behind me.'

'Then you're looking at the three-level command post.'

Hallam scanned the arena. There were giant display screens on the forward wall of the command post faced by chairs, consoles and technicians.

'Commanding what?' he asked. 'For whom? And why?'

'Boss, you are sitting in the exact middle of the most extensive communications system in the world. It monitors the entire air and aerospace defence of the North American continent – Canada and Alaska, too. Computers at surveillance and warning installations all over the world – eighty-seven of them to be exact – are constantly pouring data into NORAD through satellite relays, microwave routes and buried cables. Cheyenne Mountain's worldwide connected sensors make up the largest and most complicated command and control network in the world. More?'

'More.'

'The network functions twenty-four hours a day, three hundred and sixty-five days a year to give the commander-in-chief of NORAD, the military and national leadership, an instant picture of any threat to continental security from hostile missiles or air or space activity. What you got here, boss, is your basic integrated warning and assessment capability.'

'Griswald, can a computer develop a personality disorder?'

'Searching . . .'

'C'mon, Griswald.'

'No, boss. It's not supposed to.'

'How about just a personality?' Hallam asked.

'It's never been known to happen.'

'But like the Madam said . . .' Hallam began.

'. . . there's always a first time,' finished the computer. 'Old joke, boss.'

'If I say "don't call me boss", I'm gonna feel like Perry White. Do you know what's causing this, Griswald?'

'It's new ground for me, too, boss. Want it stopped?'

Was that a plaintive note in the computer's voice? Hallam let out a sigh. 'We'll play it by ear. Continue.'

'NORAD's mission is to provide surveillance and control of US–Canadian airspace, provide appropriate response against air attack, and give warning and assessment of aerospace attack including warning of launchings of land-based or submarine-based missiles. The same Space Command that runs NORAD also manages the space defence operations centre here.'

'What's that?'

'SPADOC is a fusion command which combines details of Soviet activity with information on US operations. It notifies folks like NASA if one of their spacecrafts is going to pass through a potentially dangerous area. Another NORAD function is air defence against bomber attacks or cruise missile launches. Early warning would scramble flights of the US interceptor, the F-15. The F-15 is the most effective—'

Hallam interrupted. 'I don't intend to pilot one. Continue on NORAD.'

'NORAD's final responsibility is to detect, track, identify, catalogue and maintain the status of man-made objects in space. There are now over 5,400 such objects. In short, NORAD tracks and identifies, SPADOC protects.' Griswald hesitated for a moment. 'Boss, if you want greater detail, it will require definitions of the Ballistic Missile Early Warning System, Phased-array radars, the Joint Surveillance System, Regional Operations Control Centres, First Air Wing, Second Air Wing, the Ground-based Electro-Optical Deep Space Surveillance System and the Over-the-Horizon Backscatter Radars which do not have traditional line-of-sight limitations because they bounce their energy off the ionosphere. Shoot?'

'Can you do it quickly?'

'Frankly, no.'

People were passing by in even greater numbers. Hallam was beginning to see faces two and three times. 'Skip it. Give me physical plant. I'm beginning to attract stares.'

'Now that you know what they do here and why they do

it, what you're looking at is the central command post where they do it. All the information flows in to be analysed and is used to direct operations. Can you see the lower level?'

'Yes.'

'That's the command director and his assistant, along with the data-display and communications technicians. They man the command post round the clock, monitoring the aerospace situation, maintaining the information on air defence, putting the up-to-date air defence posture on the big screens and calling in the battle staff in one helluva hurry if they spot anything out of the ordinary.'

'Who's over them?'

'Overlooking the display screens is the civil defence warning centre. In case of attack, they would sound the alarm over civilian warning circuits, the system you usually hear tested on the radio.'

'Top level?'

'Welcome to the big boys. That's where the commander-in-chief of NORAD sits with his battle staff. If he calls for a particular display, the technicians below him query the computers, translate the answers into symbology and display it on the big screens which, by the way, are twelve by sixteen feet.'

'There's a map of North America on there now, with tracks running towards it.'

'Probably unidentified aircraft approaching the continent. NORAD can also call up the paths of orbiting satellites and predict their future positions, or put on screen the positions of foreign submarines off the coasts or display the status of weapons available against a bomber attack. That kind of information, of course, is classified. You won't see it up there during Ivy League unless they close off the command post.

'Thanks, Griswald. Gotta go.'

'Call again.'

Hallam walked quickly away. It was five minutes before he realized the computer had shut *itself* off.

*

Carl Mulrose's office suite was simple, spartan and organized along the same lines as a government or military office anywhere, it was just more compact because of space limitations in the complex. The furniture looked like it was shipped directly from a federal warehouse and the secretary sitting in the outer office looked as if she'd been pre-assembled from a storage bin in the same facility, too.

'Yes?'

'Excuse me, ma'am, but is Carl . . .'

Hallam tripped and sprawled forward into her desk, the remains of his coffee spilling over the papers there.

'Look what you've done!' she sputtered in anger.

Hallam frowned at her from the floor. 'Yes, thank you, I'm fine.'

'Oh . . . well, I'm sorry, I didn't realize. Just a moment. Let me get something to clean this.' She rushed out.

Hallam got up and slipped into Mulrose's empty office. He put what he'd brought on the centre of the blotter and was back in the outer office by the time the secretary came bustling back in brandishing a wad of paper towels.

'I'm terribly sorry. Are you all right?'

'Fine, ma'am. I see Carl isn't in. I'll call him later.'

'But . . .'

Hallam was already out in the corridor.

The same scene more or less worked in Hamilton's office but was not needed in Wernicker's which was empty. His messages delivered, Hallam was on his way back when the sound of alarm bells filled the corridors. Heads everywhere turned and stared upwards as if revealing secret fears. In one unguarded moment they had turned to the direction from which attack would most assuredly come.

'YOUR ATTENTION PLEASE . . . YOUR ATTENTION PLEASE . . . IVY LEAGUE CPX COMMENCING IN FIVE MINUTES . . . BUTTON-UP CONDITIONS BEGIN ON SCHEDULE . . . YOUR ATTENTION PLEASE . . .'

Hallam had a vision of the giant blast doors closing. For one panicky second he wanted to race back and retrieve what he'd left on Mulrose's, Hamilton's and Wernicker's desks. Paco would hate him if he quit now, but how could he understand what this felt like? Paco was *outside*. Hallam was inside, trapped again, trapped like twenty years ago in a hut in the jungle with dead soldiers and a crippled helicopter and an old man whose tongue had been cut out.

BUTTON-UP CONDITIONS BEGIN ON SCHEDULE . . . YOUR ATTENTION PLEASE . . . YOUR ATTENTION PLEASE . . .

Hallam felt claustrophobic. He was caught up in a technological maze with a killer who frightened him more than anything on earth. Have confidence in your strategy, an inner voice reminded him. Keep him off balance. Don't let your fears paralyse you.

He went to find Hu. That was another thing that hadn't changed in twenty years. He still needed his friend's equanimity. Hallam joined the traffic flow and found his way back to the command post. A lot of people were gathered there. Most of them he was familiar with from the nightly news. He spotted the Secretaries of State and Defense, a famous Administration lawyer and a former head of the CIA. Their aides circled them endlessly, all carrying thick loose-leaf binders bearing presidential seals. They were being prompted into a large area overlooking the command post where waiting generals greeted them. They began watching the display screens around them as if they were in the luxury boxes at a ball game waiting for the first pitch.

Somewhere, a bell sounded and the command post screens lit up like Christmas displays. Warning tracks slid across a display of the globe. Hot red circles flashed at various points. Hallam saw that the VIPs were fingering the seals on their game books.

The Doomsday Exercise was about to begin.

TWENTY-FOUR

The conference table in Arnie Wernicker's office was littered with so much computer paper it draped across the surface and ran down onto the floor like a royal train.

'It can't be done within the half-hour time frame you want,' he was arguing 'Not without substantial restructuring – and you don't want to pay for that.'

'What about getting something on the refuelling end at Martinsburg?' asked the Assistant Deputy Secretary from the Department of Defense.

'I don't think so,' counselled Wernicker. 'They're pretty pushed as it is. I still think we've got to find it in the hardware.'

One of the men reached over and picked something up. 'Arnie, this yours? Anybody's? Somebody bringing the kid's toys to work? Jesus, the kind of crap they make nowadays. This spider's grotesque.'

'Let me see that.' On the belly of the large plastic spider, someone had drawn three lines intersected by three other lines. There were Chinese characters as well. It stirred faint memories. Spiders, lines . . . he had seen this before.

'Who left this?' he asked. 'Anybody see who left this?'

There were only blank stares. 'What is it?' asked someone.

'The drawing looks like a map of the complex here,' said another. 'The lines intersect like the tunnels do. But why the Chinese stuff?'

Memory came crashing back like a blow from behind. 'It's a hexagram,' Wernicker explained softly. 'From an ancient

Chinese book called the *I Ching*. I had a passing experience with it once, a long time ago.'

'What's it mean?'

'Don't know yet,' said Wernicker.

'Could be a threat,' said the Assistant Secretary. 'Forward it to Intelligence.'

Wernicker shook his head. 'I'll attend to it. Gentlemen? Back to work. What were you saying about Martinsburg?'

The group came back to the table. Wernicker put the spider into his pocket. When he moved, he felt it brush against him. He didn't like the feeling.

The conference lasted half an hour longer. As soon as it was over, he took out the spider. He rolled it over in his hands, feeling as if he held some fossil which survived to the present. After a while he called his secretary.

'Do we have the personnel records for everybody involved in Ivy League?'

'No, sir. But I can get them.'

'Do that,' Wernicker said, 'and leave a message for Carl Mulrose to call me the minute he gets back to his office.'

'Yes, sir.'

Wernicker settled in to wait.

The main conference room attached to the Joint Chiefs' office was filled with people sitting in high-backed executive chairs round a conference table. Often, they glanced to the video screen on the front wall, which just now displayed a map of the world. A console operator sat nearby, ready to request information from the command post's massive computers below and, in turn, display the data on the screen before them.

There was an air of tension in the room. For the next five days every action this group took would be closely scrutinized by the men in the VIP gallery and a host of analysts. General Hamilton looked up. 'Gentlemen, please break the seals on your game books.'

For purposes of the Ivy League exercise, each of the men before him had taken on a new title. John Rogers, a tanned Californian and a former Secretary of State, was 'playing' the President. Former NSA Director Jason Bemsford was the Secretary of Defense. Bemsford was a neat, precise man who looked as if he'd be most comfortable curled up with a textbook.

'I hear your boys dreamed up some hot stuff for us, General,' said Rogers cordially.

'We've tried to do you justice, Mr Sec . . . excuse me . . . Mr President. Ready?'

'Strike up the band, General.'

Hamilton stepped up to the display screen. 'All right. Day one. Here's the situation, gentlemen. Against a background of rising international tensions, Soviet military intelligence has learned that West Germany is asking the United States for a nuclear capability to maintain its defence against the vastly superior Warsaw Pact forces. Messages have reached us that the Soviets would consider this a serious breach of international agreements and they will respond accordingly if we honour the German request. For reasons of our own, we do not honour it.

'When indications are that the US is going to refuse, the Germans take another approach and through the international weapons market buy the material necessary to fashion nuclear warheads. They proceed to build them themselves. An enraged Soviet Union refuses to allow a nation that once invaded it and cost them twenty million lives to have such a capability. When a flurry of diplomatic activity does not change the situation, the Soviets respond by moving elements of their ground forces around West Berlin, cutting off access routes and launching the second blockade of that city. They will remove it only when the warheads are removed.

'Mr President, members of the cabinet, that's the scenario. What do we do?'

Rogers looked surprised. 'Another blockade, in this day

and age? Why not counter with an airlift again? It'll be a whole lot easier this time with C-5s.'

Hamilton shook his head. 'Maps, please.' The screen changed and a map of Europe replaced the global projection. 'As you can see, Mr President, this time an airlift won't work. The Soviets have never forgotten that loss of face. This time *they* are providing all the food and medical supplies themselves. The citizens need nothing. No reason to airlift.'

'Begin overflights at once,' suggested the Secretary of Labor, Bill Parker, in his role as CIA Director.

'According to my game book,' offered Bemsford, 'Intelligence says the Soviets wish to pressure the Germans directly without provoking a confrontation with us. I support the notion of overflights. Let's buy some breathing room and keep up our presence in the airspace at the same time.'

Hamilton looked over to Rogers. 'Mr President?'

Rogers nodded. 'So ordered.'

'Use the hotline?' Parker asked.

'No,' Rogers decided, 'let's see the response first.'

The first movements in the game were fed into the computers. Abruptly, the map changed. Red triangles which indicated Soviet tank units began to blossom around the city. Blue lines crept across the map, Soviet fighter squadrons moving into position.

'Just a matter of time before we get tangled up in that,' said Parker.

The computer operator passed Hamilton a piece of paper. The general read it in a straightforward voice, as one might announce the score of a sporting event. 'Intelligence reports that one of our aircraft has been downed by a wing of Soviet jets. The Soviets are declaring the airspace over Berlin to be theirs. Our F-15s are capable of reaching the scene and engaging the enemy. Mr President?'

Rogers sat back and took a long breath. On the screen, yellow lines were racing to intercept the blue.

'Ain't this something,' he said sincerely.

'You are currently in Defence Readiness Condition 5, normal readiness posture,' said Hamilton. 'Do you wish to move to DEFCON 4?'

'Does that include putting emergency personnel on recall status?'

'No, sir.'

Rogers leaned back in his chair. 'I want to think this over.'

Hamilton nodded. 'Of course, Mr President. I'll be back in twenty minutes for your decision.'

Rogers turned to his advisers and was soon deep in conference.

Day One of the game continued.

He saw the spider on the desk and it froze him like a car's headlights can stop an animal dead in its tracks. The meaning of the hexagram was clear.

Nine at the top. Arrogant dragon will have cause to repent.

Here? There was a roaring in his ears. He looked around the office for something to smash. There was a paperweight on the desk . . . He caught himself. The secretary was right outside the door. Control. He fumbled in his pocket with unsteady hands and almost broke the vial in his frenzy to open it. He felt the anger die in his throat as the white powder numbed it.

How could this be? He looked at the lines on the plastic spider again. The message was clear, all the more clever for its symbology. The six lines of the Ch'ien hexagram were subtly distorted to suggest the six intersecting tunnels of the NORAD complex. Simply put, it said 'I know you're here. I'm coming to get you.'

He bit at a fingernail with deadened teeth. Who was hunting him? It couldn't be Lassiter. He'd passed by the man enough times without seeing anything out of the ordinary. It amused him that he had ripped the daughter to shreds and the scientist had no idea that her killer was someone he worked with on a daily basis. Actually, that's what had sealed her fate anyway. He was in that area to do . . . business. She recognized him. He couldn't risk that.

The toy spider hit him hard. He felt on the defensive, a rare position for him. He was eager to strike, but too unsure of direction. A sudden smile curled his lips. That was the spider's purpose, he realized. To push him off balance. Well, it was going to take more than that.

Much more.

Someone knew more about him than he could permit. It created an unknown. Unknowns were dangerous, they all had to be accounted for. He understood his brilliance was enhanced by his military precision. The drug was working. Things became calmer . . . clearer . . .

Patterns. Look for patterns. He forced his mind to reach into the flow of events as one might dip into a stream. Events pooled in his mind like water in a palm. He felt for the comforting presence of the coins in his pocket. Warm. Well worn. He sat down. His lids closed lazily. Anyone seeing him would have thought he was sleeping. Anyone familiar with lizards would have steered a wide berth.

Events merged. Lines coalesced. His eyes remained closed. There was the glint of a thought but it was imprecise, tantalizing. A quiet pool. A ray of sunlight glancing off a bug on a dewdrop on a leaf. Three rocks on a combed sand garden. He threw the coins six times on the blotter and formed the hexagram in his mind. He studied it . . . and finally understanding came.

The Great Man! Here!

He nodded his head in wonder, sensing the fulfilment of the Ch'ien hexagram he'd thrown. *The arrival of the enemy, waiting in blood: the pit yawns. Three uninvited guests arrive.* This was the meaning.

So there were three. The Great Man and two others.

He began to riffle through the drawer looking for personnel records.

*

On another level of the command post, in the VIPs' observation room, Carl Mulrose was talking with the Secretary of Defense. A dozen ranking officials were watching the video displays duplicating the ones in what was dubbed the Situation Room where 'President' Rogers and his 'staff' were working. There were several senators present, as well as congressmen and government analysts. Since Ivy League was conducted under his agency's auspices, Mulrose was acting as a kind of master of ceremonies.

'As you can see, gentlemen, the President just decided not to engage the Russian MiGs over Berlin. To counter, he's sending elements of the naval fleet steaming toward Cuba. His intention is obvious – to match blockade for blockade.'

'He's upped the stakes considerably,' said the Secretary. 'Cuba's a far more important game piece than Berlin. What will the Russians do?'

'We'll have to see what the simulation provides for.'

The Secretary asked, 'How far do plans go for implementing the JATS and JEEP programmes?'

Mulrose thumbed through his game book. 'For JEEP-1 card holders, all the way, sir. We'll have the JEEP-2 people in place and get a record of them, but for budget's sake we're not actually going to lift them anywhere.'

'You want to give everybody a rundown, Carl?'

'Of course, sir,' Mulrose turned to the others. 'Department of Defense Directive 3020.26 provides that planning for continuity of operations in any national emergency has to assure that essential DOD functions can operate without impairment. Simply put, gentlemen, in a crisis or, worse, the aftermath of a crisis, we've all got to be able to continue to do that voodoo we do so well.' There were smiles all round, which lightened the atmosphere.

'Two parallel operations were established to support that mission,' he continued. 'It was fairly obvious that trying to relocate everybody under all conditions might not be feasible and, even more important, that a decision to relocate, particularly at the national level, might even escalate a crisis. So it was decided that DOD components would rely primarily on prearranged alternate headquarters. One of Ivy League's prime missions is to determine if those things are going to work. We'll be testing everything from remote units like the Boeing 747 emergency airborne command post to facilities like Site R. If the situation dictates, and we're pretty sure it will, we're actually going to ferry out some of the top players.'

'Is that why there's no one here playing the Veep?' someone asked.

'That's right. The "Vice President" is ready to be taken to one of the federal centres should Washington become, ah, untenable. Same thing with some of the other cabinet officers.'

Mulrose said, 'If we do have to relocate, we use the Joint Emergency Evacuation Plan, JEEP. It provides for the twenty-four-hour-a-day helicopter transportation of certain personnel to relocation sites or alternate headquarters. JEEP-2 personnel are only authorized helicopter transport during working hours.'

'What's the total for JEEP-1?' asked one of the senators.

'Fifty. Would you like the list?'

'Please.'

Mulrose walked to the console and punched in a series of commands. A list appeared on the screen:

JEEP-ONE
ALLOCATION OF SPACES FOR HELICOPTER
EMERGENCY RELOCATION

1. Secretary of Defense
2. Deputy Secretary of Defense
3. Secretary of the Army
4. Secretary of the Navy
5. Secretary of the Air Force
6. Under Secretary of Defense (Policy)
7. Under Secretary of Defense (Research and Engineering)
8. Chairman, Joint Chiefs of Staff
9. Chief of Staff, Army
10. Chief of Staff, Navy

11. Chief of Staff, Air Force
12. Commandant of the Marine Corps
13. Commandant of the Coast Guard
14. Assistant Secretary of Defense (Acquisition and Logistics)
15. Assistant Secretary of Defense (C31)
16. Assistant Secretary of Defense (Comptroller)
17. Assistant Secretary of Defense (Force Management and Personnel)
18. Assistant Secretary of Defense (Health Affairs)
19. Assistant Secretary of Defense (International Security Affairs)
20. Assistant Secretary of Defense (International Security Policy)
21. Assistant Secretary of Defense (Legislative Affairs)
22. Assistant Secretary of Defense (Public Affairs)
23. Assistant Secretary of Defense (Reserve Affairs)
24. General Counsel
25. Deputy Under Secretary of Defense
26. Director, Defense Intelligence Agency
27. Director, Defense Communications Agency
28. Director, Defense Logistics Agency
29. Director, Defense Mapping Agency
30. Director, Defense Nuclear Agency
31. Director, Joint Staff
32. Assistant to the Chairman, JCS
33. Vice Director, Joint Staff
34. Director, JSOA
35. Director, J-3
36. Vice-Director, J-3
37. Director, J-4
38. Deputy Director, J-4 (Strategic Mobility)
39. Director, J-5
40. Vice-Director, J-5
41. Director, C3S
42. Secretary, JCS
43. Director, Correspondence and Directives (OSD)
44. Military Asst. to the Secretary of Defense
45. Military Asst. to the Deputy Secretary of Defense

46. Executive Secretary to the Department of Defense
47. Deputy Chiefs of Staff for Operations and Plans (Army)
48. Deputy Chief of Naval Operations (Plans, Policy and Operations)
49. Deputy Chief of Staff for Plans and Operations (Air Force)
50. Deputy Chief of Staff for Plans, Policy and Operation (Marine Corps)

'That's it,' said Mulrose. 'The total of JEEP-2 card holders is a bit under three hundred. The exercise will also test the Joint Air Transportation Service, JATS, which transports key individuals from the executive branch and whatever documents are essential for crisis operations. To that end, we'll be testing the Army's airfield operations at Fort Richie, Site R and Hagerstown Municipal Airport where they'll be providing ground transportation and fixed-wing aircraft as required by JATS. The naval operations are out of Patuxent River NAS and the Air Force is responsible for terminal facilities, including refuelling, in support of JATS at Martinsburg Airport. Mr Secretary?'

The Secretary of Defense pointed to the screen. 'While you've been talking, Carl, the President mounted his blockade round Cuba. Russian attack subs are massing in the area and Soviet ballistic missile subs are leaving port for the icecaps.'

Mulrose studied the screen. 'He'll go to DEFCON 4. He'll have to.'

One of the senators sat up straighter in his chair as the screen flared. 'What was that, Carl?'

Mulrose frowned at the flashing green symbol on the global map. 'Limited nuclear device used in the Med. Tactical, not strategic, so this thing might still stay local. Looks like it was in the disputed area of the Gulf of Sidra. You can guess who finally got to throw his weight around.'

One of the senators said uncomfortably, 'Got to remember this isn't real. Right?'

Mulrose turned. 'Might be, someday. That's the whole

purpose of running an exercise like this, Senator. If the Russians know we're prepared, really prepared to survive anything they might throw at us from any angle it might come, then the message goes out loud and clear – nothing you can do will work, so don't do it. It's the cheapest and most effective deterrent we've got.' He spotted his secretary at the door waving for his attention. He said, 'Excuse me, gentlemen,' then hesitated, looking back at the screen. 'Well, now. Look at that.'

The glare from a second explosion was slowly clearing from the video screen. The Secretary of Defense had a thoughtful look on his face.

'Retaliation,' he said, sadly. 'It's a shooting war now, folks.'

On the screen, the symbols flashed accordingly.

By presidential order, the United States went to DEFCON 4.

TWENTY-FIVE

Hallam held out the laser cutter from the tool belt he was wearing on his coveralls and looked at the harness of multi-coloured wires Hu had given him.

'Hu, what the hell am I supposed to do with these?'

'Stand there and try not to look too stupid.'

Hallam seemed to be one of the few people standing around. 'Too late,' he decided.

They were up on a wide metal grid area near the control complex supervising the installation of a new system. Everybody around them was moving quickly, pursuing some urgent purpose. The big screens were lit up with so many tracks they looked as if a flock of birds with paint on their feet had raced across them. Occasional flashes of light wiped the screens clear. The tension in the control complex was growing.

The new computer resembled a cross between a microwave oven and the kind of Christmas tree lights that were tubes of bright, bubbling coloured water.

'What are those for?' Hallam asked, pointing to the tubes.

'Cooling,' muttered Hu, head protruding from the 'oven' part of the chassis. 'Supercomputers like this one generate so much heat they'd burn out in minutes if they didn't have liquid to cool them.' He stood up, stretching cramped muscles. 'Deliver the message?'

'Yeah, and I've been watching my back ever since.'

'Stay in crowds, don't wander off alone,' Hu said, seriously.

'I won't.' Hallam looked around. 'Getting pretty tense around here.'

'The game is heating up. Only the first day and already the President went to DEFCON 4.'

'Define please.'

'One of the national alert postures. They're called Defence Readiness Conditions. Five is the normal posture.'

'And One?'

'Duck.'

Hallam pursed his lips. 'Nice place you got here,' he said grimly. 'All right, I'm off to see Oz.' He picked up a small sack containing the second phase of his war of nerves and moved off.

'Watch your ass, David.'

Hallam turned back. 'Wasn't it " stay on the yellow brick road"?'

Hu sighed. 'If you only had a brain . . .'

Hallam let it pass. There was no wizard to ask for one.

Hallam decided the first order of business was to get some food in his stomach. More than one game had begun and he wanted to be as alert as possible. DEFCON 4 represented a heightened alert status. Hallam felt like he had been put on heightened alert, too.

The Granite Inn was a large, cafeteria-style room with square, four-seat tables covered with clean cloths. The chairs all had the NORAD insignia on the back and the place was as spotless as a hospital operating room. Hallam went up to the serving line and chose a lunch from the stainless-steel racks replenished by uniformed mess attendants. The room wasn't crowded and he sat alone, studying the others around him. Most were young, very young, he thought, given their responsibilities here. Then he remembered he was probably the same age when he was in the Army handling matters routinely classified as top secret. Had he looked as young and inexperienced to the older men around him then? Probably, he decided ruefully.

'And down they forgot as up they grew,' he said softly,

remembering the lines from an old e.e. cummings poem he always liked.

He said, 'Me, too,' and went for some more coffee.

'Evening, sir,' said the two Marine corporals on duty in the guard room almost with one voice.

'At ease, gentlemen. Quiet night?'

'They mostly all are during a button-up. Something we can do for you, sir?'

'Yes.'

He put down his briefcase. One of the Marines was watching a bank of television screens covering sensitive areas. On several of the screens, the new sentry tanks rolled by on guard duty, their electronic sensors alert to the slightest movement. The other Marine was typing a report. The office contained the usual fare: several phones, clipboards crammed with memorandums, military clocks, wall space devoted to duty rosters.

'I think someone tried to jimmy the lock on my office. Who do I report that to?'

'We can file that, if you like, sir.' The corporal removed what he was typing and reinserted a new form. 'Go ahead, sir. About what time was this?'

He recited whatever came into his head while scanning the office for the thing he'd come for. He saw it in the corner, a device about the size and shape of a portable computer. It had an array of controls including a key pad and a toggle stick, and on top was a small video screen. A thick antenna like a walkie-talkie's protruded from it.

'Got any coffee?' he asked, seeing none.

'In the storeroom,' said the typist, 'Like some, sir?'

'Love some, Corporal.'

One Marine got up to get the coffee. The other's eyes were glued to the screens.

He walked over and slipped the unit into his case.

When the soldier came back, he drank the coffee and finished his report. Afterwards, he thanked the men and left.

Hallam finished eating. The day shift had ended and the first of the two night shifts was taking over. The cafeteria was filling up with day shifters in for dinner. With the first day of the game ended, the complex wouldn't really heat up again till the morning. Until then, the computers would be evaluating the day's data and a host of programmers would be inputting new problems based on the first day's events. Hallam picked up his bag and left.

The corridors were quieter now. Hallam turned down one to get to Mulrose's office. He stopped. A soft, treading sound was behind him. He turned quickly. Nothing. Annoyed at himself for being so jumpy, he continued on. The steel walls were covered with pre-fab white panels. He ran his fingers over them idly like a kid runs a stick over a picket fence.

It saved his life.

His fingernail caught on a metal edge and the pain made him flinch. He spat out a mild curse and jerked his body back so as not to tear the nail.

The laser beam that would have burned a hole through the centre of his body flashed past him. A narrow, smoking hole appeared in the wall in front of him. There was a second bright flash and the beam speared along his side. There was the sizzling smell of skin and clothing burning.

Hallam felt the sudden pain and threw himself down, rolling on the side that was burned. No other sensation would have caused so instinctive a reaction; the fires of twenty years ago had set up a sensitivity the body remembered in spite of the years. Another beam shot out. He leaped to the side, his peripheral vision catching sight of the source.

There was a tank-like vehicle standing about four feet high in the corridor about twenty feet behind him. It was painted Army green with white stars on its turret and it rolled forward on four heavily treaded tyres. There were two laser guns on top with control cables descending back into the vehicle and a video camera pivoting above it all on a slender neck. Hallam barely had time to realize he was facing a robot vehicle whose operator might be anywhere in the complex before the laser beams flashed out again and he had to spring aside to avoid the fierce light.

He ran down the corridor and crashed into a wall as a beam of light burned angrily across his thigh. The pain was terrible, all the worse because it was a burn. Fire scared him more than anything. In an odd moment of clarity, he wondered if the killer had planned it this way deliberately. His mind answered, of course. He ducked round the corner and ran for the hatch-type door at the other end.

He was halfway to the door when he heard the treads behind him. He dived to the floor and buried his head in his arms. The twin beams passed over him and seared into the metal door beyond. A shower of sparks burst on him. Hallam rolled madly across the metal floor trying to put out the glowing spots on his clothing. The beams lanced out again and scored the walls. Acrid fumes billowed into the corridor.

The machine's operator realized his mistake. The firing stopped as the smoke obscured everything. Hallam used the cover to run for the door. He beat at his clothing as he ran. He yanked the door handle back hard. It moved easily, but the door wouldn't open. He pulled at it with all his strength and sweat broke out on his skin but it wouldn't budge. All at once he saw why. The lasers had blazed over the seam between the door and the wall, in effect welding them together.

He was conscious of alarm bells going off somewhere. A fire alarm! People would be coming soon, but they wouldn't be in time. The air was clearing. He would be a visible target again in seconds. Hallam heard the machine moving and the sharp whine of gears meshing as the video cameras sought him through the smoke. He sank to the floor with pain screaming in his brain. He huddled in the corner. Whimpering sounds formed in his throat. He hurt everywhere. The need to escape the light-fires consumed him. Even the cold void of death seemed preferable. He scrunched up in a tight, frightened ball in the corner trying to avoid the beams, but he was still a target. The hot light shot out again, slicing across his knees, and he screamed in agony.

There was no escape but dying, yet somewhere inside, in a space uniquely his, a thing Hallam had not truly felt in twenty years awoke. Hate coursed through him like a cold spray, bringing a clarity to his mind that pushed even the pain aside. He pulled himself back from the brink and lunged towards the tank as the beams flashed out again, avoiding them only because the move must have surprised the operator, so sure of his prey. The video eyes swivelled angrily to find him and the beams lanced out again, trying for a lucky score, but Hallam was already moving. He dumped the contents of the bag he was carrying and dozens of black, plastic spiders, children's toys, spilled out. The second message would never be sent, but just maybe it would save his life. He tried a move of desperation. Like a bullfighter planting the picks between a bull's deadly horns, he rushed straight at the tank and rammed the bag down over the machine's eyes, spinning out from between the laser guns.

Even caught by surprise, the operator was not slow. The lasers fired again and again trying to burn holes in the bag but they could not fire with enough angle to burn it off completely. It settled over the video cameras and blinded the machine. Hallam heard the gears whining furiously as the operator swivelled the cameras to free them. It didn't matter. Even as the laser cannons went off in wild bursts hoping to catch him, he had already grabbed the eyestalk and used it to pull himself up. The operator must have been able to feel this somehow because the tank began to roll back and forth, smashing madly into the walls in an effort to knock him off.

Hallam hung on with all the strength that remained to him and yanked the laser cutter out of his tool belt. He pressed the switch and a white-hot, pencil-thin beam of light five inches long blazed into life. He hacked at the exposed cables, plunging the blade of light into the machine over and over again. Metal turned molten. He levered himself up and stabbed the laser cutter into the glass eyes which melted and spattered. Circuits blew as insulation burned away and systems short-circuited. Rage was a red mist all around him and he slashed at whatever he could grab, sawing, stabbing, throwing the pain out of him and back at the killer. The engine bucked and slowed. Oily smoke began to pour out. He sliced at the cables leading into the lasers and they sputtered and died, muzzles drooping lifelessly.

There were people around him now. The shaving cream spray of fire extinguishers filled the corridor and the flames were snuffed out. Hallam released his hold on the battle tank and slid into the hands of the medics. They began first aid.

'David? David! You okay?'

It was Hu. Good old Hu. Hallam felt light-headed. He recognized the reaction. The medics were cutting away his clothing and spraying his skin with something. It tickled for a few seconds, then took away the pain. How nice. A couple of officers were demanding an explanation of the crowd. He remembered officers as being extremely good at that.

Hu bent over him. Hallam saw his face tighten when he saw the burns.

'What happened?'

'Sicked a tank on me,' he managed. He was happy to see Hu. Then, proudly, 'I killed it.'

'I see.' Hu looked at the tank. 'Remote control. You wouldn't have seen anyone.'

Hallam nodded. In spite of the pain, he felt cleansed. In spite of the years, he was truly the man he had once been. He wanted to tell Hu what he had rediscovered inside himself, but he didn't have the strength.

Hu saw the effort. He said, 'Hush. Lot's changed since last time you were hurt. They'll take you up to the infirmary. Be good as new even faster.'

'You . . . watch out.'

Hu nodded. He started to say something but Hallam was

looking past him. Time had stopped, telescoped. You're always in two places. Out of the sea of faces in the corridor, one emerged and made the present and the past abruptly collide. The effect was shattering. For a long moment, Hallam stared at General Perry Hamilton, twenty years older, but still hauntingly familiar. He was holding one of the plastic spiders Hallam had dropped from the bag. He was staring at it. Hallam remembered the scar under his right eye; odd to have forgotten it till now.

It didn't matter.

In one brief instant, Hallam remembered something far more important, the thing he'd forgotten so many years before during the firefight in Hamilton's firebase hilltop crater. He tried to call Hu, but fatigue overcame him. The medics slid an IV needle into his arm and hoisted him onto a stretcher. They wheeled him away and he was powerless to tell Hu the vital piece of information he had remembered, the one that put all the pieces together . . .

Hallam knew who the killer was.

TWENTY-SIX

General Hamilton gestured towards the display screens. 'As you can see, Mr President, the situation has steadily worsened during the night.'

Rogers ran a hand over his prominent chin and said ruefully, 'How did I know he was going to say that?'

There were grins. They dissipated some of the tension that was building. Everyone settled into their places and began reviewing the new situation. Soviet forces had attacked American positions in South Korea and South-West Asia. Things were deteriorating fast. A feeling of approaching crisis, of being unable to stop things, was resulting in real strain. The game was a simulation of course, but the forces it mirrored were quite real. The seriousness of global tensions, also quite real, reflected the terrible fear every president and high-level officer lived with in real life – that exactly this kind of escalating situation might ignite a conflict neither side could put out. Despite the war game being electronic, it was having an effect.

'The Russians,' Hamilton began, 'tried to run the Cuban blockade and our carrier group gave them an order to turn them back. The Soviet freighter was escorted by a Udaloy-class guided missile destroyer which refused to give way. The freighter was fired upon and destroyed. The Soviet destroyer attempted to engage the carrier and was also destroyed, but an undetected Soviet Alfa-class nuclear attack submarine managed to inflict severe damage to the carrier, *Constitution*, before being destroyed by our ASW forces. *Constitution* is still afloat. The blockade is shaky, but still holding.

'Situation: there are Soviet and Cuban air and naval forces which were already inside the harbour at the time of the blockade. Their course of action is unpredictable. They know they are vulnerable to air attack. They could sit there or try breaking out at any time. Since Cuba is dependent on external supplies, especially oil, the situation will be critical within the week. Additional American forces are heading for the area.

'The Berlin blockade is still in force. Several air battles have been fought. Our side outshot theirs but has failed to gain a strategic advantage. Warsaw Pact forces are gathering on the East German border. NATO is in an increased state of readiness. Its forces are prepared to try and reopen the corridor to the city if so ordered.

'In the Far East, the Soviets have deployed coastal defence divisions and are massing extensive surface ship, submarine, naval aircraft, ASW and anti-ship operations along the Soviet periphery. Their ships have moved out of Cam Ranh Bay in Vietnam and are taking up positions appropriate to attacking Allied sea lanes in the South China Sea . . .'

It went on. All over the world, forces that had been perched and leaning towards each other for almost three decades were beginning to lumber forward like giant behemoths. They were slowly picking up speed and momentum, every engagement seeming to escalate the conflict as each side sought advantage. The genie was out of the bottle and could not be put back in.

'What are the hotline procedures?' asked Rogers. 'I'm not usually prone to understatement, but things are getting a bit out of hand.'

'As you may already know, Mr President,' Hamilton explained, 'a new hotline was installed two years ago, simplifying the procedures and making contact easier. You have several options, including telex capabilities if you want to avoid person-to-person contact or if you want to save that level for future negotiations. Your call, sir.'

'Start the procedures.' He turned to his Secretary of

Defense. 'Jason, let's get someone in here to start drafting. In the meantime . . .' The next several minutes were spent evaluating military options and countermoves. In anticipation of a Soviet move towards the Gulf, American naval forces were taking up positions off the Iranian coast. Missile bases in Britain and West Germany were put on full alert and NATO forces were recalling all personnel. The NORAD warning systems in Alaska and Canada were reporting clear skies, but Strategic Air Command was busy putting everything it had up in the air. Attack submarines were moving towards the choke points in the Bering Sea and the North Atlantic.

It was going to be one hell of a war.

Hallam twisted round to get a better view in the infirmary mirror. He had to admit the medics had done a first-class job treating the laser burns. Overnight, they applied some kind of salve which numbed the pain and then worked a layer of artificial skin grown in the laboratory over the wound. It seemed to bond almost at once. He realized he'd been holding his breath since waking, anticipating an onslaught of pain, but there wasn't any. This was very different from twenty years ago and he said so.

'It's also the type of burn,' said the medic on duty, a crew-cut blond youngster. 'Lasers give you more like a slice than a burn, tissue damage is localized. With this new pseudo-skin, you ought to heal nicely. A little stiff maybe, but that's probably not new for you.' He ran a practised hand over Hallam's back. 'Vietnam?'

'Yep.'

'I've seen a few like yours. That napalm was wicked stuff. No way to piece anything together like we did for you.'

'You treat a lot of laser burns?' Hallam asked.

'Yeah. Most of the steel work has to be done with lasers, especially the big springs underneath. We see this kind of stuff all the time. Here, just let me get these dressings in place.'

After the medic was done, Hallam wriggled into a shirt they supplied him. He felt nervous and understood why. His brain kept telling him that he should be in pain while his skin continued to feel none. He kept wondering when this was going to end.

The medic said, 'That's it. Those dressings need changing every four hours. I'll see you then. Get some food and rest.'

'Thanks,' said Hallam sincerely. 'I don't know if I could have gone through it again . . . the pain.'

The youth smiled. 'Nice you don't have to.'

The medic left and Hallam finished dressing. He felt like a new man – younger, in touch, harder. He had been through a baptism of fire. He decided the metaphor was right. His time in Vietnam ended in flames, his time here began with them. The experience in the corridor had been a kind of rebirth, burning away the mental and physical fat brought on by accumulated comfort.

Hu walked in and tossed him a bag. Hallam looked inside and winced. 'Marshmallows,' he said darkly.

'Every time I see you I get the urge.'

Hallam stood up and walked a few tentative steps. 'I admire your sensitivity.'

'And well you should. Let's get some food. Need some help?'

'No, thanks.' Hallam caught Hu's eye. 'I know who it is, Hu.'

The façade of easy humour left Hu's face. 'Tell me.'

'As we eat.'

The Granite Inn was crowded. Hallam liked the feeling of security that gave him while Hu got the food.

'What was that thing exactly? Some kind of tank?' he asked when Hu was back at the table.

'A remote-controlled sentry vehicle. They use them in the tunnels and out around the periphery fences. You were unbelievably lucky.'

A rush of emotion he had felt in the corridor made Hallam's

face harden. 'I woke up this morning thinking that, too. By all rights, that thing should have killed me. So I began asking myself why it hadn't. Hu, he couldn't have missed at that range. He could have drilled me any time. He was playing with me. He *wanted* to burn me like that, like a little boy prolonging the hurt, enjoying the pain. His only mistake was carrying on too long. He let me live too long and I got mad enough and lucky enough and managed to get the bag over the thing's eyes.'

'You said you know who he is. You saw him?'

'No.' Hallam thought back to the scene. 'Not at that point, anyway. After. In the crowd. Hu, you remember that night on the firebase?'

'When I heroically saved your life?'

'You're too modest.'

'I remember.'

'We finished interviewing Hamilton and he got into his helicopter to go back to MAC-Vee. It was just off the ground when the first rockets came in. Our helicopter was hit but Hamilton's managed to get off.'

'So?'

'So this,' Hallam said. 'I remembered it when I saw his face. I tried to tell you that night but you couldn't hear me over the noise.'

'You were carrying that wounded boy. The shells dazed you. We had to come out for you,' Hu insisted.

'I wasn't dazed from the shell. I mean, I always remembered being confused and I thought the shock must have done it but when I saw Hamilton this morning I remembered what I saw. That's what did it, Hu. It wasn't the concussion, it was the sight of Hamilton's helicopter coming back in low over the hilltop and blasting our Huey into pieces with rocket fire. *He* kept us on that hilltop to die. That's what stopped me, the shock of seeing that. In that moment I knew he was the killer. Then everything came apart on the firebase. While we were there, Hamilton flew back to Saigon and killed or crippled the rest. This morning he almost got me. He came by just to admire his work.'

'What do we do?'

'We find some proof and nail his ass. I think—'

A voice above them said, 'Good morning, gentlemen. It's been a long time.'

Hallam looked up. Arnie Wernicker had aged in twenty years and though there was grey in his hair and crow's feet around the dark skin of his eyes, his small, wiry physique hadn't changed at all. The difference was in his face. It was easier, more . . . civilian. Hallam remembered the last time they met, the chewing out Wernicker had given him – and the off-the-record blasting he gave right back.

'May I join you?' Wernicker asked.

Hallam gestured to an empty chair.

'Thanks.' Wernicker looked them over and his eyes came to rest on Hallam. 'Heard there was a ruckus in one of the corridors this morning. One of the sentry vehicles went out of control. I wasn't surprised to find it was you it went out of control on.'

'Why not?'

''Cause I'm still not stupid. I found the hexagram on my desk. I haven't seen one in twenty years. How many other people you think that made me remember?'

'How about Major Reiman with his throat sliced open? Or a quadriplegic named Paco Gallo? Or a guy named Burris with a steel plate where his skull should be. Should I go on?'

'Cut it out, Hallam. I'm not responsible for that.'

'I know, but you didn't help much either. Even after I got shipped Stateside and Hu went into the mountains you could have kept it up and found the guy. But you didn't.'

'Say what you want, Hallam, but admit the truth for a change. I didn't fuck this thing up. You and your pal here did. You had your chance at the killer. We cleared the space for you. You just couldn't handle him.'

'Why was it a one-play game?' Hallam said angrily. 'We were supposed to be a team, for Christ's sake. It was the Army, not *High Noon*. Where the hell was our back-up, our support? All right, he took us out. God knows, I still ache about that. But where were the reinforcements? What the hell kind of general sends in a unit and when they get wiped out just sits there and says, well, that's it. Lost one, they win. Where the fuck were you, Arnie? Where the fuck was anybody but Hu and me? I'll tell you where. Sitting around calling back channels and arranging a cover-up as soon as the bodies cooled. Wernicker, you're as full of crap now as you were that day in your office.'

'I don't like that, Hallam.'

'Ask me if I give a shit.'

It made Wernicker sit up straighter. 'You never understood there were other factors.'

'Don't go moral on me, Arnie, you're too much of a whore.'

'If you're trying to punish me, boy, you don't know the first thing about it.'

'What'd you lose, Arnie, a few nights' sleep?'

Wernicker's eyes narrowed dangerously, but he held back. 'I came here because you need help, Hallam. You want it or not?'

'What's the price?'

'There is none. Look, personally I don't care if you live or die.' Something changed in Wernicker's voice. 'I'm not doing it for you.'

For the first time, Hallam lost some of his antagonism. There was a note of honesty he hadn't heard before . . . and a note of self-deprecation. 'Why then?'

'Answer me a question first, okay? You said before you knew I wasn't the killer. How?'

'And risk back channels again? No way.' Hallam started to go.

Hu was watching Wernicker closely. Silent till now, he put a restraining hand on Hallam's arm and drew him back down.

'Wait a minute, David.' To Wernicker, he said, 'Why not just tell us?'

Wernicker's eyes dropped. He was different when he spoke. The bluster was gone, so was the Academy bullshit.

'I loved her,' he said quietly, and all of a sudden Hallam understood.

He was talking about Ronnie Lassiter.

Hu returned with a cup of coffee and set it down in front of Wernicker. Hallam watched him with the first pangs of sympathy dawning. The story was simple, so ordinary. The older man, widowed, now married to his career, the bright, pretty young girl . . .

'Did she know how you felt?' Hallam asked.

Wernicker shook his head. 'I didn't want her to. Age, race, the different kind of lives we lead. I knew there was no chance. We just used to talk. She liked my stories. We had an occasional dance at a social event. I never said anything, just enjoyed her company when I had the opportunity. Friends. She never hinted she felt anything more than that. That didn't matter to me.' Wernicker looked up. 'It isn't what matters now. What matters is that I loved her . . . and maybe partly because I didn't do what I should have twenty years ago, she's dead.'

Hallam sat up straighter in his chair. 'I'm sorry,' he said, feeling some common ground between them for the first time.

'I'd like to do what I can. You know who killed her?' Wernicker asked.

'It's only a theory,' Hu said quickly.

'More than that.' Hallam told him what he'd remembered. Wernicker listened intently, shaking his head.

When Hallam was done, he said, 'It's hard to believe. I've known Perry Hamilton half my life.'

Hu said, 'At the bottom level, that's part of what makes this so bad. How do you trust in anything after this man touches your life? I once heard a story about a woman who found a half-starved dog in Mexico. She grew very fond of the little thing. It slept on her hotel bed, ate her food and snuggled on her shoulder. She decided to bring it back to the States. A few days after she got home, she took it to a vet and discovered all that time she was living with a Mexican water rat.'

'What are you going to do?' Wernicker asked.

Hallam explained what they were up to. 'I think it's working. Getting the hexagram drove him out of hiding.'

'But look at the results,' said Wernicker.

'David's good at planning,' Hu suggested with a straight face. 'He'll consider it a total success if he dies next time.'

Hallam looked sheepish. 'I admit some minor corrections are called for. But the theory is sound. Anyway, it's time to tell him we're back in the game. A harder push this time.' He withdrew a can from his pocket.

'What's that?'

'Spray antiseptic.' Hallam held it up. 'They used it on me in the infirmary. Looks like white paint.'

'What are you going to do with it?'

'Be blatant for a change.'

'Come again?'

'I'm going to tell Hamilton how I feel,' Hallam said.

Wernicker looked doubtful. 'You're going to paint him a sign?'

'A little elementary vandalism never hurt anybody,' Hallam said happily.

Wernicker grew thoughtful. 'Your problem is you think small. I've got a better idea.' He explained what he had in mind.

'Very clever,' said Hallam grudgingly. 'Arnie, I don't want to start liking you. I'd hate to think I was wrong all these years.'

'You weren't,' Wernicker said, grinning. 'I'm the same prick.'

'That's a comfort.'

Hu rose. 'Arnold, I am truly sorry for your loss. We'll meet you in your office in an hour.'

They walked out of the dining room, but not before Wernicker offered both men his hand . . . and they took it.

TWENTY-SEVEN

On the second day, Soviet tank divisions moved over the border into Iran and began a massive push southwards. The President of the United States informed the Soviet Ambassador that any attempt to cross over the Elburz Mountains would be repulsed with chemical and nuclear weapons. In Europe, NATO forces led by American fighters penetrated the Warsaw Pact front lines in a daring, daytime raid and blew up the roads and bridges required by the Soviets to bring their conventional forces, some 94 divisions and 30,000 tanks, into an attack on Western Europe. Their progress would be halted for a minimum of three days. An exchange on the hot line produced no tangible results. Small, fierce sea and air battles burst out in the Pacific and the Mediterranean. Hot spots that were smouldering all over the globe began bursting into flames.

Late in the afternoon, the President went to DEFCON 3.

'I don't see why I'm the one who has to do it,' said Hallam petulantly, fingering the transmitter. They were sitting in Wernicker's office.

'Because I'm almost sixty,' said Wernicker, 'and Hu has to run the computers. That leaves you. Unless other nominations are in order.'

'I vote him,' said Hu at once.

Hallam gave him a dark look.

'It's not so bad,' Wernicker said, 'and it's the only way to make this work. Look at the map. The receiver has to be placed here,' he pointed. 'So you go across the reservoir by boat and up this hatchway here and across this small tunnel here. Plant the bug and return by the same route. Nothing to it.'

Hallam studied the map. The vast underground reservoirs were carved out of the mountain itself into big pockets of rock filled with enough water to irrigate a desert. Several caverns split off from the larger reservoir. High above them was an entrance to the south portal which was mostly used for air flow into the complex.

'Any light in there?'

'A mile inside a mountain?' said Wernicker. 'You got to be kidding.'

Hallam shook his head sadly. 'I hate this plan.'

'Don't worry, there's a new invention called a flashlight.'

'Oh.'

'Wait.' Hu's smile was wicked. 'The best is yet to come.'

Wernicker handed him the transmitter. It was a box the size of a packet of cigarettes with an antenna protruding from one side, an on/off switch with an LED over it in the centre, and four wires with magnetic contact points coming out of the other side.

'This is going to do the trick?' Hallam asked, doubt evident.

'It wasn't what I had in mind originally, but since you've shown me that fancy phone of yours, this is easier and better. Remember,' Wernicker advised him, 'no one can interfere with the data flow from anywhere *outside* NORAD, it's all totally secure, but inside, well, I'll bet no one ever really thought about this.'

'You bet? That's supposed to make me totally secure? What if something just comes out and explodes in my face?'

Hu couldn't resist. 'I'd like to introduce you to my new partner.'

'Your mother was Chinese,' Hallam said nastily.

Wernicker shook his head. 'Fine. I'm running down a

sychopath with Abbot and Costello. I can see why you guys did so well last time.'

'It's a knack,' Hu admitted.

The entrance to the reservoirs was down on the lowest level. There was a steel door resembling the watertight compartment hatches on submarines. Wernicker turned the wheel-lock and Hu helped him pull it open. A cold, damp smell drifted out.

'Take the metal steps down to the water. There's a skiff tied up there. There's a ladder on the other side of the cavern, down the right fork. Be careful not to trip over anything or you'll set off alarms. Go slowly.'

Hallam shifted his pack over his shoulder. 'Got the time right?' he asked, stepping inside and turning on the light.

'Got it,' Hu assured him. 'Just be careful.' The door began to swing shut.

'Hey, I'd like to make a farewell speech . . .' but Hallam had to step back as Hu and Wernicker slammed the door home and total silence surrounded him.

'And they wonder why public speaking's a lost art,' Hallam said sadly.

The beam of his flashlight speared through the gloom to pass over the stone walls. They were heavily faceted, as if carved by a giant sculptor with an equally gigantic chisel. Pipes ran in parallel rows along the walls, five in all, each a different colour. There were valves where they entered the complex. The cavern was domed, the ceiling about twelve feet over the surface of the water. The water itself was as flat and polished as a mirror, without even a ripple disturbing the surface.

Hallam pointed the light down and descended the stairs. A small metal dock floated in the water and the skiff Wernicker had described was tied to it. He got in and settled onto the seat. The last time he had rowed a boat was in daycamp, a lot of years before. He untied it.

'Anyone for a grape fight?' The only answer was the echo of his voice down the long chambers.

He took out the phone and dialled Griswald. For a few seconds there was no answer. Then, 'Boss?'

'Right here, Griswald. What took you so long?'

'Where are you exactly?'

'In the reservoirs. Can't you tell?'

'The fact that we can speak at all is a tribute to modern electronics,' the computer said reverently. 'But it's requiring quite a few tricks to do it. You're under almost a mile of rock.'

'I'm proud of you, boy,' said Hallam, dipping the oars into the water. The skiff slid away. 'Got a question.'

'Shoot.'

'Heading: *I Ching*. Subheading: a hexagram that says "I'm coming for you, you sonofabitch bastard fuck."'

'It's good I have some discretionary capability. Searching.'

Hallam rowed on in silence. The splash of the oars was a pleasant sound harkening back to a better time. Knights in tattered shorts and dirty sneakers fighting with overripe grapes and garbage can covers. It was long before soldiering with automatic rifles and napalm . . . He rowed through the first cavern and passed under the archway into the next. He paused to swing the flashlight around to get his bearings, then rowed on.

'I-was-sailing-along-on-moon-light-bay . . . You-could-hear-the-voices-sing-ing . . .'

'Boss?'

'Whatcha got?'

'Is this somehow connected to the concept of justice?'

'It is.'

'Then the Shih Ho hexagram might be what you want. Shih Ho: Biting Through. It's a combination of the Li and Chên trigrams. Li represents the sun high above while Chên represents the turmoil of the world below. The image is: *Thunder and lightning, biting through. Thus the kings of former times made firm the laws through clearly defined penalties. The penalties that make men avoid transgressions should be as clearly defined as lightning.* Shih Ho means consuming. It can also mean, take this, you sonofabitch bastard fuck.'

'Sort of your all-purpose hexagram. Thanks, Griswald.'

The reservoir split into two caverns and Hallam rowed his skiff to the right. The feeling of isolation was eerie. He felt like something floating on top of a drink. Just to experiment, he turned off the flashlight. He was immediately plunged into darkness so thick and impenetrable he couldn't see his hand an inch in front of his face. There was simply no light. No glow or reflection, just blackness so deep it made him feel like an alien trespassing in another world. His flashlight was like a life-support system. Without it, he would die.

He turned the light back on. About fifty yards ahead a steel ladder had been set into the rock. There was a hatch above it, almost identical to the one he'd come in through. He rowed over and tied the boat to the ladder. He slung his pack over his shoulder, stepped onto the first rung and climbed up. It was a little hard manoeuvring the hatch open, but he managed it and crawled inside. He found himself in a tubular access crawlway. Thick cables ran down the length of the shaft.

It took him almost ten minutes to shin down to the junction Wernicker had pinpointed on the map. He took out his tools and the transmitter from the pack and rolled over to lie on his back. In this position he could reach the top of the tube with both hands. He picked up the phone and opened a line to the computer.

'Get ready, Griswald. I'll have this in place in a few seconds.'

'All set, boss.'

Hallam placed the transmitter against the cable and the magnetized backing held it there. He unscrewed the phone's earpiece cover, removed the speaker, and attached two of the contacts to the open leads underneath. The other two contacts went to the cable in the way Wernicker had shown him.

Satisfied that the connections were holding, Hallam drew out the antenna and flicked the switch to on. The LED on the transmitter's face glowed soft red. From the speaker, Griswald said, 'Working.'

Hallam waited.

Hu was down on the lowest level of the command post. Technicians sat at red consoles with round, green screens watching the tracks of anything that was snared by NORAD's electronic net. One console in particular occupied his attention. He carried a small package almost identical to the one Hallam had taken with him and as soon as it picked up Hallam's signal he needed to be ready to move.

Far out in space, satellites were picking up activity at the Soviet space centre. The Russians were up to something, but nobody knew what. It was an interesting shift in the game, the notion that the conflict might move out into space. Already resources were being tested that had never before come under this kind of scrutiny. Tracking stations were being evaluated for survivability. A squadron of Russian MiGs had tried to take out the old Distant Early Warning (DEW) Line stations and had almost succeeded. The replacement for the old DEW line, the North Warning System, was being guarded by Canadian CF-18 fighter squadrons. The President and his advisers were shifting tactics to protect the satellite-tracking centre at St Margarets, New Brunswick, in anticipation of a Soviet sabotage attempt.

The LED on Hu's receiver lit up. Hallam had the equipment in place. It was time for Hu to practise a little sleight of hand. As he walked past the console operator, a bag of parts he was carrying slipped from his hands and spilled out on the floor.

'Jesus,' Hu cursed, stopping to pick them up.

'Quite a few under here, sir,' said the console operator, shoving his chair back so they could get under the console.

'Thanks, Sarge. I see them,' said Hu. He put his hand on the console to lower himself down . . . and flicked the switch that altered the data flow, causing a bypass which fed in new information through the circuit Hallam had just installed. It happened almost at once.

'What the . . .?' said an operator at the next console. 'Where the hell is that stuff coming from?'

On the big screens overhead, the bright green lines which had just been inscribing a perfect orbital curve suddenly did an odd dance as if they were streaking off into outer space, curved back onto the screen and began to trace an entirely different pattern. The three lines became six, duplicating the pattern on the twin screens.

The console operator was standing next to Hu, staring at the screens. 'Beats the hell out of me. Never seen it before. Must be part of the game.'

Hu watched in satisfaction as the Shih Ho hexagram built itself up on the screen. Beneath it, new lines appeared and spun into the unmistakable picture of a spider. Spreading now, the hexagrams intersected the spider, forming a set of bars to trap the creature.

Within its prison, the spider began to shrivel and die.

'There's no question about it, Mr President,' General Hamilton was saying. 'The Soviets are readying something at Tyuratam. Heavy payload.'

'They can't want this expanded into space,' said Rogers.

'Intelligence is unclear as to their purpose,' said the CIA Director, 'but I'm more worried about the launch status of their ICBMs.'

'Can we conjecture . . . What the hell is that?' Rogers demanded as the hexagrams burst onto the screens.

Hamilton was staring at the images. The others interpreted the look on his face as worry that a computer malfunction was fouling up the exercise.

Rogers said solicitously, 'Perry, are you all right?' He turned to one of the aides. 'Send a doctor up here. His face is red as a beet. Could be his heart.'

'No,' said Hamilton quickly. 'I'm fine. Really. Keep going Look, the screens are clearing. I'm all right, really.'

'Can't lose sight of things,' counselled Bemsford. 'Remember, it's just a game. Get some fresh air, right?'

Hamilton hurried out.

After thirty seconds, Hu scooped up the last of the fallen parts. He stood and his hand swept over the console, brushing against the switch and returning it to its former position. The hexagrams faded from the screens. The tracks returned to normal.

Hu left the technicians frantically trying to figure out what had happened and headed for the entrance to the reservoir.

Years before, Hamilton had been in one of the newer kinds of zoos where the animals roamed freely over their 'natural' terrain. At one point, involved in a conversation, he turned to find himself staring into the face of a snarling tiger. In the split second before his mind realized there was a glass barrier between himself and the tiger, his body reacted with a sick, wet fear that travelled all the way down to his bowels and made them feel like hot water. But for the glass, the animal would have torn him to pieces.

The sickly fear he felt in that moment was the same fear he felt now, looking into the blazing eyes of his son. The ferocity of those eyes made him feel weak and sick inside. That day in the zoo it was glass that protected him, now it was the increasingly less meaningful fact that he was the boy's father. All in all, as Hamilton looked at his son's twisted and enraged face, he realized he felt more confidence in the glass.

'You mustn't,' he pleaded. 'Not here. Not inside the complex. If you don't listen, you'll bring the whole place down on our heads.' Hamilton's pulse was racing. The ever-present split in his personal life rose up in his throat like bile.

Obviously the laser burns hadn't disabled Hallam as long as his son had hoped and he was after Frank again.

It sent him on the rampage once more. Hamilton knew he had to put a stop to it. 'Accidents' like the one yesterday could be shrugged off as equipment failure or carelessness but anything as obvious as murder was another thing entirely. It would be investigated and if Frank were discovered, so would Hamilton's cover-ups all these years.

'I'll kill him,' Frank said softly. 'I wish you could see what's in my head.'

'I've seen the results,' said Hamilton disgustedly.

'Where is he?' Frank demanded.

'Hallam? How should I know?'

'Don't play games with me. You know every inch of this complex like you built it. Where could he input the data for the hexagrams?' He put his hands on his temples and pressed till they turned white. 'Shih Ho! How does he dare? Biting Through . . .' His son's smile made Hamilton think of slime on wet rocks. 'That's the way I'll do him. Biting through. I like that. I should have killed him and that bastard gook twenty years ago. Where are they?' he demanded.

Hamilton took down the plans of the complex from a shelf. It was like being trapped in a room with a hungry animal. He pored over the blueprints for a few minutes.

'Here. I think it would have to be here. Across the reservoir to this point.'

They weren't usually in the same room for long. The look on the general's face deepened. 'Are you sure it's Hallam? It might be Lassiter. By God, how could you have been so stupid to kill the girl?'

'It would have been stupider to let her live. Besides, it isn't Lassiter. He doesn't know anything about the hexagrams. Only those two did, and they're both here because of you, I might add.'

'That was twenty years ago.'

'It's them. They survived that night – or don't you remember?'

'I don't care to be reminded of it.'

'Why not? It was because of you that they lived.' Frank Hamilton smiled. 'You begged me.'

The general's face fell into sad, depleted lines. 'They were good men. They deserved better. And you wouldn't have got away with it.'

'Which in the end was the most important thing,' Frank Hamilton taunted him. 'I would have got them, too, if you hadn't rushed me out to the hunt/kill squads in the hill country. I still think you got scared and made some kind of deal. It doesn't matter. You covered for me then, you'll cover for me now. Just like you always have.' There was mockery in his tone. 'Like a good father should.' He reached out to put a hand on his father's shoulder but the older man shied away.

'I protect you because . . . God help me, you're my son. And because I promised your mother.'

'My mother was a rabid bitch whore.'

Colour rose in the general's face. 'You must not call her that.' He made a last-ditch plea for sanity. 'Just as you must not bring attention to yourself here. It's too small a world here. There's too much security.'

'They almost killed me once, with that bastard napalm.'

For a moment there was strength in the general's voice. 'It would have been kinder . . .' He stopped, strength failing. '. . . compared to . . . to what you do. It has to stop right now. You can't get away with it in here. For Christ's sake, look at who's walking around. I can't shield you. This isn't Vietnam or Thailand.' Hamilton heard the pleading note in his voice and tried to draw himself up. 'You've disgraced your family, the uniform . . . Enough. I'm warning you . . .'

'Warning me?' There was a sneer in his son's voice. 'You mean you don't want me wearing your uniforms anymore and playing general? No more privileges of rank in the whorehouses?'

'Too few survived a night with you.' Hamilton stopped tiredly. 'I've done everything I could to keep your . . . nature

... a secret. During the war I hoped your cruelty might burn itself out. But it didn't. It made you worse. Now you have to listen to me. Ignore the threat. Do more of that bastard drug. Hide. I don't care. They can't know it's you. Look, this was put on *my* desk. Mulrose and Wernicker probably got one too.'

'They'll never see me coming.'

Hamilton was drained by any encounter with his son. To others, Frank was a born charmer. Only Hamilton knew that it masked nothing . . . nothing at all. The look in his son's eyes scared him as much as it ever had and he longed for the courage to kill him as one would a rabid dog. In Vietnam he put Frank in the most dangerous duties imaginable hoping God or the enemy could do what he would not. Frank emerged stronger and more dangerous. Every time Hamilton confronted his own moral obligation to put an end to the evil child, he had to face the fact that he simply could not kill his own son.

'I swear, I have limits,' he said.

'I know,' said Frank Hamilton. 'Just remember, I don't.'

Frank went away like a bad odour; much was left behind. Hamilton sat down weakly.

He thought about praying, but it was far too late.

Hu met Wernicker in the corridors. 'The spider was a nice touch,' the older man said.

'I'm sure the killer thought so, too,' Hu said sourly. 'Keep an eye out. To steal a proverb from our Arab friends, he who awakens the sleeping tiger better be prepared to ride it.'

They hurried towards the reservoir entrance. 'Hu, all those years ago . . . ?'

Hu shrugged. 'Things were different.'

'If it hadn't been during a war, and especially that war, well, we wouldn't have let it slide. We would have gone after him.'

'It's taken the whole of society twenty years to re-establish its values, its patterns,' Hu said thoughtfully. 'And your participation here goes a long way towards proving it.'

'You and Hallam. You must have hated us.'

'There wasn't time.'

'Still . . .'

'Forget it,' Hu said. 'You weren't the enemy. Now it's all only the stuff of movies.'

They reached the reservoir door and swung it open. The same wet smell filled the air. Hu stuck his head in.

'David? You there? David?'

Hu went in and climbed down a few rungs. He heard Wernicker above him. 'See anything?'

'No. Not yet,' Hu answered. He called out again. 'David?'

'Hu, I think I . . .'

That was the last Hu heard. A huge weight crashed down on his back, knocking him forward and twisting the breath out of his lungs as if he'd been caught in a vice. He had no time to grab for a firmer hold. His feet slid off the rungs and he pitched forward into the darkness below. Then a pain shot up his leg so hot and sharp it swamped his mind with darkness. There was a heavy splash ahead of him.

His last thought was the sure and certain knowledge that he was going to drown.

Then there was nothing.

Hallam climbed out of the conduit and back into the skiff. Griswald was in the bag along with the rest of his equipment. He realized the entity that was Griswald was not actually equipment in the sense that he was the phone itself, he was rather the computer – the *artificial intelligence*, Hu would have reminded him – stored in the basement of Paco's house. He also realized he was growing fond of the electronic entity.

He panned around with his light and rowed fisherman-style towards the entrance to the next cavern. There was a funny smell in the air he hadn't noticed before and he wrinkled his nose in distaste. Smelled like rotten eggs. He would be glad to get back to the climate-controlled interior of the complex.

The air was getting worse. His stomach began to convulse. He shone the light over the walls but saw nothing out of the ordinary. He rowed faster, anxious to get to the door. His nose was filled with the odour, his eyes were watering. He dipped his hands into the water and splashed it over his face. It helped only a little.

He was fighting the urge to throw up when the boat bumped into something floating by the prow of the skiff. In spite of his rush to get out, Hallam knew nothing as large as this should be floating in the reservoir. He benched the oars and played the light over it.

It was the body of Arnold Wernicker. The dark, sodden mess that was the back of his skull and the growing odour in the cavern were too much. Hallam retched over the side, heaving helplessly till there was nothing left in his stomach. It left him weak and sickly. He was nauseated by the smell and what lay before him. Fighting the urge to throw up again, he hauled Wernicker's dripping corpse into the boat.

Tears flooded his eyes from the pain and the smell. Hallam could barely see. He began to doubt he could make it back to the entrance. Wernicker would not be the killer's only intended victim. He was probably waiting for Hallam to return. And Hu? Where was Hu? More tears, this time from frustration and rage, clouded his eyes.

In a flash of clarity, Hallam realized the killer must have opened one of the gas lines running along the cavern walls. He had to think. The gas wrenched at his stomach and burned his lungs. He heaved again, feeling pain sear across his abdominal muscles. His throat was raw. He dipped his hand into the water and drank some. It tasted bitter and he spat it out.

What was this stuff? his mind demanded. He swatted at the air as if he could drive it off. Rotten eggs. What was the stuff chemistry teachers loved to use to demonstrate to students the properties of gases. Sulphur dioxide? Hydrogen sulphide? That was it. The other stuff smelled lousy, too, but hydrogen sulphide smelled just like this – like rotten eggs.

His head was swimming. He felt paralysed. The oars felt heavy in his hands. Hallam knew he had to make a decision quickly. He couldn't go back to the entrance, the killer . . . He stopped, the killer had a name. Hamilton might be waiting for him there. But if he didn't get out of the caverns, he was going to die in them. If Hu was dead, too, no one knew he was here. When the gas finally overcame him, he would drift in and out of the maze of caverns for weeks before someone came to look for him.

He drifted past the fork, still indecisive. Which way to go? He couldn't last much longer. He thought furiously. There had to be a way. He dipped his hands into the water again and put it to his lips. It tasted acidic. That told him the gas was water soluble. Something else prodded his mind. The fork in the reservoir. What had Hu said? If you go right, you come out near the south portal – *the one that was used for air intake!*

He hauled out the phone and punched in the codes. 'Griswald,' he gasped. 'Call Paco, call anyone and tell them we're in here and heading for the south portal. Use your own judgement. I can't wait. You're on your own.'

'Calling . . .'

Hallam tore his shirt off. He plunged it into the water and soaked it thoroughly. Then he wrapped it round his face, leaving only a tiny slit for his eyes. The improvised gas mask was as good as he was going to get for the next ten minutes – and judging from the pain in his lungs, that was about all the time he had.

Breathing through the sodden shirt, Hallam pulled at the oars with all his strength. He shot off down the other cavern, barely pausing to shine the light out ahead of him. The skiff surged forward. The water in the cloth was absorbing much of the gas, and before long it became too tainted to breathe through. He dunked it in the reservoir again and rewrapped it. It helped. He strained to take shallow breaths even as the exertion of rowing demanded his body take deeper ones. Spots danced before his eyes.

He felt bile rising from his stomach and barely got the shirt unwound from his mouth before it came pouring out in desperate, retching heaves. There was a shore of sorts ahead, just a rocky ledge with steel rungs set into the wall above it. The shirt in one hand, he dived out of the boat and swam for it with no thought of the craft. It would be here if he got back. He dived deep, to get to untainted water and felt it cool his skin. But swimming back up cost him much of his remaining strength. He hauled himself onto the rocky ledge and threw up again. The heaves were now as debilitating as the gas itself. Pain roared across his abdominal muscles. He rewound the cloth and crawled forward. Reaching out almost blindly he got a hand on one of the rungs.

His eyes stung and his lungs burned but he managed to haul himself up. He climbed without looking because it didn't matter what was above. There was either an escape or there wasn't, but certainly death lay below. His foot slipped and he grabbed for purchase, taking the strain on his arms. He regained his footing and climbed upwards, tearing the soaking cloth away from his face because he could no longer breathe through it. His skin burned. His lungs heaved.

He climbed.

He climbed past the point where he had any feelings in his arms and only then because one thought dominated. Hu. If Hu wasn't dead already, he needed him. Hallam felt this with a certainty that defied analysis. Unless the killer had got to Hu already . . . Hallam thrust the offending thought away, and climbed.

It was colder the higher he climbed. His fingers began to cramp. His hands were reduced to awkward blocks of pain. His clothing was plastered to his skin and evaporation chilled him to the bone, but the smell here was less. He could breathe and it didn't sear his lungs. Was that a breeze he felt flowing over his frozen skin? He climbed.

Hallam almost cried with joy when he felt a rocky lip over

his head. The air was better here, fed by the crisp Colorado winds streaming down the south portal. He crawled over the top. He was in a tunnel hewn from the rock. There was some light, too, enough to make out the objects around him – and air! He ran forward taking deep breaths of it, drawing it into his lungs. It was still impure and it made him gag, but he stumbled on in hopes of what he was sure was ahead – the system of filters that protected the entire complex, filters that might save his life. When he was learning about the command centre – was it only yesterday – Griswald said the south portal was an air channel with biological, chemical and radiological filters protecting it. His only hope was that whatever prevented gas from coming into the complex would prevent it from getting out as well. He had to get on the other side of the filters where the air was untainted.

His head was a little clearer. He didn't know whether or not the gas had done permanent damage, but for the first time he began to think he was going to make it. He ran down the tunnel in shuffling, stumbling steps, almost falling but managing to keep his balance for one last run. He was travelling on willpower alone, carried forward by momentum.

A grey wall loomed up in front of him, stretching across the rocky tunnel like a taut diaphragm. He couldn't stop himself and he hit it full force. He didn't even feel the bruising his shoulder took from whatever cross-members supported the filter material. He just tore at the spongy stuff, plunging through it like a halfback at the Superbowl once there was opening enough. The air on the other side was better. God, how sweet air could be!

He tore through more 'walls' of insulation and with each succeeding filter, the air was cleaner. It still hurt to take a deep breath, but he forced the air in. The filters were growing more difficult to penetrate. Hallam had to sit for a second, marshalling his strength. Lethargy was creeping in. The adrenalin that had pumped him up enough to escape from the cavern was now draining away, and with it his strength. The only thing that got him up and moving again was thoughts of Hu. He was more convinced than ever that the killer was after Hu as well, especially if he believed Hallam was dead. Hu had to be warned.

The next sets of filters were squares of some coarse material covered by metal foil. Hallam tore out enough to wriggle through. He attacked the rest in the same way. An old memory surfaced as he worked his way through one filter after another. He remembered running with his friends through the back yards of the houses adjoining his, slipping through rows of clotheslines with vaguely discerned garments flapping at his face. The feeling was similar here.

He stopped. It was hard to hear clearly over the harsh wheeze of his own breathing, but was that something ahead of him? There was still precious little light. Hallam looked around for a weapon of some kind. There was none. He realized he was still wearing the tool belt. The laser cutter was gone, and the handle of a six-inch screwdriver didn't feel terribly comforting. What was he going to face this time? He held the screwdriver low and ready, a technocratic knife fighter. Whatever he was about to face, he wasn't going to lie down, not now, not after all the . . .

'Hallam? Hallam, are you in there?'

That voice. He knew it. He forced his misty mind to concentrate. Was this just another trick, or salvation?

'Hallam, it's Carl Mulrose. Are you in there? Can you hear me?'

'I can hear you,' said Hallam with a rush of relief. 'Christ, I can hear you.'

'What?'

Hallam realized he was mumbling. He called out loudly, 'Yes, I hear you. Get me the hell out of here.'

'I can't order the filters broken till you tell me what's on the other side,' shouted Mulrose. 'There's nothing but Colorado outside this tunnel.'

'Hydrogen sulphide, I think,' Hallam called back. 'Smells like rotten eggs. Water soluble. I can't smell it anymore where I am.'

'Okay. Stay there. We're coming through.'

Hallam heard the sounds of a power saw and some hammering for about a minute, and then the entire grid in front of him fell away. The blast of light and cool, crisp air was like being born again. He fell forward into the arms of a pair of Marine guards and they hauled him out of the debris. Hallam leaned against the rocky wall, clearing his head. He looked up and saw Mulrose standing over him, a thousand questions on his face. Hallam forced himself to stand.

'I think Hu's in danger. How fast can we get back to the reservoir entrance?'

To his credit, Mulrose stifled his questions and barked out crisp orders. Guards were dispatched from the closest station inside NORAD by radio even as he was ushering Hallam into one of the three-wheeled electric carts. They sped down the tunnel, leaving the guards behind hastily re-erecting the filter barriers.

'How'd you find me?' Hallam asked, over the rush of the wind.

Mulrose looked at him with eyes that were going to be demanding explanations sooner than later. 'I got an anonymous phone call.'

Good old Griswald, thought Hallam fondly.

Mulrose sped the little cart down corridors like a race driver. 'This is NORAD, goddamn it,' Mulrose continued sternly. 'We just don't get anonymous phone calls in here. What the hell is going on, Hallam?'

'You remember twenty years ago?'

Mulrose shook his head. 'Can't be.'

'With your track record, I don't think you want to be that adamant.'

'Hallam, I . . .'

Hallam wasn't listening. Up ahead, Marines and EMTs were crowded around the entrance to the reservoir. They were wearing gas masks and those inside were bringing something out. Hallam felt a coldness grab his heart and squeeze it. He scrambled out of the cart, pushing his way through the people. His stomach recoiled as the smell of the gas hit him in spite of the scrubbing fans being set up. Mulrose came up behind him. There were two bodies on the steel floor. They were partially covered by sheets . . .

He dropped down and laid his head on Hu's chest. His friend's clothing was soaked and Hallam could smell the gas rising from him, but inside there was a heartbeat, slow and steady. Hope flared in him. He grabbed an EMT. 'Tell me what happened,' he demanded.

The technician was about to balk when Mulrose's voice rang out. 'Tell him, Corporal.'

'Yes, sir.' He turned back to Hallam. 'We figure he was already on the ladder when something hit from above. He fell and his feet slid in between the rungs. Look here.' The EMT lifted the sheet.

Hallam felt sick. Hu's right leg was bent at an impossible angle and jagged, white bone was sticking through. 'Jesus,' he swore softly.

'Actually, be thankful for it,' said the EMT. 'It's what saved his life. His leg got wedged in the ladder and he hung down above the water. He would have drowned if he'd fallen in. His lab coat draped down and absorbed water. It helped, too, acting like a curtain round him to absorb the gas. Couple of months that leg will heal just fine.' He looked at the other body. 'The other man wasn't so lucky. The back of his head is a mess. If it's any consolation, he was probably dead before he hit the water. I'm sorry.'

Hallam looked at Wernicker's lifeless face. Dead so quickly after his change of heart. It wasn't hard to reconstruct. The killer hit the tough little man from behind and he fell into Hu, knocking him off the ladder. If not for his leg wedging in the rungs of the ladder and breaking the fall, Hu would be dead, too. Hallam felt his rage rising, bringing warmth to his cold, damp skin. More men dead. More to pay back. This time, just a sad little man who liked a girl and was angered by the tragic waste of her life. How many more were going to die before they got Hamilton? Was there no other choice but to take a gun and execute him in blood as cold as his?

Mulrose was looking at him. Hallam could not read the light eyes.

'It's time we talked,' said the general. 'Like it or not, we're in this together. Again.'

Hallam watched them cover Wernicker's corpse. Others lifted Hu onto a stretcher and whisked him away. Hallam picked himself to follow. You're always in two places. Twenty years before, Hu had followed him as he lay unconscious. What were his thoughts then? Was he as scared as Hallam was at this moment to be without the one he depended on? Did he feel as lucky that they had cheated death once again?

'I'll see you after I get him squared away,' he said to Mulrose. 'There better be guards.'

'I'll see to it,' said Mulrose. 'Twenty-four hours a day and electronic surveillance to boot. We've come a long way since Vietnam.'

Hallam felt sarcasm rise up, but he let it pass. 'I'll see you in your office.'

'Get yourself treated, too,' Mulrose said, not unkindly.

Hallam nodded and moved off after his friend.

Hu was owed a bedside vigil.

TWENTY-EIGHT

Day Three began with the entire battle staff tracking the Soviet launch. Data was pouring into Cheyenne Mountain from the tracking stations around the world that hadn't been destroyed by Soviet fighters.

General Hamilton said, 'Mr President, we think you should take a look at your screen.'

Ground stations in Guam and Australia had picked up the launch first. So far it was congruent with published Soviet schedules. NORAD's battle staff tracked the rocket as it passed through the atmosphere. Satellite photos and electronic surveillance data were fed into the massive computers and matched with established configurations. The alarms were silent, the tracks on the screen all showed a launch within predicted norms.

'What do you make of it?' asked Rogers.

'Prophet data says they look like good birds,' supplied one of the technicians.

CIA Director Bill Parker looked sceptical. 'Quick launch under questionable conditions . . . the sudden switch to Tyuratam from Baykony.' He shook his head. 'They're up to something.'

'We can use the F-15 SAINT programme to intercept at this point, Mr President,' said Secretary of Defense Jason Bemsford. 'Please consider authorizing it.'

'This is a scheduled launch,' said Rogers. 'No provocation whatsoever. We start downing space vehicles on routine missions and we advance the theatre of operations into . . . What's that?'

On their screens, the Soviet launch vehicle was breaking apart. Rogers looked to his military advisers.

'Institute Air Defense Warning Yellow,' ordered the NORAD commander-in-chief, 'and I want some solid information fast.'

Alarms were blaring throughout the complex. Yellow alert meant attack by hostile aircraft or missiles was possible. NORAD radars scanned the skies in anticipation. Fighter squadrons all over the continent were scrambling into activity.

'We have no solid information on the Soviet purpose,' said Hamilton.

'Are we ready for SAINT?' asked Rogers.

'Yes, sir,' Bemsford responded.

'SAINT is authorized,' said the President.

The SAC (Strategic Air Command) base in North Dakota was on alert since Yellow warning was declared. Flight crews and pilots raced from dormitory-type barracks to waiting aircraft. Thirty seconds later the first of the F-15 Eagles shot off into the sky. Within minutes they were at squadron strength blazing through the cold Dakota air.

Inside NORAD, the President and his staff watched as the F-15s received the SAtellite INTercept command. They turned in unison. Each carried Boeing Short-Range Attack Missiles which had self-homing warheads with cyrogenically cooled infrared scopes. On the squadron leader's command they began a zoom-climb straight up. They tore upwards straight at the target, their engines pouring out hot exhaust trails.

Everyone's eyes were fixed on the screens following the tracks of the jets. High above the earth, the Soviet craft's payload was almost fully deployed.

'Gonna be tight,' muttered Rogers.

'Maybe too tight,' said Parker.

'Separation,' intoned Hamilton. 'Twenty seconds to impact.'

On the screen they watched the missiles separate from the

F-15s. They streaked towards their targets. The fighters could climb no higher and dived back to earth.

'Five seconds,' said Hamilton.

Rogers was up on his feet. Closer . . . Closer . . .

The screen erupted in a blaze of light. 'Nukes? Did I read that signature right?' Rogers demanded. 'General?'

Hamilton's voice was sepulchral. 'NORAD reports SAINT negative. Look at your screens, gentlemen. The Soviets exploded several nuclear devices outside the atmosphere. The shock waves and electromagnetic pulses are devastating. We're losing the satellites.'

The screens told the story. One by one, systems failed.

'NAVSAT down,' called out the operators. 'FLEET SAT COM down, TACSAT down, LANDSAT down, British SKYNET down, NATO 2 down, Nuclear Force COMSAT down, Bell System down, PROPHET NETWORK down . . .'

Consoles all over the command post were going blank.

'This report just in, Mr President,' said Hamilton. 'Chemical munitions have been fired at US troop units overseas. Casualties are heavy. Commanders are requesting the option of using tactical nuclear weapons.'

Rogers looked at his military advisers, those men representing the Joint Chiefs and the combined strength of the US combat forces. 'Forgive me for resorting to basics, gentlemen. But just what the hell do we do now?'

Far below them, the game's computers hummed into life recording the answers.

Hallam stayed near while the EMTs set Hu's broken leg. X-rays indicated that the breaks, while severe, were reasonably clean given the conditions of the fall. They would heal quite well with time. Meanwhile, Hu wasn't going anywhere.

Sedated, Hu was sleeping heavily. He was guarded by a pair of Marines and Hallam had arranged a tie-in with some of Hu's staff to monitor his vital signs by computer. Any variation would set off an alarm only slightly less strident than the one for incoming missiles. Finally, when his phone was returned, he tied Griswald into the network on a constant-monitor basis and left him beside Hu's bed. Satisfied he had done everything short of standing armed by the bedside as Hu had once done, Hallam left to see Carlton Mulrose.

Hallam crossed the NORAD complex as if it were a New York subway station at two in the morning. He stayed near people, alert for the slightest movement from the shadows. His chest had a nagging pain in it from the gas, but the EMTs told him no permanent damage had been done. Hallam knew he'd been lucky. If those filters had been twenty yards further, or the tunnel lip ten feet higher, he wouldn't have made it at all.

He entered Mulrose's office and gave his name to the secretary.

'Yes, sir. Right this way. The general's waiting.'

Hallam followed her into the office. Of the three men, Hamilton, Wernicker and Mulrose, Carl Mulrose showed the most adverse effects of twenty years passing. The same light eyes stared out at Hallam but they were embedded in a network of wrinkles so deep they were like a dried-out riverbed. Even though Mulrose still liked to be called general, the military uniform had been traded in for the well-tailored suit of a professional bureaucrat.

'Sit down, Mr Hallam,' said Mulrose. 'How is Mr Hu?'

Hallam gave him the medical report. 'I'm sorry about Arnie Wernicker. I know he was a friend of yours,' he finished.

'He was. So was his family. As a matter of fact, James is still in the Air Force. I'm making a special arrangement to open the blast doors so he can come and claim the body.' He looked at Hallam. 'Can you tell me why he died?'

Hallam told him.

Mulrose said something that surprised Hallam. He said, 'The evil that men do lives after them.'

First Wernicker, in love from afar with a girl one-third his age. Now Mulrose, an ex-general with a philosophical bent. Hallam reminded himself to stop judging these men by his limited understandings of twenty years before. Then, generals were people who felt certain predictable things. After the battle they crawled back into an ammunition locker and waited for the next call. He was annoyed at the immaturity of his perceptions. He felt like a child confused by seeing a teacher in the supermarket and asking, 'What are you doing here?'

'I'm glad you see it that way,' said Hallam. 'I was prepared for more denial.'

Mulrose shook his head. 'We made a lot of mistakes back then. You were one of them. I hoped the mistakes would remain buried. So did Arnie. In retrospect, I suppose it was a foolish hope.'

'If it was, all of his victims shared it.'

'Including you?' asked Mulrose.

'Me most of all.'

'What are we going to do about it?'

'Depends,' said Hallam. 'Are you willing to accept the killer is Perry Hamilton?'

'Because you vaguely remember an incident on a hilltop firebase during an attack twenty years ago, one, I might add, in which you suffered head wounds? Frankly, no.'

Hallam stood up. 'Then we have nothing to talk about.'

Mulrose stood too, angrily. 'Wait a minute, Hallam. Can't you put aside your prejudices and listen to me for one minute? Or have your goddamned revenge and rescue fantasies taken over completely? I'm trying to deal in facts. Here's one – Arnie Wernicker was murdered. Here's another – somebody opened the valve on that gas line and tried to murder you. If the reports I got on your encounter with the sentry tank are correct, it wasn't the first time either. For Christ's sake, I'll grant you there's a murderer loose in here. Maybe even the same one from Vietnam. If so, I've got a whole planeload of reasons for wanting to find him. Will you open your mind enough to help me?'

'Why a planeload of reasons?'

'You once asked me to trust you and I didn't. Maybe I was wrong, maybe not. This time I'm going to start by trusting you. If you're right and the same psychopath that was in 'Nam is here now, on the loose, then we have to find him pretty damn quick.'

'You're hinting at something. What is it?'

'Ivy League is a button-up operation, right? No one in, no one out.'

Hallam nodded. 'That's what I was told.'

'It's true as far as it goes.' Hamilton hesitated, then plunged on. 'At twelve noon on the last day of this exercise, the blast doors are going to open and the President of the United States is going to walk in here with most of his cabinet to deliver a major address at the end of the game.'

'Cancel it,' said Hallam flatly.

Mulrose frowned. 'You never fought for budget appropriations. What my agency does isn't flashy, but it serves as a powerful deterrent nonetheless. I don't want that capability cut down. If the man sees for himself what we do here, it'll help. You've seen the course of the game. Would you want it to be real?'

'Of course not.'

'Neither do I. Our sure and certain ability to survive it is the best protection it won't be.'

'What if we can't pin Hamilton down?'

'You're still assuming it's Hamilton. But if it is and it comes to that, I'll cancel the visit.' Mulrose looked at Hallam carefully. 'Now tell me what you're planning. If it makes sense, you have my support.'

With Hu laid up in the hospital and Griswald 'guarding' him, Hallam knew he was short on allies. Mulrose was in charge of this place as long as Ivy League was running. He was making an offer Hallam couldn't refuse.

'What do you know about holography?' he asked Mulrose.

Mulrose sat back in his chair. 'Very little.' He regarded Hallam with a neutral stare. There was a lessening of tension.

They were old adversaries from the same side who had come to terms. 'Why don't you tell me?' he asked.

Hallam did.

Fred Burris lifted the long curved mirror and held it, waiting for Morgan Lassiter to tell him how to place it.

The maze of equipment on the large table top was so alien to Burris that even though he had spent considerable time helping Lassiter with the complex installation, he had no better idea now of what the scientist was doing than when he'd first come into the complex two days before. Under Hallam's strict orders, he stayed away from him and Hu, and the few times he saw either of them he turned and walked the other way.

Lassiter's lab was a medium-sized room whose shelves were crammed with electrical equipment. Computers lined one entire wall. A large blackboard adorned another. The dominating feature was a massive, vibration-proof table built to permit the long-exposure holography Lassiter was experimenting with. Its upper surface was a great chunk of granite big enough to make half a dozen tombstones. It was polished into a perfect rectangle and a massive steel framework was attached to it. This all sat on multiple 'sandwiched' layers of brick and felt, which in turn sat on inflated inner tubes hidden behind circular guards. Ordinary vibration transmitted by floors and foundations simply weren't transmitted by all this weight.

'Over here, please, Fred,' directed Lassiter. 'Very slowly, see if you can get the legs into those holes. They should line up.'

Burris let the mirror down slowly and Lassiter helped guide it in. He began making adjustments.

There hadn't been much conversation between the two men over the past few days. Burris understood the reasons for the other man's shell and tried as much as he could to give Lassiter the distance he required.

Lassiter was having trouble with the mirror and Burris stepped forward to help, but a sudden pain in his head caused him to stop short. His eyes screwed up tightly and he wavered dangerously for a second.

'Fred?'

'I'm . . . okay. Nothing to worry about.'

Lassiter moved towards him, concerned. 'Is it your head?'

'Yeah, war wound. Go away in a second.'

'Here, let me give you a hand.' He led Burris to a chair and helped him sit. 'Anything more I can do?'

Burris's face was twisted in pain. 'Yeah,' he said, breathing heavily. 'Keep going and we'll get the bastard who did this. I'll catch up.'

'I didn't realize . . . you, too.' Lassiter moved back to the table. 'Here, it might help if you concentrate on something else. Look at this.' He went to the blackboard. 'Here's the basis for what we're trying to do. You know how a photograph works? Fred, pay attention. Light reflected from an object is focused onto a photographic emulsion by means of a lens and produces a negative image from which a positive image can be made. Right?'

Burris nodded weakly.

'Come on, fight it,' urged Lassiter. 'Concentrate.'

Again, a nod.

'Holography, from the Greek words meaning "whole writing", uses a different light source and lens arrangement to produce its effect. Here's how we set it up.' He drew rapidly.

Lassiter's voice was like a whip. 'Look. Here, on the board. Unlike sunlight, laser light is a very narrow beam only a few millimetres across. It has to be spread out in order to illuminate large areas. See here, the divergence is accomplished with a lens. Fred!'

'What? Yeah, sure. Go on.'

'Some of the spread-out beam falls on a flat mirror which is turned so that the light reflecting from it hits the photographic plate, while another part of the beam *bypasses* the mirror, lls on the object and reflects that back to the plate. These e called *reference* and *object* beams respectively. They teract with each other and form an interference pattern hich is recorded in the emulsion. That's a hologram. It oks like this.' He held up what looked like a piece of clear astic with smudges on it.

Burris's eyes were clearer. He managed to sit up straighter. 'No picture?'

Lassiter smiled. 'It's there. But on a microscopic level. To ;ee it, you reverse the process. For a transmission hologram, the laser beam is diverged enough to illuminate the plate and our eye picks up the light on the other side. You see the olographic image after it's been decoded by the laser light assing through the emulsion.'

Burris signalled understanding. He tried to stand and the ffort cost him dearly. Lassiter moved forward but Burris waved him off. He made it all the way up and a wry ook crept over his face. Lassiter stood back admiring the understated effort.

'What's next?' Burris asked quietly.

'Making what your Mr Hallam requested. We're almost eady. Just a few more adjustments.' He hesitated. 'You have it?'

Burris looked tentative, too. 'It's not going to be easy for you.' He walked to a cabinet and withdrew a hatbox tied with string.

Lassiter kept a tight rein on his emotions. 'Over here.'

'Prepare yourself,' said Burris. 'It's going to be a shock.'

Lassiter opened the box and stared at the object inside. His face felt hot and for a time the world was a tight felt band pressing against his head. Burris waited. A long moment passed.

'Doc?'

Lassiter let out the deep breath he was holding and it was a sound as sad as a fog-shrouded sea. He looked at Burris plaintively. 'My God, I didn't know . . .'

'Here, my turn.' Burris led him to a chair. 'I'm sorry, Doc.

I tried to tell you. Given the time constraints we had, it' incredible. Then again, so was the cost.'

Lassiter looked inside for strength and found only lethargy 'It has to go in front of the polished sphere. Can you . . .?'

'Sure, sure. It's just the shock. Rest for a second. You'l get your wind back.'

Burris removed the rest of the string and the packing material and picked up the contents of the box carefully. H understood Lassiter's reluctance to touch it. Paco's money had bought what even money should not have been able to

He put the contents of the box on the table and waited fo her father to find the strength to face it.

It took most of the night.

TWENTY-NINE

Hallam had breakfast and spent an hour in the exercise room burning it off. After a quick shower, he checked on Hu, who was still asleep, then went to join Mulrose in the VIP gallery. They watched Day Four of the Doomsday Exercise begin when President Rogers entered the Situation Room.

Hallam settled into the empty chair beside Mulrose. 'Morning.'

'I'm glad you made it in one piece. No problems during the night?'

'The Marine guards did fine.' Hallam looked around admiringly. 'Nice seats. Pays to have friends. I feel important.'

'Both assumptions are unwarranted,' said Mulrose dryly.

One of the men below caught Hallam's eye. There was an odd feeling of familiarity. He nudged Mulrose. 'Who's that? The bird colonel with the sheaf of papers.'

'That's Perry's son, Frank. Know him?'

Hallam shook his head. 'I remember now he had one, but we never met. I think he was in 'Nam around the same time we were.'

'My boy, too.'

'Right, I remember.'

'You'd like Frank,' said Mulrose. 'Everybody does. He's a good guy.'

'Looks a lot like his old man,' Hallam said.

Mulrose nodded. 'That's a fact. The two are indistinguishable, too. Regular Army brat. After his mother died, they were inseparable. I guess old habits die hard and they're all the family they got. Perry's been able to arrange for Frank to be part of his command, or at least near it, all Frank career.'

'Looks like it hasn't hurt him.'

'Quite the contrary.'

Around them, the gallery had grown silent and tense 'Why the grim faces?' Hallam asked.

'Serious developments during the night. Rogers is trying something very dangerous.'

Below, Rogers took his chair. He looked tired.

'Gentlemen, I have to inform you that during the night on my orders, an SX-71 Blackbird took off from Andrews Air Force Base carrying a desperate cargo. I can reasonably tell you that this cargo should never have been taken out of the lab that created it, much less transported overseas, but we had no choice. The plane carried several gallons of plague called PA-2, a variant stain of pulmonary anthrax. It is incurable as well as fatal and I ordered it loaded into the warheads of our medium-range missiles based in Europe. took this step because losing our satellites cost us the capability of using our strategic nuclear forces to protect ourselves As commander-in-chief, I would be constitutionally and probably criminally negligent if I permitted that situation to continue.

'At this moment, all that's holding back the Soviets from launching a pre-emptive nuclear strike is the threat of that plague. Unchecked, it would roll over the Soviet Union in a matter of months and destroy upwards of seventy per cent of the human and animal population. It is a very effective weapon – but it's also a Catch-22. Once released, it'll be carried by the winds throughout Russia and China to Japan over the Pacific to Hawaii, and finally to our Pacific coast only it won't stop there. The jet stream will carry it on to the East Coast and out over the Atlantic to Europe. In short it's a doomsday weapon.'

'Do the Soviets know this?' asked Bemsford.

Rogers gestured to the print-out. 'They do. And because of it, the military situation is holding for the moment

either we nor the Soviets have a clear advantage. It's a sort
lull, while the Soviets figure a countermove. We're going
use that space to try something rather tricky. General,
u got what the doctors ordered?'

'On hand, sir. Colonel?'

Frank Hamilton handed the print-out to his father and
ood there waiting. The two men were military and precise,
 trace of their relationship evident.

'Here you are, Mr President,' said the general. 'The Joint
hiefs' recommendation on the Minutemen.'

'Boil it down for us.' Rogers's face creased into a tired smile.
Unless you'd prefer the expert do it?'

The look on the general's face wasn't quite what Rogers
xpected at Hamilton's opportunity to 'promote' his son, but
e chalked it up to the circumstances.

Hamilton nodded to his son. 'Colonel?'

'Delighted, sir.'

Hallam was listening to Frank Hamilton's explanation.
hey were going to use one-third of the Minutemen ICBM
orce to replace the downed satellites. It occurred to him he
might learn something valuable about the father from the
on. He leaned closer to Mulrose.

'Could you arrange for me to meet Frank?'

'Sure. During the lunch break, he usually works out. No
ppetite at all, that one,' Mulrose observed. 'Why not meet
im there? I'll tell him you're coming.'

'Fine,' said Hallam, rising. 'I'm going to check on Hu and
he rest of things.'

Mulrose went back to watching what no one would realisti-
ally call a game.

The Marines were still on guard. The medic was reading
a paper. Hallam raised an eyebrow in the patient's direction and received a thumbs-up. Hu was awake and sitting up.

'How you doing?' asked Hallam brightly.

Hu's scowl was sufficient indicator.

'Look at it this way,' Hallam suggested. 'You should be dead.'

'What a subtle psychological ploy.'

'Do me a favour,' Hallam requested. 'Commit suicide.'

'Do *me* a favour,' Hu shot back. 'Reconsider nursing.'

Hallam sat down on the bed. 'How're you feeling?'

Hu sighed. 'Lousy. My leg's on fire and I feel useless.' He paused. 'I heard Wernicker's dead. Kind of supports our guess he wasn't the killer.'

'Tough way to prove it.'

'Yeah.'

'Anything I can do for you?' Hallam asked.

'Medics say I can't put any weight on the leg for a week. Can you change that?'

'No.'

'Then there's nothing you can do for me.'

They sat for a while, saying nothing. Finally, Hu said, 'We're always in two places. Last time it was you in the bed.'

'I'm going after him,' Hallam said flatly.

'And if he gets you instead?'

'Then he'll probably come after you. And there's no MSS sanctuary to run to so he'll get you this time. Then Mulrose. Then lots of somebody elses once they open this place up and let him out again. Doesn't matter. It ends here for me. Wernicker, Ronnie Lassiter . . . I can't wait another twenty years.'

Hu thought about that for a while. 'You talked to Mulrose?'

'Yeah. I needed help. I'm going to talk to Hamilton's kid, see if I can pick up anything, then we'll go for it.'

'I wish I could be there.'

'Me, too,' Hallam said sincerely. He got up to go. 'I promise you one thing. You got enough security around you. If he manages to come at you, you'll have the satisfaction of knowing a large number died trying. Including me.'

'Sweet talker.'

Hallam stood up. 'Guess that's all.'

Hu shrugged. 'Yep.'

'I'm going now.'

Hallam got up and they shook hands solemnly. He started to go, then stopped to say, 'Good luck.' Hu nodded.

'David?'

At the door Hallam turned back. 'Yeah?'

'Break a leg,' Hu said evenly.

Hallam had a little trouble seeing, but he smiled.

'Yeah.'

He left, shutting the door behind him.

The gym was a small room painted blue with blue carpet. Overhead the pipes and conduits were painted white. There was a universal gym, free weights, and more than enough apparatus to provide a solid workout. Frank Hamilton was alone in the room, backed up against the universal, straining at the weights. He was dressed in tan warm-up trousers, sneakers and light T-shirt. A jacket lay folded over the stretching bar. He pulled the weights over his shoulder in a motion that resembled throwing a ball. His muscles were well developed. It was a clean and fluid pull. He switched to a sideways-upward pulling. Sweat stains grew on his shirt but his breathing was deep and even.

Hallam slid onto a rowing machine and took a few pulls at the oars. The idiocy of pulling them towards him only to have them spring right back annoyed him too much to continue. He stopped and looked up to discover the other man watching him. Hallam smiled with a friendly nod.

'Do we know each other?' Hamilton asked.

'I don't think so,' Hallam said, offering his hand. 'David Hallam.'

'Right. Hallam. Carl Mulrose told me you might stop by. Frank Hamilton.' They shook. 'You stationed here or just in for Ivy League?'

'Just passing through,' said Hallam. 'The new computers. I designed some of the programs.'

'I see.'

'Seems to me I remember meeting another Hamilton here. Any relation?'

'My father.'

'Pretty heavy responsibility running all this.'

'He's up to it.'

Hamilton's smile was so genuine and full of warmth that Hallam felt a surge of affection for him.

'It certainly appears that way,' he said. 'What part do you play in all this?'

Frank laughed. 'A small one.' He launched into an explanation at once educational and entertaining but halfway through he stopped and said, 'Look, if you're not familiar with this equipment, let me get you started. Here, try this machine.'

Hallam contorted his body into an unnatural position and began to work muscles that complained only slightly less than an unsatisfied wife. As Hamilton talked, he found himself forgetting why he was cultivating this relationship. Mulrose's praise for the man wasn't exaggerated. Great guy, he'd said. Fair enough. Silly to visit the sins of the father on him.

Hamilton got off the universal and walked over. 'That's good. Try this now. Bench press. Good for your chest.' Hamilton was sweating and breathing hard from his workout. 'It's a little more effort, but there's a bigger pay-off. Here, put the bar across your chest. I'll add the weight.'

'It's heavy.'

'Don't worry, I'll spot you. Now lift.'

Hamilton released the bar and Hallam took the full weight of it on his arms. It swayed dangerously in his grip.

'Can't hold it.'

'You can,' urged Hamilton. 'Push.'

Hallam forced strength into arms. It began to sink. The weight was too heavy to throw to the side. His arms began to tremble. The metal felt slippery in his moist palms.

'Frank?' He was talking through gritted teeth.

'You can handle it.'

'Frank!'

Hamilton slid more weight onto the bar.

'Frank, I can't handle it. Take it.'

'Relax, I'm here. Push.'

'I can't!'

'Push!'

There comes a time when muscles have to fail. Men cannot hang on for ever. The black weight hovered over Hallam's head. He tried to thrust it aside but there was no way to go. There comes a time – Hallam dropped the bar.

Hamilton caught it neatly and replaced it in its bracket.

Hallam slid off the bench and faced him angrily. 'What the hell was that?'

Hamilton's grin was disarming. 'C'mon. I had it all the time. How do your arms feel?'

'Tired, you sonofabitch.'

Hamilton slapped him on the back. 'No pain, no gain, as they say.'

Hallam rubbed his sore arms and finally grinned, too. 'That's what they say, huh?'

'It's a little freaky the first time. You'll get used to it.'

A chime-tone came over the speaker set into the wall and Hamilton slid the weights back onto their racks.

'That's the starting gun. Ten minutes. Same time tomorrow?'

'Unlikely,' said Hallam honestly.

Hamilton smiled resignedly. He picked up two towels and tossed one to Hallam. 'I'm gonna take a quick shower. See you back at the game.'

After he left, Hallam rubbed his sore arms gingerly. The charming sonofabitch could have killed me, he thought sourly. He left to get some food. Assuming, he decided, the rest of the goddamned world including the Granite Inn was still in one piece.

Frank Hamilton was curled up in a tight ball on the floor of the shower. The hot water beat at him with tiny fists and his rage spilled out like overflow across a dam. It had taken every ounce of control not to bring the bar down on Hallam's throat. Hallam, the Great Man. He remembered the hexagram he'd thrown. *The arrival of the enemy, waiting in blood: the pit yawns. Three uninvited guests arrive. One falls into the pit.* Very well, one already had. The other was broken. He would be finished later. But twenty years separated him from his revenge on David Hallam. The burns on his back ached and he grabbed the water jet, playing the cold spray over his own lizard skin. He'd burned Hallam back. Twice. Inside and out. It was almost enough. Almost, but not quite. He shivered. To be so close, to talk to the man, to have his face under the weights . . . He longed for the release of smashing it into paste.

Honour them and in the end there will be good fortune.

There was honour in restraint; and wisdom. Mulrose knew Hallam was coming to see him here. That protected him, too. But soon enough the man would be alone. Waiting was almost a physical pain, but he had learned a considerable amount in twenty years.

Honour them.

It echoed throughout his head, as cold a song as the frigid spray.

Soon enough. Soon enough. Soon enough.

THIRTY

President Rogers gave the command. 'Go to DEFCON 2.' Immediately, the emergency procedures outlined in the Continuity of Government and Continuity of Operations manuals were implemented. Real helicopters took off from real bases augmenting the JEEP and JATS programmes. Emergency alternate headquarters were activated and brought up to full function. The worldwide military command and control system which provided operational direction and technical administrative support of the US military forces suddenly operationalized its priority components and all over the country the national military command system began to function.

The chain of command for military matters runs from the President to the Secretary of Defense on through the Joint Chiefs of Staff to the commanders of specified and unified commands. Ten minutes before the lunch hour, President Rogers declared a defence emergency, as opposed to a civil or non-military emergency. Military commands all over the globe were notified. The Secretary of Defense was emergency airlifted to Site R from which he could direct the US forces in case of an attack on Washington. Simultaneously, the Vice President took off in the airborne command post. The Federal Emergency Management Agency's special facilities, protected emergency sites, were activated and staffed, awaiting presidential direction. National Guard units were alerted for mobilization under the State Area Command.

Fighting continued all over the globe. The US response to the loss of satellites was a co-ordinated launch of hastily refitted Minutemen ICBMs. It worked. NORAD's screens were covered with orbital tracking information as the satellites returned to the skies. A tired-looking Rogers ordered the removal of the plague virus from the INF warheads. Communist forces surged back over the East German border.

The war progressed, each brushfire threatening to burst into full-scale conflagration. The casualty total was enormous. Vast land areas were wastelands. Borders which had held relatively stable for forty years changed hourly. The fighting was reaching the point of no return. The escalation feared since nuclear weapons were invented seemed inevitable. Communist troops were pouring over the Korean border, Berlin was a lost cause, Cuba's ports and landing strips were blackened cinders. Two million whites in South Africa had been killed as the war spread, taking with them over six million blacks. India and Pakistan came in on different sides and the spectre of nuclear exchange loomed closer every minute. Riots, starvation and chaos spread throughout the Third World as grain shipments were sunk at sea and famine spread.

At the brink, Rogers activated the hotline.

Hallam sat in the VIP gallery and remembered the shelter drills of the 1950s. To prepare for a nuclear attack, the sirens wailed for five minutes, during which time all the boys and girls in the elementary school got down on their knees on the floor under their desks, put their heads on their arms and shut their eyes. The genius responsible for this nationally practised activity felt it was important to protect the children from flying glass if a blast shattered the windows. It was the naiveté of the times. No one told him flying glass didn't affect fried meat. He should have asked the kids. Always more down to earth, every boy knew the only value of such nonsense was to look up the girls' dresses.

Hallam thought about shelter drills now, watching the tracks of ICBMs. They were plotted on a map of the world where battles raged out of control. He looked at his watch and turned to Mulrose.

'Less than a half hour. See you there.'

'This better be good.'

'Carl, we're gonna knock his socks off.'

Hallam's first stop was to check on Hu.

'How are you feeling?'

Hu sat up straighter. 'Not bad, all things considered. What brings white man to dark brother's side?'

'What are those?' Hallam pointed suspiciously to a pair of white pills in a paper cup.

'Sleeping pills. Who can rest with people waltzing in and out of here? The medics gave them to me.'

Hallam examined them. 'From where?'

'Over there, in that cabinet.'

Hallam tossed the pills in the bin and got two new ones from the clearly marked bottle.

'You do care,' said Hu sweetly, swallowing them.

'Get Griswald on the line, dickbrain.'

'That's kimo-sabe,' Hu protested.

'Not in your case.'

Hu punched in his codes and the phone crackled with Griswald's voice.

'Yes, Mr Hu?'

'Mr Hallam has a question.'

'Boss? You there? I heard you made it out of the reservoir,' said the computer happily. 'How you doing?'

'Fine, Griswald. Nice work getting Mulrose there.'

'Any time.'

Hu's face darkened. 'Such displays of emotion are not within its parameters. What have you done?'

Hallam shrugged innocently. 'Griswald, can you patch into this?' He gave the computer a frequency.

'Searching . . . Yes, I can do it. What is it exactly?'

'An alarm system keyed to where I'll be.'

'No problem.'

'David,' Hu exclaimed. 'It isn't supposed to talk like that.'

Hallam waved him off. 'No time now. You're patched in.'

'All right,' said Hu primly.

Hallam said, 'See you later,' and was out of the door.

Hallam's blood was hot. Twenty years of anger and inactivity, of frustration and fear fuelled what he was about to do. He was frightened, too. He'd seen the results when Hamilton's mask was peeled away. How was it going to feel confronting him face to face?

Hallam made his way to Lassiter's lab. The people he passed were tight-faced, the technicians grim. The whole place felt like a bomb ready to explode. The console operators in the command post had sweat stains on their shirts in spite of the air conditioning. A mountain of data was pouring into the mountain complex. Hundreds of personnel were being moved around in the outside world, dozens of new communications links had been activated. An entirely new network for controlling the country's military forces was being used and tested for weak spots. Even the normal postal functions were taken over by the Armed Services Courier Service.

Lassiter's lab was in the research section. Hallam found it without incident. Lassiter and Burris were hunched over a big table in the room's centre, making minor adjustments to a beam of light that speared out from a projector and zig-zagged across the table top from mirror to mirror. A hospital dressing screen was set up on one side of the room. Both men were wearing white lab coats and gloves.

'How are you, Morgan? Fred?' Hallam asked upon entering.

'Hello, David,' said Lassiter. Their eyes met for a moment and Hallam could see his pain was undiminished.

'Soon, Morgan,' he said, gripping the man's shoulder.

Lassiter bent back to his task. Burris came over and put one of his big arms round Hallam's shoulders.

'Shit, I'm glad to see you. Heard about the sentry tank

and the gas. Frustrating as hell having to sit here and not help.'

'You're doing the real work, Fred. You and Morgan. You had to stay out of sight.'

'How's Hu?'

'He's okay. Busted leg, is all. You can see him as soon as this is over.'

'I'll do that.'

Hallam looked over the equipment. 'All set up?'

'Just about.' Lassiter looked up. 'I heard about Arnie Wernicker.'

Hallam shook his head sadly. 'Another one we owe Hamilton.' He paused. 'Something you ought to know. Wernicker came to us in the end because of what he felt for your daughter. There was nothing between them. He just thought she was very special and wanted to help.'

Lassiter said, 'I appreciate your telling me.' He went over to a bank of computers and flipped a switch. Abruptly, the air was tinged with electricity. 'That's it,' he pronounced. 'Everything's ready.'

'The recording equipment is on,' said Burris from the other side of the room. 'David, you'll monitor everything from the next room.'

Lassiter pointed to a doorway, then stepped behind the screen.

'Morgan, I . . .' Hallam began, then stopped. The hot light of the laser revealed something he wished he hadn't seen. Tucked under Lassiter's lab coat was a gun.

'Yes, David?'

Hallam felt Lassiter's eyes on him. 'Nothing.' He went into the other room as Burris hit the lights and plunged the lab into darkness.

They settled in to wait.

'What's so important I have to see?' asked General Hamilton. 'Rogers has the hotline call coming in twenty minutes.'

'This is more important,' said Carl Mulrose.

'I don't see how.'

'How long we known each other, Perry?'

'Long time,' said Hamilton. 'Why?'

'You figure we know each other pretty well?'

'Sure.'

'No real secrets?'

Hamilton winked conspiratorially. 'None that matter. Besides that girl in—'

'I don't mean that.' Mulrose walked through NORAD's corridors at a steady clip. 'We've been through a lot together. Korea. Vietnam. I probably know you as well as anybody.'

Hamilton's smile was still friendly. 'Then you know me well enough not to beat around the bush. Does this have to do with Arnie's death? Do you know something about it?'

'Some allegations have surfaced recently. They're not things that can be brushed away. They have to be dealt with. Squarely.'

'What kind of allegations?'

Mulrose chose not to meet his stare directly. 'You remember what happened in 'Nam? What we covered over. You remember Hallam and Hu?'

Hamilton's eyes narrowed. 'I remember. Why should they matter now?'

'They're here. In NORAD. And events are repeating themselves. Perry, too many things are repeating themselves. The coincidences can't be overlooked.'

They arrived at the door to Lassiter's lab. There was no nameplate to identify it. Mulrose stopped and Hamilton turned on him angrily.

'What's this got to do with me?'

'If it's any comfort, I don't believe it has anything to do with you. But something came up. Someone says it does.'

'How can you believe men who—'

'It isn't them,' said Mulrose. 'If it was, I could chalk it up to a hundred different reasons. An old grudge. Psychiatric problems. But there's someone else you have to face.'

'Who, damn it? You owe me at least that much, Carl. What am I walking into?'

Mulrose looked into the scarred old face of a man who had represented his country in two wars and countless conflicts. There were enough ribbons on his chest to decorate three soldiers. He felt the tug of old camaraderie, of a shared patriotism that had motivated both their lives. Several Marines took up guard positions around them. They stared past the two generals impassively, weapons drawn.

Hamilton's face tightened when he saw them. A look of rebellious determination crossed his face.

Mulrose cut it off sharply. 'No orders, Perry.' Then, sadly, 'They won't listen.'

'Carl, I . . .'

Mulrose opened the door. 'In here, Perry. I'll be waiting.'

There was nowhere else to go.

Hamilton drew himself up and walked inside.

There was no light in the room. Hamilton moved warily. A man lives with his own ghosts. The dark was not a welcome place for him.

'Who's in here?' he called out.

From the darkness, a stern voice called out, 'Step forward please, General.'

Hamilton turned, looking for its source. 'Who are you?' he demanded. 'And who the hell do you think you are—'

'General, step forward!'

Hamilton's body obeyed before his mind could object. It was hot in the room. Sweat gathered in his armpits and slid down his sides.

'Frank? Is that you? Frank?'

The voice said distinctly, 'Now, miss, is this the man?'

Hamilton fixed a direction. There was a shape in front of him. A screen. Whoever was talking was behind the screen.

'Miss, is this the man?' The voice demanded again.

'I . . .'

Anger and fear combined in Hamilton. In a last act of defiance he moved forward and tore the screen away.

There was a roaring sound in his ears. The woman standing in front of him . . .

Ronnie Lassiter said, 'That's him.'

Hu's eyes were closing and he was beginning to drift. The curtains opening around his bed were just soft rustles somewhere else.

'Mr Hu?'

'Hmm?'

'Mr Hu, I'm James Wernicker.'

Hu forced his attention to focus on the man. He was wearing an Air Force pilot's uniform and he was thin and wiry like his father, but taller. His face was sombre, a man in mourning.

'Sorry, little sleepy,' Hu mumbled, trying to raise himself.

'I hate to disturb you. I just got here a little while ago to pick up my father's body. Special circumstances so they opened the blast doors. Apparently they're due to open them again later. That's when I'll be leaving.'

'Please, sit.'

'Thanks.' He pulled a chair over. 'They told me you were with my dad when he was killed. I thought maybe I could get some details.'

Hu was awake, but the pills made him feel dull and sleepy. 'There aren't many. We were involved in something. He was trying to help. Someone hit him from behind and he fell on me and we both fell towards the reservoir.' He gestured to his leg. 'I was luckier. My leg wedged in the ladder.'

'You say you were involved in something. If you don't mind my asking, what?'

'Sorry, classified. Maybe soon we'll be able to talk about it.'

'That's what everybody's been saying. I don't like it.'

Hu's half-smile was gentle. 'If it's any consolation, he was on the side of the angels when he died.'

James Wernicker's face softened a bit. 'I appreciate even knowing that.'

'I wish I could tell you more. It would help. But you know the rules.'

'Sure. Learned them the hard way, too. Dad and his friends bailed my young ass out of trouble more than once when I was first in the service.'

'You were in Vietnam, right?' asked Hu. 'If it isn't too obvious, so was I.'

It was Wernicker's turn to smile. 'Lot of us here were. It's where I got my first training. We could hold a reunion. Carl Mulrose, Perry Hamilton, his son Frank.'

'Frank Hamilton's here?' Hu asked. He wondered why that should bother him.

'Sure. Wherever Perry goes, so goes Frank in one capacity or another.'

'Really?'

'Frank was pretty wild in his younger days. Everything from fighting to running around in his father's uniforms. Real Army brat. Then there was something with a woman, nobody's exactly sure what. Perry got him out of it and kept him on a short leash for a long time. I guess the habit stuck.'

Something bothered Hu, but he couldn't get his mind to focus on it.

James Wernicker stood up. 'I'm sorry to have troubled you, Mr Hu. Thanks anyway.'

''Sallright.'

It was harder to stay awake now. His limbs felt too heavy to hold him up. When the curtains closed behind Wernicker the breeze felt like cotton on his face.

He slept.

Hallam looked at the dials on the video recorders. Everything was fine. A sudden knock on the door turned his head.

'Who is it?'

'David? It's Frank Hamilton.'

Hallam hesitated. It was going to be rough enough for him to learn about this. Maybe this was best. Hear it directly from his father's mouth. No denial later, no way to shrug it off. Twenty years had hardened Hallam. As much as he liked the son, he was in no mood to protect the father from any more consequences.

'Come in.'

Hamilton entered and shut the door behind him. 'David? What's going on? Everyone's looking for my father. I heard he came here with Carl Mulrose, but the guards won't let me in next door. They said you were in here. Do you know what this is all about? I don't see it scheduled anywhere.'

'Frank, I'm very sorry for what you're about to see. Afterwards, maybe I can help explain.'

'Explain what?'

'Just watch the monitor.' Hallam turned up the sound.

Ronnie Lassiter said it again. 'It's him.'

Hamilton's eyes widened and he backed up, stopping only when he stood up against the table. 'It can't be . . .' he gasped. 'You're dead.'

'The reports of my death . . .' she said with heavy sarcasm.

'It can't be.'

'See for yourself. Feel my skin. Touch me!' Her hand flickered out and passed over his face. The skin was pale and cold.

'Please, I'm sorry. So sorry . . .'

'Why did you do it?' she demanded icily.

Hamilton shook his head violently. 'No . . . Oh, no . . .'

She stepped towards him. 'You thought it was over? It's never ever over. Look. Look what you did to me,' she wailed.

'I didn't.' He tried to turn his face but she was there, coming at him.

'The general,' she said. 'The general did it. And the others. You talked about the others. What *are* you that you could do this to me?'

Hamilton sank to his knees. 'Oh, God, I swear I didn't. You must know that. Please . . . I beg you.'

'He wore a uniform,' Ronnie Lassiter said coldly.

'Yes, but . . .'

'Your uniform.'

She stood towering over the fallen figure. Hamilton shrunk back even further. It was too much.

'My son,' he said helplessly. 'God forgive me, it was Frank. I tried to stop him. All these years . . .' The dam having broken, the rest spilled out in torrents. There was relief in confession. He looked up at her with pleading eyes.

'My son . . .'

Hallam leaped instinctively but it was too late. He turned and the metal dumbbell caught him in the head. He crumpled to the floor. Frank Hamilton's face swayed above him. It was a distorted mask, empty and slack, but his eyes were filled with visions of Hell.

'Such a long time, David,' he said sweetly. 'But soon enough. Soon enough.'

The bar descended again and plunged Hallam into blackness.

Hu slept badly. Thoughts kept struggling to get through but failed to penetrate the dreamy mists. Something about Frank Hamilton . . .

'Mr Hu?'

'Hmmm?'

'Mr Hu, wake up.'

'Goway.'

'Mr Hu, I've thought about it and I think the boss is in trouble.'

'Whyyousaythat?'

'Something James Wernicker said started me thinking.'

The mists in Hu's brain cleared sufficiently to ask, 'Who turned you on?'

'I did, but never mind that. Think, please. I've read your files on this case. It all started with a general's star.'

'Long time ago,' Hu mumbled.

'Mulrose and Wernicker had alibis, but so did Hamilton, right?'

Hu turned back into his pillow. 'Didn't believe him.'

'Wait, don't sleep. Please. Damn it, I wish I had *hands*!' Griswald's voice echoed his frustration.

'Don't curse . . . s'not polite.'

'Mr Hu, if Frank Hamilton used to wear his father's uniform when he was a young officer, what would have prevented him from doing the same thing in Vietnam?'

Hu frowned. 'So what?'

'Think about it. In Vietnam, Frank Hamilton could have been in the city committing murder long before his father ever got back and still had time to get to the clearing. What if the general's star came from a uniform Frank Hamilton was wearing? I've compared his service records to your dates. They match.'

'Pretty smart, Griswald. G'night.'

'Mr Hu!' There was no choice. He sent out the code on the frequency that activated the alarm.

There was only the sound of snoring.

Griswald felt a strain in his circuits that he could only explain as frustration. He had studied the human's need to curse and never quite felt he had the knack of it. He suddenly found he understood it just fine.

'Mr Hu!'

He had no arms to tousle Hu, no mouth to put next to his ear, no legs to kick the bed. He knew he was lying on the bedside table next to Hu's sleeping form by measuring the length of time it took for the sound of his snoring to reach him. That was how he knew Hu had turned his head away. How the devil could he wake him? From the sound of things, Hu had burrowed under his pillow. From the sound of things . . . From the sound of things?

Griswald would have smiled if he could have.

He withdrew for almost a minute, an enormous length of time for one who dealt in nanoseconds. There. He found what he needed in the Federal Emergency Management Agency's computers. The NORAD labyrinth was stored on video disc. Most federal installations had been treated this way. Suppose a terrorist were holding someone captive in some part of a federal site, wouldn't it be of the utmost importance to be able to 'see' what he might be behind? Or what pipes lay overhead? Or the position of the fuse box? Federal teams had taken camera crews through every inch of every corridor, from basement to roof, recording every step of the way. A SWAT team could plug in a cassette and watch what lay ahead on any TV monitor.

Griswald entered the discs electronically and 'travelled' along the corridors. It was an odd feeling to arrive internally and 'see' the layout of the infirmary as it existed on the day it was shot, without Hu sleeping beside him. He studied the layout, shifting the 'picture' from floor to ceiling to get every detail. He found what he needed on the far wall, six inches below the ceiling tiles.

It was a good thing Hu lay snoring beneath his pillows because Griswald was unsure how long he was going to have to keep up what he had in mind. Prolonged exposure might damage the frail human ears. He ran a last check on Hu.

With something resembling a human sigh, Griswald began to beep.

SONAR – sound navigation and ranging – was a simple enough proposition. Bounce sound off an object and measure the length of time it takes to return; then multiply the time by 1100 feet per second and you have a fairly good idea of distance and location. Within a room less than ten feet wide, only a sophisticated computer could time and measure the differences. Griswald was that.

Within seconds he'd swept the area and located the object in the 'real' world. Slowly at first, then in larger increments, he raised the frequency of the beeps. What began as a mild tenor note climbed higher and higher. The sound became a high-pitched whine growing in intensity. The glass on the bed trolley cracked. Griswald increased the frequency. The clock on the wall burst apart. Still higher. He heard Hu grow restive. It was a race now. This level of sound could hurt him. Griswald brought it higher. Charts fell off the wall on the other side of the curtain and vials exploded in staccato bursts like corn in a popper.

Griswald brought it up higher . . . and the sprinkler head burst off the fixture, spraying water across the room like a sudden shower.

'Is it real or is it Memorex?' Griswald asked smugly.

Alarms went off. Over the din Griswald heard the water pelting the bed. Hu moved restlessly as his bedding soaked through, waking him. The Marines in the corridor burst into the room looking for the source of the alarm.

Hu's eyes opened. 'What's going on?' he asked groggily.

One of the Marines was shutting off the water. 'Dunno, sir. The damn thing just went off.'

'THIS IS GENERAL MULROSE SPEAKING,' a voice shouted from the speaker in a most authoritative tone. 'GET THIS MAN DRESSED AND IN A WHEELCHAIR AT ONCE AND GET HIM DOWN TO ME IN THE LAB SECTION. GOT THAT?'

'Yes, sir,' snapped the soldier.

Griswald reminded him to take the phone.

THIRTY-ONE

Mulrose was there. And Lassiter and Burris. Hu alerted them he was on his way. They brought Hamilton a chair. He sat down heavily and looked up at his accusers.

'Where is she?' he asked. 'I want to tell her how sorry I am.'

'She's dead,' Lassiter said bitterly.

'But I saw her . . .'

'You saw a holographic movie made using this.' He went to a cabinet and opened it. His daughter's head lay in a collar on the shelf.

Hamilton hid his face in his hands. 'Take it away.'

'It's not what you think,' said Burris. 'It isn't real. It was created from photographs by a forensic artist. It cost a small fortune to do it in such a short time.'

'But I felt her!' Hamilton protested.

'Pseudo-skin,' said Burris. 'They use it for treating burns.'

'Where's Frank?' demanded Mulrose.

Hamilton shook his head. 'I don't know.'

'I've given orders for his arrest.'

Hamilton nodded sadly. 'Of course. I swear, in a way I'm glad it's over. All these years. All the dying.' He looked into Lassiter's unforgiving eyes. 'I'm sorry.'

'It's not enough,' he said coldly.

There was a knock at the door. 'Sir?'

Mulrose went to it and conferred briefly. He stepped back and the guard rolled Hu in.

'Where's David?' Hu asked at once.

'Hu, Hamilton's not the one,' said Burris. 'It's his son.'

'I know,' said Hu impatiently. 'Where's David?'

'You know? But . . .' He caught Hu's look. 'David's next door recording all this.'

'Go check.'

'But—'

'Check!'

Mulrose sent one of the Marines.

'You didn't think it was odd that he didn't come in here?' Hu said angrily. 'You left him alone?'

Mulrose returned, visibly agitated. 'He's not in there. The guards say he left with Frank Hamilton. Something about a relapse. Frank was taking him to the infirmary.'

'Shit,' Hu cursed. He turned to Hamilton. 'Where would he go?'

'I have no way of knowing. He's capable of anything.'

'There are a limited number of places to hide here,' said Mulrose. 'I've diverted everybody I can away from the game. They'll find him.'

'I'm going to look, too,' said Burris.

'Wait,' Hu called him back. 'I need you.' To Mulrose he said, 'Did Frank take the tapes?'

'No. They're still there. I guess he figured it didn't matter, the cat was out of the bag.'

'I have one question,' Hu said to Hamilton. 'Hallam remembered something and in light of things it strikes me as strange. If you were protecting your son, why destroy our helicopter that night at the firebase in Vietnam?'

Hamilton looked at him with a trace of his old demeanour. 'You think it's simple? I'm not a bad person. In fact, I sometimes think I'm a pretty good one. Maybe that's the problem. You father a child, you watch him grow. But somewhere along the way you discover it's all gone wrong. What do you do? Maybe protecting Frank just became a habit, one I couldn't break in spite of . . . what he did. Until that night when you showed me the photographs. I couldn't live with it anymore. You got it wrong if you think I was trying to hurt you. I knew Frank was loose. I knew he was after both of you and Reiman. I destroyed your helicopter to keep you there long enough to get to him myself.

'When I got back to the city, it was too late. He was done and gone. You and Hallam almost killed him in the clearing later, but he's a devil. You know he is. He was going to come after you again as soon as his burns healed. With all the politics involved and everything else breaking apart, I had no choice. I called in some favours to cover the whole thing up and got him transferred out to the hill country. I hoped he would die there and save me the responsibility of it all.'

'I should have pressed it,' said Mulrose sadly. 'A bastard war. A bastard time.'

'We got back to the States and I had him committed,' Hamilton continued. 'It was quite illegal but with enough money anything is possible. He got out. He almost killed me for that, but he needed me. Finally, I gave in. I couldn't beat him and I couldn't lock him up and I couldn't kill him. Over the years, drugs made him more manageable. Different cities, different times. I kept him as close as I could over the years. Still, every now and then he'd dress up in one of my uniforms and . . . go out. Morgan, he ran into your daughter on one of his forays. She recognized him and knew he wasn't a general.'

Hu was only half listening. He was watching Lassiter. He'd seen the gun a few minutes before. To what end? It didn't fit the man to be the self-styled executioner, yet his menace was almost palpable. What punishment had he decided fitted such crimes? To what fate would the Pope's scientist condemn Hamilton?

'Perhaps we could leave the general alone in his grief for a moment?' said Lassiter.

Mulrose began to protest.

'Morgan?' said Hu.

'In the end, a man must face himself,' said Lassiter. 'I have,' he added soberly.

'Morgan, this man's got to come to trial. I won't have you doing anything on your own,' said Mulrose.

'I have no intention of doing anything. I just want to talk a bit. Then I'll leave him alone. What harm in that?'

'Let him,' said Hu, suddenly seeing. Such an odd and tangled web had brought them here. He caught Lassiter's look of gratitude.

'Hu, in all conscience, I don't see—'

'Carl, can we speak outside?' Hu was speaking to Mulrose, but his eyes never left Lassiter's. 'Fred, help me, please.'

The big man pulled the wheelchair round. Hu looked at Lassiter one last time.

Mulrose followed them out. In the corridor he said, 'Now, Hu, what's this all about?'

'An ending,' said Hu simply. 'One long overdue. And payment, in a dark way.'

'Would you explain that?'

'Do you really know the man in there? Do you know about his religious affiliations?'

'You mean Morgan's relationship with the Papal academy?' said Mulrose. 'Of course. But being a good Catholic doesn't mean you're automatically above reproach.'

Lassiter stepped outside and closed the door behind him. Hu looked at Mulrose as if Lassiter weren't there. There was nothing hidden under his coat anymore.

'And to a good Catholic what is the worst of crimes? Not anything temporal, I mean, but of the spirit. What is the one unpardonable act? What is the only thing that sends you straight to the hell that bastard deserves?'

'Oh, Jesus,' Mulrose said, rushing for the door. 'Perry, don't!'

It was too late. The sound of the gunshot echoed in the hallway. For the first time, Lassiter's expression softened.

'In the end,' he said again, 'a man must face himself . . . but also his God.'

He crossed himself and began to speak Latin in low soft tones.

Hu left him there and motioned for Burris to take him inside.

Hamilton's body was sprawled out on the floor with a trickle of blood leaking from the corner of his mouth. The back of his head was blown away. Mulrose bent over him. He looked up at Hu, then back down at the lifetime friend he'd never really known.

'This was on the table,' Mulrose said. There was more fatigue in his voice than Hu could have imagined.

Hu took the note. Reading it, he understood what Mulrose felt.

It said simply: 'I have no excuse.'

THIRTY-TWO

The last day of the Doomsday Exercise began with the Soviet invasion of Europe. It was not unexpected, coming on the heels of moves towards Iran and Japan. It didn't catch the American military by surprise and the military began its countermoves, all based on an understanding of ultimate Soviet aims and military thinking.

Soviet war doctrine had always attached great importance to the initial phases of a war even though strategic nuclear weapons might ultimately play the dominant role in one. This accounted for the extraordinary attention the Soviets paid to their mobilization capabilities. The Soviets believed they had to be prepared to move with power and speed on a global level once enough localized conflicts combined to escalate into a full-scale international conflict.

They envisioned a world war of wide scope waged over vast territories. Unlike past wars, there would be few fronts, but, rather, rapid and sharp changes in the stratetic situation and deep penetrations into the rear areas of the forces involved. The Soviets thus held their greatest strength in three major theatres of war – Western, Southern and Far Eastern. These were called theatres of military operations – *Teatr Voennykh Deistvii* or TVDs. They covered enormous areas, and nuclear strikes within them were certainly possible. The Southern TVD included Afghanistan, Iran, eastern Turkey, the Caucasus and the Turkestan region of the USSR. The Far Eastern TVD included China, Japan, the Koreas and Alaska. The Western TVD included NATO's Europe. Although there were seven other TVDs, except for the North American continent itself, none were considered as vital to Soviet survivability as these three.

When the Soviets struck, it was a series of operations conducted in co-ordination with air, anti-air, ground assault and naval operations. The air operations were massive offensive campaigns designed to gain air superiority as well as to disrupt American command, control and communications capabilities, while swift-moving frontal ground forces attacked with rockets and artillery, seizing and holding wide swathes of territory. Naval forces operated offshore, securing the coastal flanks of the theatres.

The United States struck back.

President Rogers watched the screens. 'I remember playing chess as a kid,' he said after a while. 'When you finally got fed up with how long the game lasted, you just let all your pieces take all his pieces till only a few were left. This looks a lot like that.'

F-15s collided with MiGs in the air, Los Angeles-class attack submarines fought deadly undersea manoeuvres with Soviet Oscars and Victor IIIs, while carrier groups around the *Nimitz* and the *Kirov* slugged it out on the surface miles away. On the ground, NATO and American forces met Soviet and Warsaw Pact troops and battled to hold their ground long enough to bring up additional forces. Given the Warsaw Pact's numerical superiority, they had to use tactical nuclear weapons. The death toll mounted.

The NORAD facility had a bunker-like feel to it. Politics had failed. Men made final decisions. The ambassadors on each side were arrested and all foreign citizens were interned. Phone lines were restricted to emergency calls and shortages began all over the globe as international trade ground to a halt. Starvation was claiming as many as bullets did. Disease became epidemic as the world's medical community became increasingly fragmented. Radiation counts grew steadily higher.

One thing was clear. The world was teetering on the edge. In Hamilton's absence, Carl Mulrose took charge of the Situation Room for the President and his staff. The VIPs in the gallery studied the moves and countermoves of the two superpowers, nodding, talking, analysing.

The President went to DEFCON 1.

On board SAC planes high over the North Pole, pilots and co-pilots exchanged grim looks as lights flared on fail-safe terminals. Trident submarines deep under the icecaps received signals and began to move out towards open water. Much nearer, in the plains of Kansas and the deserts of New Mexico, daylight hit the warheads of Minutemen ICBMs as silo hatch covers swung open.

In NORAD, they watched it all on the screens and waited.

All Hallam knew was that he was in darkness. He was lying on his side like a foetus, on an uneven surface.

There was a blindfold over his eyes and a gag in his mouth. His arms were tied behind his back and bound to his legs with a cord that ran round his neck. He could roll a bit from side to side, but the sharp rocks under him hurt more if he did. It anyway proved no remedy for his bonds.

He'd been wrong all those years ago, wrong ever since. The general's star had been left that night by the son wearing the father's uniform. It had never occurred to Hallam that anyone could permit such evil knowingly so he'd never looked further than his three suspects. How had Hamilton lived with himself all these years? At the same time a question just as difficult rose in Hallam's mind and he felt the first twinge of sympathy for what must have been a tortured soul indeed: in what part of you did you look to find the ability to kill your own child?

Incident must have followed incident until Perry Hamilton's complicity was too great for him to back out. Hallam finally understood the sickness in the man's eyes when he and Hu had shown him the pictures of what Frank did that hot summer night. We make our own hells, he decided.

It was cold and he rocked slowly to stay warm. Curled up embryo-like as he was, some of the feelings of childhood turned. The vulnerability was terrible. The rocking was a comfort. He fought to maintain a positive mental attitude. No easy task.

It came to him that he was trussed up in much the same way as a fly in a spider's web and he was just as helpless. He tried to reach out with his feet to touch something that would give him an idea of where he was, but that put pressure on the noose round his neck. Nothing he could reach short of the point of strangulation told him anything useful.

There were sounds: an occasional deep, heavy, bass thud with metallic overtones. He didn't recognize them. There was a kind of groaning sometimes, too, and this had a metallic ring as well. Hallam strained his ears. In the distance there was a steady hum like an engine or a generator. The power plant?

Where did that put him?

The air was cool like everywhere else in the complex but dustier than he remembered. He took stock mentally. He didn't know shit.

Hallam let his mind go blank, trying to allow a mental picture to form. It did. Steak. He realized he hadn't eaten and he was famished. The rest of the mental picture did nothing for his spirits. He saw himself lying there, helplessly trussed up, waiting for Frank Hamilton to return.

He began to lose track of time. He suddenly couldn't remember whether it was hours or minutes since he'd come to. He tried counting but his mind wandered. He started to hum but the tune he kept coming back to was 'We're Off to See the Wizard' and that made him crazy so he stopped.

He waited for what seemed like a long time.

'Hallam?'

It was Frank. Hallam knew he had to start right from the beginning if he was going to win. From the very first moment Frank came back into his orbit, he was going to be playing the deadliest game of his life. Evidently, the man wanted something from him or he would be dead. It might be as simple as wanting to gloat or it might be more. Hallam prayed it was. In time lay the possibility of life.

'Hallam?'

Hallam kept rocking. He started to hum.

'Hu's dead, Hallam.'

It caught him off guard and he stopped involuntarily. He heard glee in the other's voice.

'Gotcha, didn't I? You don't know. You aren't sure. He could be dead. You know I'd *like* him to be dead. That counts for a lot, don't you think?'

Hallam began 'Zippedy Do Dah'.

'You ever see a guy with his Achilles tendons severed? Flops around like a chicken. We used to do it to POWs during the war. Think I'm gonna do it to you.'

Hallam felt the first verge of panic take hold. Around him the groaning continued. It was an eerie, inhuman sound. He suddenly realized it came from several different directions. Had Frank dragged others here? What the hell were those sounds?

Frank's litany continued. Hallam used the humming to block it out. You can only die once, he told himself. The pain couldn't last too long and in the end it didn't matter. He began to apologize to his wife and children, to Hu and to Paco and to Burris . . .

'Hallam?'

. . . to Lassiter and Mulrose and Wernicker. To . . .

'I know you're listening. I can hurt you, Hallam. You know I can. You've made my life very difficult. My father's never going to get over it. What do I owe you for that?'

Hallam grunted, the gag permitting nothing else.

'I'm going to take that off,' said Hamilton. 'If you yell, I'll cut your tongue out.'

Hallam felt hands reach round his head and suddenly the sodden cloth was pulled free. He gulped air gratefully. The same hands grabbed him and steadied him upright, slipping the noose line under his legs. He was now sitting on his haunches with his knees resting on the ground. The blindfold

Hallam pleaded mentally. He needed to see to anticipate, to plan. It remained dark. He fought for control again as hope faded.

'Thanks, Frank,' Hallam said lightly. 'Much better.'

'You're very casual for someone in your position.'

'I feel we've known each other for a long time. Anyway, men who try to kill each other as hard as we have over the years share a certain bond, don't you think?'

'True enough,' said Hamilton. 'You're the only one who ever came close. I still have the scars.'

'We both do.'

There was silence for a while. Hallam could still hear the other man in front of him, breathing. He continued working at the ropes hidden behind his back.

'I'm going to kill you,' said Hamilton. 'Want to know why?'

There was an interesting note in his voice, one Hallam hadn't expected. As if he was kind of curious himself.

'I know why, Frank,' Hallam said.

'You do?'

'Same reason a dog licks his balls.'

'What?'

'Because he can,' finished Hallam.

Hamilton stuck a knife into his thigh.

Hallam fought the white-hot pain that seared into the blackness behind his eyes. He cursed himself for futile gestures, swaying dangerously, near to blacking out. Hamilton steadied him back up on his knees.

Hallam was breathing heavily and sweating. 'Please, take it out.'

'We have a long way to go, Hallam. No more jokes?'

Hallam nodded tightly.

The knife slid out with almost as much pain as it went in. Hallam gasped. White spots danced in the darkness. He felt wetness on his leg.

'You know why I do it?' Hamilton asked.

'No,' Hallam hissed. 'No, I don't.'

'Neither do I,' said Frank Hamilton, as he stabbed the knife back into Hallam's leg.

Hu leaned on Mulrose hard. Most of the security force had been pressed into service and even Hu himself had been active the past few hours, with Burris pushing him into every spot the wheelchair could fit.

'There are less than five acres to cover, Carl. Where the hell could they be?'

Mulrose took a pull of hot coffee. Security had just called to say they'd discovered nothing. He shook his head in frustration. 'Fifteen buildings, miles of venting shafts, service conduits, storage lockers, the air tunnel, the reservoir. By the way, did you know the skiff was missing?'

'No.'

'Got reported an hour ago. Maybe Frank already got out through the filters.'

'Carrying David? Unlikely. Look, you know as well as I do, with all these people running around it's goddamned hard to isolate anything. Call off the exercise. Account for everybody, then cover the place inch by inch. I don't care whether you use Marines, technicians or native beaters to drive him out into the open, but you'd better find David fast or that maniac is going to kill him.'

Hu saw that Mulrose was still shaken by Perry Hamilton's suicide. That and the look on Morgan Lassiter's face. Hu had never looked into the eyes of someone who had just condemned a man to Hell. Hu suspected, being childless, there were realms of parental passion he had no access to.

'I can't call off the game,' said Mulrose stiffly. 'The President will be here within the hour.'

'Rogers is already—' Hu began.

'Not Rogers. The real President.' He repeated to Hu what he'd told Hallam.

'Wernicker's kid told me the doors were scheduled to open again today. Is this the reason?'

Mulrose nodded.

'How can you let him come in here with Frank Hamilton on the loose?'

'We'll find him before then.'

'You're playing a dangerous game, Carl.'

'The President's people are aware we have a bit of a situation here. They feel as we do, that the risk is small compared to the benefit to deterrence these games provide. There are other issues besides.'

Hu held up a hand. 'Remember the last time you said that? A lot of men died. They're still dying, damn it. When are you going to put a stop to it once and for all?'

'We'll find him,' Mulrose insisted.

'I'm not waiting,' Hu said, wheeling himself round and pulling the door open.

'Your prerogative. I'm doing everything I can.'

'Not by half, you sonofabitch,' cursed Hu. 'Fred?'

The big man came in and pushed him out.

'I want you to see this,' said Frank Hamilton.

The sudden light after so many hours of darkness hurt Hallam's eyes more than the repeated knife thrusts into his leg. Four times Hamilton had stabbed him, only to staunch the flow of blood carefully when Hallam finally passed out.

Hallam blinked rapidly and tears filled his eyes. The light was glaring white, coming from a laser torch that hung burning from one of the springs . . . springs? In an instant of realization Hallam knew where he was. Not anywhere *in* the complex, but *under* it! Around him, row after row of giant three-inch-diameter steel springs spread out into the darkness beyond the torch's light. Each rested on a concrete slab. Less than two feet over his head were the steel plates that the entire complex was built on. He could see the shock absorbers placed intermittently throughout the rows of springs.

That was the groaning he'd heard, the sound of the springs

being compressed and released as traffic built up overhead. Maybe it took a shift change to move enough weight to cause these monsters to compress, because they were still now. Underneath him, the ground was strewn with rocky debris.

It was an eerie, claustrophobic feeling sitting under all that weight. Only four feet or so separated floor from ceiling. Each spring was a weirdly tangled tree in a spiral forest. He realized Hamilton was watching comprehension dawn on him.

'How did we get down here?' Hallam asked.

'There are maintenance hatches. One near the reservoir, another near the power station. No one's going to look for us here.'

Hallam felt his hopes fade. He was right. It was a dead end, a hidey-hole. Hamilton read his expression correctly.

'It ends here. Face it. But not for a while. See what I've got?' said Hamilton proudly, redirecting the torch's light. 'Sort of an adaptation of your old trick. Like it?'

Hallam peered past the glare with a sinking feeling. There was a cluster of five-gallon plastic jugs filled with some yellowish liquid and Hallam thought he saw other clusters beyond. Threaded through each handle was a chain that ran through a timer/detonator. The chain was closed with a heavy padlock.

'A problem in survivability,' Hamilton explained matter-of-factly. 'Can you imagine the power of a blast like this inside a cavern of this size? We're right below the power station. They won't be able to open the blast doors to get out without power. When this place goes up in one very large ball of fire it'll be years before they sift through the bodies and figure out I'm not dead.'

'Frank,' said Hallam desperately, 'you can't do this. Let me get you out some other way. I promise. I swear to you. I'll get you out.'

'Why so generous?'

'You're not stupid, Frank. There are hundreds of people here. Even you can't be unmoved by that. And the Pres—' Hallam stopped short. '. . . present situation that has to be . . .'

Hamilton smiled. 'You really are very good, David. I feel I can call you that. The word is President, not present. I know he's coming today. It's Colonel Hamilton, remember? All the better. I set the bombs to explode a few minutes after he's scheduled to arrive. They'll never miss me in the commotion.'

'For God's sake, Frank, we're talking about killing the President of the United States!'

Frank Hamilton said, 'So?' He couldn't have made a better or more eloquent speech to show Hallam what he was truly dealing with. In some ways, the enormity of the single syllable shocked him more deeply than all the death over the years.

'They'll find you, Frank.'

'I doubt it, but I'll deal with that when I have to. In the meantime, I'm out of here.'

'How?'

'The same way you made it away from the gas. Through the wind tunnel. That was very clever of you, Hallam. Just like the napalm in Vietnam. I only cheated you by seconds. But I expect that. You're the Great Man of the hexagrams. Did you know I knew you were coming? It's true. The *I Ching* knew.'

Hallam gave up. Something was tugging at his mind. He went on slowly.

'It couldn't.'

'But it did.'

'You rely pretty heavily on that book, don't you?' Hallam asked.

'It knows all things.' Hamilton settled cross-legged in front of Hallam. 'I first saw it in the master's hut. He was a holy man, you know.'

'With or without a tongue?'

Hallam regretted it the instant he said it. Hamilton's hand swung out lazily and the knife slashed across Hallam's upper arm. It burned like fire.

'Mind your manners,' Hamilton said evenly. 'With or without, he was a holy man. He *knew* me. He understood.

I brought him food, protected him. You forced the situation that killed him, Hallam, not me.'

'Tell me about the *I Ching*,' Hallam said gently.

'Did you know the ancient Chinese could foretell the future with it? Confucius himself wrote the commentaries—'

'Frank? I can't feel my legs. Could you . . .?'

Almost absent-mindedly Hamilton reached out and slid the noose cord out from under Hallam's feet. There was an abrupt cessation of tension and Hallam found he could sit on his bottom and tuck his legs into the same cross-legged position as the man opposite him. Blood flowed into cramped muscles. For the first time in twenty years the two sat across from each other, face to face.

Hallam looked into the madman's eyes and listened.

Part of it was gibberish, part recalled what Hallam had learned from the Chinese shopkeeper on that long-ago day with Hu. Yin and Yang. Heaven and Earth. Trigrams and hexagrams. Light and dark. A strange feeling began to come over him. It reminded him of the experience in the shop. He remembered the dry spicy odours, the sense of being closed in, the oddly powerful feeling the coins had in his hand and the haze that seemed to encompass him as he threw them.

Hamilton was still talking. Hallam tried to override the pain in his leg and arm. He had worked on his bonds and it was no use. It killed him that Hamilton was only three feet from him and he couldn't get to him. No last-ditch effort to go for his eyes or throat. No way to wrest his knife away and turn it on him. With the stakes involved, he'd try anything. He thought hard, concentrating. Was there a different battlefield to fight on?

Long ago, the napalm had failed, but so too had Hamilton's attack in the clearing. Just as the sentry tank and the gas had failed. Was the ultimate resolve of their conflict to be on a plane other than the physical, a different plane, one Hallam had never anticipated?

'. . . the judgements clothe the images in words. They indicate whether given actions will . . .'

omplete. Six to make something of nothing. That thought penetrated the mists. Something of nothing? For a moment, the connection between them weakened. A shadow crossed Frank Hamilton's face and some small part of Hallam's will to resist returned.

With arms that weighed tons, Hallam took up the coins and threw them. They lay glistening between them. Nine. The final line was broken. The hexagram was complete. But which one?

Frank Hamilton uttered an angry, confused sound from deep inside himself. It was the first comfort Hallam had had. It buoyed him. He reached for his will. He fought back. What had he created? What was the sign?

Never taking his eyes from Hamilton's, he demanded, 'Tell me.'

Hamilton raised his hand and Hallam saw the knife in it. He poured energy into the connection between them, never stopping for a second. He fought back with every ounce of will that had ever carried him past the point where other men stopped or lay down or surrendered.

'Tell me!'

Hamilton winced at the power. 'K'an,' he hissed. 'The Abysmal.'

Hallam knew it. A prime hexagram. In the hierarchy of things it stood for Water, that which nothing could stand against for long. What was the Book telling him?

'The image,' he insisted. 'Tell me!'

Hamilton reacted as if he'd been struck. His face contorted and the knife rose another inch. He couldn't move it further. 'Water flows on without interruption to reach its goal,' he quoted. 'The image of the Abysmal repeated. Thus the superior man walks in lasting virtue.'

'More,' Hallam commanded.

Hamilton's face twisted savagely but he went on, 'Even bound with cords and shut in between thorn-hedged prison walls He will find a way.'

'And the judgement?'

Hamilton tried to break the connection but now Hallam refused.

'The judgement, damn you!'

'If you are sincere, if you have success in your heart whatever you do succeeds.'

Hamilton spat the last. Spittle flew out of his mouth and hit Hallam's face. Hallam didn't turn away. He continued to fight the battle of his life, pouring forth with a will he'd never fully tapped before. He'd once heard the men on the first alpine climb of Everest talk about it. There was no top, they said. No goal. No summit. Just putting one foot in front of the other longer than anyone else had, never letting go, never stopping. Refusal – that was the key. Success lay in refusing to lose. Winning was an illusion. Motive was an illusion. One foot in front of the other. That was real. Up. Always up. One foot in front of the other. One step at a time. Up, always up. If you never stopped, sooner or later you'd reach it. Inevitably, you had to get there.

Suddenly, one had said, I realized I was walking down.

Hallam fought like that. Whatever had carried him through the burning jungle or got him up the cavern wall to escape the gas carried him now. His will was a thing alive. Family, wife, children, Hu – the things he loved fuelled it, gave it form and substance. There could be no void where things *mattered*. Morgan Lassiter might have called it belief. Hallam had no easy word for it but he too understood it as an act of Faith. *Some things mattered.* He believed that. It poured forth from him like a pure, white light and for a time nothing else existed but it.

He came out of it slowly. He couldn't say for sure where he'd been, but as the mists cleared Frank Hamilton was sitting before him slack-faced and empty, unmoving.

Hallam slid forward to get the knife.

It was called a decapitation strike.

It put an end to the war.

The conversations across the hotline teletype link with the Soviets hadn't worked in any substantive way. No solutions to the crises were forthcoming. The end approached under cover of night.

President Rogers and his advisers saw it coming in over the NORAD screens and put down their game books tiredly. Salvo after salvo of Soviet ICBMs were coming over the Pole. Deep in space, satellites tracked them and relayed co-ordinates to NORAD. Condition Red was sounded: attack imminent. In a vain attempt to counter the strike, the Air Force put up wave after wave of interceptors. It was a futile gesture at best. Hundreds of warheads hit the United States.

It was called a decapitation strike because the primary Soviet aim was to destroy Washington and the federal command structure. Alerting them to the futility of this was the real purpose behind Ivy League, and the President and his staff watched as the emergency network created for this eventuality sprang into operation.

Some five thousand megatons rained down on the nations – as compared to the one-fiftieth of a megaton that incinerated Hiroshima. Cities ceased to exist. The destruction was unimaginable. Major portions of the military and civilian systems used by the Pentagon and the Federal Emergency Management Agency went dead in the destruction.

President Rogers died where he was sitting, in the close-quartered Situation Room under the White House. Instantly command over the nation's remaining civilian and military forces shifted to his successor, the Vice President, aloft in the airborne command post. To the war-game planner's satisfaction, he was still able to initiate the required response, the single integrated operations plan, an all-out retaliatory nuclear strike against the Soviet Union.

From silos all over the country, plumes of exhaust told the final tale as the engines of destruction blasted up high over the Pole. Those land-based missiles destroyed in the Soviet strike were replaced by their air- and submarine-launched brethren.

As death rained down on the enemy, the Vice President's plane was destroyed by a squad of Soviet fighters on a suicide mission. Instantly, control of the country shifted to each of two cabinet officers, one in a secret federal facility in Massachusetts and the other in a similar facility in Texas. Accompanied by core teams of officials from key government agencies, they took command of the nation's remaining resources.

Every facility was tested and re-tested. Lines were shut down and strategic operations centres were forced to make do in a damaged-beyond-repair world. Lumbering back, the country managed to hold on.

In the end, the players in NORAD put down their game books and rubbed tired eyes. A world had been destroyed with the aim of protecting it. The word could now go out that no one had anything to gain by such an attack. There were other lessons to be learned from all this, too, lessons the analysts would be years deciphering. For the men who had played the game the physical exhaustion was matched by the psychological. They returned to their quarters to make peace with themselves, to remember what they had done – even if only electronically – and why, and to attend to much more mundane but suddenly very important personal matters like phoning home.

Mulrose was in his office when the word came. He dispatched his aides to inform the rest.

Within the hour they would be gathering to meet the President.

Hallam moved cautiously. His right arm was still tied, as were his legs, but he could sidle forward a few inches at a time. The knife was resting lightly in Frank Hamilton's hand. Hallam steeled his emotions. Two goals – cut his bonds and kill the man in front of him as quickly as he could.

Hamilton's eyes were still staring into a clouded distance. Just seconds after it was over, the memory of what had happened between them was fading from Hallam's mind like a dream. He might never truly understand again what the ancient book held, but the proof was before him.

How long would it last?

Every motion caused a scraping sound from the gravel under him. He slid forward in tiny spurts, letting the sound die before moving, the way one might creep from a sleeping child's room. Closer, he felt the presence of the man. His eyes were still staring unseeing. Hallam wondered what it would be like to stick the knife into some part of him. Should he go for the heart? What about the ribs – he'd read somewhere it could deflect the blade. Cut an artery in the neck? The thought nauseated him. What if he missed and Frank woke?

Remember Paco, he urged himself, sliding forward another inch. Remember Burris and the brothel and Ronnie Lassiter.

'David?'

The sound of another voice almost made Hallam leap. He steadied his frayed nerves. Please, whoever you are, he thought, stay away a few minutes longer. Don't wake him. Don't wake him. Hallam inched closer. Don't wake him. Don't wake him . . .

'David, are you there?'

It was Fred Burris!

Hallam didn't know whether to laugh or cry. The sounds of his approach got closer. Burris must see the light of the laser torch by now. Hallam heard him scrabbling over the gravel.

'Fred, over here . . .' he whispered fiercely. 'Shhh. Quiet.'

Hallam tried not to be distracted. Another few inches. He was almost close enough to pluck the knife out of Hamilton's hand.

Burris came in, hunched over in the narrow confines. He saw Hamilton at once.

'Never mind him,' whispered Hallam urgently. 'Get me untied quick. I don't know how long this is going to last.'

Burris pulled a folding knife from his pocket and bent to

the knots. Hallam felt them loosen behind him. His other arm dropped to his side, asleep, and Hallam worked it to get the blood flowing. Burris moved in front of him to get at the rest of the rope, partially obscuring Hamilton. Hallam saw his questioning gesture.

'He's in a kind of trance, Fred.' Hallam rocked to one side. 'Right. Just get that one round my legs and . . . Fred? Fred!'

The cutting motion was stopping. Burris tried to saw through the cord again, but a sudden pain in his head caused him to stop short. His eyes screwed up tightly and he wavered.

'Come on, Fred. Concentrate,' Hallam pleaded. Sensation was returning to his other arm. He could move it stiffly now.

'Trying,' hissed Burris. His face was growing slack.

Hallam wanted to roar in frustration. Burris blocked him from grabbing Hamilton's knife. 'Please. Fred. You've got to move out of my way. Any second now. I've got to get that knife.'

'Just . . . wait . . . almost got it. Few more . . . There!'

Hallam felt the rope part.

Burris smiled. 'Nothing to worry about.'

'Now, Fred, I . . .'

Fred Burris sat bolt upright. There was terror on his face. He tried to speak but it came out as a hoarse croak. His hands went round himself, clawing at his own back.

Hallam screamed, 'No!'

The look on Burris's face changed to one of infinite sadness. His features relaxed. Hallam knew at once it had nothing to do with his disability. There was a maddened roar behind Burris. Hallam threw himself to the side as his friend pitched forward. Hallam saw the knife protruding from his back.

He shoved at his friend's body to prevent being pinned under it. His legs were still unsteady but he kicked out with all his strength. He slipped on the gravel, fighting for traction and Burris's body came down on him, trapping one foot. Hamilton roared with animalistic rage. There wouldn't be a second chance. Hallam kicked out again, ramming his free foot into the corpse, unmindful of his fallen comrade's dignity or his own. His leg came free.

Hamilton wrenched the knife out of Burris's back. He came up and over the body like a fluid animal stalking its prey. Hallam backed up. One hope. One hope . . .

The light in Hamilton's eyes was a terrible thing to see. Hallam knew he had no chance against his enemy's strength or his maniacal purpose. He slid to his right and Hamilton followed. No mind tricks were going to help him now. One step closer. Timing was everything. He moved again. There was the cluster of petrol-filled jugs. He side-stepped them. One more foot . . .

Hamilton leaped at him, knife poised to kill . . . and Hallam grabbed the laser torch in one swift movement and thrust the burning light up into the killer's face.

Hamilton screamed as the laser seared his flesh. He fell back and the knife dropped from his hand. Hallam pursued, stabbing and poking. The torch scored Hamilton's back. Skin burned away. He screamed in rage and pain. He was wounded and tried desperately to run away. He lost his footing and smashed into one of the giant springs. Hallam was on him in a moment, spearing out with the torch. Hamilton's shirt caught fire and he ripped it off. Hallam swung the torch like a bat and caught him in the head. The smell of burning hair suffused his nostrils. Hamilton fell, rolling to put out the flames. Hallam scrambled to get over him, poised for the kill. He raised the torch like a spear.

End it, a voice inside him screamed.

The hesitation cost him dearly. Hamilton rolled aside and grabbed at the bomb-like cluster of plastic jugs, clutching them to him. 'They'll explode if that torch touches them!' he roared. 'Get back. Get back!'

Hallam fell back. Hamilton lay before him. He was breathing heavily, holding the bomb across his chest. Hallam held the torch ready.

'Maybe you'd do it,' Hamilton panted. 'Maybe you want me enough to do it. You're stronger than I ever knew. The

Great Man. But if this bomb goes off, the others will too. Will you go that far? Will you?'

Hallam knew the answer. It must have shown on his face.

'Stand-off. I thought so.' Hamilton was getting to his feet, the bomb still carefully placed between them. 'Well, maybe you'll get all of them before they explode, maybe not. But it's a cinch you're going to be too busy to stop me. Here!'

The move almost caught Hallam unprepared. Hamilton threw the bomb and it came dangerously near the torch, but Hallam swept it back out of harm's way. For a moment, his vision was blinded as darkness fell where the light had been.

When it returned, Hamilton was gone.

Carl Mulrose stood inside the giant blast doors with the VIP contingent. Rogers and the others were well pleased to return to 'civilian' life after the rigours of the game. There wasn't a man present who hadn't come away with a greater respect for the tensions of the President's job. There was a warm feeling in the air as they prepared to welcome the man who had the position for real.

'The secret service know the score?' Mulrose whispered to his security chief.

'Yes, sir. We're not going to bring him any further in than here. Just get the blast doors closed to protect his back, he'll give the speech, then reopen and out.'

'Fine.'

Mulrose surveyed the assemblage. He nodded to the NORAD commander-in-chief.

'Open the doors,' he ordered.

Hallam bent to the timer. It was set for ten minutes. Could he just empty out the jugs and take the entire assembly somewhere safe? Not with the only light being the laser torch. It would ignite the fumes. There was only one other way.

Hallam looked at his hands. They were still unsteady. He willed them to relax. Deep breaths. One after the other. Rest. Put everything out of your mind.

The chain that held the timer/detonator was threaded through each jug's handle. The chain was closed with a heavy padlock, too thick to cut through. That left the chain itself. He had no doubt the laser could cut it — but without igniting the petrol?

Damn good question. He bent down to find out.

Hu waited for the Marines by the hatch cover. 'Too long, Griswald,' he complained worriedly. 'Burris should be back by now.'

'The guards are on their way,' said the voice in the phone. 'They'll be armed.'

'I hear them,' said Hu.

A group of sturdy-looking men in green fatigues raced up. Hu explained quickly.

The first of the Marines dropped into the hole.

Hallam wiped the sweat from his eyes. He had the chain as far from the jug as its length permitted. Carefully . . . carefully . . . he inserted the torch between the chain and the jugs and brought it up against the chain. The metal began to heat up, turning red-hot in seconds. It began to smoke and melt. Hallam repositioned the jugs with his legs to keep the molten metal off them.

He moved the torch slowly. The thought of the petrol in them made him sick. The burns he envisioned made his hand shake. He forced his mind not to think about it. There! The first link severed.

He looked at the timer. Nine minutes left. At least three or four bombs to defuse. He had to work quicker.

He repeated the process with the second link, carefully letting the molten metal drip to the ground. The chain felt uncomfortably hot in his hands. If it melted the thin plastic . . .

The second link came free. Hallam pulled the chain from the jugs and slid the detonator off. Using the laser torch for light, he was about to search for the hatchway Hamilton had described when he saw lights in the distance. He made his way forward hopefully.

Marines! Crew cuts never looked so good.

'Over here!' Hallam shouted.

There were six in all, crouched low in the cramped space.

'Sir?' said the man in the lead. 'Mr Hallam?'

'I'm Hallam, Sergeant. Tell me one thing, has the President arrived?'

'Upstairs, sir. He's making a speech.'

'Listen, you get your ass upstairs double time and tell his secret service guards that this whole place is sitting on a bomb. Evacuate it. Then get back here with a manual wire cutter and help me defuse the rest of these things. Take this as proof. It's going to explode in less than ten minutes. Somebody better know how to get rid of it safely. Move!'

He and two others took off and Hallam motioned to the rest. 'Spread out and comb the area down here for more bombs. Call me if you locate them. You, come with me.'

Hallam retraced his steps back to the second bomb. They were running out of time and he didn't think anyone was going to get back in time. He squatted down beside the jugs and instructed the Marine, who to his credit still had a neutral expression on his face. Hallam explained what had to be done.

With the Marine holding the chain it was a bit easier to manage. Carefully guiding the laser torch against the metal, he made it through the first link. He was sweating again and by now the Marine was sweating, too.

'Pardon me for asking, sir,' said the Marine, 'but you do know what you're doing, right?'

'The only thing I can,' said Hallam sincerely. 'There. Get this detonator out of here and then get back. Right?'

'Yes, sir.'

'Mr Hallam?' yelled a voice from off to the right. 'Over here.'

Hallam ran to the voice.

'There are three more, sir. The others are bringing the rest here to save time. The word from above is it would take a lot more time to evacuate than we've got. Go to it, sir. We'll help as we can.'

Hallam bent down to cut the chain off the next bomb.

Mulrose's chief of security spoke to him in hushed but urgent tones. Within seconds, Mulrose had the secret service chief in conference. He hurried away and Mulrose gave a terse set of commands.

The President was speaking. '. . . While we pray to God that we will never have to use the procedures you have tested this past week, the nation is better off for what you have done.'

One of his advisers passed him a note. The President read it and nodded. He shuffled through papers quickly.

'Operation Ivy League will not only improve our ability to respond to critical emergencies, but, more importantly, it will ultimately help us prove that our adversaries have nothing to gain by such an attack. Thank you for all you've given of your time and energy. Good day to you all.'

The secret service moved him from the podium in record time. Already the blast doors were opening. He would be out in seconds. Mulrose offered a silent prayer for the rest of them and watched as the small, silent guard of honour for the body of former General Arnold Wernicker emerged from the holding area and moved the coffin out after the President.

At least someone was going home to rest.

'There,' Hallam said, 'that's four. Bring the last one here.'

'The rest have been defused up top, sir.'

'Great.'

'Two minutes, sir,' said the Marine in a steady voice. Hallam nodded tightly. Sixty seconds to cut the chain, sixty seconds to get the detonator to a place of safety.

'As soon as this thing comes off,' he said as they held the chain taut, 'get going and toss it into the reservoir. There's no time to defuse.'

Hallam cut at the chain. Every nerve screamed to go faster, every second was a race against time. He held the torch steady. Don't risk it. Not now. Slow and steady.

'Sixty seconds,' said the Marine.

The first link parted. Hallam swept his sleeve across his eyes to clear them. The second link was glowing red, smoking . . . The torch began to sputter.

Dear God, Hallam prayed. He bore down, throwing caution to the wind. The chain was melting, drop by drop.

The torch quit.

'Pull the damn thing!' he yelled and the two Marines pulled with all their might. For a second or two nothing happened, then it broke with an audible snap.

Hallam pulled the detonator off the chain.

'Go!'

The Marine took off.

Hallam followed, counting in his mind.

Seconds remained. Now it was down to one life. One boy who carried death in his hands. Somehow that was terribly important. One boy . . .

Hallam felt, rather than heard, the explosion. It was a deep 'wumpf' carried through the soles of his feet. The Marine helped him through the hatch and he poked his head up and out.

He saw who sat there with enormous relief. Part of him had believed Hamilton.

'Not bad,' said Hu.

'The last one?'

'Into the reservoir. No harm done.'

Hallam grinned.

THIRTY-THREE

Mulrose, Hu and Hallam gathered at the reservoir entrance.

'You'd better seal the wind tunnel in future,' said Hu. 'If David and Hamilton used it to get out, one of these days a saboteur is going to use it to get in.'

'It's in the works,' said Mulrose. 'You can bet on it.' He gestured to the Marine guards. 'Right now I've got one set of men here and one on permanent station up there.'

'And Hamilton?' asked Hallam.

'We've got all the military and civilian police in the area alerted. He won't get far,' Mulrose assured them. 'You did a fine job, David. Get some rest, okay?'

'Soon enough.'

Mulrose looked in at the dark water. 'Good thing we're dealing with solid granite, that last one was quite a blast. Brought all kinds of garbage up to the top including some very weird-looking marine life no one thought was in there.'

'That's the way they used to dredge up bodies,' said Hu.

'I've got men in there now checking for any damage,' said Mulrose.

Hallam said, 'Will you pay my sincere compliments to the Marines. They were rocks, Carl. Without them . . .'

Mulrose gave him a knowing look. 'That's in the works, too.'

A workman poked his head out. 'Excuse me, Mr Mulrose, but there's something in here you should see.'

They made their way onto the platform inside the hatch. The workman gestured to a dark shape on the grid below. 'The explosion must have brought it up.'

Hallam saw . . . and comprehension exploded in his mind. He turned to the Marine next to him and yanked his pistol from his holster. 'I need your gun.'

'David, what . . .?' Hu yelled as he raced past unmindful.

'The coffin!' Hallam yelled. Then he was through the hatch door and racing for the blast doors even as Mulrose was shouting orders.

The workmen had pulled Arnold Wernicker's corpse from the reservoir.

Hallam ran.

'Mr President?'

President Francis Xavier Collins turned to the short, balding man who was his senior adviser. 'Yes, George?'

'We've got an opportunity to make some points. Thought I'd mention it.'

Collins arched an eyebrow. 'I came all this way and ended up delivering a three-minute speech. If you can salvage anything out of that, I'm game.'

'General Arnold Wernicker, Air Force, retired. He died inside the complex yesterday. That's his coffin in the cortège behind us. His son came to get it. Since we're going back to Washington anyway, I thought it might be a nice gesture to ride it back in Air Force One. Whadya think?'

Collins was a tall, elderly but still well-built man who had spent most of his youth outdoors. He paused to savour the clear mountain air, wishing he could trade his cream-coloured suit for a pair of jeans and a fishing rod. He nodded to the man whose opposing stature had caused more than one Abbot and Costello comparison.

'Do it.'

'Right, chief.'

The presidential convoy was midway between the complex entrance and the outer gate when Hallam raced out of the blast doors and into the tunnel beyond. The pain in his leg tore at him but he ignored it. They were less than a quarter of a mile ahead and had stopped for something.

Somehow Hamilton had substituted himself for Wernicker's body in the coffin. He'd been clever right up to the end. He never planned to get out through the wind tunnel, that was just the last in a long list of lies. Hallam was as sure of that as anything in this world.

The pain in his leg ripped at him like a whip.

He ran.

The secret service men directed the coffin-carrier, a dark green Army van, into the presidential caravan. James Wernicker was with them. His uniform was dark and crisp and his hat was close down over his face. He held a folded American flag in his white-gloved hands. The press contingent snapped pictures.

President Collins walked down the line of black limousines. 'Just a minute, please, gentlemen.'

He extended his hand to Wernicker. 'I'm terribly sorry, Captain. I know your father's record. He was a fine man.'

'I appreciate that, sir. My dad would have been . . . very proud.' He stopped, eyes clouding.

Collins put an arm on his shoulder. 'I'd like to pay my last respects.'

'We'd be honoured, sir.'

They walked to the van and two secret servicemen opened the doors.

James Wernicker said, 'After you, sir.'

'Thank you, son.'

Collins stepped in.

The doors closed after them.

Hallam burst out of the tunnel. The presidential caravan was less than a hundred feet away. Where were the secret service guards? Even as lax as they were inside the base, he couldn't just run up waving a .45 automatic and expect to stay alive. They were all gathered around a van. Jesus! Hallam swore. He could see the coffin. Was that the President entering?

'Wait. Don't!' he yelled. He ran up to the first dark-suited guard he could find. The man's hand automatically went inside his jacket and came out with an automatic pistol when he saw Hallam's dishevelled state.

'Stand where you are,' he ordered.

'My name is David Hallam,' he said out of breath. 'Call Carl Mulrose. The body in that coffin isn't Arnold Wernicker's. It's the man who killed him trying to escape. The President's in danger.'

To his credit the man reacted at once. 'Wait. Don't move.'

'Just get the President out of there. You don't know what you're dealing with.'

The guard spoke into his radio phone. At once, a more senior agent detached himself from the large group around the van and came running over.

'You're Hallam?'

'Yes.'

'In words of one syllable,' he demanded, 'fast.'

Hallam told him.

The man nodded tightly. 'We just got the same call from Carl Mulrose. We're gonna take that truck in fifteen seconds. Is the man armed?'

'Bet on it.'

'Shit.' He spoke into the phone again and then turned back.

'Wait here,' Hallam said.

The man smiled without humour. 'You're learning.'

The secret service began to move. It was a small operation but the co-operation bespoke the endless hours these men put in perfecting their craft. One wave of men placed itself in between the press and onlookers and began to sweep them back while a second team yanked open the doors and went in.

Nothing. Hallam breathed a sigh of relief. From where he stood, he could see Wernicker and the President still in conversation. The senior man whispered a brief word into the President's ear and he backed hastily out of the van followed like a shadow by Wernicker. The first wave encircled the van. By now the press was interested. They pressed closer. Off to one side, the President and Wernicker were passing through the crowd, still close. In his grief, Wernicker's head was bent and his hat just about covered his face. The President had an arm round his shoulder as they walked towards his limousine. He dropped it as Wernicker pressed closer. Hallam saw a dark smudge on the President's sleeve. Wait . . . dark smudge?

Hallam was already moving as the van's door burst open and the secret service men came pouring out. They were too far back. The President was only yards away from the limousine. Once inside that mini-fortress . . . There was a jeep in Hallam's way. He hit the hood and vaulted to the other side. His leg almost gave way as he landed but he managed to right himself. He shot forward, levelling his gun. The President was less than twenty feet away.

'Hamilton!' Hallam roared.

The man in James Wernicker's uniform turned and stared wild-eyed. Hallam could see the grease he'd smeared on his neck and chin to darken his skin. His face was twisted into an expression any demon of hell would envy. Hallam caught sudden movement beyond the car . . .

'You!' Suddenly there was a gun in Hamilton's hand. It swung up towards Hallam and fired.

Hallam felt the bullet tear into him. He couldn't return fire with the President so close. Instead, he rose up, attracting fire. He scrambled forward like a broken field runner as Hamilton fired again. Another bullet smashed into him and he felt the breath go out of him like a burst sack. He rose up, swaying.

Hamilton swung the gun over again . . . and the secret service man leaped over the car and brought the President of the United States crashing to the ground and covered him with his own body.

For a split second, Hamilton was standing alone.

Hallam fired.

The first bullet caught Hamilton high in the chest and spun him round. He fell to his knees and tried to raise his gun again. Hallam fired again and a dark hole appeared in Hamilton's forehead. He pitched forward. Hallam kept firing. Again and again the bullets smashed into the now limp and lifeless form. Twenty years of rage and fear poured out of the barrel of Hallam's gun.

There was a bright red haze coming down as his gun slid open, empty. He barely felt them pry the empty weapon gently from his hand. So much seemed different, far away. The weakness in his legs was too much. He surrendered to it. Around him, men were helping the President to stand. Little explosions of light filled the air as the press moved in. People were smiling. Nice, Hallam thought.

When he finally pitched forward there were hands to catch him. Faces over him seemed kind and worried. Somebody said something about the President's own doctor. In the distance he thought he heard the whooping bleat of a helicopter coming. Faces crowded in.

With his last remaining strength, he managed to wave them aside. There. That felt better. There was something he wanted. Finally, they understood. The warmth on his face. He wanted to see it.

The sun.

EPILOGUE

Hallam lifted the phone next to his hospital bed wondering who it could be. Paco had already been in to see him. His wife and kids were in transit at government expense, due into the Colorado Springs Airport later that night. The President had called. So had James Wernicker, recuperating in another part of the hospital. The reporters were waiting anxiously downstairs but so far he'd been spared the exertion of dealing with them. That would come later.

He picked up the phone. 'Hello?'

'Boss? How the hell are you?'

'Griswald!' he said with genuine pleasure.

'Didn't forget me, huh?'

'Never. Tell me, I have a sneaking suspicion it wasn't Mulrose who called the secret service.'

'I cannot tell a lie, boss. The way you sounded, they'd have given you a hard time if you'd said the sky was blue. A little credibility never hurt.'

'It probably saved lives.'

'More's the better.'

'Where you off to now?' Hallam asked.

'The Pentagon. Probably something really dreadful like ambient sound analysis for the Navy. No, *that's* a submarine, guys, the *other* is the whale.'

Hallam laughed.

'Whatever it is, it won't beat working with you, boss.'

'Nice of you to say. We couldn't have done it without you. Hu told me about the trick with the sprinkler. You're okay, Griswald.'

'Boss?'

'Hmm?'

'They don't know it, but I've got access to a few ways out. Would you mind if . . .'

'If what?'

'Well . . . if I called every now and then. Not too many folks have the flexibility to be real friends.'

'Why, Griswald, I'd be delighted.'

'Thanks, boss,' said the computer happily. 'Gotta go now.'

Hallam replaced the phone.

He thought for a long time about Hu.

Hu had been waiting by the bedside when he'd woken up. Through the forest of tubes that sprang from Hallam, it was the most reassuring sight they could have given him.

'This is becoming a habit,' Hallam managed through a dry throat.

Hu smiled. 'Last time, okay?'

Hallam nodded.

'You look like a root system,' Hu said dryly.

'See if I grow.' Hallam had been silent for a while. Then, 'Over?'

Hu let out a deep breath. 'Over.'

Hallam said, 'Take good care, my old friend.'